IGNATIUS VALENTINE ALOYSIUS

REPUBLIC OF WANT

REPUBLIC OF WANT

IGNATIUS VALENTINE ALOYSIUS

Tortoise Books
Chicago, IL

FIRST EDITION, MAY, 2020

©2020 Ignatius Valentine Aloysius

All rights reserved under International and Pan-American Copyright Convention
Published in the United States by Tortoise Books
www.tortoisebooks.com

ASIN: XXX
ISBN-13: 978-1-948954-11-2

Excerpts from the novel first made their appearance in a different form in the following journals: "One Small Victory," in the *The Sunday Rumpus*; "Tabernacle for Drinkers" and "Greeting Cards" in *Third Coast Review*; and "Rain" in *La Tolteca 'Zine*

Cover design by True Ideas, Evanston

Tortoise Books Logo Copyright ©2020 by Tortoise Books. Original artwork by Rachele O'Hare.

For Rosalind and Robert
For Cynthia

Feed-Fed

∞ }

garnish } served up } as decoration } plate platter pickle } commodity
} thrown away } discarded } fish head } who eats? } who eats fish? }
not a vegan } and who else? } not a sufferer } nor aversionist } yet, a
carnivore } who eats fish heads? } the poor } needful } cats } predator
} it's a garnish } nothing more } cover it up } with parsley } lettuce }
a spoon } sliced tomatoes } something, just don't } don't show it }
fishhead } hide it, him } make it disappear } in the crowd } among
us } does not exist } meaningless } everything is } meaningless, yes }
why bother with it? } this fishhead } nothing left } what's there
anyway? } why, the smarts! } so smart } soft flesh } meat } of the sea
} soft sweet } soft sweet cheeks } soft sweet cheeks and gills } and
the eyes? } what eyes? } clear } @ || @ } not white } nor milky } he
feeds on them} the heads, the eyes } is fed them} feed-fed } what,
eyes? } no, not the eyes } please } gross! } it's reality } fact find
fumble} the inevitable } nothing wasted } in a soup } tchala kadi }
this reality } of spicy soup } of being in a soup } climbing out of the
pot } bowl } this is Destiny } Destiny wants } makes } happen } this
is broth } the base } of something } the story } elements } structure }
spice } it moves } does the fish fly? } does it } talk? } sing? } cry? }
plead? } want? } or walk? } on land? } scrambles } for air } soak }
drown } starve } face up } face down } sunburn } shame } survival }
tomatoes } food } water } love } waves } waste waster } feed-fed }
pakoras } see-feel me } fishhead } republic } of want } so many }
people } matter } people matter } a public matter } this life } place }
old world } country } consent } contrast } of one, all } being } Destiny
} ∞

Toolkit:

Fathomless: a matter of what came first, the will or the way. or what's formidable.

Id or Ishtar: understanding the fates, Brahma, the Moirai, Aka, Takdir, and Qadar, Norns, too; let's not go to the underworld now, when crisis occurs at eye level on the streets.

Silence: is sensible and senseless, architect of seduction and isolation.

How many? see Notes on Conditions of [...] Among Children of Global Populations.

Hunger: empty vessels don't make the most noise. they have heart, urgency, silence.

Experiment: everything is that, restless, wanting change, a natural trial through time.

Assemble: all the parts with care, this isn't complicated. or is it? wrap them like a ball inside your head, dear reader.

Denouement: final strands drawn together in surprising ways. use sentence fragments, and long sentences open. close. lowercase it, lowercase.

PART 1

"[T]he ride home is not as long as the way I came, two centuries of hunger brought me along many detours before I recognized your house."
~Sonia Sanchez

"The most fleeting thought obeys an invisible design and can crown, or inaugurate, a secret form."
~J.L. Borges

Between Home and Elsewhere

If life mattered to nineteen-year-old Fishhead now, it meant much less to him than it had when he'd moved from innocence to adulthood in hunger's grip and crushed by his family's indigence, as if Destiny imposed suffering on him alone, while all the world moved ahead with success born from ambitions that escaped distress or dying.

From here at the water's edge in downtown Bombay, Destiny seemed unfair. He looked to the distant horizon as if things made sense there, as if somewhere beyond that line fate had an answer as to why he'd lost Anupa so suddenly, just when he'd begun to enjoy her presence, all the things she'd given him which he'd lacked and longed for at home. Ambition kills or saves, so it appeared to Fishhead. Which one claimed him, the killing or saving? He could not say, could not distinguish one from the other. And why should he choose either? Destiny now forced him to pick between home and elsewhere; he believed it. But did he have a choice? If his father, his mother, and the stench of their shared life in the tenement had not pushed him away, he still had the unendurable memory of Anupa's passing. He moved with bitterness and misery because he'd led her to her fate, and now memory chained him to that dizzying place, no matter whether he visualized his escape on land or at sea. He wanted to make good, although he possessed more honest intentions than means during this late January of 1977. He had a plan: leave home and work on an offshore oil rig. A plan borne of desperation, yes, with uncertainty rippling out to the edge of water and sky where Destiny thrived and watched, but perhaps from there one could see a more benevolent horizon to the west, which had everything one could want.

Before him, the Arabian sea moved in all its majesty. From behind the high seawall and jetty steps, it looked far safer than he imagined it would from the oil rig. The Gateway of India monument towered over Fishhead as he stepped near the basalt Victorian arch and gazed out at the sea with its bumpy jackfruit-like skin. He'd come through his Bombay, a city so challenging to cut through, always overcrowded and sticky, just to see this. A promise of the future along every bit of coastline in this sea of ages.

He tore the contents of his father's handwritten letter and let the pieces fall away into the sea. Fishhead didn't need the added numbness of another re-read. And how could he have responded? After all, he *had* been critical of the man responsible for creating him, this man who refused to endear himself to his children. He'd found fault with Dad from the very start, from his first moments of awareness. And as the years had sped by in increased turmoil, his disappointment in Dad had increased with equal measure. Fishhead visualized all of it (his confrontations, reactions) and wondered if he'd been too hard on this man who'd always kept a tight hand on his family's way of life and its spiraling direction of misfortunes; perhaps, for reasons Fishhead did not yet understand, Dad could not express love and care. He'd read Dad's long letter three times and become intrigued by the graphic on the last page, the one showing arrows facing north, south, east and west. Dramatic Dad.

Dramatic man. Fishhead thought he had some of that in him, too. He did not regret what he'd done with the letter, having stored its contents in his mind anyway and hoping he'd forget them in time; but if soon could only come sooner.

The ripped pieces of the letter floated away before him, some taken down by the waves which climbed and crashed and tossed the boats about. Waves fell like plasters of rain that swept mercilessly across the city throughout the summer monsoons, pelting arrowheads of downpour, summoning floodwaters that had pushed him to helplessness and surrender. The city became like the sea then, waist-high waters unyielding and hungry and unreliable. He trusted the land more and knew it well under his feet, for better or worse. And yet he had no sense of any future at home as he set his mind toward the sea; he couldn't fathom it, and yet it lay in his path like a cow he touched on the street to grace his heart.

He owned a secret: his fear of deep water. Feared it like Dad's debtors who came one after another to the front door almost daily with their regret and expectations, their demands and undeclared threats. Fishhead understood their capacity for primitive justice, and he imagined their strength in numbers, the greater danger. Destiny allowed that, it did; he felt sure of such outcomes.

He should have spent more time with Anupa, Fishhead realized it now, and loved her as she'd wanted him to, loved her more for bringing Cervantes, Mary Shelley, Borges, Phyllis Wheatley, H.G. Wells, and Rumi into his life, for filling his heart with songs by the Yardbirds, Joan Baez, Dylan, Edith Piaf, The Supremes, Simon and Garfunkel, and others. Yes, he should have loved Anupa more. Explored the mystery of her warm sunsets, her lush thighs, small breasts, a stomach smooth as rose petals. Run his fingers through her long black hair combed through with coconut oil. Anupa's eager hips, like gates leading to a universe he'd never known and only imagined, an image of desire woven in the paralysis of his private hours. But something always held him back. Unanswered questions: Why did this girl reach down and choose him? His poverty embarrassed Fishhead so much, but she'd welcomed him into her life. A commitment from him, isn't that what she'd hoped for? He'd been awkward with Anupa, even when she allowed his unpracticed hands to touch her. She wore a welcoming smile for him, always a smile like a white flash from the sun illuminating the darkness of his hunger and heart; still he held her at the edge of his reality, never wanting her to know its shameful truths, how his hard life had shaped him into a raw, stealing demon. Destiny sewed them together and called on them to take in life's carnival, their quiet defiance pushing against the walls of convention which marked the haves and have-nots, because Anupa came from privilege. He came from nothing. Had nothing. He had no right, he thought, to step into her world and make it his own.

Fishhead regretted that his family blamed him for her death and perceived him with a critical eye, unaware of his pain and future plans. Too much to bear. Any beauty he'd perceived of Bombay had vanished, so that more and more, he'd been taking himself away from home to work long hours inside the city, or to while away his time at the water's edge. He'd been to Juhu Beach, Bandra's Bandstand, Worli Seaface, Chowpatty, Marine Drive, and now the Gateway of India, always wishing for a new morning elsewhere, across the ocean or on it.

More pressing matters kept occupying his mind. He'd struggled to focus at work, where he made illustrations in a small greeting card company tucked away inside an industrial complex too unsanitary for its massive size, a brick and concrete shoebox of pale whitewashed walls and long hallways that appeared as tunnels needing more light and clean air. The smell of gunpowder, dyed fabric for shirts and jeans, animal glue, reams of paper. Floors shuddering under his feet from machinery. Sounds of progress trapped in central Bombay, an area called Lower Parel. Fishhead spent his days there before coming home each night with a heartache. His emotion stifled his creativity, and he needed a job that did not make him think so hard or work so much unpaid overtime under constant fluorescent lights. He earned a modest income but not enough to break away.

Go to another city if suitable work came along, *that* had been a thought: New Delhi, Hyderabad, or Bangalore. Madras on the opposite coastline, perhaps, but so far from home, and he did not speak or understand any southern dialect, like the native tongues which his parents used in private. He might find a job in Surat, his birthplace in the north and an overnight train journey away; he had been there to visit nana. But Fishhead liked the high energy of Bombay more than anything. He considered work in the film industry, although he had no inside connections in Bollywood, and no related skills. The Hindi and little Marathi he spoke in Bombay helped him get around well among the unimaginable swarms of people pushing through the city all day long. Fishhead moved silently in these crowds, a nobody, a boy on the verge of adulthood and as inconsequential as commuters hanging from overloaded trains that fled through tenements and slums choking the city and the developing countryside.

Work in another town needed more attention: he hadn't made an effort to apply or even understand how to move his intentions past the classified ads. Matrimonials and advertisements flooded them, ate space, and bored him too much, but he had at least scanned the papers at work during his lunch hours, never imagining that Pradeep, his oldest brother by three years, carried good news to change his life and point his attention towards the sea.

And what did Fishhead know about the sea now? Any seaworthy job required him to face deep water, go offshore, train his feet like a seaman and hope to god that he didn't throw up all day long like some mangy tenement dog. Nothing on land carried more danger than deep sea drilling and life on an oil rig. And yet he knew little about such an existence. He would earn a lot of money, much more than a fair Indian wage. Help him afford those foreign cigarettes and jeans. Impress girls. Anupa wouldn't mind him moving on, she wouldn't. Should he do it? Get work as an unskilled roustabout or roughneck? And what location at sea, what points under the stars?

Work on the rig assured Fishhead's distance from everything but the memory of his loss. He stood under the protective shadow of the Victorian arch and tightened his jaws, hoping he had enough courage for such a move. Then he stepped away and leaned against the stone wall overlooking the seaface. The wall rose a few inches above his kneecaps, but dropped about thirty feet to the active waves on the other side. Several mid-sized wooden ferries bobbed up and down beside each other, engines running, coughing smoke, drawing attention with their decorations, flowers, and paint, their gaudiness and wear. At times, port and starboard sides went knocking into each other, their gunwales flushing spray and foam. The distinct smell of the sea. Its odor of age-old moss in the salted water stung Fishhead now and then. He placed his hands against the too-warm, flat top of the wall and leaned forward to look down at the waves. Toss Anupa's memory into the foam and pretend her death had never happened. Let the water absorb this memory of her. He blamed himself. Debris bobbed on the waves in one corner of the barnacled jetty, waste from the tourists visiting this airy waterfront with its tall ancient palm trees. (Had these coconut palms seen the Queen of England on the stone steps, or her Viceroy, and Britain's nobility and gentry? Had these palms witnessed the ordered movement of uniformed guards and sepoys? Or firm, cruel officers on their horses? Had they smelled the rifles and cannons? Heard commands now obsolete in effect and power? The clap of hooves? Had they breathed in history's air?) Paved, marked roads ran clean and black, as if an extension of the immaculate Taj Mahal Hotel behind him. This area, Apollo Bunder, had no beaches, just rocks and the seawall, and yet it brought Fishhead here, even though he didn't care to be among its crowds, the daily tourists. On the other side of the monument, several visitors worked the time-worn coin-operated metal telescopes. Minutes later, a bus pulled up with more tourists who crowded around, taking impatient turns to look south through their red paint-chipped telescopes into the distant aura of Elephanta Caves. But Fishhead stood alone, preferring his isolation, his regret.

Church bells from the grand cathedral nearby began ringing, as if echoing the guilt and remorse in his heart. Well past noon, and not yet six in the evening. They rang at this moment to mark another soul's passing, and Fishhead bowed his head in silence, held his breath for this person, and Anupa, too. He made the sign of the cross. A shroud settled over him like a fishnet. He hoped Bombay had shown that dead person a good and decent life, if it was possible in this hectic and uncaring but enterprising city. Had that someone tasted *falooda* from Harilal's boutique snack shop downtown? Had he or she put a fork through a silky pastry from La Patisserie at the Taj Mahal hotel? Had that person eaten *aloo chaat* and *samosas* from Fishhead's favorite snack stall at Azad Maidan? Had that person enjoyed the carnival? Fishhead wished for these simple pleasures, too; his family's poverty did not keep him from wishing for them, and it had pleased him to spend what he could of his small salary to treat his sister, his ailing mother, and even Anupa to these things.

With its distinct rumble, a Royal Enfield motorcycle roared past behind him on the wide road, and the gunned engine made Fishhead turn, its sound flooding his awareness and increasing his sense of regret.

The Enfield rider wore no helmet, and the sound of his racing engine demonstrated the man's aim to impress the tourists there; but the roar did not excite Fishhead, who passed no judgment on the rider. Fishhead moved about with an empty head, as if indisposed from the weight of his emotion; his head and heart pulled him down, cleared of everything but for Anupa's memory and his desperation to leave home.

When he'd turned eleven, he'd wanted his own motorcycle, not a plastic toy but a real one, just like the used red Norton a resident in the neighborhood owned and fixed. But if the cost of a Norton stopped him from affording a bike, then why not have a Royal Enfield or Honda? Plenty of those around. Put joy into his life and improve his status. A reasoning young boy. He'd figured he might even lower his expectations and get a moped or Bajaj scooter if it came down to essentials, if he had to pare down. His dream, a wish, a need, and only if he had money. His family never had money. He never had money, never enough.

Yes, this had been his boyhood desire, his want, his one ambition. Own a motorcycle. A wish for adventure and speed on land, for the sound of roaring engines, rumbling trains, and sputtering rickshaws; and speed in the air with low-flying airplanes coming in to land at Santacruz airport, or those MiG jets booming across the city overhead. Have money, own a motorcycle, and get as far from the insecurities of his stricken family, peeling away from life like old molding paint in the tenement.

As he'd grown, he'd imagined rides through the city on his own two-wheeler; he could take a girlfriend or his sister everywhere, and mother too, if she agreed to sit side-saddle behind him in her sari. His sick and overworked mother. Fishhead kept his eye on her, cautioned by her fatigue and illnesses. If he had a motorcycle, he could take her to see the doctor. Even when he turned nineteen he did not lose his dream of owning one. He wished to slip away to lover's lane with Anupa on his motorcycle—that famous lane at Bandra's Seaface—and show her a good time. If he could afford a bike, he'd also wear good clothes and shoes, smoke foreign cigarettes, put his collar up, and show off a fancy hairstyle to match; eat at a rooftop restaurant near Churchgate Station with Anupa, listening to live jazz and swing performed by a piano trio while they dined.

How his ambitions changed. He looked at motorcycles differently now.

He wore a pair of patched and darned light jeans, and a white, long-sleeved shirt with a frayed collar; he rolled the sleeves up to his elbows to hide the rips in them. The sunlight darkened Fishhead, although life kept him too thin for his age and height. He passed a hand through his thick black hair, his straight and short hair, and he wiped the oily sweat off his forehead, his high cheekbones, and jaws. The left cheek held a pimple demanding a scratch, and his deep-set brown eyes burned from the tropical heat.

With his back to the water, he continued to stare in the direction of the biker, long after the Royal Enfield disappeared from view. The image of the motorcycle locked in his sights; it came into focus as he viewed it again in his mind, and he got a closer look: Great gunning pistons. Crisp clutch. Steel chain link and shine. Murderous wheels! Yes, motorcycles had power and aroused a sense of excitement, but their riders did dangerous and foolish things with them. The few traffic rules did not stop these riders on Bombay's chaotic streets. Motorcyclists in a hurry often disobeyed these rules, but their racing machines never won a race against the constant, pooling rain, which choked their pistons and carburetors like animals drowning in a flood. Water slowed those two-wheelers down and took control of them. Fishhead remained sure of one thing: *that* Enfield rider's overconfidence would cause problems in a downpour, stalling his motorcycle in a modest flood. Fishhead saw life as water, as one. Life like the sea, life and water as one. And yet he became fearful of the sea, afraid of its tremendous depths. Both life and the sea had their risks.

Calling on Destiny

If you ever paused to wonder about your life—its form and light, its voice, purpose, and gains, but surely its losses, then it's likely you have taken Destiny's name, to acknowledge it, thank it or appeal to it, to ask Destiny for help, whether in prayer or in moments of desperation or gratitude, in silence when alone, at play, when success blossomed in your hands. Perhaps Destiny's name passed through your lips when you faced loneliness, depression, or hunger; or when fatigue overwhelmed you while you worked under pressure at your job, at home; when anxiousness and bouts of panic clawed your back as things appeared to go wrong, those wrong turns that made you desperate, grasping for the right answers, for peace and resolution. You look up towards the sky with hope flooding your eyes and senses. At other times you may have called on Destiny with an egoistic and overconfident trance, or with the occasional dose of shame or insanity. Have I run the full gamut of situations, dear reader? Maybe, just maybe. In any case, I feel that you may have called on Destiny with philosophical questions that are typical of such personal inquiries. You know the ones I am talking about: *Where am I going? What am I doing here? What is my future and why is this happening to me? Why me, why not someone else?* These are inquiries that, at some time or the other, have passed through head and heart, through sinews of living, sentient flesh, going back and forth within marrow and tunneling bones; and you have asked them a hundred times—no, a thousand times or more, unable, however, to keep count, I am sure.

Please forgive my bad manners. I don't mean to be rude, or encroach on your views and lifestyle. I put these notions forward from mere curiosity and without meaning to show you or anyone else the slightest form of meanness, disrespect, or cruelty. Maybe you haven't experienced any such thing. Nah, not so, never, you want to say. Maybe you can't remember every instance, although Destiny has made sure to give your few significant life-changing events a permanent place in your memory, although I suspect that you have come to respect Destiny's influence over you in some form or the other, in some manner whether consciously or inadvertently, asking questions as Fishhead asks those same questions. After all, who in their right mind keeps count of such uncomfortable circumstances and inquiries, let alone the good ones? No one wishes for crisis. No one wants to remember moments of despair, although distress thrives at the core of your living world and from its very beginnings. No one wants to remember any of that. Neither did Fishhead while he struggled through his family's hardship. I am reminded of *The Stranger* and Camus' protagonist Monsieur Mersault, who also admits to his crisis while facing a most unusual and impulsive situation as a prisoner; Mersault considers his use of the gun on an unnamed Arab youth at the beach and says, "I was assailed by memories of a life that wasn't mine anymore." Camus' unfortunate protagonist reached a juncture of pure uncertainty and darkness in the story of his life. But what about the young Arab? Don't you want to know his identity? Have you not wondered about this mystery? The question has remained unanswered until recently. Now Kamel Daoud has investigated this incident and handed us the truth. The Arab boy has a name, you see, he does; it's Musa, and he left behind a brother and mother in Algiers. So, no matter what reason Mersault had for using his gun on Musa and then calling on Destiny later for forgiveness or help or to settle his rattled conscience, he had no purpose for killing Musa, except to relieve his fear of the unknown and his own ignorance. Between those two men then, who do you suppose felt despair more? A good question, yes? Perhaps the answer lies in favor of society's biases, a burden for any writer.

Who am I? You ask. You want to know, and I will tell you. I am a storyteller, a storymaker, and let me say that I understand despair, and respect it for what it does to the soul and to those embers fanning curiosity at the back of my protagonists' eyes. They think of death often, and I know they believe that Destiny took them to a threshold over time, much time that has escaped their awareness, as if they have just woken up from an impossible and shocking dream. This is Fishhead's case. Despair is the dark theater a character enters, ticket in hand, the confluence of "just being" and "living," that space between *existing passively and being entertained* or *coming truly alive.* Perhaps you have found yourself caught in between both circumstances often, unaware of everything and everybody, your surroundings, just as Monsieur Mersault also felt trapped in that doubtful space. This is also Fishhead's desperation, but in his own particular way that is typically Indian. It's a realm of hunger, his Republic of Want. Personal despair is also a manifestation of social despair, that unconscious despair which chips away the senses bit by bit as it pushes the body and the bodies of the masses into a mechanical fury, a drone-zone, if you will. Fishhead's path of despair is a legitimate one. I say this only because I understand it all too well, as I said before, just as I also understand the act of living. I hope that Destiny keeps you from the path of despair, dear reader.

The questions I pose are the very questions Fishhead asks as he grows into a young and ambitious man, an innocent soldier of misfortune billeted in the filthy tenement in Bombay and in the tenement of his soul, while Destiny depletes his physical and empirical power and holds him firm with destitution, hunger. But this is Fishhead's story, and he is fortunate to be embraced (or should I say included) in *Notes on Conditions of Hunger Among Children of Global Populations*, a volume of exceptional value that a man called Iva holds while he sits in a quiet reading room at The Cliff Dwellers Club, overlooking Chicago's famous Grant Park and Lake Michigan. The Museum of the Art Institute of Chicago there at his left. Buckingham fountain up ahead. Iva reads Fishhead's story with a keen interest. Fishhead seeks Destiny, the abstract, unseen and animate storm brewing in his life, like boiling, steaming aromatic *chai* made from fresh milk and spiced ingredients that he can barely afford from roadside tea-stalls. Tea is consumed in India like water; I'm sure you know that. It is cheap to say the least, but he cannot order a glass if he wanted to, not without containing his guilt and shame as he borrows a few *paise* from a co-worker or classmate, unsure when and if he can pay them back. Lessons learned from his father. Fishhead doesn't understand any of it; he fails to recognize that Brahma has marked his forehead with a sign of naiveté and confusion, determined his path even before he knew it, before he opened his eyes to the world and walked this life of suspicion and hesitation. If Karma is the consequence of a journey, Destiny is the journey itself, everything we know to be true and wanting in work and life. Destiny is Brahma, the Three Fates, the Moirai, Norns, Fa, and Qadar in Islam. Every culture has a name for Destiny, even crucial but silenced cultures like the Mayans and Native Americans—and they all point to the same face, the same unseen power, which leads them to their futures. Confucius and Mencius regarded Heaven's will in marking the path and decency of human beings. Maybe you have an interest in philosophical matters, with a fascination for such methods of thought, or maybe you don't; but surely you do not see yourself as a failed pragmatist striving for a place in a self-absorbed, driven and violent world, hoping to earn a name that you can attach to your door, a sign of success to hang over you, and a partner who will continue to love you as you are, expecting the same from you in return. What else is there in life but love and understanding to fight all hardship?

What is Destiny's wish for Iva's life? He is still searching; he feels something and has a private sense of this, but he cannot articulate it well. And what is Destiny's wish for you? Iva knows that he cannot affect or ignore Destiny, a power that is at his side and in his very being, prevailing so far ahead of his path, leading him gradually or in haste, and determining his thoughts, his moves. It does not matter whether Fishhead believes any of this; they are both choice-less in the matter, pulled by Destiny's current in a particular direction.

Why does no one speak of Destiny anymore? I ask you. It appears that humans move away from the center of their beings with each day that they pursue their wants and cravings, with each day that they are willing to hold a gun or idolize its power over life and living. Even Iva will admit that he has failed in this regard, failed to pay attention to the path he has taken, and situations continue to challenge him. They have spun out of control for Fishhead, who contemplates Anupa's death with seriousness; he wonders: *What is my direction? Why does this have to happen to me and not someone else?* These are significant questions. They might be for you, too. Concerns of fate have inhabited Fishhead's thoughts. Yes, Destiny has the answer before Fishhead can even think of his question. Destiny knows what he will do in response to his question, and he does nothing more, but all the while lives to accomplish Destiny's will.

Iva is a selfless and caring person, not a selfish one, a human unfit for these "I" times, you know, this period of the *id*, which also happens to be the very I.D. of the self, that singular "passport" required just about anywhere in this interconnected and multi-cultural world, this hyper-linked world of problems and terrors. Peace is a finger resting on a trigger. As Iva reads Fishhead's story, he might even wonder if sometimes he is like Fishhead, mirroring the painful crawl of the young boy's life, although Fishhead is locked within it, and to him it feels fast and unrelenting (which is untrue), so much so that he is unable to catch up with it or control its direction.

There is confusion and growing alarm there for Fishhead. Destiny knows this, and what you hear and know is true in the voice of my narration, because *I am Destiny*:

All that happens to Fishhead must and will also happen to you, and to any living and sentient soul that has touched the earth and felt her heat and cold, her prowess and creativity, her heart, her magic. I am the deep intuition residing at the periphery of your every instant. I am true, and I know that you have called on me from your place of disquiet, your moment of distress, and also from the comfort of your chair, bed, car, your run or walk, for I am everywhere, a source of ages, a source of thought and actions, an endless fountain of motivations, both good and bad, virtuous and terrible. Perhaps you believe none of this. There is no such thing as fate, you may insist; and I will not begrudge you for holding such a view. Then let me ask you this: What is the speed at which you move? Is your life racing ahead at breakneck speed, or do your days crawl, throttling the dreams which speed through the fist of your brain at night? Perhaps, unlike Fishhead's life, yours moves at a pace agreeable to you, and that's good, very good. It makes me happy to know this about you, because I have willed your path, as I have intended the path which Iva takes. I am an essence of his being as I am an essence of yours, even if you do not believe it. I am with him in a great city like Chicago. I might choose any city around the world for that matter, any town or village, any slum and tenement, like Fishhead's tenement so far away in India, his Republic of Want. Instead, I pause in Chicago. Iva has been striving for success and fame (dreaming of it, as a matter of fact), and I have fed his dreams and stifled them too. Is he ready? Perhaps only he can answer this question. He is at his wit's end and entangled by moral questions, although he does not show it. A life with immorality imposed on it; he has learned how to adapt to its scrutiny and unfairness, and I will spare you those details, because this is Fishhead's story more than anything. In presenting these characters beforehand, I merely suggest that human nature is the same naked iteration of enigmas winding through time and space, covered in different clothes, conditions, and climates; it presents a unique narrative, living dust carried through one universal air of experiences. These lives have already been lived, I insist. Do you believe me? They are celebrated again and again.

Iva reads his volume now (the one with Fishhead's story in it), and soon he will get in his car and drive through the city as he always does; the car is a mid-sized sedan, white and clean, and not quite near its end. Let's jump ahead a week from The Cliff Dwellers Club where he reads about Fishhead, and let's show him as he sips his coffee while driving too fast for the roads, because he is running late for work on a weekday morning. He can think of nothing else expect the consequence of arriving too late at a private ad school just west of downtown, where he teaches part time. He drives, later than usual this morning (but then he's always a few minutes late), predicting his reprimand that may or may not come, although he believes it will happen. I know it will not, but I must let Iva believe what he wishes to believe. I will not interfere with his choices and course of action. It's a sunny day in Chicago, and I know how this ride is going to end even before he has time to slow down. He does not slow down, and, in fact, presses hard on the pedal and swerves from lane to lane quite dangerously, confident but hurried and reckless, cutting sharply between unsuspecting cars and their drivers on the southbound 2-lane main street called Western Avenue. At some time or the other, every driver feels a sense of power and control behind the wheel. Why is that? How do you control a few thousand pounds of shiny, rushing metal with your foot? Why such arrogance? At Pratt, Iva catches the changing stoplight and wants to beat it, but he must slam on his brakes because the light has turned red quickly, and the car in front of him stops without warning past the pedestrian white line of his lane, coming to a screeching halt with half the vehicle sticking out into the intersection; and Iva is lucky for wearing his seatbelt, but not so lucky that he can keep the airbag from exploding in his face, or stop his coffee mug from shooting off the dashboard cup holder that has jerked it loose with the impact of the collision. The front of the sedan folds like an accordion, making the sound of thunder or a mortar assault. Yes, Iva is a creature too desperate to manage his life, too worried about future's consequence. He fails to enjoy where he is in the moment. The present, although oblique and offensive to him, is the safest and surest place.

Fishhead knows that same feeling of desperation. I see it in so many faces, as I see it in that girl, that young adult who waits after lunch at the 35th/Archer train station on the CTA's Orange Line. Let's call her Daniela. Why is she nervous on Monday afternoon, shaking, muddled up inside and confused when she should be on the train that takes her to that English Composition class at the Community College in Chicago's Loop? Her school-issued Ventra card has no money left on it, no balance, not enough to get her a one-way ride, which costs over two dollars, and she has no money in her pocket, at least not enough to fetch that ride; she is frustrated, poor and hungry, dizzy. Fishhead knows this feeling. Their paths will never cross because they come from different times and places, but he'd understand that she, like him, is also penniless with pockets full of air, because her mother is poor, separated in marriage, and struggling to feed her two daughters. A single parent. Daniela is the oldest child, and she understands her family's true circumstance, although she is still quite innocent and waits to find her path in life; but she is determined to succeed, even though much gets in her way, her poverty and hunger in particular. She is a small girl with shiny black hair down past her shoulders, a lean girl with a slight lisp. You see, discovery is a painful pleasure, that moment between night and day, between dreaminess and realization, an awakening. I know Daniela will realize her purpose and fulfill her mother's wishes for a better existence. She loves her mother and understands her sacrifice, just as Fishhead also understands his mother's sacrifice. So Daniela suppresses her pride and asks one commuter after another at the turnstiles to help buy her ride on the CTA, until an older woman feels bad for her and stops, not wishing to be identified; her gesture of kindness is enough for her. This is Daniela's lucky day.

Fishhead too has his lucky days, as you will soon see, but he doesn't grow fast enough; he remains naïve, unable to realize when his luck changes for the better or when luck moves him in the direction that I wish to take him. Many like Fishhead are not so fortunate at all. As for him? Anupa's death has pushed him to the water's edge at The Gateway of India monument and marked his moment of madness. What did he hope to reach for by going there? What did he wish to see and touch beyond the horizon that his city could not give him? He had never planned on going there before, and behaved as if his city pushed him to its very limits or bored him. Can a city actually do that? Or do people do that? What do you think? There are things I refuse to interfere with, situations I will not alter. Fishhead seemed confused, unable to tell the difference. His family's indigence corrupted him, and he remained unconscious of his own moral corruption. This form of corruption or distress could never happen to you, you might be inclined to say, not where you are, not in your place of comfort. That's okay, I understand. But it can, I know it can, and it is happening all around the globe. Immorality challenges everyone and changes a few irreparably. And perhaps it will ease your mind to know that even Iva resisted such prompts and denied their existence, often moving blindly through life's understory to get somewhere in Chicago's glass and brick forest by the lake, hoping to make a name for himself, be somebody, cleaving his way through career and challenges rising before him like stubborn vines, like those tall invasive grasses of the prairie, and groves of young dogwood and English holly; and all the while, wolves of opportunity howl outside his door, and cold, intolerant paradoxes in the flesh scoff at him and give him the stink eye. But I dressed beads of kindness around his neck, I did that. Ask Iva, if you meet him on the street; he'll say that I did. He remembers them—people performing acts of generosity in his favor—and he holds on to those memories.

My intervention here is necessary, because, like Iva and Daniela, even Fishhead would be impossible without it. We are all involved here, including you, dear reader. There's much to consider about his story that will be nothing until all the parts come together. Even I must depend on you and your willingness to indulge in Fishhead's world, a place so alarming and troubling. I've dragged you into it, I know, a story that's half a century old. Yes, I'll admit, I have waited far too long for your interest in this narrative. So allow me to continue in the only way that his life can be told, with its starkness and honesty, its simple vocabulary, because no fancy dictions are required for the tenement life which Fishhead lives. A fitting usage of speech, yes?

His homeland is a geography of growing wealth and urban waste, a post-colonial hotbed of trade, talent, and corruptions. Fundamentalist leniencies and terrors refuse to go away, and there is a price for everything and on everything. His Republic of Want knows no bounds. Everyone's an entrepreneur here, every man, woman, and child, despite the stark poverty separating the haves and the have nots; even the pariah dog and pauper move as hustlers, looking for opportunity, food, and shelter from the heat and relentless monsoon rain. I might have chosen India as my true birthplace, for how could anyone not care to walk on this epic, animated land or belong to it? I belong here and everywhere. I am born within the soul of every human being and creature. I am a citizen of worlds known and unknown, undeniable and certain across all borders and time. And India in Fishhead's time remained as much an enterprising place as it is now; his homeland draws you in with its deepest senses and trances, and with its tastes, sounds, and smells. Each event so distinct and memorable. All color is cosmic and chromatic here, like diamonds raining down from the sun, and many languages to braid the cleverest tongues. If songs from this country's heart can move its many millions, then should it not move you as well? A span of fifty years or so is too small, too minor to separate Fishhead's days from the present, from yours, and yet there is that distance, that separation from what took place then and life as it is now. Modernity in India bloomed impatiently in his time, racing fast into the future with its eyes on the West; and without this hunger for growth emerging from its chaos, India might appear as secondary now as it did before its crucial independence. Such is its predestined path, you might say, on which I chose to plant Fishhead—this naïve, dreamy, but determined protagonist, whose beginning and early life is just as mixed up and troublesome enough to pave the way for his youthful heartache.

A Family Happens

In an ideal and gracious world, Fishhead and his siblings should not have been born. They owed their existence to the resolve of their parents, Eshma and Balan George, who married each other against both their families' wishes in 1951, at a time when a newly independent India began untying itself in its fourth year of freedom from British rule. Eshma had been promised to someone else, not Balan, the boy she loved. Instead, she followed her heart. As high school sweethearts in Coimbatore, South India, she and Balan often met secretly behind the girls' school compound walls and even wrote letters to each other, agreeing to burn them or rip them into pieces and toss them into the Noyyal River, so no one could find their notes.

Eshma's widowed mother and Balan's father—a still-married man under employment with the British telephone and telegraph service—knew each other intimately, thanks to a chance meeting years before at the postal service station in the southwestern coastal town of Cochin, where the unhappy, struggling widow examined incoming and outgoing parcels during the war on a scant salary, a hardship that had forced her to change the unchangeable, and then break with strict local customs by putting down new roots with Balan's father and moving to Coimbatore with her deprived children. Both parents had placed their offspring in boarding schools to make time for themselves, away from watchful, judging eyes, and from wagging tongues always ready to lick the wrapper off a scandal.

Eshma and Balan attended different and strict Christian boarding schools (she'd landed in the convent school closer to home in Coimbatore, and Balan found himself in an all-boys school in Madras run by Christian fathers), and despite their great distance, they kept up their veiled relationship, hiding it from their siblings, parents, and friends. Balan came home to Coimbatore often, whenever school closed for the summer or during holidays, taking the seven-hour train journey deep inland from the eastern coastline with two of Eshma's three younger brothers, who also attended the same boarding school in Madras. Balan and Eshma nurtured their feelings for each other, and through high school and graduation they proceeded to make their relationship more public.

A sudden job transfer for Balan's father caused both parents to move their families north to the port city of Surat, an overnight train journey from Bombay on the *Flying Ranee Express*. Young Balan found a job in the police department; he flashed his seasoned bamboo policeman's *lathi* stick, and relished the power his khakhi uniform presented. Eshma obtained work as a telephone operator, thanks to Balan's father, whose influence remained steady with his departing English bosses and the changeover department of the new Indian government.

Eshma soon faced the inevitable: an arranged marriage to another boy, Sudhir, an Anglo-Indian youth like her who came from the neighboring village of Nanpura. But she cared little for this arrangement or for this safe and hardworking Christian boy who would have made her a very happy household. She struggled to entertain the notion of their growing old together dutifully without love and going about their childrearing in peace, in mercy's untroubled vessel—a dull journey, she imagined, because she did not know Sudhir at all. Marriage could not guarantee the love she needed. Eshma prayed hard for the strength to fight the stress of this temptation; she begged for a different path in life, a hopeful destiny, one with Balan that she believed she knew and wanted, even as she became more and more aware that, given the nature of their parents' relationship, their own course was somewhat incestuous. No matter, she wanted it, just as he also did. They'd fallen in love and offered themselves to each other. She felt lucky, like her name suggested, and became desperate to derail the arranged union between her and the boy from Nanpura, but she didn't know how.

Then Balan revealed a sinister side of himself that no one had yet seen; he threatened Sudhir physical harm if the boy went forward with his marriage to Eshma. This had all been done semi-legally; he solicited the aid of lathi-bearing sympathizers on the police squad by falsely labeling Sudhir a *goonda,* a local thug, and convinced his fellow collaborators on the force to teach the boy a lesson, but only when he, Balan, gave his word. A gamechanger, this twisted threat; an unexpected and terrible provocation so insane, it provided an ideal script for an Indian movie. No one questioned Balan on this immoral and shady manner, certainly not Eshma, most innocent and naïve, who, although she would live to see more of such behavior in the years ahead, did not yet have reason to question her future husband's maneuverings. Instead, she saw in Balan the making of an action hero, a villain committed to stealing her heart.

Now she faced an upside-down world full of craziness and judgments, fear. No one dared challenge the young upstart Balan in his khaki uniform. To question him meant to question the police force, and any blame of the law risked its retaliation, however small, and produced awkward consequences and sore inducements. Balan failed to acknowledge his wrongdoing, or this grim and unlikeable side of his character. So young, so bold and brash, he did not understand or see the germ of madness twisting slyly through his bloodline from his mother's side, even though it was now manifest, this woven chaos, in how he threatened anyone who chose to upset what he and Eshma had started. He claimed her for his own. But to what end? To what lifeline in the future did their union aim?

Eshma and Balan's parents regretted the social crime in this defiant relationship and broke off their own intimate alliance. Their bitterness sealed the future. A curse for permanent unhappiness burned in the parents' defeated hearts. No one deserved to be happy if *they* could not be happy, the widow swore. Eshma saw her mother burn with a searing obsession ruled by unforgiveness. Christian or not, the widow declared, no one deserved happiness, no future child of this union, unchaste as it stood before God, had a right to be happy or successful.

Then, as efficiently and surely as passing clouds on a rainy day, Eshma and Balan got married. They wasted no time in ushering their own offspring into the world, so that five years and two boys later, one late summer night in the mid-1950s, Fishhead's infant cries rippled through the maternity ward at Nanavati Hospital.

This young and tired mother slipped a hand-sewn dress over the dark brown puddle of flesh in her arms, because she wanted this third male child of hers to be a girl—poor, poor Fishhead (Oh, the cruelty of parents to impose their dreams on children!); she'd borrowed an Agfa Isola camera from a female friend from work, and she made sure it captured good images of her third new son, with his curly hair and chocolate skin.

Eshma kept her job and trusted it more than anything, and soon an offer for a transfer to the telephone exchange in Bombay came her way, and she took it. The young couple and their three boys left Surat and its Old World aura for good. The family rented a corner house in the distant suburb of Malad, just north and west of the growing city. Balan, however, struggled to gain employment. Having left his police post in Surat, he could not find work good enough for him in metropolitan Bombay, where every aspect of city living became a real and inescapable cause for anxiety; he began drinking more and more, borrowing small sums of money to keep his family afloat, money he could not pay back with ease. Meanwhile he spent more and more time at the city's thoroughbred racecourse, Mahalaxmi, known famously for its Indian Derby. Then came a job interview with the British Council, which at last gave him the work he wished for and enjoyed. Balan became an assistant in the classical music library. The family moved away from the distant, northern coastal suburb of Malad, and rented a small duplex apartment in Collectors Colony, better known as Sindhu Colony, in Chembur, where Fishhead's early story takes place. This move brought them closer to the city's edge and within three kilometers of the school that Fishhead and his brother would attend until graduation.

Three years later, Balan became manager of the council's music library, a title that allowed him to borrow a stereophonic record player, and bring home as many 33 1/3 RPM and 78 RPM vinyl records as he could hope to review. He hired a local carpenter to build two sturdy shelves on the wall above the record player, and he lined them with a variety of borrowed albums; as his collection increased, he stood the surplus on the corner of the floor beside the gramophone. His new job pleased Eshma and gave her momentary relief from the day-to-day demands of her family, and she took full advantage of the government-issued ration card. But while Balan's modest income contributed to the upkeep of the household, he kept portions of it for himself, to placate his creditors, buy his drink, and fuel his weekend racetrack gambling. He added Rummy to his indulgences, playing against his sister and her husband (the childless uncle and aunt lived elsewhere inside the city and visited Balan and his family on weekends), betting five or ten rupees per round.

Balan's success at work brought him face to face with many well-to-do patrons of the British Council, but he asked for no special favors. Nor did he miss a step at work—he kept his personal indulgences more or less in check, because he wanted no one else to control them, Eshma least of all. He walked a thin line between tasting privilege and succumbing to his want; he struggled to give up his temptation for one, the want, even as his proximity to the other assured him a decent life for his family, which remained incomplete without a daughter. So on the hottest night of the summer, their narrow mattress and stained mango-wood bed frame burned for a few minutes with their muffled cries of passion, while Fishhead and his two older brothers slept from the day's exhaustion.

"I'll pray that God gives us a girl," Eshma whispered. "I am tired, Balan." She let his weight and heat cover her.

He hooked her shoulders from behind her back, breathing hard, breathing into her hair, the side of her neck. "It will be our Destiny, not God's choice," he muttered, drifting in and out of sleep as strength left his bones. Then he slid his body away from her with the quietest rustle; the bedsheet moved when he edged his body over and eased himself back onto the bed, and Eshma clutched the thin sheet before it bared her naked Anglo-Indian skin.

"I'll pray for a girl," she whispered again, and made a quick sign of the cross in the dark as she stared at the ceiling and its old, turning fan. "Hail Mary, full of Grace..." she began, words barely escaping her lips, but Balan did not join her, and instead turned away, eyes closed.

He avoided any talk of God, fought it almost, although he never admitted to being an atheist or agnostic. These words meant nothing more to Balan other than an absence of belief, any belief, and particularly belief in the Church, Eshma's belief. He preferred Marxist socialism and argued its cause at the slightest provocation, and yet Balan remained careful to point out that he did not care to contribute communally and surrender his labor to the state. "The Russians and Koreans can keep their communism, and China and Fidel's Cuba can do that, too," he'd said to one nodding British Council patron, adding, "I'm all for democratic socialism." He hinted at his secret fondness for personal wealth, which eluded him. Balan hadn't meant to indulge the young patron with such a distraction as politics in the quiet space of the music library; he had no good reason to do so, given that the man in his black turban, who went by the name of Jagdeep Singh Gawalia, had only visited to take out a few long-playing classical records, among which, Balan noticed with some curiosity, Ligeti's "Atmosphères" and "Lux Aeterna" stood out for their remarkable disassociation from formal elements of music composition that, somehow—and despite the reposeful arrangement of this music—reminded Balan of other bold thinkers and talents from around the world. He told his patron what he thought, that great music always comes from within the depths of mankind and that it can be profound and moving without drawing its instructions from the church, a monarch, or from God, and Mr. Gawalia nodded the first time, smiling and offering up a simple "Indeed, if you insist" out of respect for the library space. Balan's next informal question about the man's personal affairs ("What do you do, sir?") while checking out the patron's vinyl records, prompted Mr. Gawalia to reveal with hesitation that he did advanced research at Bombay's oldest university, the prestigious Wilson College. Balan replied at once, *"Fides, Spes, Caritas,"* uttering the three words with an air of pride as if *he'd* authored them or attended Wilson; somehow the college's motto of *faith, hope, and love* meant something to Balan, but he gave no reason. In response, Mr. Gawalia said "Yes, although for me it will always be *vishwas, asha, and prem."* Balan nodded, rebuffed by the patron's sense of Indian pride. He pressed Mr. Gawalia for further details and learned that the man had been corresponding with another graduate scholar from The New School for Social Research in New York; they focused on the subject of global poverty and its immediate relation to rice growth, labor, and consumption in Asia. But not willing to be one-upped by a formal academic, Balan felt it necessary to launch into another diatribe about labor and Communism, upon which he finally lost the interest of his cordial patron, who departed a few minutes later with the records pressed against his chest.

But I digress, dear reader, and must offer my sincere apologies, as we are still in Eshma's nighttime company. And did you pay attention to Balan's words in bed? He mentioned my name. "It will be our Destiny, not God's choice," he'd said to Eshma, as if he believed it in his heart. He does not care to know me. In fact, he even fails to acknowledge my presence and influence on him and his family. He does not talk of Destiny, of life's path or outcomes, whether it is his or anyone else's fate, but he seeks it and poses those questions in the silent structure of his body's cells; this much I know, almost as if Balan moved among the city crowds as a wildcat foaming with a want for success and wealth, but frustrated by his intelligence and by what it cannot do for him. And that tiny bit of his mother's madness lurking in his veins… Daily, his feet take him through this jungle of people and contracts built one on top of the other by words, promises, needs, and actions. Agreements working as glue to bind humanity and keep it in place. Balan is concerned with the possibility of his escape from life itself (because he struggles to have his success); drink will do that, drink with its fiery twists of *fate*, so that he can forget for the moment the depth of his conflicted existence. He can live in stasis.

I want to write about him, I do; however, this story belongs to Fishhead, who turns his body now from one side to the other on the bamboo *chattai* under him, which separates him from the cool tiled floor as he sleeps just a few feet from his parents' bed. A pair of mosquitoes, *moisies*, on the skin near his anklebone have disturbed the boy's confusing and strange dream of food. A monster made of food and waste. Running ahead of him and getting larger, fatter. Things Fishhead could eat and want. Food he reaches for but cannot obtain.

I am intrigued by the word *becoming*. There is movement in this word, a suggestion of living and happening, engagement, which can either be a happening that awakens a body's cells or a happening that subdues these cells and reverses them back to a state that is before-being. Religions point to this word, and philosophies address it and give it due respect. The essential notion of Fishhead's story is, above all else, one of *becoming*. I choose my words with care, picking them and placing them before you with absolute intention—my emerging, patient, and renewed narration, and its *becoming*, which does what Balan refuses and what Fishhead is learning. The boy learns how to seek and expect. *Becoming* is that movement away from stasis, the stasis which the father reaches for when he drinks and which the son rejects when he leaves home to go play outside from sunset to sundown, while Eshma prefers neither *becoming* nor stasis at any cost, having placed her unquestioning faith in God's hands to lead her through life with the effort of her prayers, rosary, and Christian gestures.

There is something fascinating in my process, which is more methodical and purposeful than humans can imagine, because my presence is vital to the *becoming* of this known world in which Fishhead and his family belong, and you, dear reader, who reads this text in current time. Now is a time of great vitality, production, and consumption, with computers, smartphones, notebooks, texting, social networking, and a more reachable world than during Fishhead's time. My own reach is a limitless framework of connections and fulfillments, meant to indulge the interactions of living things with each other, humans with humans, and humans with other creatures, with plant life and vice versa. Even manufactured objects live with the core elements of life—you name them, cars, trains, bridges, furniture, shoes, shanties, homes, microwaves, light stands, glassware, guns, knives, coffeemakers, combs and Ziploc bags, hairspray, lipstick, money, eggs, parsley, carrots, and the terry towels you use and clothes you wear, just too many things to mention here—and I am in them all, energizing them and defining their paths and interactions through history, especially when hunger exists, like Fishhead's hunger, with the passions and desperations of a pariah. Things that appear dead, however still or cold, aren't dead at all; they continue living in new forms and are very much alive, perhaps more alive than some humans.

I work unseen, in the background, like a novelist, your narrator, engaged in a sincere imitation of the world with its active species, as for instance, protagonists as Fishhead, and his supporting cast of characters who make up his parents, relations, associates, and siblings. My interference with Fishhead's narrative, however, has its purpose and rests on many necessities, one of which is to insist that the Destiny you call on is forever in touch with current time, always present, tied to all life, including the past and future; and I wish to bridge the gap in time between where Fishhead is from fifty years ago and where you are today; my interference provokes a deep mystery that is full of possible questions and varied reactions in all humans. Another reason, if you look at it this way, is that I hold up a mirror to reflect the walls and windows of this story and to make them less opaque, less limiting, more reflective and reflexive, and fused with other realities waiting to work their way into Fishhead's life, in much the same way as time and air are limitless and fused with every aspect of existence. I will show you how my manifestations appear in his life in most unexpected ways and occasions, always to become a matter of consequences. How do you suppose my manifestations appear in your life? Can you imagine that and express it? I become the very fabric of Fishhead's existence, and remain the absolute energy behind his actions and thoughts that lead him to the many consequences he faces now and is about to face. These are all stories of value, stories of truth and even fabrication, as fabrication always wants to mimic reality but pushes reality's boundaries like a stubborn and persistent child who does not understand its own limits, or obedience, courtesy, and acts of patience. You may wonder if there will be other stories within Fishhead's story. Perhaps, but I am hesitant to admit to such a proposal now, and yet I can say that this work isn't meant to be an exclusive product study of Andre Gide's *mise en abyme*, but a slight look into it; more than anything, I wish the novel to be a layered narration of this world of interiority and outwardness that possesses Fishhead and surrounds him. My voice, my narration becomes a *diegesis*, that occasional word which academics and literary figures like to use, and it comes with eternal wisdom that exists beyond our protagonist's awareness. A voice such as mine moves through time in a parallel plane, an unseen "other" crest and web not known to humankind, unreachable in fact, except when I wish an encounter, as I do now, engaging with you in this way. This web is an intricate one, so enormous in scope and scale to confound any mind that attempts to comprehend and explain it, but that is exactly how the brain works, isn't it? And the very act of studying the marvelousness of the complex brain by humankind is an act of reflexivity and self-examination, of narcissism, if I may add. My sincere wish is that my words do not seem insensible to you, and I ask for your engagement, as I endeavor to make Fishhead's story worth your while.

Fishhead had a little brother one day in late October 1959, as he reached the curious age of four and a half. Almost overnight, the one-room duplex apartment in Collectors Colony became crammed and restless with the new addition of little brother Kishore, but the family of six had neither the means nor the intention to move to a larger place. No matter, the attention Fishhead had been used to receiving until now turned to this dark and unusually plump infant, so unaware of the family's overburdened state upon his arrival. Life outside the apartment, even on the graveled street in front or at the edge of the pond a hundred feet or so away, offered our protagonist more pleasures, more freedom than anything the indoors could offer, especially the freedom from little brother Kishore's endless needs. Kishore had a natural gift for consuming all the attention, Fishhead reasoned, although he thought nothing of the attention his aunty, his father's sister, began to shower on him; it seemed she had a particular liking for Fishhead over his brothers. Did aunty see him as the most agreeable and the least independent? A child she might mold at leisure for her own needs?

- Fishhead. Republic of Want. -

"Come, sit here," Aunty often said to him, as now, during a weekend visit with her husband to see the infant Kishore. They still had no children of their own.

Fishhead began to understand his own growing hunger for attention from her, and in some strange way which he seemed unable to explain, he often found himself standing next to her whenever she visited, waiting for this invitation to sit on her lap, wrapped in her arms, pressed against her body's heat and breasts, her flattened stomach, hips, and thighs, which she opened a few inches to make a soft, cushioned seat for him. He began to understand his growing need, although he had no means, no sense, to use the right words for such feelings. He liked the attention, that's all. What pleasure did *that* bring her? Did the other adults at home notice anything unusual? Did they wonder but hesitate to ask? Then she let Fishhead go without so much as a warning, and he ran outside to play, unwilling to stay indoors but still thinking of the image of his aunty's shape and warmth, which clung to the back of his body and on the underside of his legs, as if that woman's body, that sensation of pleasure from his contact with her, burned itself against him, lived in his memory, so that he might never forget it. He had no way to explain this feeling and awareness, but he looked forward to it, her invitation of "Come, sit here," even if it appeared to mean nothing at all to her. He took the invitation just as calmly as it came to him, without confusion or bother. Play soon distracted him and made him forget. But could he?

Cuts You Like Needles

Fishhead's life involved water, whether he played shipwreck at the pond with paper boats and baby frogs (as passengers, alive or dead), whether he stuck a vessel under an outside spigot to catch water for home use, or ran for the train in a hard downpour. He'd understood the price of water early in life and discovered its joys too, because that's how he first came as close to Anupa, came to touch her in just the same way as when the rain clutched his body and didn't let go. He'd met Anupa long before he entered high school and joined the social club for boys and girls, and by then he had begun to recognize his family's hardship more, but his awareness came slowly in his early years as Dad's troubles at the British Council grew. The things Fishhead didn't know: a few of the wealthier patrons of the cultural institution began to complain of Balan's reddened eyes in the morning and the smell of alcohol on his breath. Although he never shirked his responsibilities at the music library and enjoyed what he did very much, Balan liked to go drinking after work, and, during the long monsoon season, returned home under dark rainclouds without an umbrella (he didn't like using one), the sound of his footsteps lost in the thrashing. Fishhead found humor and disappointment in the sight of his father at the front door, a figure unreachable and desperate for a dry towel. Dad appeared no less distant on dry and hot summer days. At home, the boy only paid attention to his father's interests when circumstances in the household put Fishhead face to face with Dad's behavior: when uncomfortable exchanges of stress took place between his parents, or when the occasional creditor (often men in pairs), came knocking on the front door at sunset and sometimes on weekends, asking to speak with Dad, who managed to pacify these unthreatening men somehow. They wore simple street clothes and *chappals*; they looked as any neighbor might, so Fishhead simply assumed them to be Dad's business associates.

Even as he turned eight, his family's status seemed unclear to Fishhead. Small and lean, always hungry, he faced hardship without complaint. He faced the heat and rain without complaint. He enjoyed playing in rainwater, and let his mother worry about his getting sick from it or from his surrendering to snakebite (always *that* risk in the monsoons); the snakes emerged from everywhere during the wet season, flushed out of their holes and wanting higher ground.

The rainclouds brought a different mood to the day. With light and thunder sparking the guilt of sin. Lightning whips tearing through dark pillows which hung low, pressing down. Fishhead disliked this menace of the clouds, this one thing, and what the rains did to his family on the ground, and yet he liked when it poured. The rains came as sure as another day, a rain thick as people moving about in the marketplace. That strong smell of the earth, and moisture pounding, dancing furiously with the oil and dust on the ground, drenching everything in minutes. Scattering life. The furiousness of the noise, drumbeats rifling through the things he did. And, suddenly, a clearing of light in the clouds, a pause, but just a pause.

Fishhead had trouble sleeping during the nights of hard rain; it disturbed the mosquitos; they pestered him, bit him, and he slapped them and scratched himself. Then the pelt, pelt, pelt of water shot down from the skies again. The screech of this assault, a war. One side winning. Not his. When flood waters touched the verandahs, they rose to the doorsill and entered his family's living spaces on both ends of the apartment. He feared the invasion; it made him uneasy. What could the family do? Watch for snakes. He lived on the ground floor, not always a sensible level. His family's small rented duplex apartment—that one-room concrete and brick structure with its verandah in front and a verandah at the back— sat in a grid-shaped colony of residences that occupied a large tract of land with one paved road in the middle that ran west and met the main road to the east. A home for Fishhead, home in the northeast corner of Bombay proper, this ancient metropolis surrounded by water on three sides, a city not unlike anything Italo Calvino might imagine as he prepared to write *Invisible Cities*. And Fishhead endured in this dreamlike space, a fantasy, his Bombay, which seemed to be all things to him, as if I, Destiny, insisted on it; you might say that Calvino himself chose to help Fishhead and describe his thoughts from a different place and time, offering descriptions like *Cities & Desire, Thin Cities, Cities & Names, Trading Cities, Cities & the Sky, Cities & Signs*, and so on until the endless rumble of Bombay resided inside Fishhead as a plastic reality that became his *Cities & Memory*.

One particular morning, the rain seemed unstoppable; it had fallen throughout the night, in spurts and stops; it kept on when Fishhead woke up, and rained much more when he put on his school uniform: khaki shorts, half-sleeve white shirt, a Prussian blue school tie with two diagonal stripes of primary color (his choice of yellow), and unpolished black shoes. He stuck his feet into old, white socks, his only half-decent pair. He brushed his teeth, rinsed his face, and pulled his hair back without a comb. Then breakfast came in a hurry, as he sat down before a bowl of hot porridge, which Mom made from *sooji* and water. He liked her porridge, the way she cooked it from cream of wheat. He enjoyed *elaichi* banana slices with his hot porridge and the lumps Mom left in there. The yellow banana pieces kept their sweetness and tasted as if ripened with the natural essence of cardamoms inside them. Always this hot and sticky porridge, cheaper than corn flakes from a box, which cost more and which needed milk. His family could never afford enough milk, even though the obliging milkman offered to run a monthly tab. (The vendor pulled up to the front door most mornings with two large aluminum milk barrels strapped to the rear and front of his Hercules bicycle in a precarious way; he came down the graveled street and flicked his tiny bell repeatedly with a thumb, crying out *dudhwallah, dudh-w-a-l-l-a-h* at the top of his lungs. Mom turned the milkman down, knowing the outcome of keeping another tab she couldn't pay. Nana, who was visiting, always accused the man of thinning his milk with water.)

When Fishhead wrapped his school books in his plastic raincoat and put the load on his head, he knew Nana would disapprove; and yet he did just that, ready to step out in the rain just after seven, trailing behind his brothers; they would not wait for him.

"The raincoat goes on your back, not your head, child," Nana said, worried for his health.

Fishhead didn't listen to his maternal grandmother. And Mom took his side (Eshma knew how he liked to play in the rain). School had its own set of strict rules to follow. School = discipline. Buy the books; use them. They are useless wet. But how did this requirement suit Fishhead? Do you not also recall your own schooldays, dear reader? Did rules hamper you? Did you worry about getting to school on time or facing your classmates as Fishhead did in his condition? He hoped to keep his books dry, and off he went into the gray, the day's ashes, his cheeks and mind flushed with dread as he faced the two-and-a-half kilometer trek to school. He kept to the left side of the two-lane road. Rain pounded his chest, his bum, and shoes. It whipped his arms and the back of his legs, draining into his socks. The squishing between his toes and under his arches, like mango pulp. He dreaded his destination: the school's suffocating gates, the harsh treatment of the unkind teachers: Mrs. D'Cruz, the math teacher, and Delgado Sir, the geography teacher, and Mrs. Hassan, the science teacher. He raised his left arm to hold up his books now and bent it like a handle on a cup: didn't think of this move, and his arm became a downspout. In a matter of minutes, the rain soaked him through and through, but Fishhead walked on in the heat and the dull hour. The water soon climbed past his ankles, and then came up to his knees. Skies came crashing around him, deafening. He ignored stalled vehicles, and the two double-decker buses that plowed by, making cautious waves. A pariah dog inched across the street to his right, its nose up in the air, ears like wings. Bicyclists pedaled no more. The power in this water, the quake at his shins and feet; Fishhead stayed on course. He moved alone among a few strangers making their way through the risen waters; a woman hiked her brown sari up to her thighs, and a stray goat raised its head to keep it from taking in water. *Baa, baa,* a sad bleating now and then. Fishhead wondered if Pradeep and Prem had taken the bus or walked, made it to school on time, or not. He delayed them and knew it, but wished they'd wait for him. They always walked faster, took big steps: so focused on their destination and getting there before the bell. They ran for the crowded bus and jumped on, hanging for dear life at the rear door like tumors. Fishhead liked to look about him, study things naturally, find his love of life in the dreams of his walking free time, in the gentle time before school's demands. The rain imposed quiet on the marketplace, and forced him to keep his eyes half-closed. He stuck out his tongue as a frog would do, then drank each thundering drop from the honeyed sky. Savored the sound of its menace. Most shops still had their shutters down, the *mithaiwallah* across the street, too—sweets like carrot halvah and *laddoos* would make Fishhead feel better about himself now, keep out the cold under his sunburned skin. He shuddered at the thought; nothing dry on him, except books and bones. The raincoat on his head hadn't come undone yet. He should go knock on the *mithaiwallah's* shutters, stand there for a moment under the store's corrugated roof, shake off the rain, and take in the smell of sweetened milk and cardamom boiling down in large vats behind the shutters. Nothing like it! The stores appeared safe, built three or four steps above street level. A few more loose dogs. Garbage floated everywhere. But all this didn't matter and remained an afterthought. Must push on, push on.

A real bother, this rain, this moving, living water. Persistent! A short time later, the flood met Fishhead thigh-high further up the road just before he reached the fork that marked the midway point. *Keep going, keep going,* he muttered. *Even if the rain cuts you like needles.* But there it came, a sudden dip of the pavement, and he hadn't covered half the distance to school yet. He had to get to the other side, but saw no road. He fought the current that pushed against his thin legs. His flesh had begun turning into prunes. Should he step back and return home?

Can you see here, dear reader, the moment when the archaeology of survival in an unstable being forces its mind and heart towards prudence, if for a mere second? What intuition will Fishhead follow at the right moment, what prompt from me will he pay attention to? The need for survival is essential and kinetic. You might blame Destiny for such an outcome, yes, but the decision to turn around or step forward is always yours to make, not mine. Would you tempt fate? Adversity is the wisest counsel, and you must act, however. I am certain you, too, have faced your share of crises, small and large. A moment then for Fishhead to take. School pressured him, expected his presence even today. He kept his body still in the water, thinking about his next course of action while currents stirred below his neck, walls of motion pressing against him and pulling or pushing him. He leaned ahead, placing his feet forward with more care and making sure he felt the road beneath him, as the current showed its strength at his ankles. The water took his shoulders, and he started to lose control. He went on his toes.

Out of nowhere a drowned ox drifted toward him, stiff and pale on its side. A bloated ox with an open mouth, a limp tongue, and gaping, soulless eyes: a punching bag for God. The water turned it, showing Fishhead the many sides of death. He could not react fast enough to the animal's approach. Too fast, too fast. Never before had he shut his eyes for anything this world had to offer him, but he closed them tight now, just as the vanquished beast sailed towards him. He did not duck when a hoof tapped his forehead like a hammer and caught his upturned arm. Panic set in and a stiffening began in his blood. His heart thumped, echoing inside him and between his ears with the hawk of a mewling star, despite the clatter of raindrops making craters the size of his porridge bowl. Then the animal left his space, gone, like his own father whom Fishhead saw so little of, so little that he didn't miss the man at all. That kind of gone.

So you think you know this water, but no! You don't know what it tears away and brings through your part of town without warning. How many homeless, how many threatened by drowning and disease, made airless? Crops washed away, huts taken. Households possessed for graveyards. And the animals, what can they do? This water has a longing, a need, and it grows angry for some kind of satisfaction. Blood of the universe, not red. Rare. Not the way you know the corsage of life that pushes through your veins.

Little did the boy know when something flicked his shoulder that he'd touched a snake. Right under his nose! Didn't see the creature submarine between the droplets. Live and futile, a thick patterned snake with a promise of venom. It stayed behind the ox and came hurrying toward it in search of some secure level. But where, how, through what orifice? The open mouth of the ox perhaps, because Fishhead did not see a gash on the animal at the water's surface. He sucked air and pulled his nostrils closed, and he pressed his lips together with the rainwater lodged in his throat. The reptile rippled fast, fast. Did it want him? It didn't. It did!

Touched him again. Startled, Fishhead jumped back in the thick water and dropped his arm, exhaling, and the books and raincoat skidded off his head and plunged into the flood.

He almost lost his footing, but down he went splashing and grabbing in a panic, because his books mattered most, more than his own life. Can't worry about the snake. He held his breath underwater and forced his eyes open; the water stung, the world around him changed, dirty and thick with the muffle and drone of the unstable, the formidable. Bubbles everywhere. He did not think of the water's strength and snatched the raincoat before it came undone in the current. He did not think at all but simply moved with the reaction of a cat, a bee, a boxer. Cassius Clay. The boy believed in the new champion of the world. He wanted to be like Ali or perhaps not; he looked up to the champion, the dancing, stinging bee whose voice came through All India Radio after a heavyweight match. All India Radio, broadcasting from shortwave radios in shops and from loudspeakers put up in public areas. Fishhead heard the fight there. Move fast like a butterfly, sting like a bee. Save the books. He tried to save them.

He tore through the surface and gasped for air as the water pulled him several inches off the road and onto the sidewalk. His toes met the road. With his hands above his head, he turned his body to face east again, and without unwrapping the raincoat to check the condition of his books, he placed the pile back on his head. It made no sense to open it now—unsound, a word they often used in school; doing *that* would be unsound. He wanted to get away from this water, and he began to push his body through it while he held the books up high with both arms. Still raining. He kept moving forward with slow and careful steps until the water slipped back to his waist then fell to his shins. It took time, but it happened at last. *Thanks,* he said, because he hadn't lost his place on the road or sunk into a ditch or gutter, but the rain washed him like bread in a crow's bath. In spite of his victory, Fishhead had an awful feeling, a sense that he might never be free of this water, never safe from its anger, and that someday his body would feed its hunger.

He turned north at the fork in the road and picked up his pace through the divided golf course. Splish-splash, splish-splash! The sound in his shoes, loud enough to silence the frogs and pillage a conference of crows on the expanse of grass, now water-logged in places on both sides and held back by waist-high wood fences, painted in white. Unpaved shoulders of gravel, stones hammered down to size in nearby quarries with *Adivasi* labor. Petals of yellow poinciana and pink cassia lay waste alongside pods torn from tamarind and gulmohor trees in the rainshower. Soaked pieces of old newspaper blown here from the marketplace. He suddenly remembered the lunch in his pocket, unable to save the roti and banana. Wouldn't touch it now. He still had a kilometer to go, although his right foot started to burn, as the wet leather of his shoe rubbed his skin under the lace and against his heel bone. The skin would peel away and make fresh red scars in place, but Fishhead had no time to check that now. Lone pedestrian for a little while. He walked faster and stayed focused on his steps; soon he left the golf course behind and entered a residential area as the road continued north past Sion-Trombay Road and the oblong roundabout which contained Diamond Gardens. He crossed the intersection and cut through the gardens, walking a few hundred yards more before he spotted the church and school building to his right. He turned east to face the church, about two hundred feet before him; soft curtains of rain kept his holiness at bay. The belfry, granite steps, and carved wooden doors. Stained glass everywhere. The cross. Redemptorist officiants. All confirmed symbols of this mixed neighborhood, in which a Portuguese legacy had risen strong among the Hindus and Muslims. Fishhead could almost detect the smoking essence of frankincense and myrrh from Sunday service.

Saint Anthony's Road split off on either side of the church like an inverted wishbone. He avoided the main wrought iron gates and followed the wide curved pavement to the right instead, which led him around the compound wall. Before too long, he approached the U-shaped building for the boys school. The church and school stood as one, joined not in single file one behind the other, but offset from each other, like the shackle of a padlock swung the other way. Fishhead took the south entrance. He sighed, then walked past the gates, and sighed again when they didn't squeak, and he went up the smooth steps, the sound of water pushing around in his shoes. Feet like prunes in there. Glad the rain didn't pelt him anymore. He paused at the entrance to the hallway, its doors held open. Welcome, latecomer! Those revered, silent corridors around the quadrangle where everybody assembled on important mornings, not today. He'd missed that, again. Drops of water fell from him like cherry bombs going off at Diwali, a moment of cruelty for his lateness. He'd make a laughingstock of himself in class, he knew it; take in his classmates' jeers and taunts, and his teacher's scolding. He had already started shivering beneath his clothes. Sit in the classroom all day shaking.

Just ahead to his left, a corner, the long south hallway facing the quadrangle. Fishhead pulled his weight forward until the principal came in view there. Father Brendan stood at ease in his ballooning white cassock, white socks, and black-laced shoes with their polished look. He had thin brown hair, fair skin, a face and paunch, and fingers thick with power. A man who ripped the air out of the soccer ball when he kicked it high. The red fountain pen in his hand meant something. The well-oiled bamboo cane inside his left sleeve waited, ready.

Fishhead said nothing as he turned the corner and approached Father Brendan. What could he say? He knew the principal had heard it all before, many times before, his reasons for being so late. Wordless, he put the wrapped books down on the shiny floor and made a puddle there, and then he stepped in front of the principal, holding both hands out at his sides. Father Brendan reached for his cane with its ball end. The ball side mattered more than the opposite slender end, because it showed how Father Brendan felt about you, about what you did, what you deserved. The ball end touched Fishhead and nudged his forearms from below.

"You're late again!"

"Yes...yes, father."

"Open your hands, face up. Raise your arms, raise them...there."

A simple request, an order the boy did not refuse. He opened his hands, and all the problems of his world spun down to those few sharp cuts that descended hard, swiftly. Show no pain. Keep yourself together. Show no pain. He tightened his face and pressed his teeth together with each downward strike. A feeling of bitterness grew in his nerves, as if he'd dipped his hands in hell and its fire had eaten them away. His blood screamed inside him, a body fighting back, a violated land. Nothing he could do about it. Almost to tears, this boy. Then, stinging from the whip, and seeing the red pen in Father Brendan's hand, he bent down before the principal and unpacked the raincoat, his books. Difficult, so difficult. He began to free them with trembling, burning hands, as he peeled away the raincoat and pooling water one plastic fold at a time; he released those printed pages, imagining the worst outcome for his books. Surely they'd turned into soggy leaves by now, rare corn flakes in his bowl of watered-down hot milk.

You see, I am not without compassion, dear reader, as I understand all too well the fragileness of the good human heart. I give your protagonist his respite. He does not know me yet, does not know Destiny enough. He inherits his mother's simpleness, slow to grasp the schemes of the world. I will reveal truth to him, if he should ask about the outcome of his life. What more does a hapless boy have to go through to show his strength of character or name his growing realization that the world he occupies isn't right? Fishhead must learn to deflect the tyranny of the adult realm, which he cannot reject. Inside his raincoat, and to his surprise, the books stayed dry as feathers, including *The Adventures of Huckleberry Finn*. One book got unlucky: his *Don Quixote* took water on its back pages, which stuck together. He'll work hard to save them, dry them. He picked up his calendar (the school's datebook that every student carried), and, ignoring its wet side at the base, he presented the calendar to Father Brendan, then looked on as the principal marked another day late, very late, with his red pen.

Fishhead shook the raincoat and gathered his books. He waited for Father Brendan to leave before he trudged off to the large common bathroom down the hallway. He undressed in haste there, and, without emptying his pockets, squeezed the rainwater out of his clothes while he stood in the center of the lighted space. Shower stalls and urinals reaching to the tiled floor all around him. He wore no underwear. His skin had shriveled up, fingertips too. He did not look forward to walking home at three in the afternoon, when the bell rang to end the school day. The rain paused and resumed all morning; it threatened to accompany him with equal intensity later. The shy sun deserved a scowl. When the lunch bell rang, Fishhead did not care for the usual roti and banana mother had rolled and packed for him, now in his right pocket. He reached for it anyway. As he feared, the rainwater ate through the newspaper wrapper and turned the roti into mush, so he threw his meal away. No lunch at lunchtime. He left his classroom on the second floor and came down the flight of steps in the center of the U-shaped school building; once he reached the ground floor hallway, he stood on the fringe of the cafeteria stall at the bottom of the steps; he stood there in his damp clothes and took in the smell of freshly fried snacks: hot samosas and potato *bondas*. The aroma of fried chickpea batter coating spiced potato dumplings teased him and made his stomach growl, but he'd come to school without enough money. He wouldn't borrow any from a classmate, and although he had his pride, it did not feed him. Mother gave him ten paise, but what did such a small amount buy him except candy to sweeten his mouth. He needed fifty paise or more for a samosa or a bonda sandwich. Hard to beg, but he stood around as hunger clenched his stomach, and he studied the boys while they clamored around the stall to place their lunch orders. Beneath the racket, hot oil sizzled in two large vats on the other side of the counter.

Sometime later, Fishhead wandered off to the sports field behind the school building. A few boys wandering here and there but none on the spectator stands, just as he imagined. They would be out soon. He needed to get away from the temptation of the cafeteria; it served him no good to hang around there. The rain had subsided, but water dripped, tears spilled, from the old fruitless mango tree towering between the south gate behind him, to the right, and the concrete stands rising four tiers at his left. The tree offered respite from the sun and heat, but not now. He decided to cross the rectangle field despite the wet patches on the dirt, and soon reached the far end of the grounds to the east. He aimed for the common wall and climbed it, picking an area near the big tamarind tree, which grew on the other side of the girls' school playground and spread its branches over the wall. Girls! He eyed them now. He forgot his hunger, if only for a minute or two, because he became distracted by a group and their teacher about seventy feet ahead of him in an area spared by water; other groups of girls gathered elsewhere across the playground. Primary school girls in gray pinafore dresses, white short-sleeved shirts, blue ties, and sashes around their waists. A pretty sight. The group near him held an animated discussion about something, the girls' voices rising into near screams across the dampened grounds. Fishhead understood their pleasure at being outdoors again. His wet clothes still clung to him. The cotton changed its appearance into a darker, coarser shade of color when wet, and he became bothered more by the wet uniform the girls had surely noticed than by the altered shade.

"Anupa, pay attention!" he heard the teacher say to a girl in straight black hair that fell down past her shoulders. Anupa had faced away from the group and fixed her eyes on him. He didn't know her but he liked her clean uniform, black saddle shoes, and white socks that went up her nice smooth calves. She had dark eyes and pretty legs, a square-ish head with long and straight hair, silky black hair. Some of her classmates started to giggle, and they too looked at him. One girl reached over and pulled Anupa's shoulder back to make her face the teacher.

"Come on, *yaar*," the girl said to Anupa. "Don't upset the teacher."

Fishhead turned a corner of his mouth up and swung his head back in the direction of his school; he made sure to keep his balance on the wall, as he extended his reach to grab on to a branch. Then he stepped off the wall with the branch in his grip, saying "Anupa, pay attention…Anupa, don't upset the teacher! Anupa, pay attention. Come on, yaar." His weight took the branch down and bent it. He never let go and pulled his body towards the thinner end of the branch, until his feet touched the ground several seconds later and even as the branch began to resist. The branch meant to spring back and slip through his grip. He held on to it as it went away from him gradually, and he pinched off six long tamarind pods in the process, dropping them at his feet. Then he clutched some leaves just as he let the branch whip back to its original place above him with a whoosh. It cut through the air, leaving a bunch of tiny leaves in his fist. That fresh, tart smell.

He liked the name Anupa. Didn't forget it. He named the tamarind tree Anupa. Anupa, fresh like the leaves in his hands. A sweet and sour girl? Sweet and sour worked well for tamarind, but he didn't think he'd like that in a girl. Anupa had better not be sour, not to him. Sour girl, sour girl. No, not for him. Or was he the sour one? He wondered. He held the leaves close to his face, their small and narrow oval shapes closing in his hands when he blocked the light. The sharp odor of young tamarind washed over him and entered his senses, so that he had to close his eyes to acknowledge the lure of this natural world. The leaves never tasted as tangy as the fruit inside these hard-shell pods; the leaves tasted sweeter in fact. He opened his eyes and stripped some leaves from their mid ribs (many had already come away from the swinging branch), and he pressed the leaves together into a loose ball then pushed them into his mouth, against his molars. His body awoke when he started to chew, the sweet and sour sensation sweeping through him like a new sunrise in a foreign place, a paradise in his heart. He became more alert now, a naked, primal pulse beating in his chest and under his clothes. He swallowed the morsel then put the rest of the leaves in his mouth and chewed again. His jaws tightened from the cut of tartness in the chewed leaves. He swallowed his saliva, mashed the leaves between his teeth. *I am a cow; don't you see? I am dheynu, gai.* "I am a cow, Anupa," he said. Then he reached down and took a pod and he broke the hard brown shell by pressing it between his fingers. He tore off bits of shell from around the pulp. Thick and pale yellow veins held the dry pulp together. You didn't eat those, Mom had said once before, so he picked on the veins and pulled them away to one side of the pod, and he closed his teeth around it. The pulp and a black seed came away, stretching with light resistance like toffee. He used his tongue to dislodge the seed, the size of his fingernail, and he began to eat the pulp, allowing the sourness of the tamarind to cut through him like the principal's well-oiled cane. The sourness forced him to shut his eyes as his temples tightened and shrunk on either side of his head. Those jaws, clenching again. He chewed and let his spit loosen the pulp and he passed the mixture down his throat while his tongue pushed away the tougher parts and veins, which he spat out. Spat right out. And when his spit and veins hit the dirt, he used his right foot to cover the veins with the dirt. His stomach growled again but settled soon enough. He did not move until he ate the entire pod, and the tamarind left a gritty sensation in his mouth and against his teeth. Fishhead picked up the other five pod shells and put them in his pocket. *Take the raw tamarind home to Mom.* She loved tamarind and used it to make her rare fish curry or a tart lentil soup, *sambar,* which he enjoyed with rationed rice.

He went through the afternoon without a meal and waited until he returned home, his stomach a starved well. Days like this, full of uncertainty and hunger: his life paled in comparison to the other schoolboys. He picked out the poor kids, the down-and-out kids, from the hundreds that came from better homes and privilege, but even these poor boys moved with some pride and dignity. Why did he not feel the same? They ate their simple meals with satisfaction and without formality, they enjoyed their roti and pickle, their *bhaji,* which their mothers had made. But did they not also face hardships at home? Fishhead kept silent about his own family's problems and did his best to get his homework done, although hunger distracted him. He strived, a slightly-more-than-average student burdened by his tardiness. He had a good head for memorizing pages of text, but hunger made him want to forget everything he learned. Cramming didn't make him smarter, just more prepared for his exams. Trouble at home kept his mind away from his textbooks and pressed him to escape with play.

He desired Darren's companionship at play more. His new friend wore neat clothes and lived in a big rented house with walls at the south end of the large, square pond. Fishhead played with Darren a few times; the experience with this new friend pleased Fishhead, and he wanted more of that. Darren came from an Anglo Indian family; he had sisters, had a fair Indian mother, and an English father who wore suits to work. Then Darren stopped coming out to play altogether, week after week, even when it did not rain, and Fishhead failed to understand why; he recalled his friend's unhappy mood the last couple of times they hung out together at the edge of the pond. Trouble there, too? Darren revealed nothing. Perhaps his folks did not want their son to mingle with neighborhood kids after all. Upper class, upper crust; white and brown won't adjust. Still, Fishhead kept an eye out for his fair friend, another reason to while away the daylight hours at the pond just beyond his front door.

Waltz of the Flowers

He walked away from his parents' arguments, words exchanged often in Tamil or Malayalam, their native state languages of the south, and sometimes in English, or in Hindi, the national language they all spoke in public. Fishhead blamed himself. He soon learned from brother Pradeep that Dad had lost his job in the music department at the British Council; his creditors had started showing up and pestering him at work.

Dad's job there had had its privileges: he'd kept a gramophone at home and brought records home to review for the British Council's Indian members. A passion: he'd pull up a chair beside the stereophonic player on evenings and weekends; he'd drop a long-playing record on the turntable and call for silence in the room. The New World Symphony. Marian Anderson at the Lincoln Memorial in 1939. Segovia. Larry Adler on the mouth organ. In this restless home, music demanded silence, attention, understanding. Fishhead received it all with curiosity and interest, his head in a slow turn; he wondered how Dad could appreciate such music while showing no regard for the popular *filmi* soundtracks one heard all day long throughout the city, on radios and public broadcasts.

But the gramophone and records were due back at the British Council soon. Fishhead found it hard to read his father's dejection;

Dad kept a straight face and controlled his expressions in hard times. But Fishhead knew when his father had a good mood; music from the West brought out the man's emotions and conductor's gestures, almost as if Dad had composed each work. The gramophone and vinyl records meant more to him now, especially since the British Council wanted them back. Did Balan see the inevitable and fail to acknowledge it? Yes! I should say yes, Destiny's crisis that brewed early in his head and heart, churning like monsoon clouds through the labyrinthine folds of his awareness. Desperation is hell, a blacksmith's poker reddened by fire, which Balan held too close to his eyes. Fishhead wondered about Dad; the man did not wish to talk about this loss with his family, although a part of him did not seem to care at all. Life had a nasty habit of running away from the man's grip, and so he drank and gambled, escaped into tunnels that sucked light and air, tenderness. Nothing new or unusual here, I insist, another drop falling in history's bucket of ills. Balan had run up a drink and food tab at a restaurant near the British Council. Unable to pay back his tab, he figured he'd get it from Eshma. She did not help him and could not, so they argued.

Mom had no time or desire for romance now. The meager monthly salary she earned from working at the telephone exchange paid for rations, the rent, schoolbooks and uniforms, train and bus tickets, and helped to feed the family. Fishhead listened and asked few questions, although he did not understand why Mom complained about Dad. She complained more when Nana visited, although Nana had returned to her home in Gujarat, much to Dad's relief. Now the only visitors were the strange men who came to the door uninvited, asking for payment from Balan Sahib. (The men added Sahib to mean Sir, out of respect.) Somehow, Dad managed to send these men away with promises; he spoke of actual days and dates. Fishhead couldn't help noticing that, when those dates arrived, his father stayed out all day, returning late at night.

The square pond had answers. The still water behaved as a window to the universe, appealing and mysterious, reflecting clouds and sky in the daytime, and distant stars winking at night. If the pond knew his family's troubles, it would also reveal the answers, Fishhead believed this. The pond also knew why Darren stayed away, even though the boy's family hadn't moved out. Fishhead still needed someone to play with; he chose Prem.

On the opposite side of the gravel road, the pond occupied an entire street block diagonally across from the rented duplex apartment and just south of it. This body of water had its secrets, deep enough to drown a cow, goat, or adult, and far more dangerous for a boy like Fishhead. After days of rain, the pond disappeared under overflowing water, a brown liquid that rose inch-by-inch to reach the front porch steps. On good days, the pond glimmered in the heat and daylight, clear, full of reeds and cattails pushing up in clusters near the edges. There, the lotuses and submerged algae grew, then came debris, frogs, bottom fish, snakes, even the few paper boats Fishhead and Prem launched and steered with gentle branches. The boats always took in gulps of water.

The boys' natural brutishness reigned. Fishhead skimmed stones and aimed at anything that poked its head out of the water. He also used sticks. The frogs made deep-throated sounds, their lives appearing undisturbed and so natural beyond the family's saga of survival, its pitfalls and struggles. He wondered if they read his troubles, if the pond shared what it knew with them. The frogs stopped singing at the slightest disturbance; any sound interrupted them. Keepers of the night. Fishhead wanted to know their secret to living without worry or pain, without the need for money or cruelty. He wished to know this, imagining for a moment dressed-up frogs in a crowded marketplace, shopping and negotiating prices down like Mom did, or complaining with each other about his behavior with stones, with sticks. He looked into the water. He looked up. Smacked the water. Smacked it again. Heard sounds, cries, whistles. The crescent moon showed its face above him like a queen stepping out into the emerging darkness with her subjects, an entourage of dotted lights and dreamy white. Away from the horizon to the west, the sky blushed with the last caresses of orange. The end of summer.

Then Darren came out of hiding one morning, and Fishhead stirred, moved, walking barefoot to the south end of the pond to greet his friend, and glad he'd worn a shirt that day; it made him look somewhat decent, despite the lack of footwear. Darren mumbled something. His father had fallen seriously ill, he said. He didn't have long to live, he added, as he stood facing the pond. He gave no further details. This news saddened Fishhead, but he didn't know how to express his feelings to his friend, and could not say for certain if he'd heard the truth, a half-truth, or if Darren had made up the story as an excuse for his absence. Then Darren left a few minutes later, unable to stay outside much longer; he offered no explanation. Fishhead knew he'd never see him again. He wouldn't go after that friendship; no, he would not. He joined Prem at the north end of the pond and told his brother the sad news. They hung on to the warm afternoon in silence, their unease becoming visible in the energizing ripples their sticks made on the water's surface. Then Fishhead began slapping the water. He hit hard, aiming his stick at every tadpole or silverfish that dared rise to the surface. They jumped, died, or dived underwater. He beat frantically at the reeds rising from the pond and bent them, wrecked them.

He had his fill and left the pond. He left his brother behind and went for a walk alone. As daylight changed, he turned for home and saw Prem still at the pond with his back to the road. Fishhead said nothing. Mom and Dad shouldn't know that he did not like to wear his *chappals*, as the flip-flops slowed him down and kept him from running. He washed his feet under the faucet at the side. Washed up for dinner, assuming there would be a meal worthy of the name. Hunger hit him now, and he needed food, something to eat. No leftovers after lunch, only dry, stale bread. And Dad refused to cook. Pradeep stayed out until bedtime.

Fishhead caught the hint of music just before he stepped over the threshold. The open front door, always open, except at night when the family slept. The soft, familiar notes of *The Nutcracker*, a record Dad had played before. And the scratch of a needle being pulled by the record. Such a sweet piece of music, playful too; it brought the night in like a familiar guest. Fishhead paused at the doorway and studied his father. When had Dad come back home? Fishhead wondered how he'd missed it. Dad sat in his metal chair, arms folded, feet tucked under him. He wore a white singlet, which he slipped inside his dark slacks; he'd hung his light blue long-sleeved shirt on the back of the chair. He liked to move about the house without his shirt on. Now Dad closed his eyes and tilted his head back, absorbed in the music, carefree.

Soon someone from the British Council will show up at the door with a small truck to haul everything away in blankets. It's been arranged. For Balan, who cares more for the gramophone and records than he does his family's welfare, this will be devastating. That's fate, you might conclude, just the way it goes. Here again I must step in and say that a person in charge of a family must consider the outcome of choices made. Balan failed in this matter; a circuit in his brain appeared to have malfunctioned, although he regarded this situation as normal. He is unable to notice this crisis; he will not acknowledge it, even for the sake of his own survival. In his blood is that thread of madness from his mother's side. He has become too attached to his gift of music. No longer will he have the gramophone and records in his possession, and this realization has caused him to sit by the player with the impression of a bereaved parent grieving next to the body of a dead child. He gives the player his undivided attention, spends more time with these musical objects than he does with his wife, his children. Some kind of deprivation.

Fishhead did not understand why his father drifted so far away, so connected to the source of music—a veneered oak case with four tapered legs inspired by Sputnik. The record player's square lid is lifted up like a car's hood. *Grundig,* it said in raised letters, brushed in chrome on the front of the case. Fishhead had always fought the temptation to explore the gramophone in Dad's absence, but he knew now that he would do so at the next opportunity. He needed to know the source of Dad's silence, why this music meant more to the man than his family.

Fishhead stepped forward and faced the player, a box as wide as his outstretched arms. Dad there to his left and behind him. In the center, the black 12-inch vinyl disc turned. 33 1/3 RPM, it said on the printed label. Round and round Fishhead's eyes went, a game he liked. It challenged him, reading the finer print on so many records. Dad had more of these than his heavier 78 RPM records, but this one, this disc playing now, claimed a special place in his heart; one of his favorites. Fishhead knew not to interrupt his father with questions. Soon a thing of the past, this knowing. Suspense cut through the air and weighed down the room. Fishhead wondered if Dad had any regrets at all. Why did Dad say nothing? It brought him so much pleasure, this unreachable world of the West now in his living room. This player with its automatic movements: arms rising, swinging, as if oiled, levers moving up, down, sideways. Soundless, almost. Two discs awaiting their turn, balanced at the top of a slim metal post with a ledge that held them up in the center of the turning record. Fishhead enjoyed this privilege too; he'd seen this action many times. The first disc fell on the spinning rubber plate, and a needle swung inward then came to rest in the outermost groove. At once a warm crackle radiated from the stereophonic speakers in the case, and then music flowed. Later, when their turn came, the other records dropped one on top of the other, and the gramophone kept playing. Dad sat this way for hours.

The records stood pressed up against the wall or against the case on both sides, a collection of composers, musicians, vocalists, and choirs. Beethoven, Bach, Chopin, Mozart, Brahms, Strauss, Vivaldi, and Tchaikovsky, and others like Rimsky-Korsakov, Paganini, Dvořak, Clara and Robert Schumann, Segovia, Elgar,

Mahler, Sibelius, and Shostakovich. Gershwin and Ellington, Scott Joplin and Samuel Coleridge-Taylor. Fishhead tried to learn these names, this music. Strange and foreign places, a world out there. He knew little about it, about them. But did they know about him, that he lived like this? Dad hummed passages from symphonies, instrumentals, operatic pieces, musicals, folk songs, ballads, maritime tunes, minstrels, and spirituals. He played Marian Anderson and Maria Callas a lot. Nat King Cole, too, and Billie Holiday. Voices with soul and earnestness, heartache. He played recordings directed by Arturo Toscanini and performances by Yehudi Menuhin, by Julian Bream. Dad kept a few Jazz performances, and a Blues record of Charley Patton.

The Nutcracker turned and turned, a flawless plate of plastic, flat and burnished as feathers on a mynah. At the center, a picture of a handsome dog stared into a big horn, the words *His Master's Voice* printed next to it. Fishhead followed the name, the dog, and horn as they spun around. Heaviness weighed on him, on his vision. He brought his hands up and placed them on the edge of the open case near the record. Did Dad catch his movement? Fishhead turned to his left. No: eyes still shut, arms still crossed, good. Then he moved his fingers along the dull green fabric, small ridges in a pattern covering the case, a feeling like thick paint. He ran his hands along the case, thinking of Darren. Might not see him again.

"Stand back!" Dad said. "Don't touch that when it's playing! You'll scratch the record!"

Surprised, Fishhead retreated. Dad took his shoulder and motioned him to sit on the floor, then sat back in his chair again and closed his eyes as before, irritated. He swirled an imaginary stick in his hands now—the conductor, the artist and composer.

Movements of his head, his wavy black hair, the form of his hands, slender like *moringa,* the tasty drumstick vegetable, and his dark, bare feet. Clean toenails, changing color. A handsome Dad, striking, but as far as Fishhead knew, he did not play any instrument.

Dad's face became dramatic and expressive. Fishhead thought his father cried inside, with sadness or joy, but always without tears. Why should Dad be happy? Did he want happiness? What joy did life bring him? He did not care to share it with anyone. Dad went somewhere else at times like these. Fishhead wanted that, wanted to take from these records what Dad also took in, so he got on his knees without a sound and approached the wooden case of the record player again. He turned his head to the left and looked at his father, then leaned over the player, his shoulders almost touching the edge of the case. Dad's eyes stayed shut. Fishhead remained in front of the player with equal fascination for a minute or two, but then he moved his right knee a bit and set it back down by mistake on a tiny pebble that had been tracked in from outside; the sudden, sharp ache made him stumble, and he grabbed the gramophone case with his right hand to keep his balance. Then he heard Dad's chair squeak; the slap to the back of his head shook him hard. Startled, Fishhead turned to face Dad, bumping against the case with his shoulder, and the needle jumped back, scratched the record. At once Fishhead got to his feet, fear gripping his face with the unthinkable isolation of Dad's anger now focused on him.

"What did I tell you? What?" Dad sat up, pushed forward, and shouted over a repeated section of music. "Come here!"

"No!" Fishhead said. "No, I'm sorry."

"Come here! I asked you, didn't I?" Dad got up and grabbed the back of Fishhead's collar and dragged him towards the back of the room. "I won't say it again! Stay away from the player! I have to return it! But now you've scratched the record! How should I punish you?"

Fishhead pulled down desperately on the front of his shirt to keep from choking. "I'm sorry!" He repeated, hurt and ashamed.

Dad let him go and returned to the player; he lifted the arm and advanced the needle's position on the spinning record. Then he returned to his chair in front of the gramophone case. The *Nutcracker* played on, full of mirth, as if nothing had happened, and Fishhead coughed, nursing his hurt and body's prickly heat.

The slap of his brother's feet echoed through the darkness outside. Prem came running, taking wide leaps, across the gutter first (the one that ran between the street and front yard, some grass), and then along the short flagstone path leading to the open door. He slowed down once he landed on the low cement porch. A cheetal fleeing in the night from some sound, a bit of news that snapped like a twig, alerting him. Take safety now, tell others. Night's silence amplified his movements, the high arches in his feet pushing air, pressing down on the porch. Thin Prem, a year older and lean as Fishhead. They fought and played, but they watched out for each other, reading each other's natures as twins did. Prem had a disadvantage though, a boy unthinking and prone to accidents.

He showed up dusty at the front door, wearing an old shirt that hung over his khaki shorts. No shoes like his brother, not on graveled streets while playing.

A dance called *Waltz of the Flowers* began. A beautiful passage from *The Nutcracker*, one of six dances that played near the end of the ballet. The music expanded. *There!* Dad closed his eyes tighter. The harp's warm ripple dashed across the room, across an imagined landscape far away, building anticipation and release. The static air failed to hold back this ecstasy shifting up and down, to the right and left, and forward…a flight of pleasure. Then wind instruments rose to join the harp, sounding off a broadcast of what followed: horns unwilling to keep still. The sound from violins leaped like flowers drenched in sunlight before a bee. The violins made a weave, they soared—and in this way, the waltz commanded attention, as it lifted and moved through the room to enter Fishhead's consciousness. From his place at the rear of the room, the boy took it all in and tried to understand it. Fishhead sulked, disappointed in Dad and in his hunger. Dad dropped his head from side to side, and waved his imaginary baton as if to free his tensions. His shoulders moved and his body did, too. He kept his eyes closed.

Prem waited on the porch, hands against the doorframe. He leaned in, not wanting to disturb the moment and upset his father, unaware of what had just happened. He stood there, breathing, catching his breath, looking in, observing Dad in motion. Dad had his back to the door and sat near it. Then Prem wiped his feet on the jute doormat at the threshold. Scrape-scrape.

"Shh!" Dad cut in, pushing the sound from his lips, eyes shut to declare his concentration. He frowned. His upper body straight now against the back of the chair. He wanted this, to keep listening to *The Nutcracker* undisturbed. *Undisturbed!*

Fishhead gestured, as if to ask Prem: Is something wrong? Be quiet!

"It's Darren's dad…" he started to say. Couldn't wait any longer.

"Quiet!" came Balan's command, more stressed this time. A roar. Displeased with his second son's intrusion. Fishhead moved closer and brought a finger up to his lips, a caution to Prem. At the same time, Dad opened his eyes a little and moved them sideways, turning his head to hold Prem's attention, cutting air with sight. Had he seen Prem as a problem child from the beginning, a stone too heavy for progress, too difficult for success and good health? Prem, least favored by Dad.

"Didn't Darren tell you?" Prem repeated. "I just heard his sisters…talking about their dad's cancer. He's dying." Prem crossed the threshold. "They walked by," he added, "but didn't…didn't see me at the reeds." He came forward, one soft step at a time, came around Dad and edged in between them. The living room shrank, and Fishhead sat on his haunches; he made space for his brother, eyeing Dad. Balan got up, agitated, determined to keep his focus despite the intrusion. He raised a hand to smack Prem on the back of his head, but Prem ducked, moving away. Too fast, that boy. So Dad pulled his chair forward and fell back in it with a scowl—those eyebrows, gates down, let the fuming train go by. Prem aimed for the kitchen at the rear; he went past the back door, his news lost to the music. *The Nutcracker* played on, that dance, the *Waltz of the Flowers*. Fishhead thought of it, this sad truth of Darren's family, carried out of darkness in Prem's hands. Even Darren could not confess it. Fishhead had an aching for his friend. Suddenly, the music didn't seem happy to him at all. He got to his feet and faced the wooden case of the player, and he let his eyes rest on the needle as it rode the endless groove of the spinning record. The life of that man, Darren's father, there in that groove, his veins, and the low pressure of his pulse against his wrists. Fishhead turned around and stepped past the back door, where Prem searched for food, anything, in the narrow and bare kitchen.

Love's Treason

Balan has an innate artistic talent, but who will detect it? His isn't making art to impress his family, and he must do something else to keep his interests as he faces the imminent loss of the gramophone and records. But he is an artist today, perhaps tomorrow, too. What does art mean to him as he considers his family's growing indigence? I want to get behind his desperation. So let me ask you, dear reader: What does art mean to you, and can you describe it for me? I know it's a loaded question, but I'd like to hear your opinion. And tell me what art does for you if it does anything at all? Why make art in the first place? Is art life, death, Destiny, or all of it? Mine is an honest inquiry, and I don't mean this as an intrusion. You might say with a burst of instinct that there is no simple answer to any of these questions, no brief answer, and I am being ridiculous to even expect a blanket response. Art is an experience, a consensus, discord, but perhaps a question, an assertion, or a reaction. Isn't that enough? Then again, it is madness, joy, endurance. A test, something to be done without the expectation of riches, although there is a reward: its beauty. Art cannot be described entirely, you might say, it cannot be explained, because it is one thing and everything—a feeling, a moment, that spark, a sublimation, an idea, a connection, or subjective reaction that relies on what's within and without. Ah, yes, and can you live without art? I insist that art grows from the heart, from the ground and below it, grows through us all, resonating with a deep sensitivity in the time and space I occupy. *Patience, patience!* There are no walls on earth to hold time and space. *Suffering can do that, only suffering can do that.* Perhaps, you know someone who doesn't care for art at all, who has no patience for it, no inclination or capacity to perceive its value. Art is never the same for two people, they'll argue, and there is much to discuss and disagree about it. Through your forms, art aims to imitate life or dismantle it. So why should I expect a straight answer, a simple answer? Of course, you are right, I shouldn't expect a simple answer at all. Your views are different than mine. So be it. But why, you are thinking, do I bring up the subject of art when we need to keep our attention on Fishhead? I apologize, but this concerns his father. Balan is a man who struggles with himself. Can we talk about all that's within and without this man, these tensions he will pass on to his children, to Fishhead?

Consider this for a moment: There is a doorway, an important and imagined doorway that draws the line between the conscious and subconscious, and you exist on this conscious side of that doorway, drenched in your senses, just as Balan and Eshma also do. Just as Fishhead exists in all his senses. I am interested in talking about what's on the other side of that line. Say you are an artist. Or the beholder. You have a passion for art, a skill for engaging in its practice, appreciating complexity or the minimal. Avenues of experimentation and application, with wood, paint, plaster, or just pencil and paper, rubylith, bytes, perhaps words, a song, a movement, clay, fabric, glass, stone, wire, an instrument, beads, anything that helps your soul plead or sing. What touches you or connects you with your dreamstate: the formless, or the divine? Does art not first emerge in your subconscious before you approach it with your senses? The answers you pursue to questions residing beyond the other side of that line? Art is all that comes alive there: the seed of ritual, ceremony, portrayal, process, or provocation. The formless takes form in your hands. Does it not? I ask you, reader. Art *is* life, death, Destiny. A bridge to cultivation, to confrontation. Something grows, something dies. Mirror for the self and the other. Need I also say that art is the sound in a river, the song of the cardinal, of a cathedral, a minaret, electromagnetic frequencies, the shape of air through the leaves and your clothes, an intrepid bike messenger, the motion of a highrise crane in Chicago, a car navigating tight streets and lanes in Bombay, an aircraft over the Atlantic, your sunrise, raked clouds, the lust of a feather, a movement of a knife, an old paring knife that Balan George uses to carve forms from bars of soap, which his family cannot afford.

Yes, he is the artist today and perhaps tomorrow as well. Who will care enough to detect his talent? Not Fishhead, who can only ask: *What is Dad doing to our soap?* The artist functions nevertheless. He's a being embraced by the irrational, determined to pull off the imagined and give it form, some meaning in a confusing world. How it challenges and manipulates him! Balan has been drawn into the vortex of his subconscious; I know this, I am there. His space on the other side of that doorway remains unsettled, an unbearable magma culled from rust, from bacillus growing uncontained in his corruptible essence. His attempt to make small art in time and space is a compliment to me; after all, he must do something to forage his Destiny, because he has no self-made path. Years wasted as a rebel youth in South India defending his patriotism, breaking rules, pushing good people against themselves, up against imaginary walls. He is creative nevertheless. Somewhere is a purpose Balan knows he will possess and believe in, a purpose he hopes that his family can understand and accept. Opportunities for income, wealth. He contemplates his future and sees it taking seed now; he is sure his soap art will do that.

Fishhead's curiosity got the better of him. He stood by his father's side to observe in silence, but Dad would not have it and put his left arm out to create a barrier. Fishhead obeyed, wordless. Dad in the chair, leaning over the card table, on which he spread an old newspaper. Soap in his left hand, knife in the right. A glass with liquid nearby, three fingers high, clear. His drink? Dad spared no bar of soap, placing his collection on the newspaper away from him, a half dozen pieces in all; he put the ridged, dried remnants at the end of the row to his right. Go at those last. He drew on the soap with the pointed end of the knife, using light, unbroken indentations to mark the shape of his form. Will Dad make something holy? Fishhead wondered, although he never saw Dad in church. Dad pressed down harder along those lines to make deeper channels. Shavings fell away from the bar one by one and dropped onto the newspaper—thin strands, twirls, and slices the size of his fingernails.

Fishhead wanted to understand his father. And his burdened mother; he sensed Mom's frustration and inability to help Dad find work, another duty Eshma did not want on her plate. Fishhead wondered why his father made no effort to find a new job; maybe Dad did not care enough to do that, and appeared comfortable with his new pastime at home, spending hours in his chair, carving soap on the weekend, too. Fishhead could not pull himself away, unlike his siblings; he kept a good distance and watched Dad go digging for soap with an old paring knife in hand, snatching up any soap from the kitchen or bathroom before he settled at the table. Dad wanted new bars, because he grumbled about the used pieces, the smaller ones; he took them all anyway, determined to make his knife unmask every piece of soap, which the family depended on for washing and cleaning laundry. This work took hours to complete and left an odor in the room that lasted through dinner, lingering even when the family slept through the night in the heat with windows open.

What shapes did Balan have in mind? What had he hoped to discover about himself through this creative exercise? I can assure you that his art did not threaten to sell his soul to the devil, the demons; he also had no intention to carve out miniature wayside icons like those religious stone gestures visible throughout the city. No expressions of sacredness here for this man. His life, this labyrinth, held many mirrors; it harbored his habits, seeded his corruptions, and lit his vision. Now more than ever, the beholder also made beautiful things. The hours he spent at the table seemed insufficient to him, never too much, always too little. Fishhead watched on as Dad made rough human carvings, and chiseled forms attached to geometrical shapes, as if to show someone alighting a bus or train, perhaps emerging from within an irregular box! Could Dad do more? Fishhead wondered. Could Dad do better? Searching, searching for deep answers, for form and style, that family man. Dad's wrists began to hurt, but he kept on, resenting any disturbance or distraction. Fishhead noted that his father only spoke when he wanted help to clean the table, often before Mom came home, but she knew soon enough. And because she did not complain at first, Dad kept it up on the weekends. The soap bars cost a few *paise*, more than she could afford, and soon she grew tired of the extra expense Dad put her through. The added headache. Soap had its purpose in the bathroom and kitchen, nowhere else.

Uncle and aunty came; it had been a little while. Fishhead could never be sure he liked their visits, because Dad got caught up with them and ignored everything else, including lunch, the home, his art. They brought drink, playing cards, a portable shortwave transistor radio, and cigarettes; at times, sweet or salty snacks to share. Dad put away his interest for soap carvings to enjoy their company; he really looked forward to their visits. Fishhead noticed a change in the mood at home: Dad groomed himself, shaved, wore fresh clothes which Mom washed, tucked his shirt in, walked upright, and seemed more alert and conscious of his appearance, his wavy black hair, mustache, and goatee. Dad used coconut oil and combed his hair straight back, and he spent all day training loose locks of hair to stay in place, because he didn't like them falling across his face. Fishhead had no doubt that uncle and aunty came home to see Dad more than anyone else, more than Mom, and often they visited on Sundays. Dad played Rummy with them, sometimes with real money, using small change that aunty, his younger sister, loaned him; he won a few rounds and lost others. With their encouragement and help, Dad also started betting on horses at Mahalaxmi.

At such times, Dad and his visitors created a world of their own, removed from everything else surrounding them. A time for adults, a serious time for adults engaged in their own pleasure: Fishhead realized this, convinced that his brothers felt the same. While Prem also stayed behind and watched from time to time, Pradeep made it clear by his absence that he disapproved. Fishhead would not disobey Dad's requests, and he did not expect Prem to, either; he went to the kitchen at the back, brought glasses for three, served water, placed kisses on the visitors' cheeks, emptied ashtrays, placed his ear near the radio, and hoped for a dip in the snack box.

"Don't move the antenna!" Dad said. "You'll upset the reception!"

"I won't!" Fishhead replied. He stepped away.

He got a hug from aunty, a bit too long, but he didn't mind the lingering softness of her warm breasts afterwards. He couldn't be sure if he wanted more of it. He wanted more. Then off he went beyond the edge of their circle, formed by his questions and hunger. If he failed to understand his father, his uncle and aunty remained a mystery to him altogether; and yet he began to feel as though he might like them better. Their mysteriousness, their private lives, interested him more. There they all sat around the small card table, behaving as if no one else lived at home. Trails of cigarette smoke rose to the white ceiling and drifted across the room, stirred by the overhead fan; jokes and serious conversations ruled when silence failed. Dad did not offer his thanks when Fishhead helped, and Fishhead did not expect it.

In fact, he could not recall a time when Dad thanked him for anything. He couldn't remember when Dad had carried him in his arms, or if Dad carried him at all. "That's for weak men," Dad had once said, although Fishhead didn't think Dad referred to physical strength, because exercise and fitness did not suit him. Fishhead received no softness or affection from his father, and he remained sure his brothers shared the same outcome. So he turned to his mother more. Mom wore the appearance of a parent pushed to the edge of fatigue from her duties at work and home. She had her full-time job at the exchange, the government telephone *bhavan* near Churchgate, more than an hour away by train. Strong willed, determined, she took every breath for her children, although she did not say so out loud, as far as Fishhead could remember. But he caught her sobbing when she cooked alone, her housedress smeared with spices and traces of food that she wiped off her hands. Mom sat on her haunches, with knees under her chin, the wick stove in use before her, a pot with a lid on it. Steam rising. She worked in that bare kitchen with its bare shelves, but preferred the partially-open verandah. The slow kerosene stove, now desperate for a new set of thick cotton wicks. Dad said things to her. Dad made promises, like when he swore he'd get her a primus stove and a pressure cooker after he won at the racetrack; he shared his time between carving soap and studying facts about horses, jockeys, stables, and their owners. Uncle and aunty made sure he did his homework. For his daily reward, Dad kept a small bottle of moonshine at home and drank while he pored over race results.

Fishhead liked the few times when Mom smiled, like she did after Dad made his promises. Mom meant something else in her smile though, Fishhead reasoned. Dad's promise impressed her in much the same way as the government-issue ration card did, with its severe limitations of supply and quantity. She liked the ration card and stayed married to it, but she did not care for her total dependence on it, even though it came to her rescue often. Life at home tied Mom down with chores, and Fishhead gave his help when she needed it. At times he protested. Mom did everything: she washed, cleaned, cooked, and went to the market with the ration card. Fishhead accompanied her and helped bring home small bags of rice, sugar, and wheat flour (sometimes whole wheat grain she had to grind into flour). Kerosene to last a week. He hated the smell of this fuel because it hung in the air and stayed on his skin, his clothes; it stung his nostrils and threatened to soil the food. He often went alone with Mom to the market, although sometimes she took Prem or Pradeep instead. And when Fishhead did not help his mother, his feet sometimes took him to the streets, to play with his brothers or with other neighbors.

But more often nowadays, his interest in Dad's soap enterprise kept him inside. One Sunday morning, before uncle and aunty arrived, Mom snatched the square bar of soap from under Dad's hands, although he'd spent the day before carving it down to a crude animal shape; it resembled the head and neck of a common brown bear. Why the bear? Fishhead wondered. An interesting choice Dad captured from memory. Such a curiosity, the Indian bear. (Once in a while, a brown bear, the size of an overweight schoolboy, came through the streets, leashed and trained by its owner to do tricks inside a ring of bystanders.)

By nine o'clock, Dad had poured his moonshine, mixing it with water, a blend so clear one might think he drank plenty of water; even so, the pungent odor of the alcohol filled the room, no matter how he tried to hide his habit. Now the added smell of soap, from the shavings that piled up minute by minute. All of it bound for the trash. After returning from church, Mom had changed into her housedress and complained about the work piling up for her on the weekend, the cleaning and cooking. No rest. She resented the sight of Balan hunched over her soap. And when she snatched the carved soap from under his nose, it startled him.

"I need it for the laundry, Balan," she explained, half smiling but serious. "I cannot afford to have another bar of soap wasted like this." And she turned around, intending to make her way to the verandah at the back, where she scrubbed and beat the family's clothes on the floor by the shallow sink in the corner.

"Give it back!" Dad dropped the knife on the table and jumped to his feet; he pushed back his chair and grabbed her arm just before she could get away. But when he pulled her towards him, she freed herself, wrenching her body away with such force that the soap flew from her hand and hit the floor. The bear's head snapped off; the grape-colored bar broke into pieces.

Fishhead stepped back: so much tension he forgot his hunger.

"Now look what you've done!" Balan shouted. "All my hard work!"

"Look what I've done?" Eshma glared into his narrowed eyes. "Balan, I have no more soap for the house! I have no money to buy any! I work all day and all you do is sit around and waste—"

Dad cuffed Mom with the back of his left hand, and she choked on her words, spittle flying, some blood; she almost lost her balance when her head spun around.

"Mom!" Fishhead shouted. "Dad, please!" He stepped down to the verandah and hid behind the wall there, clutching the doorframe. The threshold just below his knees. Kishore started crying, then got to his feet and ran to join his brother. Fishhead did nothing to stop Dad, who had Mom up against the wall, one hand pressed against her chest and the other wrapped over her mouth, even as she turned her head from side to side to catch her breath, her speech. Hot cheeks, smears in red. Dad did not let go. Mom, no longer pretty, just defenseless, bullied, hurt. Her old house dress with short sleeves and buttons in front that suited her good form, now untidy, a popped button. Mom's ankles showed unusual veins on her well-formed legs, which Pradeep had explained before as some kind of defect; Fishhead thought of it now.

"You're embarrassing me in front of the children!" Dad said, his voice firm and stout, his hand away from her mouth now and turned into a fist that he pushed up against her chest, pinning her against the wall.

Mom broke into sobs as soon as he lifted his hand from her mouth. "I didn't mean to. I didn't, Balan." She wiped her stains with the bottom of her dress and moved away from Dad, while he rubbed his hands clean on the newspaper and remained standing, looking at her, his fire subsiding. Mom went down on her knees to pick up the broken pieces of soap from the floor, and Fishhead rushed forward to help her; Kishore came and stood near him, in tears. The heat and humidity fell away into a cold and unhappy place marked by this betrayal, by love's treason. Dad watched, stiff arms at his side. Mom reached for a piece of soap right in front of her; but just before she could grab it, he kicked it across the room. Mom scrambled on her hands and knees to pick it up. "Oh, Balan, don't!" She did not look up at her husband.

Fishhead couldn't contain his exasperation; he rushed towards his father, wrapping his arms around Dad's waist and grappling with him, hoping to bring him down; but it felt like he wrestled a tree. Dad pushed him away. Kishore screamed, cried.

Fishhead clenched his teeth and went down on his knees to help his mother; she remained speechless. "I'll get you soap, Mom," he said in her ear. "I promise. I promise!"

Did she even hear him? Mom said no more, and Fishhead knew he'd find her sobbing alone in the kitchen later.

"I'm sorry," Balan said afterwards, before she left the room. "I'm sorry I hit you, dear. I'll make it up to you, I promise. I'll find work. Just some bad luck I'm going through now."

Mom said nothing; she just went about her housework.

Fishhead did not know what to make of the act or the apology. He did not understand Dad, could not tell sincerity from insincerity, did not know how to settle the confusion and anger swirling in his own head and heart, pulling him further into a firmament of hunger for food, love, and lost caresses. His Republic of Want. He had no right to encroach on this incident, no right to stay as witness, or to let Kishore share this awful memory. Tidal. Absorbed. The things children do at their own peril. Did Mom want consolation? Would she accept it from him? Fishhead did not mean to interfere, but he wished to react, with a touch, an arm locked with hers, a tug of her dress. Would she put her hand on his head? He would take that. If she did it now, he would like that very much. He remembered her arm across his shoulder once or twice before; her hand through his head of hair when they went to church, school, the marketplace. He wanted more of these touches now, ached for them, even as he had a sense from the unsure expression on her face that she needed a moment to herself. Why could he not console her? He would get her some soap somehow. Something evil had just occurred, a corruption of his senses and innocence, a drowning of trust; Dad's eruption coughed up injustice from the depths of human darkness. What did Fishhead learn? What understanding could he gain from this instruction of force? While he watched in silence and confusion with little brother at his side, a strange energy hummed in the firelight, filling the boy (and little brother) with doubt, resentment, and hesitation.

Mom and Dad both withdrew to their own corners of the world, combatants bruised under hot lights of the ring, and thirsty for this face-off to end. Fishhead wanted happiness, a morsel, some assurance that life in hunger's grip didn't always mean there would be aggression, too. Hours passed in silence, an easing of his parents' strained relations; a few days advanced this way, then a week. He found happiness in play outside, but already his body and heart began to show the dulling, disquieting burden of his family's crisis.

The lingering thought of his promise to Mom. He never realized until now the value she placed in soap: this need for cleanliness without fussing. A pure necessity like food, and now so scarce. But there was a solution: an unconventional solution, one requiring quick feet and nimble hands, but a solution nevertheless.

Fishhead felt his anticipation rise as he made his way to the main road just outside the entrance of this residential colony. A hot weekday afternoon. He aimed for the shops, all lined up next to each other selling magazines and paper, kites, vegetables, fried snacks on large trays, readymade garments for children, shoes, hot chai, household goods, sacks of grain, spices, and soap. Yes, that's what he wanted: soap. His mother's welfare mattered most.

He came around from the back of the smelly shop, stepping past its two massive over-used cooking vats with long stained wooden ladles, and he reached into the closest burlap sack by the front door; the sack contained generic bars in pink and brown. He grabbed three bars of soap, then spun around to make his getaway, sure he hadn't been seen.

But at the back of the shop he ran into two older boys, employees. They apprehended him without trouble; one held his wrists behind his back in a vise grip, while the other darted inside to fetch the owner, who emerged in a huff and grabbed Fishhead by the collar. "Where do you live, little runt?" he demanded.

Fishhead said nothing, just squirmed reluctantly.

"Shall I call the police? Or we could just beat you right here. How about that instead?"

"I'm sorry!" Fishhead pleaded at last. "I'm sorry!" He coughed up his address, and the owner dragged him home by the collar.

Dad met the man at the door and listened to his explanation. Fishhead could see his father's jaw clenching as the shopkeeper spoke. Then: "I must apologize," Dad said. "I am…absolutely mortified. I have no idea why he would do such a thing." Dad started loosening his belt. "I will make absolutely certain it will never happen again."

At last the shopkeeper left. Dad slammed the door but made sure to empty out the living room before he instructed Fishhead to pull down his pants and turn around with his hands spread against the wall.

Notes on Conditions of Hunger Among Children of Global Populations

I wish to converge now on the landscape of the contemporary Western Canon, to show you that such a condition as Fishhead's is prevalent throughout the world, with societies old and new, full of assailed and deprived children. His situation, like theirs, is demonstrated as the consequence of a passive-aggressive though flawed and unshakable patriarchal leadership in the family unit, which has spread conveniently beyond itself into most, if not all, facets of life, including business, religious practice, and industry. This compelling argument is presented and updated with adequate historical evidence in a hardbound scholarly work of eleven editions called *Notes on Conditions of Hunger Among Children of Global Populations*, co-authored by three experts, namely Gunnar Sevrinsen, Sahaan Shihaabi, and Jagdeep Singh Gawalia, and published—with the web-based listserve assistance of numerous research and cultural aides—by The International Rice Institute, co-headquartered in Malmo, Sweden and New Delhi, India. All editions of this work, while being available among leading booksellers, major libraries, and in numerous other vital advocacy institutions, also exist in the permanent collection of The Cliff Dwellers Club, where Iva now reads. *Notes on Conditions of*

Hunger Among Children of Global Populations is a remarkable achievement: over 600,000 entries including data from regional hunger studies, statistics, and predictive analyses, as well as essays, stories, poetry, drawings, and photographs in the companion collection. This hardbound work, with its award-winning design, is also available today with an Internet subscription for streaming or download with podcasts, or as a boxed CD collection, and as an acclaimed supplement: a recent documentary DVD film put together by two alumni of the College for Creative Studies in Detroit, Michigan. This film on human suffering through hunger premiered on the World TV channel in 2015, and has been shown on BBC, PBS, Al Jazeera, and other worldwide broadcasts since then.

The authors of this volume bring with them academic distinctions and years of merited experience in their fields of study, for which The International Rice Institute remains grateful. Gunnar Sevrinsen and Jagdeep Singh Gawalia work side-by-side as senior researchers and professors at Malmo University today, while Sahaan Shihaabi carries her purple pride as a professor of Predictive Analysis from Northwestern University and its School of Professional Studies in Evanston, Illinois. Her work and life coincide in most creative ways in the classroom in Evanston and at Wieboldt Hall, the school's sister location that lies east of the Water Tower on Chicago Avenue, just a half block or so from the lakefront.

Once each year in March, The International Rice Institute puts out a companion collection of fiction, essays, and poetry with humanist themes that relate one way or another, either directly or indirectly, to hunger and the eradication of poverty around the world, but always with an inclusion of children in these creative works and with subtexts that continue to question the role of patriarchy, politics, and business in the cause of human suffering. With a generous UNICEF grant, The International Rice Institute engages senior design students from Parsons School of Design (The New School) in New York to layout, illustrate, and produce the creative writing collection: around 300 pages of original material received from around the world through the Rice Institute's proprietary online submissions portal, edited and selected by The New School's Department of English. Some pieces make their way by any means possible from oppressed regions like Somalia, Syria, Cuba, Eritrea, and even from Burma, and, thus far, two from North Korea (published anonymously for fear of government retribution against the authors and their extended families). Fishhead's story emerges from just one of these collections from six years ago, a work of fiction titled, *Chawal aur Chini*, which when translated from Hindi, means "Rice and Sugar," much-needed dietary ingredients for the poverty-stricken characters in the story.

Allow me to visit, for the moment, a flash of Fishhead's mythical past, the ancient wonderlands of the Ramayana and Mahabharata, texts which have formed India and moved through time to birth his present state. While Fishhead wished for a morsel or two of happiness despite the conflict between his mother and father, his Republic of Want is a slice of India itself. A morsel or two of happiness brought perfect balance if you lived the life of an ascetic, a *sanyasi,* earning a few coins each day by playing the *vina* under a canopy of trees at the forest's edge. An ancient kingdom. Macaws, monkeys, and curious, smiling village children surround you; they have crossed little streams to come see you sing then laughed at you or even served you, on few occasions, milk, *srikhand*, and ghee, because it brought their household good luck. Simple meals of roti, lime pickle, and raw onions strip your body of its fat and keep the mind alive with a fire that burns with sacrifice, with devotion. Life at the edge of madness. The *sanyasi*, avatar of the divine.

Young Fishhead, young post-war child, understood the asceticism of these men and women, as if this knowledge grew deep in his heart and awareness, and yet he turned his eyes away from *sadhus* and *sadhvis* who sat along dust-ridden shoulders of the streets, playing miniature tambourines shaped to their fingers and divining the futures of passersby in the name of the pantheon of gods; sometimes the *sadhus* stood on their heads or contorted their white-painted bodies, their lean orange-robed bodies, into infinite variations of disbelief and awe while they chanted and hummed, as if clinging to some energy of the living world crisscrossing everywhere about them. Bombay rumbled on in its own vitality and entrepreneurial drive; the city did not appear to stop. A *sanyasi's* manner in a metropolis like Bombay left Fishhead with a poor impression, suggesting an awkward contradiction unfit for his liking; he often teased or ignored them, and regarded them as being no different than the poverty-ridden children who, starving and dirty, near nakedness, also took to the streets with open palms and unclean faces, hands, and bare feet. Did Destiny intend his life to be like them? These children also begged for food and money—alone, but often in pairs or gangs—and they made the reserved, sidewalk manner of the *sanyasis* seem pale in comparison, because the city bred these children and held them close to its breast, made them dependent participants in its industry of survival, and unwilling to release them to the countryside.

Fishhead accepted neither reality of the poor children or *sanyasis*. Such a Destiny belonged to them and not to him: his mantra. His family would never end up like them, never. He wanted to believe it; but more and more, the opposite threatened to come true, and he began to push this realization away from his head. He could not accept his growing hardship even as it forced him to confront it. Protagonists need contradictions, and Fishhead had them, I made sure of that.

Burned Like Fire

His relationship with little brother Kishore grew.

The four-year gap in age between them allowed for a natural and timid association, whereas Kishore's needs as a toddler bored Pradeep and Prem; they could not be bothered with caring for the little one. As the middle child, Fishhead showed care and understanding, especially in the absence of their parents. Fishhead began to feel responsible for Kishore's welfare, a task he resented sometimes. Dad spent little time with the child he'd made, and Mom went right back to her fulltime work at the telephone exchange after giving birth to Kishore; she relied on her family to care for him while she worked long and tiring shifts.

When Kishore asked for a piggy-back ride, Fishhead let his five-year-old brother climb on his back and wrap his arms around him. Then Fishhead hiked Kishore further up on his back. Little brother laughed, and off they went to the empty lot on the other side of the graveled street.

To get to the empty lot, Fishhead had to cross the front lawn and step on a concrete slab placed over the drainage gutter. About two or three feet wide and knee deep, gutters like this one bounded all streets and emptied into natural canals and bodies of water elsewhere. Gutters overflowed during the monsoon season and became dangerous traps for the unwary. (This drainage system of gutters exists throughout India, first introduced to the country during the time of the Indus Valley Civilization in the Bronze Age—a history of early India, China, and Europe, which Fishhead studied in school with some intrigue.) Fishhead moved across the graveled street and the dry gutter on the opposite side, careful about the cargo on his back. He leaned Kishore forward and then redistributed his weight before entering the empty lot with its dirt, piles of construction gravel, stones, wooden planks, rope, rebar, and sand piles.

Fishhead remained in the corner of the lot, bouncing Kishore now and then because he liked to hear his brother's laughter. Kishore's weight bore down on his thin legs and made his knees tremble, and his lungs burned: asthma. Fishhead tried to ignore it. Kishore giggled, delighted at being so high off the ground.

"Want me to put you down?" Fishhead asked. "I have to do that."

"No!" Kishore cried.

"I have to put you down for a few minutes."

"No, no, I want to stay here."

He hiked Kishore up on his back again. His trembling knees pained him, so he walked to a pile of wooden planks and eased his bottom down, careful not to release his brother.

"I have to rest a little," Fishhead said.

"Okay, then will you run?"

"Shall I run? Want me to run?" Fishhead asked, and his brother nodded, full of excitement. "We'll be one of dad's horses?"

Kishore screamed. "Go!" little brother said. "Dad's horses, go! Dad's horses."

Fishhead got back on his feet and walked to the far end of the lot. He turned around and started to trot, then burst into a full gallop. Like dad's horses. He ran the length of the empty lot and turned around to repeat his feat. He paused, tired now in the late afternoon heat, and hoping he could put Kishore down again, but little brother pressed him to keep going. Fishhead didn't want to, he didn't. His knees trembled more and the pain ran up his thighs, his hips; his lungs burned.

In the distance, Pradeep stepped onto the front verandah, looked at them, and then went back inside. All seemed right with the world. Brothers at play, and all the time in the world to grow, laugh, discover. But Fishhead did not want to become like the adults. They never explained anything and did whatever they wanted to. They came and went as they pleased, and paid no attention to the little ones. Too busy with their own needs. Too busy with their cards and horses and drink, too busy to ask even if the little ones needed food or water; the adults never got up to get the little ones any water. They expected service instead. They kept secrets and filled the house with cigarette smoke, horse-chatter, and the odor of their alcohol, sweat and perfume, dabs of Old Spice and baby powder. No, Fishhead, did not want to grow up like them. Brothers at play and play alone; he liked that.

He turned his head. Prem stayed low at the reeds. The large pond lay still with a face of blue sky and cotton clouds, an invitation to surrender, enter caresses of glee, the praised, lose sense of time, and trust in memory. Go neither forward nor back in mind, everything present at once, and selectable at will, in no particular order. I am there, Destiny, your drink, your intention and place. A pair of black oxen approached the pond; they paused to study the water then went down the steep embankment one behind the other. A series of splashes, their closed nostrils desperate for air. Such happiness! Prem came out from near the reeds; he sat on his haunches and began pushing the end of a long cattail reed into the water; he beat the water and talked to it, shouted at the oxen. What did he say? Fishhead wondered; he found the pond more attractive now and wanted to join his older brother there. Perhaps he should put Kishore down, smack his bum and send him home. He tried.

"Go, big brother," Kishore pressed him instead and tightened his hold. "Don't stop, please don't."

Fishhead almost began to choke. He stood there, of two minds about his added load. Little brother came first, he had to admit. *Finish what you started.* He hiked Kishore further up his back and fastened his grip around little brother's thighs.

"Hold on tight!" he said, panting. "Stay close, very close, and don't let go of me whatever I do."

Kishore's voice rose, "Yes, yes, I won't let go, whatever you do."

Fishhead took a deep breath and leaned into a sprint with all the weight of little brother on his back, and their bodies rose and fell. The ground shuddered beneath them and went the other way fast, and Fishhead did not speak or ask his brother anything, because he breathed hard and his lungs blew hot fire like bags of cement left out in the sun too long. He ran faster, believed he flew. The brother on his back, no obstacle at all. He flew, they did.

But then the dry shallow gutter came up before him. Fishhead didn't see it, failed to anticipate it. Unable to stop in time, he dropped his right foot in it. No obstacle at all, that gutter, he thought: easy enough to get past it for a champion horse. But his tired right knee buckled, and his left foot got hooked on his right calf. A heavy slap. And Fishhead's eyes widened as he fell, and terror drew all reason out of him: Kishore would not let go.

Fishhead pitched forward head-first, down into the gutter like a flung rock. And something snapped so fast when Kishore at last came undone from his perch. A thud. Moving gravel. A cry. Fishhead's head spun when he fell, as if the ground had kicked it, and his left forearm burned as if it had touched acid, trapped under him in an uncanny way.

Kishore, Kishore! He'd lost little brother. How much time had passed? Wordless, Fishhead scrambled to his feet with effort and fell back down into the dry gutter in a daze, his arm turned all wrong. Heavy breathing. So much pain.

At last he saw Kishore on his back in the street, in tears, the gravel, crying, so full of shock and surprise, tortured. Fishhead did not understand the world at all, did not understand why it did this to them. His warped arm. So fast, so fast and pissed on by curses. Kishore seemed okay, but Fishhead couldn't say for certain. No blood in sight. *Go check on little brother.* Fishhead did not speak; the pain crippled his side. He shut his eyes tight, unable to cry at all. His arm turned red and swelled. Not the same as before.

He got to his feet and scrambled up to Kishore, feeling nothing on the left side of his body, only lurches of failing and regret. A loose lower arm. *What would Pradeep say? Go to him, take Kishore to him. Go home now.*

"Kishore," he said in pain. "Are you okay, are you hurt? Come on, get up, let's go. I don't know what happened. I ran into the gutter and...I don't know what happened."

But little brother lay still, face down, and he refused to talk. He sobbed, he made an effort to turn and rise. "Are you okay? Give me your hand. I'm sorry. Give me your hand, Kishore. I don't know what happened, but I'm hurt." Kishore looked away instead, and Fishhead added, "You want to be a girl like Anupa? A sour girl like Anupa?" He shook his good hand in Kishore's face, urging him to take it.

Little brother shook his head. Shook it. No, not like Anupa. He took the hand Fishhead offered and got to his feet. He cried, sniffled, and pushed the snot away from his nose with the back of a hand. He had bruises on his face, forehead, and right wrist, but seemed otherwise unhurt. No split head, no tap of blood; his body and clothes smeared with dirt. A miracle. But was he injured inside? Fishhead brushed Kishore off then turned to face Prem's direction; Prem remained unaware, preoccupied with the pond, off in his dreamy state.

Fishhead examined Kishore again and tried to pick him up, but Kishore refused his help. "I twisted my left arm," Fishhead said as he led his brother home, taking baby steps. "It's swollen and red. Here, see here. It hurts a lot. But probably not as bad as what happened to Prem. You didn't break anything, did you? Answer me, Kishore. You'd be in big pain if you broke something."

Little brother shook his head, still sobbing. More snot.

"That's good. Here, I'll wipe your cheeks with my shirt."

"What happened to Prem?" Kishore asked.

"A motorcycle ran over him and broke his leg. Prem did not look both ways when he crossed the street. Dad sent him to buy cigarettes."

"When, now?"

"Not now, no. You were two. He was seven."

"Is Prem okay?"

"He is, doctors put his body in a cast up to his chest."

"Will you be in a cast?"

"Maybe, but do you even know what that is?" Fishhead laughed.

Kishore shook his head.

"I may need a cast. I'll go to the doctor. Somebody will take me to the doctor."

"Dad will."

"Pradeep will rub ointment on it."

"Dad can."

"And where's Dad?" Fishhead said.

"Where's Dad?"

"No sign of dad, you get that, Kishore? No sign at all."

Kishore nodded. "Who's Anupa?" he asked after a measure of silence.

"A girl I know. We never talk but I see her in school. I climb the wall of the school's grounds and see her there with her friends. Now shut your mouth about it, or I'll break your head in two for spilling that to everyone."

Fishhead returned from the Chinese bonesetter with his left arm in a sling. Mom took him there. The outer bone of his forearm had twisted out of place from the fall, but after Dr. Lee treated the injury, the swelling and pain began to die down. Unable to use both hands to play marbles, Fishhead spent his days reading his textbooks or kicking around an empty can on the street, as if playing soccer. Mom did not buy him a football; and no storybooks at home, just textbooks. Good storybooks and a football cost money, and Mom used every *paise* she earned to keep her family going. Pradeep had borrowed *The Swiss Family Robinson*, *Gulliver's Travels*, and *The Scarlet Pimpernel* from a classmate, but he returned the novels. The school had no library, and Jailal Ram Book Stall, the only book shop in the area, gave no books away for free, although the shop's location a mile away on the same road to school drew Fishhead to it more often than he cared to admit. He picked up comic books of war, classics, Flash and Green Lantern, Archie, and Sad Sack from foot-high stacks on a pair of tables in front of the store, and he read until the storekeeper told him to go home and do his homework. Fishhead wished he had the money to buy a book and a few snacks. Instead he faced his homework and read his history and geography textbooks with less interest. He wanted what Pradeep had, if only he knew how. He'd like to take a peek under Anupa's skirt, too.

Indian Derby

Fishhead struggled to understand why Dad spent more time at home on weekdays. A place without records and gramophone. On those hot afternoons, Dad sat in a metal chair by the window and looked out, as if the view from the window gave him a more hopeful reality—some life essence or far-away horizon he seemed to touch with his memory and unstated passion, for he had passion and showed his emotions when he listened undisturbed to music from the gramophone. But that belonged to the past. No more vinyl pleasures. The soap carver gone, too. A South Indian man of taste he'd rather be! A man of taste above all, above others. The influence of the long-departed English sizzled him and teased his frustrations. Fishhead did not understand why his father behaved in an aloof manner, saying less and less each day, it seemed. Dad never sat on the floor as the others did; he always appeared to dream, deep in thought about something or the other. He sat with a glass of drink in his hand or on the windowsill, and, on rare occasions, with the glass propped between his thighs. He sipped his drink all day.

Aunty let Dad borrow the transistor radio, a little plastic box with a dial in front and its telescoping metal antenna. Fishhead turned from his homework many times, from his place on the tiled floor, to see his father with the radio on beside him. Dad never listened to Bollywood film music and regarded such music as trash, and he did not talk about Indian movies. He preferred classical music and Western show tunes instead; he talked about Marx, Satyajit Ray, and the horror of the split between India and Pakistan. The horror of Britain's flight from his country. He played with the radio dial until he landed on the news or local broadcasts about horse racing from Mahalaxmi, Pune, or New Delhi.

The Indian Derby, a big day. Uncle and aunty did not come to visit Dad that Sunday afternoon, as they attended the races at Mahalaxmi racecourse on Bombay's western coastline. Betting for dad, too? Fishhead's nose led him to this conclusion, and he asked Mom the question, but she neither confirmed nor denied his suspicions. She resented any form of gambling, and the influence of aunty and uncle on her husband. Aunty helped Dad: brother and sister, those two; she liked Balan and spoke kindly to him, showing him more affection than she did anyone else in his family. Mom didn't care for aunty and ignored her; they spoke on rare occasions.

Dad spent his day at home in a white singlet and dark slacks listening to the broadcast on All India Radio while he sipped his drink and studied racing index cards he'd made; he pushed his dark hair back over his head from time to time when wavy locks came loose and dropped across his forehead. The Indian Derby. All that mattered. A lot to lose, but so much to gain. Fishhead stepped out to play outside, unwilling to listen to the broadcast and not fully understanding the details of this sport. Hunger reached him soon enough, and he returned home, dashing through the room to the extended verandah at the back, his fingers pressed against his ears, although he heard the sound of his body's rumbling more. He paused when he reached his mother, who washed clothes at the edge of the tiled area by the shallow ground-level sink.

The radio continued its broadcast behind him; a marching band at the racecourse played an English tune slightly off key, and Fishhead smiled. The tap ran near Mom, water gushing down on a pile of clothes with suds in the basin. She leaned forward on her haunches, and, with the weight of her arms and shoulders, rubbed a deep blue soap bar against a cotton shirt, scrubbing the collar, inner sleeves, armpits. She placed the long-sleeve shirt flat on the floor and hiked her house dress past her knees. Then she scrubbed some more. She would do the same for underwear, pants, her saris. Fishhead came up behind her and put his lips to her cheek, and Eshma uttered a sound to acknowledge him but did not smile or stop her work. She studied his feet. He counted the sweat beads on her forehead. Her work, this heat.

"Barefoot again," Mom said. "Wear your *chappals* when you're outside. I told you many times. You'll cut yourself, and then what?"

"Okay, but can I have a *paratha*?" he said.

"Why do you have to ask, because you want me to get it for you?"

"No."

"Then what? Get it yourself, child."

He stepped into the kitchen's dark narrow space in the adjacent corner there, and he reached under the lid of a vessel on the floor. Found his flatbread, still warm. Then he slammed the lid closed and it rang.

"What's that for?" Eshma said, her head raised. "Practicing for the marching band?"

"Sorry, Mom," Fishhead replied, then giggled. He bit into the still-warm flatbread and tore off a piece with his teeth. Started chewing. He loved these oiled *parathas,* which Mom made on Sundays—rolled soft flour with water and salt, oil, sugar, folded over and rolled flat again into squares with more dabs of oil, sprinkled flour, a process she repeated with each flatbread. Mom cooked them on a hot *tava* with a light drizzle of oil on both sides, and the bread flaked off in layers when eaten. Crisp and brown just off the griddle. Eat them with anything, a curry, or banana, yogurt, more sugar, murabba.

Fishhead walked over to the doorframe; silent Kishore sat by the door, preoccupied with his toys. Dad hadn't moved in his chair by the window. The marching band continued over the loud noise of the crowds, and the announcer gave a running commentary of the events on Derby day. A few minutes later Dad reached for the transistor radio and turned it off, and he wrapped his hands around the back legs of his chair, tapping with index fingers. He drew his feet under him and crossed them, deep in thought, always. A man and his mind. What would one do without the other, I ask you, dear reader? And is one cognizant of actions in the other? Separate them, exchange them, scrub them down with Eshma's blue soap bar, and what you do have? Did Balan's mind know his third son watched from twenty feet away? Clearly, the man did not. Moments later, Dad reached for the index cards on the side table nearby and took up his pencil to make notes on the cards. He turned two cards over and wrote some more, and then he collected his index cards and lay them flat on the table. He would not be disturbed.

Fishhead remained still on the top step, wordless. He chewed softly, leaning against the doorframe as if to hold it up, transfixed, idling time, curious about his father, about the things he might learn or not from Dad, about promises he'll make to keep himself from repeating Dad's breaches. Sundays are. Sundays are open fields without outposts, without markers; roam, child, roam…shed those minutes, seconds, drink sunlight, touch fate, pick seeds of emotion. Outside, three crows on the parapet of the residence made a racket. Through the open front door ahead of him, Fishhead spotted a pregnant bitch on the street. Her teats hung low, swollen. He'd seen her before. She had come through the neighborhood looking for food. Male dogs stayed on her tail, their noses up against her rear, and she snarled at them and bared her teeth but did nothing else to keep them at a safe distance. One or more had mated with her. They continued to fight for her and she stayed on the move, but she'd been limping. Perhaps a boy had struck her with a stone just for the spite of it. Fishhead imagined this spite, this need to hurt living things. Break the unbroken, weaken it. Senseless acts without reason. He'd done it too, and felt in control whenever he acted that way. Mating dogs, a goat, a fowl on the street deserved little mercy, although he could not say why; but he never harmed a cow or kicked it, not a cow, not a deity. Laughter and screams came from next door. The neighbor's three daughters called each other in a game. A car went by in front as the bitch scuttled out of view, and the vehicle left behind a trail of dust. A dry summer heat.

Then Dad rose to his feet and crossed the room. Fishhead stepped down on the verandah to move away from the doorframe; he placed his body between the steps and the arm of an old sofa there, but continued to look in. Dad aimed for the almond Godrej steel cabinet, the almirah with its mirror and two doors, which stood against the south wall in a shallow alcove forming a corner with the east wall. The cabinet spared a few feet of space for movement near the doorway. Across from the cabinet, Mom and Dad's bed of cheap *Deodar* wood took the corner and ran lengthwise along the north wall; the warm-brown bed frame and its thin cotton mattress, now covered with a thin sheet and a pair of small cotton pillows, plus Mom's Bible and rosary, her purse, her folded clothes in the corner. Her prized Singer pedal sewing machine pushed up near the footboard. The south wall had no windows. The single room became everything: a living room, a bedroom for six, a study, a dining room, closet for six, Mom's sewing room. A place, this home, but for how long before they'd have to move again?

Fishhead slipped past Dad and slumped down on the floor near Kishore, who played with a starter Meccano set, although little brother didn't quite understand how the metal construction parts and the nuts and bolts of the crane came together to make it roll on the floor or swing its hook, its thread. Pradeep had no trouble with the paper plans that came with the set, and he made a wheelbarrow, a truck, and seesaw; but Kishore wanted a crane. He got a crane, and played on, curious. Fishhead reached for his textbooks, one eye on little brother, glad that Kishore's fall in the gutter hadn't damaged him. Or had it?

Dad turned the right handle on the cabinet and pulled the door open; as it squeaked, he caught a decent glimpse of himself in the mirror framing the left door. With eyes locked on the mirror, he dropped his chin and moved his face to the left. Studied his hair. A handsome man, tall and dark, with an oval face, a mustache, and high cheekbones. Sharp, shifty eyes that went red when he drank too much. A slow and thoughtful drinker, a smart drinker who sipped his drink and delayed the outcome, in control of time and fate, his balance. Fishhead couldn't take his eyes off the man. The cabinet's doors squeaked again. Dad failed to oil the hinges, even after Mom had asked him repeatedly. So she'll do it herself, she will; cooking oil to the rescue around the house. He pulled a set of used index cards from the top shelf, and, getting up on his toes, he reached deep inside for a pint he kept hidden behind everything there. The shelf had newspaper clippings, used betting stubs, paper clips, pencils, empty index cards, racing booklets, seasonal timetables, magazines, a near-empty pack of Four Square cigarettes, and playing cards. He shut the cabinet and returned to his chair, where he dropped the index cards on the table and twisted off the bottle cap to pour a shot. He returned the bottle to its place in the cabinet. Fishhead kept his head down and moved little brother's crane. A cry.

"Get me a glass of water," Dad said, taking his place in the chair again. Pushed his words out into the air.

Fishhead jumped up. Of course, his father spoke to him, hadn't he? To the kitchen then and back with an aluminum glass of warm water. Dad thinned his drink without lifting his eyes or offering a thank you, but Fishhead didn't mind, didn't want a thank you; he turned away when his father began pouring from one glass into another, the sound of liquid falling as if Bacchus sat in his fountain in some old European town, collecting coins and personal wishes from tourists, or as if Bacchus had his name on a hip bar near Churchgate station downtown. Dad had talked about the expensive Bacchus Bar at Churchgate, which made Fishhead curious about that place, a fancy place, only for foreigners and Indians with money and prestige, influence. The things his father knew, places he went. Where did Dad go? Now Fishhead took his place on the floor near Kishore again, and did not stir until Dad began pacing the room. Something brewed; Dad became impatient, but not annoyed or angry. He paced, anticipating something, some unexpressed outcome from Mahalaxmi. He teased the small tuft of hair that had started to grow below his lower lip. As he paced, the room became a lot smaller now. Fishhead did not stay. He got on his hands and knees and went to the alcove with the Godrej cabinet, reaching for his stack of clothes, shoes, and personal items on the floor there. A small jar with marbles. He opened an old shoebox under his school uniform and removed a handmade slingshot, his catapult. He called it a catty because the boys at school called it a catty, although he did not know why or where the name came from. He shoved the slingshot in his back pocket and stepped outside, but not before he stuck his left foot into the Meccano pieces and disturbed them, as if by accident. Kishore protested, and Fishhead rubbed little brother's head. Dad had his back to them and said nothing as he lit a cigarette; he remained preoccupied with the races. Fishhead shoved off in a hurry.

He found Prem three houses away to the north, nowhere near the pond; his older brother squatted on the dusty street and played a game of marbles with two boys from the neighborhood. Lousy at marbles, Prem lost to the boys in the neighborhood almost every game he played, and gave up the few marbles Fishhead shared with him. Fishhead hated seeing Prem lose to these boys. He wanted to win himself.

"I'm in," he said, and the boys moaned, unable to keep him from their game. The fall in the gutter with Kishore had put him at an advantage, because his left arm now moved an extra quarter turn, which allowed him the added reach of the marble, the striker, as he hooked it back against his right middle finger in a way the boys had not seen before. He sprung power from his hands in this game, and learned how to use this power, although he could not say how it emerged from inside him. He focused well, better than Prem did. Somehow, Fishhead understood the precise geometry of this game, the shape of the scratched triangle on the ground, and the marbles arranged inside it. He understood the trajectory his striker should make from any distance—a foot, two feet or three— and the force that would push marbles outside the triangle so he could pocket them. He felt like a snake spying its prey when he went down on his haunches and leaned forward between both knees, the striker in his hands like a cobra.

Crack! Fishhead's striker sent the nine others in the triangle flying into each other and pushing them outside the lines. That chain reaction, the way of the natural world. A feast so unique to him, a thunder call pushing his clouds apart. The group of marbles in the triangle dispersed in a charged frenzy. Turn by turn, he put his winning marbles in both pockets of his shorts and gave a few to Prem, too. Then, just as quickly as it started: game over. No, not another one. The boys had enough.

Fishhead got bored and wandered off with his catty, while Prem stood and watched the boys play. Hunger seized Fishhead. The last time he used his catty, he hadn't much luck with birds, and he hadn't wandered far enough from home to find green mangoes.

He reached for the catty, and walked south on the road past the pond until he approached a wild rubber tree at the edge of the colony. A wide gap (the width of two houses) opened up there between the last house to his left and a familiar house to the right— the one Darren's family occupied. The wall at the edge of the property dropped straight down into a gully and stream. Undeveloped land as old as time. Fishhead stepped into the gully, following a path of small and large stones, some rocks. Frogs and lizards thrived, and, in calm catches of water, tiny fish, too. The stream, unpredictable in the high monsoon season, ran east to west and marked the division between the colony Fishhead lived in and a rustic village to the south, which consisted of huts with thatched roofs and straw walls covered with dung, and goats, cows, and chickens on a soft, trampled earth.

He paused under the rubber tree with its long and tapering dark green leaves, its thick ficus leaves, and he raised his head to hone in on sparrows chirping away on its branches. The thick cover of leaves sheltered the birds from above, although Fishhead had a clear view of them from where he stood just inside the reaches of the high tree. The sparrows used the liveliest calls and chirps. A pair of mynahs flew in, those dark-feathered starlings with yellow beaks and matching rings about their eyes. The birds prattled on, and except for their active sounds, the area remained quiet, the air too hot and still between the leaves, around Fishhead. He became aware of the houses on either side of him; now alone, unwatched, he examined his catty, the rubber strip that had come loose on one side before, but tightened since. Then he bent down to pick up a small stone, and pinched it in the leather sling and raised his arms. Pointed them at the tree. He took aim at a sparrow in the branches and narrowed his sight. He caught the rapid blink of the sparrow's left eye, the soft skin, as the bird hopped to the side. Sad thing; it failed to see through his intentions. The smooth round head of the bird, like Fishhead's marble. Feathers picked from clouds and woven, cloaking its small body. The bird, right there in his sight, now magnified. Soft, innocent eyes. The stone in his grip meant for flight, fast and straight like a meteor. Strike it, that bird. Fishhead's aim so true, cheered on by his hunger.

He pulled the sling and pinched stone toward his right cheekbone. He locked his left forearm, although it shook with the tension of the stretched rubber strips; he picked up the quaking in his ears as his heart went still. Ready now with feet spread one behind the other, he stood ready on the verge of a most profitable crime. But then it happened. SNAP! He held the tension too long. The right strip of the catty quickly came undone, and it sprung back with great force and speed. The flat, thick uncoiling piece of black rubber hit his face hard and bounced off, stinging the lid of his open right eye and missing his pupil by a hairline. He let out a cry. He winced and let go of the pinched stone and leather sling. His pain, this disgusting pain. The birds scattered in a flurry, and the tree went naked and quiet again. Fishhead dropped his head and shut his eyes, and he pressed a hand to his face. It burned like a roti that sat too long on mother's hot griddle. He spat on the ground, frustrated. "That's not evil, what I want to do," he mumbled, looking up at the sky, addressing me directly. "That's not evil, not evil! I'm too hungry, don't you see? That bird's fate is in my hands. Make it so, please." Too hungry. He threw his catty to the ground and kicked it away from him. He'd become careless. His desperation, so sure of himself, too hurried. Too determined to pursue this meal.

He stepped up to the catty on the ground and bent down; he took it in his hands again. Hunger toyed with him and raked his body on the inside, and he suffered a dizzy spell when he straightened his torso again. The world turned black, so full of orbiting streaks and daylight behind his eyelids; an ache inside his head, sickening. He closed his eyes tight to keep his balance and stay on his feet. Did not move. He placed his hands on his head to hold it straight, because the world threatened to go upside down that instant. This giddiness, he couldn't explain it, but it came unannounced from time to time, and he blamed his hunger and body's weakness. A growing boy, not growing well enough.

Moments later, Fishhead opened his eyes, still wishing for that meal. He wanted a bird. So he attempted to tie the undone strip back to the prong of the Y handle, but the thin securing rubber band broke as he pulled it tight around the prong. Frustrated, he screamed, swore, and returned the weapon to his back pocket. One part dangled. This damned catty, back to his shoebox when he got home. He swore to fix it on a better day and claim his bird, just as he did with marbles. For now, he would go home. Didn't want to waste random shots in the air like those fools. Lucky birds, lucky this time, and the passerines too; his teacher Ms. D'Souza called the mynahs "passerines," although Fishhead didn't care to know too much more about them. Lucky birds. How did they mourn a death among their kind, those mynahs?

He turned for home, wondering about Ms. D'Souza, wondering what she looked like at Anupa's age—well, at his own age for that matter. Young Ms. Monica D'Souza, his attractive teacher with round eyes, straight shoulder-length brown hair, and flower dress that hugged her hips, buttocks, and waist so perfectly. The top of her dress hugged her, pressed against her back and chest, held up her small cup-shaped breasts like new sunflowers glowing in the dust. He became curious, full of wonder: Did Ms. Monica keep a passerine under her flower dress, there between her legs? He liked her classes, simply because *she* taught them. The boys and girls school should be one, yes, they should join together, Fishhead thought. Then he'd sit near Anupa in the same class and find ways to smell her skin and dark hair, talk to her, touch her while Ms. Monica spoke to everyone in her soft and friendly way. A perfect life, a very perfect life that might be. All the food he really needed.

Fishhead went home. He ran up the two steps in front and jumped onto the tiled front verandah, and then he entered the apartment, saw uncle and aunty. He'd missed seeing them arrive somehow when he went off with his catty. Did they bring sweetmeats—halvah, laddoos, barfi, gulab jamuns? Yes, he saw the small gift box with its gold wrapping paper on a chair off to Dad's side, the knotted twine still wrapped around the box. Sweets and whiskey don't agree. The box sat unopened. Perhaps uncle and aunty knew that Dad never liked sweets. They joined him in a game of Rummy now, smoking and sipping a new bottle of booze with the casual busyness of sand crabs at Juhu Beach. Fishhead liked Juhu Beach, the two times the family went there last year. Sandcrabs, yes, Dad with uncle and aunty, their playing cards in hand, elbows up, shuffling and making talk to win, lose, or fold. Then sip, chat, and smoke. Fishhead kissed uncle and aunty on the cheek, but he didn't like to do that anymore. A growing boy should not have to kiss adults on the cheek. Dad did not acknowledge him when he entered the house, didn't lift his eyes, but Fishhead expected a smile or nod and got nothing. Dad seemed in good spirits, as if he'd won something at the derby. They left clues: their chat, the new bottle of whiskey, empty packs of Charminar and Four Square cigarettes, the filled ashtray, Dad's mood and smile, sweets, potato chips.

Where did Mom go? Fishhead wondered. She'll have nothing to do with this. Must be in the back, cooking. Where else? The things a child witnesses and rejects as false—the unpaid duties of a parent, those round-the-clock confrontations with time to do the needful, to meet expectations, say a prayer, pay a bill, bandaid a finger, the unfairness of it all. "Mom are you there? Why aren't you playing Rummy?" Fishhead called. The things a child witnesses in a parent. Scrub, clothe, feed, commute, work. Believe, believe, believe. A life cycle for one is a life cycle for all. This is your nature, too, and I have seen you raise your walls, impose expectations on yourself, and build your defenses as Eshma has.

Fishhead joined Mom on the verandah. The tiny, hot kitchen, and she sat there in front of the kerosene wick stove just outside the door. The open verandah, always better for daylight, for circulating the heat and smoke. She cooked her flour rotis this time. Strands of black smoke rose from under the hot tava on which she roasted the flatbread. Mom rubbed oil on one with the back of a teaspoon. She dropped the spoon back into a cup of vegetable oil then flipped the bread over with a flat utensil. Fishhead came and sat next to his mother. He took the utensil from her and began working the flatbread, pushing it around now and then to keep the bread from burning, pressing down on it to fill it with air and make it rise. Black spots tasted good, but a burned roti fed stray dogs that crossed neighborhood yards as they went looking for food. Mom did not smile; she smiled less nowadays. The rotis piled up on a metal plate nearby, about two to three inches high, just enough to feed the family.

"Mom, will you make murabba?" he said. "You make good murabba."

"Not this week, son. I've used up the tomatoes, and it will take a lot more to make the jam."

"I hope you'll make it," he said.

"Your nana taught me few things, because I spent most days growing up in a boarding school."

"I'm glad I'm not in a boarding school."

"Dad would have sent all four of you to a boarding school if we could afford it."

"Dad would do that?"

"Yes, he would, I know him well."

"Going to school is hard, Mom. I don't ever want to go to a boarding school."

Eshma nodded. "The nuns were very strict with me. I remember that much. I used to cry a lot."

"Like you cry now?"

His mother faced him with compassion, sadness written on her face and in her eyes. Fishhead looked away. She said nothing and returned to her cooking, and he continued to work the fresh rotis on the tava. A few minutes later, he reached under the pile of cooked rotis and eased one out without dislodging the others. He rolled it, then took a bite. Mom smiled. She got up, her knees clicked; she paused halfway to check her discomfort before standing up straight. Fishhead reached out and touched her narrow wrist, wrapping his fingers around it; she brought her other arm across her body and patted his hand gently. Flour settled on his hand. He let go and studied her as she moved away through the door of the kitchen. Her housedress fell down to her knees. Those shapely calves, strong knees, and swelling ankles with their emerging varicose veins. She returned with the small glass jar of sugar, but took it to the edge of the verandah and dusted off the few ants, sending them flying onto the un-mowed grass of the backyard. He took the jar from her, unrolled his roti, and poured a little sugar. Rolled it up again and took a generous bite, and the flatbread flaked between his teeth. He offered her some, but she shook her head.

Uncle and aunty poked their heads through the doorway, waving, and aunty spoke, "We're leaving now. Have a good evening."

"You won't stay for dinner? It'll be ready within the hour," Mom said.

"Mom's making eggplant and potato *bhaji*," Fishhead explained. "She already made the *dhal*."

"Oh, we'd love to stay, but we can't," aunty said.

"Okay," Mom replied.

"Balan won at the races," uncle added. "You should be celebrating."

"Yes, we brought *mithai*," aunty said, although she did not care to show Eshma the box of sweets that sat near Balan.

"Did Dad win a lot?" Fishhead interjected.

"Why don't you ask him yourself?" aunty said.

"That's wonderful!" Mom replied, smiling. Conversations overlapped. Then she turned to Fishhead and said, "You have no business asking such a question." She smacked his thigh, and a cloud of flour went up in the air. Mom looked up at her guests again. "Celebrate with us then," she added. "We can celebrate together."

"Perhaps next Sunday," aunty replied, smiling. "Bye, again." They waved and turned around for the front door, and Dad appeared on the verandah.

"I'll walk them to the train station," he said. "Have your dinner. Don't wait up for me. I'll be back shortly, okay?"

Mom nodded but didn't raise her head to address him. She asked, "Will you close the front door?" But Balan did not answer. "Go check the front door," she said to Fishhead.

He got to his feet and stepped up to the doorway. In the front room, Kishore played with a wooden block set of painted ABC letters. Fishhead entered the room and locked the front door. Then he picked up the box of sweets and made his way to the verandah again. Kishore interrupted his play and followed his brother, curious about the shiny box. Fishhead placed the box of sweets on the floor of the tiled verandah near his mother and waited to catch her reaction, but Mom only glanced at it, unwilling to begin a conversation about the gift.

"Shall I open it?" He asked.

"After dinner," she said. "Leave it in the front room but don't place it on the floor, or the ants will get it. Take a saucer and small bowl from the kitchen."

Fishhead did as told. He took a saucer and filled a bowl with some water. "Here, hold this," he said to Kishore and gave little brother the box of sweets, as he made his way to the front room while Kishore followed with the box. Fishhead placed the saucer on the card table and poured some water from the bowl into the saucer, and then he put the bowl in the center of the saucer. The water rose in the saucer but did not run over. He took the box of sweets from his brother and balanced it on the bowl, making sure the box did not tip over and make a mess of the water and dishes. The sweets tempted him too much, and dinner seemed so far away. He wanted to untie the knot and feast his eyes on the contents of the box; its fresh sweetmeats made with ghee, milk, sugar, nuts, and aromatic spices, with their edible gold and silver foil that dressed the top. Did uncle and aunty buy them? His mouth watered.

"Shall we open it?" He asked Kishore, winking, and little brother grabbed for the knot, but Fishhead stopped him. "I'll do it. But you can't tell Mom." He lifted the box and laid it on the table near the dishes. He quickly untied the knot and pulled the string away. The lid came off next. Fishhead pinched the corner of the wax paper covering the sweets and moved it aside, careful not to dislodge the delicate edible foil on the pieces of pink and orange *barfi,* his favorite sweetmeat made with pistachios, cardamom, and saffron. The fragrance caught him in the nose, distracted him. His stomach growled, but softly, as if to acknowledge his unexpected discovery. This treasure. He moved the box under Kishore's nose. "Smell that? Wow, I could eat this every day!" he said.

"Me too!" Kishore said, his slightly plump cheeks widening.

A gentle breeze came through the open windows. Fishhead had an idea. No one would know, not if Kishore kept his mouth closed. "Want a taste?" he said. "But you can't tell anyone. Promise me." He waited for little brother to nod in agreement, and then he stuck his fingers into the open box and picked up the few crumbs around the cut sweets. They nibbled, both of them. Fishhead broke off tiny portions from the bottom ends of a few pieces, and they nibbled some more. He did not touch the ball-shaped *laddoos*. So delicious, all of it, the sweet agony of curiosity and temptation. Should he get caught. If Mom knew.

"Fishhead, I need you. What are you doing?" she asked from the back verandah. "I hope you didn't open the sweets."

He put the wax paper and lid back together in haste and re-tied the string then knotted it, but he did not do a very decent job with the knot. He put the box back on top of the bowl then opened the front door and stepped onto the narrow front verandah. Kishore followed him. Fishhead licked his fingers, wiping them on his shorts until they went dry. They stood there doing nothing for a minute or so. A late afternoon in this quiet section of the colony. No sign of Prem; he'd likely wandered off. And Pradeep liked to spend time with friends on the school's sports field. "Mom needs me," Fishhead said a minute or so later, turning to little brother and reaching for the doorframe. "Go play with your toys," he added, and stepped inside. Kishore squeezed past him, and Fishhead buried his guilt and shame as he returned to the back verandah. Mom had rinsed the six palm-sized brinjals and placed them on the cutting board near an accompanying paring knife. Everything on the tiled floor. Everything spread out from the only wick stove. Smoking kerosene. Fishhead took his place near her again, but this time on the other side. She rolled out the last few balls of dough and cooked them on the hot tava, spooning oil on both sides of the browning rotis. When done with the last flatbread, she took a pair of small iron tongs and pulled the hot tava off the stove and placed it in the sink among other dirtied dishes. Fishhead kept his eyes on the griddle as it sizzled and smoked when it touched water. More dirty dishes after dinner, many more to come.

One by one Fishhead cut the tough stems from the purple vegetables and began dicing them. Then he tossed the raw brinjal cubes into a vessel and sprinkled salt over the cubes while Mom guided him with the amount of salt. She liked salt, as nana also did, but Dad complained once at dinner, and now Mom took more care to control her use of salt. She put a new aluminum vessel on the wick stove; took onions, ginger, and garlic from a hanging basket in the kitchen and joined Fishhead on the floor again. She began slicing them. Suddenly, she paused and placed her right hand on her stomach while she continued to sit on her haunches.

"Mom!" he said, freezing his action on the cutting board, and he stood up.

She shut her eyes briefly and nodded, but said nothing more. Fishhead nursed his panic, although he had no idea how to read his mother's discomfort. "Put some oil in the pot, son," she said.

"Mom, are you okay?" he asked.

"I'm fine. Put some oil, three to four tablespoons, and turn up the stove's heat."

He did that and sat back down, unaware of the passing time. He studied her, studied her as if the world stood still and she alone moved in step towards fate.

Pressure Cooker

At twilight, still bright, the sound of shuffling and creasing paper emerged from the front room. Moments later, Dad stepped out on the back verandah holding a package at his side. Kishore followed him, filled with curiosity. The package brushed against Dad's dark slacks. He whistled to the tune of "Camp Town Races," and then switched to "Daisy, Daisy." Something more romantic in mind. He smiled, life sparking through his reddened eyes. His whistle had a trill at the end of each musical phrase; Dad did that well. He had a talent. Soon enough, he stopped whistling and began to sing:

> *I'm so crazy, all for the love of you.*
> *You gave me your hand in marriage,*
> *though I can't afford a carriage.*
> *But you look sweet, upon a seat,*
> *of a bicycle made for two.*

"You're crazy all right," Mom said. "And what bicycle? We can't even afford that." She wore a frown, but there behind her seriousness, a hint of sunlight made her blush. "We're going to eat dinner soon," she added. "It took longer than I expected."

"I'm not hungry," Dad said. "But I got you something."

"Wish you'd join us. Especially on Sundays," she said. "Is that Prem kicking the can about in front?"

Fishhead stepped around his father and led Kishore back up the steps to the front room. And right through that front door just ahead, a clear view of Prem on the graveled street in the distance. "Yes, he's out there. Prem's there," Fishhead replied, and gestured for Kishore to sit down and mind his own business. Mom and Dad, alone on the back verandah now.

"Get your things ready for school tomorrow," Mom called out. "We'll eat soon."

Fishhead checked on his school uniform, the blue tie with its two yellow diagonal stripes, his socks and shoes. His schoolbooks and folded raincoat. But his curiosity got the better of him, so his attention wandered back to the verandah, where Dad still stood, back towards Fishhead. Mom did not get up as she stirred the eggplant and potato curry. Dad shifted the package to the other side and slipped two fingers through the jute rope that held the package together.

"I have something for you," he repeated. Did he need an answer?

Mom ignored him again.

"Would you like to open it?"

She put a lid on the pot and turned off the wick stove, and steam pushed through the lid. She held her stomach as she rose to her feet. Dad approached her, showing a hint of impatience. "Open it." Mom washed her hands in the sink then wiped them on her housedress. Fishhead stepped behind the doorframe, unwilling to make his presence known. Mom moved slowly, tired. She came up to Dad and quickly ran her fingers through her short dark hair to set it straight. He gave her the package, and she took it from him without raising her eyes. What did the package contain? Fishhead wanted to know. Mom never refused a gift. This difficult ritual of human courtesy. Forced expectations.

"What is it? How did you get it?" She looked into Dad's eyes, but he quickly turned away.

"Just open it, darling. Open it." He hummed.

Mom smiled, a faint smile, and studied the package in her hands, held it level with her hips. The box appeared heavy, a foot high and deep, but a few inches longer. Fishhead moved to the opposite side of the doorframe to get a better view, and his actions inspired little brother, who shuffled to the back door. Fishhead kept Kishore behind him, shielding him from the exchange.

"Go on, I'm waiting," Dad said. "Think of it as a blessing."

"From God, then?" Mom said. A touchy subject in this household. She moved aside and made her way to the old sofa behind Balan. An old cushioned seat with square wooden feet, one turned a few degrees in front.

Dad took a step back to let her pass. "What God?" He pushed up the corner of his mouth to scrunch his right cheek. Showed his displeasure. The pale green light of the translucent corrugated walls fell on them. The walls covered half the verandah to the north and east, and framed a wooden post in that corner for privacy from the neighbors on that side.

Mom placed the package down on the sofa and pushed the sofa back until it touched the rear wall. She looked up at the sloping corrugated roof. This extra room, a makeshift room, not safe for sleeping at night. The old sofa suited the verandah and had many uses, as now, a table for her gift, but it had a gaping rip on one side.

A pair of springs showed through; the rip had started as a small tear, a cut, but Fishhead and Prem had pulled up most of the foam and cotton fillings over time. The other side of the sofa still invited use, being firm and cushy as a bag of dry construction sand.

Mom untied the jute rope and rolled it around the fingers of her left hand; she tied the ends together, and put the rope aside for future use. (She wasted nothing, because she had nothing to waste. The jute could be recycled as a light clothesline, or a tie for newspaper bundles she'd sell in the marketplace for small change. A few rupees here and there mattered, they always mattered to her. Whereas Dad discarded the daily papers as soon as he'd clipped his horse racing facts and figures.)

Finally Mom had the gift in sight. "A Prestige cooker!" She reached into the box to pull it out. "I've wanted one for so long." Her face gleamed. She held the cooker up to study its metal, its sturdy heat-resistant black handles, the black rubber gasket, and heavy pressure regulator that fit in the palm of her hand.

"That's why I bought it for you."

"Thank you." She reached into the box for the instruction manual. The rope slid off the sofa and fell to the floor. She bent down to pick it up, but he took her shoulder and held her back. Mom got up on her toes to kiss Dad on the cheek, and he tried to pull her closer, but she took a step back. Placed a hand on her stomach. "Thank you, how thoughtful." She held her smile, but his face seemed without expression, almost emotionless. Disappointed.

Fishhead backed away from the doorframe and took Kishore with him into the living room, although he kept his attention on the back verandah.

"You must get a haircut," Mom said, facing Dad now. "Your hair is overgrown and the gray is starting to show."

"Okay, I will."

"Shall I wash your shirt? I can add it to the other dirty clothes."

Dad's sleeves and collar looked stained with sweat from the heat, but he seemed like he did not want to talk about his hair or washing clothes.

"Come, let's all have dinner. It's ready now," Mom said.

"I'm really not hungry," Dad replied. "You and the children go ahead."

Prem entered the house. He spoke into Fishhead's ear: "I know Dad. He's eating outside." Prem sounded upset. "Meat, I'm sure."

Fishhead frowned and stepped back to let his older brother cut through. Prem watched as Mom began to put away the box and wrapping materials, while Dad stood to the side and stroked his tiny goatee, thinking. Finally he made his way toward the back door, but Prem just stood there, unmoving.

"Let your father pass," Eshma said.

"What's that, Ma?" Prem asked, but finally he pressed his body against the doorframe sideways and allowed his father to walk by. "Hi, Dad," he mumbled.

Balan turned the corner of his mouth up and sniffed. "Take a bath," he said. "You're starting to smell."

"Okay." Prem jumped down on the verandah. "What did you get, Ma?" he asked.

Fishhead followed his brother and put his head down as he went past Dad, displeased. Dad always won around here. Had Prem forgotten? And, yet, Fishhead too began to consider how he might be able to stand up to his father and deny the man any respect, just as Prem had done. Pradeep did too. Lessons learned. Fishhead reached for the plates from the kitchen shelf; he did this without instruction or prompt by his mother. Prem always needed someone to tell him what to do, and he never offered to help unless asked. A lazy boy, too lazy.

"Your father got me a pressure cooker," Eshma explained.

"Mahalaxmi then?" Prem asked.

"Be quiet, Prem!" Eshma answered. Back to seriousness, life.

"Uncle and aunty must have won, too," Prem said. "Time for boozing."

"Prem!" Eshma stated. "Don't spoil a good thing."

"Okay."

"Shut up, yaar!" Fishhead cut in. "Why all this? Let's eat." He placed the dishes on the floor near the wick stove and started to serve little brother. Soon they sat around Mom and the stove, crossed their legs in front, and had dinner while Dad occupied his chair by the window in the living room.

Protein

A few weeks later, Fishhead decided he'd catch a local soccer match at school. An eager crowd had gathered around the field on this particular Saturday afternoon, although more people packed the four-tiered concrete spectator stand. Fishhead slipped past the crowd and got up close to the goalpost on the north end of the grounds; it put him near the girls' school wall at the far end of the field, the wall he liked to climb; it put him near the tamarind tree that fed and teased his hunger.

In fact, as soon as the game began, he abandoned his spot to look for Anupa; she might be over there with her girlfriends. No such luck. He returned to the goalpost, and then he spotted her in the stands across from him; she, a cousin, and a girlfriend. How had he missed her when he came in? He didn't have the courage to approach her now and start a conversation. Pretty thing; a prettier cousin though.

Anupa dressed like she belonged to a well-to-do family, so much so that Fishhead noticed anew his own shabbiness. Again, her straight and long black hair, gleaming in the light and smooth like coconut oil. Ghee, golden cream of butter. Yes, the delight of her hair, like ghee; and he stared at her across the field while the soccer match continued. Made a dreamer out of him. Then the football came flying past the goalposts, and everyone else jumped out of the way. Fishhead caught the ball hard on his left thigh and abdomen then fell back from the thrust. The crowd laughed at him, and he jumped to his feet, embarrassed and soiled by dirt, a scrape on his palm, the right one. At once, he looked in Anupa's direction, and caught her whispering something to her friend, giggling, while her cousin looked on. The prettier one. Her name? Anupa caught his eye, and he turned away and moved to the outer edge of the crowd by the goalpost. Hard to take, being called out by a stupid football in front of everyone. Hard to take. So stupid. He left the game altogether and slipped out from the sports field by the side gate.

The girls' school and its grounds led deeper into the rustic village community in the interior; the two feeder roads skirted the grounds and came together into a single lane to meet the main road. Houses with terraced rooftops surrounded the church and both schools. Jasmine, roses bushes, lilies, and bougainvillea grew everywhere. Banana plants, and guava and mango trees, too. A tall tamarind here and there. The dry heat and dust. Fishhead took the north road circling around the church until he returned to the main road and walked south for home. He didn't care to face Anupa for a while. She might forget the incident. Better if she did, he hoped she did. But his thigh still hurt from the soccer ball. How he wished he didn't wear shorts anymore! Growing boys shouldn't wear shorts in public. What if Anupa and her cousin didn't care for boys with shorts? Fishhead made up his mind to ask for a new pair of slacks.

Hard times kept getting harder. Dad continued to borrow from his mysterious contacts; his debts increased, and he struggled to keep his creditors at bay. He still hadn't found a job he liked, not that he searched with any earnestness; that ideal job resided in his head like a cancer he could not tamp down or trim. That ideal job, slippery as Destiny entreating him in a dream, slippery as protein pushing around the yolk of a raw, exposed egg he broke in the kitchen. The egg, his life. You can only nurture something if you know what it is. Balan could not put his finger on it, he could not. His dreams exceeded his skills and basic education, and he might never be satisfied with a job. What bored him? Did he want to pursue art, music? He'd become a father of four so soon in life, his adulthood riding in a pram his family cannot afford. What bores human beings like Balan, I ask you, intellectuals like him, who seem dissatisfied with their lives hour after hour, so much so that they can never change their situation nor contribute to the welfare of others?

Never a job out there that fit Dad perfectly, and yet he left home each morning without breakfast and came home after dark, around the same time when Mom also returned home from her work at the telephone exchange downtown. Her stomach grew, and it seemed impossible, this routine of hers, this tricky and difficult new life she faced, again. The only person holding a full-time job, and now with a full-time baby on the way. Nana came for a visit again from out of state and begged her to leave him, begged Mom to take the boys and go away without him. But some secret reason kept Mom home with Dad. He spent long hours at home working on his horse racing stats, even when his pockets yawned with emptiness, with air.

Fishhead failed to understand Dad's bad luck. He disliked his father, but he might have been less confused about everything if he'd had the slightest indication of what kept happening between

Mom and Dad. Such seriousness and lingering. They never spoke openly about their feelings, and said less to each other nowadays. Mom's stomach got bigger. Stress carved itself into her face, while her stomach enlarged and slowed her down. Did she even want the baby? Fishhead wondered. She looked defeated, broken, overwhelmed. He became sad, unmotivated by his textbooks and homework. He didn't like to see Mom this way. Most boys at school and in the neighborhood appeared to have lives that kept getting better, not lives that went the other way, like his. Wish he knew why. What stopped Dad from being a good father, a responsible father? Dad seemed well-fed. How did he manage that? And his secrets? Fishhead became determined to find out. He thought of Prem's words in his ears a while back and remembered: Dad liked eating outside and didn't care to join the family at lunch or dinner. Surely, he kept a tab wherever he ate. But what sensible restaurant owner would allow Dad this privilege? No money at home; hunger prevailed, the language of false reasons that guided Fishhead. He began to lose interest in school and homework. Something wrong here; he could see that, but he had no way to know for sure, unless Mom talked. She did not.

His body pressed him to find other means for adequate food, protein. Not enough flesh between his bones and skin. Too lean. He felt this in his cheeks. He needed meat. Just like Dad, he needed meat. He found his means in the slingshot, the catty, which no longer sat in the shoebox on the floor by the Godrej almirah; he shoved it in the back pocket of his shorts and took it everywhere he went. He tested his luck. Summer months opened up to freedom. He borrowed a few matchsticks now and then from the box Mom kept on a kitchen shelf, and dropped them in the breast pocket of his shirt. He fixed the ties on the ends of the catty by tightening the rubber bands and knotting them securely so they wouldn't come apart in his hands and sting his face again. He went looking for mynahs and sparrows at lunchtime when life quieted down; people rested or took long naps, safe from the blistering sun. The chirping of birds ascended, swelled, and consumed Fishhead's attention. He loaded his catty with small stones and aimed high and true into the trees; he hit a mynah and watched it fall to the ground while the trees went silent.

He approached the bird and snatched it up. He studied it.

That mynah, still breathing in his hands, eyes fixed on his as it blinked again and again—he knew he'd never forget its face and the image of its chest rising and falling, pleading for his mercy, it seemed, as he cupped its warm body, those soft feathers. He waited until it went still.

Hunger encouraged him to waste no more time. He made a mound of twigs at the end of his street, but made sure to light the fire behind a brick wall to conceal his actions. He added dried leaves, and struck the matches on a stone until it sparked then burst into flames. The fire caught without fuss under the crisp twigs, and he placed the lifeless bird on top, then let it scorch in the flames. The smoke and odor of cremation, soul of a passerine. Its fate. Hissing flesh, crackling leaves. Too hot to touch, steaming, steaming. He moved the bird across the flames with sticks he held in both hands. Then he juggled the hot bird, tossing it from palm to palm, and he pinched its feathers while it continued to hiss, its sound like the fury of rioters on a weekday *bandh* in the city. Hands burning, hunger burning, stomach pinching him. Wasting no time, he tore the bird apart, pressed his teeth down on the meat and did his best to keep it from burning his lips and gums. He ate the darkened flesh, the soft and cooked protein so sweet under the crust. And his body spoke, satisfied, relieved of its desperate need for food. He could not think about tomorrow or the day after that.

Fishhead licked his fingers clean and hoped to rid himself of the smell of cooked meat still present on his hands and around his mouth, in his teeth. He walked north along the gravel street and went past his apartment until he reached the road leading out to the main thoroughfare from the center of the colony. Near the gates, he stepped over the gutter on his right and entered a small shop, part of a residence, which sold a variety of everyday household products and edible items like bread, crackers, and snacks. The shop occupied one half of a small concrete and brick shack along the west side of the residential structure; beyond it, a *dhobi* ran a small laundry and ironing business. Fishhead used the faucet in front of the shack on the dhobi's side and rinsed his hands and mouth; then he wiped himself dry with the bottom of his shirt. He took the three steps into the shop, where the owner's wife stood behind an enclosed glass counter.

"My mother needs a box of matches," he said. "I don't have any money."

"Where do you live?" The woman asked, and he told her. She nodded. "I've seen you around. Tell your mother she can pay me back later. I know your face."

Fishhead smiled and kicked the back of his heel with the other foot. When she turned around to get the box of matches from the back of the store, he reached over the counter and grabbed a few pieces of candy, which he crammed into his pockets just before the woman returned. She gave him the matches, oblivious, and he left quickly, pleased with himself, but the dhobi confronted him outside.

"I saw you!" the older man said in a cold whisper, squeezing Fishhead's arm, pulling him close, away from the shop. He slapped Fishhead across his left cheek and behind his head; he reached into Fishhead's pockets, grabbed the candy, threw it into his face. "Don't let me catch you doing this again. I'll turn you over to the police. Now go!"

Fishhead ran off without a word, smarting from the slaps. He needed to keep an eye out the next time. Hunger had made him careless again.

Darren and his family moved away without saying goodbye. Dad sold the Godrej almirah, the small table, and two of the four chairs. No more table to play Rummy. No table to eat at.

"Please don't sell the sewing machine," Mom pleaded. "Take my wedding ring if you need to, but please don't sell the sewing machine. I'm begging you. Mama bought it for me. It's the only thing that is truly mine. Please!"

Dad pawned their wedding rings, Mom's woolen shawl, the gold chain, and two bangles she kept in the almirah. He possessed nothing of his own, except for the clothes he wore, and a small plastic comb he always tucked in his breast pocket. He found a buyer for the Meccano set and wooden block kit that kept little brother busy. "Kishore will grow up," Dad insisted. "He'll find other ways to amuse himself."

Pradeep took old newspapers and empty bottles to the market for cash. It was never enough.

Dad pawned off the shortwave transistor radio he kept on the window sill, the one aunty had let him borrow. He pawned off the pressure cooker. He had his eye on the sewing machine. If he had a choice about *that*, if he had a choice.

Mom gave birth to Lily through C-section. A difficult birth. A sweet little baby girl who cried and cried. Mom took time off from work to heal and raise Lily, even though it became clear to Fishhead that Mom did not care for her only daughter, now four years younger than Kishore. As if she meant to reject her.

Lily

When the landlord increased the rent in the new year, the family moved with newborn Lily and minimal possessions to a remote corner of the colony, settling in another rental duplex far north and west. A light, tiled courtyard, a private gate, and decorative wall in front overlooked a marshland with tall grasses, cattails, lotuses, and several bird species. Groups of loud ravens sat on electric wires raised high on wooden poles along the outside edge of the gravel road in front. Five houses west, a resident ran a plastic molding business for making fountain pens out of his home, and the odor of hot liquid plastic drifted eastward in a constant rash. Three houses to the east, a family conducted a diamond polishing business in a residence with high walls, gates, and two dogs that barked at the slightest provocation. An area so removed from people, Fishhead ended up spending more time with the inhabitants of the marshland. Too far from his former neighborhood friends; too far to play marbles with them on a whim. A new kind of loneliness.

The family occupied the east unit of this duplex. Its tiled front courtyard offered plenty of room to play. An eight-foot-wide dirt compound ran down the side of the unit from the front gate and around the back, where the verandah took on a similar look and feel as the one in the previous apartment, but this verandah stayed level with the ground, separated only by a low stone threshold at the entrance, where a broken rusty hinge testified to the past presence of a gate. A waist-high concrete wall and corrugated roof plus wall sections separated the back verandah from the natural elements of the compound. (Mom did not like this gap at the entrance; she feared for Lily's safety as her daughter learned to walk and talk.) In the back, the property opened up to neighboring houses beyond the line of bushes growing at the edges of the compound. A few plantain trees showed their fruit, raw pickings that would have tempted Mom to make coconut curries with diced plantain, if she had the luxury of time and energy; she cooked less these days, and asked Dad to spend his free time in the kitchen, which he preferred not to do.

Aunty and uncle had their own new baby and made less time to visit. Horse-racing conversations suffered, and the playing cards disappeared from sight; Fishhead supposed Dad had earned a few rupees selling the pack, or perhaps he'd given the cards to a creditor to help pay down his debts. No matter, Dad began to lose his attachment to Mahalaxmi and his dependence on the racetrack; he gave aunty and uncle his collection of racing index cards. He smoked less, too, but did not give up drinking.

Fishhead decided they had moved to put the family closer to his school, if only by a quarter mile or so. The shorter walk to the main road made a difference, although Fishhead and his brothers now had to cut through a shabby slum-like area and jump across gutters to reach it. Pradeep did not approve of the move or the new area, although he too had no choice in the decision. He disengaged himself from life at home and began to spend more hours with his school friends. A teenager now, he kept his eyes open and began to reach out for support from others more willing to advise or help him. He possessed a private sense of determination and drive, a character that Fishhead did not detect in his parents, although perhaps Mom showed some in her willingness to overcome her daily challenges while keeping her full-time job. Had the move unsettled her? He wondered. Surely she'd considered his welfare, and that of his siblings. Nothing else mattered to her, right? Surely Mom understood the consequence of leaving place.

Place is everything to you, I know. Place is Destiny, a mainspring of life, your shelter and need for belonging; it is the cause of origin and memory, the centrifuge of all your stories that mark your character and that stamp you with reason and a sense of purpose. Without place, where would you be, dear reader? If you're lucky, you'll pass the very foundations of place to your offspring, and they to theirs. Place is recreation and pleasure, the carnation of your pride. Place is history, security, a destination of numbers and characters unique to itself in all geography, and it is yours alone. Place is care and nurturing, and pets. Nothing could be more important to you, nothing offers more comfort. I float through your spaces, turn every corner, reside in every room, crevice, object, and cooking pot. Yes, place is Destiny. This is where you return to when you get off the bus, the train, your bicycle; where you hurry to after your mind and body have trudged a million steps into managed time at the office, at the university, at school. Place knows family well. Fishhead needed this security of place, and more and more he began to feel less assured, because he sensed in his family an unsettling, like earthquake tremors.

Dad found a creative partner in a young man half his age called Sachdev who knew screen printing, and they began a small creative venture, hoping to make and sell greeting cards, flags, banners, and other items with decorations for Hindu temples. Dad introduced Sachdev to the family one Sunday morning, just after a mild earthquake had shaken the neighborhood; he brought the young man home for breakfast. Mom wore a disapproving face but still served Sachdev fried eggs and bread, and a cup of hot coffee made with chicory. On Dad's face: pride. Sachdev wore a red bowtie over a white shirt and dark slacks, and in his polite manner, ate until he cleaned his plate, picking up the final strokes of egg yolk with his last morsel of bread. Then he explained his skill at screen printing. Dad did not mention a business plan. Perhaps he had none.

Fishhead became intrigued by Sachdev and the few small tins of screen printing ink the young man opened in the living room, the squeegee with its used and stained wooden handle, and the clear, framed silk screen the size of a notebook, with shoe tacks on the side and back of the wood casing. Fishhead drank in the aura and odor of these materials. His mind swirled with ways it could help them escape this crisis, this misery. Art. He liked it, even though he did not yet have a sure sense of its many forms. So novel, this art, so different than anything he learned and drew in school. Sachdev the messenger, the young man with some evidence to show that a different world of creativity thrived outside the family's tight ring of hardship.

The lack of business experience or resources, however, ended Dad and Sachdev's partnership dream in a few months, and the young man never visited the family again. Still, the effort seemed to inspire Dad to search for work in a similar field. He wore a tie some mornings (Did uncle let him borrow a tie?) buttoned his washed shirts, tucked them into his dark slacks, and even flashed a pair of cufflinks (Uncle's, again?)

Meanwhile, Fishhead struggled at school. He spent weekday afternoons hanging out on the sports field in his only school uniform; there he imagined a life of soccer, cricket, art, enough food, girls, and Anupa. But sooner or later he had to return home, where conditions never improved. Mom could not shake her fatigue. Her job at the telephone exchange paid the bills, just barely, while her retirement pension materialized on the distant horizon, but slowly, with effort.

From April through September, Bombay soaked up enough rain to resemble a rice paddy in the countryside. Ominous clouds hung over the city, issuing thunderclaps that shook foundations, rattled double-decker buses, and made Lily cry and cry. Lightning bolts of such accuracy and power; two ravens sitting on the electric lines in front of the duplex disappeared one afternoon in a cloud of smoke and feathers. *Boom!* Nature's war. Fishhead studied the scene in awe and fright. Lily cried again, until he settled her and comforted her.

He'd been taking the main golf course road home from school, cutting through the slum, emerging on the other side of the marshland with slushy feet, his body fully drenched as the rain continued to beat the earth like a yoked bullock dragging a plow under a whip. For an entire week, the clouds issued unending volleys of rain; big and dense drops hammered everything, so that the marshland in front began to overflow onto the street and enter the compound. Schools closed in affected parts of the city that

Tuesday and Wednesday, traffic got washed out in many areas, commuter train services stalled from inner-city flooding, and Mom stayed home for two days. And the gutters in the slum overflowed, rendering the main road impassable, clogged with filth and feces. Fishhead and his brothers had no other option but to start taking the long way to school by following the graveled roads out of the colony.

Then the rain stopped, offering a momentary sense of relief, although the sky stayed misty-eyed, unyielding and temperamental; throughout the monsoon season, the sky threatened to resume its punishment. There were welcome blasts of sunshine and azure skies, but the moisture lingered. Fishhead shriveled up like a prune; his clothes refused to dry in the soggy air. Such discomfort! Sticky, sopping. Insufficient dry towels. He walked about with his footwear in his hands, kept his books wrapped inside his raincoat. He rolled his slacks up past his shins, so they wouldn't slow him down in the floodwaters. He wanted summer more than anything, a break from school and those long walks. And summer hovered around the corner, but not yet.

But where did Dad go during the daytime when the family needed him in this crisis? No telephone, no other way to reach him; his whereabouts remained a mystery. He explained nothing and disappeared for hours, then returned at night, the smell of drink on his breath. Mom endured long hours and heavy travel schedules. The slowest transportation during these heavy rains. She relied on commuter trains and connecting city buses to ply between home and work; she waited in long lines while passengers shoved, pressed against each other, swore. Sardines in every can. The heat, whiff, and clamminess of daily city travel. Mom walked a lot; her varicose veins worsened; her strong and shapely calves began to lose their firmness, and her knees clicked now and then. The hard rain and extreme dampness brought on the damnedest cold, and she began coughing. Dad fed her lit cigarettes to keep her warm (How did he afford his cigarettes?) and although Mom did not care to smoke, she shared a puff or two with him. When she didn't improve, he asked her to see Doctor Advani, and she brought home tablets and syrup from visits to the doctor's small clinic in the marketplace. Fishhead worried about Mom and resented his father's deliberate absences. He wanted Dad around. (And why not? Dad remained jobless, but where did he go each day?) Fishhead began to fantasize about following his father.

Dad and Mom argued about religion one late and wet evening just before dinner. Mom had started to pray, to ask God for help. Dad always heard her, but this time he erupted in rage. "There is no God! There is no God, there is no God, there is no God! Could there be a God, if we are living like this? No. There is no God."

Mom cried. Fishhead clenched his fists and held them under his folded legs. Mom and Dad argued. Back and forth they went. Mom's voice became louder the more Dad upset her. He, they, forgot the children listening to them. Lily sobbed. Prem started to tease her for being a crybaby. Pradeep asked him to stop. Fishhead came and stood near his mother and then followed her to the kitchen after she stormed out of the front room, quaking with anger.

Butcher

Under cover of a dark morning sky, Fishhead leaned on the courtyard wall and studied the marshland, now swollen with rainwater. He mourned the emptiness inside him, pale and raw, ashes of regret littering the lightless spaces in his heart. This darkness outside, a monsoon day, all day. The sun denied.

What did the birds have to say? Nothing. The storks, ducks, crows, and mynahs stepped across the vegetation, pulling their bodies over lotus leaves and other greenery with the greatest care. The cranes stayed close to the edges even with their long legs and necks. So graceful, their motion, Fishhead thought. In the silence of the looming downpour, he could hear the soft sounds of their morning routines. No one else seemed to care.

He waited for his father to leave. Mom had risen early and departed in humble and weary silence, using the safe way along the streets of the colony, because she refused to take the shortcut through the rain-affected slum. Dad seemed in no hurry, but he too would leave home, now that the rush hour had subsided. The sun hadn't been seen for days, and the marshland hummed. A water-bound snake crossed the road as it left the neighbor's compound. Clouds held back the rain. And then at last Fishhead heard footsteps. Dad approached the gate, nodded. The gate screeched closed behind him, monsoon's ghosts howling. Several birds took flight then landed again. Crows squawked.

Fishhead waited for Dad to reach the end of the road; Dad went east towards the other side of the marshland and disappeared into the slum there. Then Fishhead pulled the gate open and squeezed through the narrow space. No sound. He made haste after Dad.

At the entrance to the slum, he jumped over a gutter full of stagnant, dirty water and debris, and ducked into a tight alleyway, pressed in on both sides by rows of tin and wood shanties. The dirty children, dirty; the wandering dogs, goats, calves, and chickens, all dirty; and the foul air. Fishhead knew this shortcut well. The stench of stagnant water and feces displeased him more than the meat and fish stalls did in the marketplace, and the earth at his feet behaved like a mudslide. He took care, stepped cautiously; he didn't like walking in the soft, wet dirt. Dad's shape came in view far ahead, followed close behind by a ragged dog, its wagging tail curled up tight. Dad spat. So rare, his spitting. The pariah dog lapped up the ejected saliva.

The slum alleyway opened up to the paved main road, which led to a different market further up in the interior, west and north of the golf course. Fishhead hung a left and followed the main road. He had almost caught up with Dad when Dad looked over his shoulder; Fishhead ducked behind the wall of a sidewalk shrine.

Dad entered the crowding market, which mushroomed around the local commuter station there (a place too dynamic and chaotic for a tender soul). He went into the building that housed the fish market; he walked through the stalls, and Fishhead stayed right behind him. That thick smell of the sea, and crisscrossing conversations of customers haggling with vendors; voices drifted up toward the high ceiling and echoed as if in a narrow underground chamber. Knives fell hard, chopping bone, fins, heads, and tails. Crushing ice, and ice being pushed around in wicker fishing baskets. Vendors sat next to each other on the dark tiled floor, traces of rinsing water at their feet everywhere, water emptying into shallow channels, carrying blood, bits of bone, flesh, innards, eyes, and gills. Crows and gulls in the rafters, on the floor, active and restless between shoppers, their cycles, bags. So many varieties of fish that Fishhead had never seen before. Mackerel piled high on painted display boards placed on the floor or on top of baskets everywhere. Sardines, pomfret, and squid-like "Bombay Duck" too. Kingfish and shark. Lots of bay shrimp and red-back crab.

A young boy came around with a hose and washed the floor clean while customers stepped to the side; he moved blood and pieces of seafood waste into the channels, which ran down the length of the floor between each row of stalls.

Fishhead didn't want to lose his father in the chaos; he stayed on Dad's heels, but kept out of view. Crows ducked and hopped about him, looking for fish scraps. Dad pulled up his slacks and dragged his flip flops on the wet floor of the long open room; he didn't lift his heels up too high or risk wetting the back of his slacks. Fishhead pushed through the crowd, now twenty feet or so behind his father. Held his place. An image of his father in clear sight: Dad's curly hair pressed against the back of his well-shaped head, those slightly protruding ears, and inclining shoulders. His old white shirt. His height, an advantage.

Fishhead drew closer to Dad, who entered a similar room, just as large, with six rows of meat stalls divided from each other by walls. At once the odor of bared flesh and drying blood cut through the air. So different from the fish stalls, this smell of beef and mutton, and of ducks and hens. Live birds in cages. Everywhere, slabs of red meat, suet, and tripe hung on iron hooks dangling from the ceiling. Heart, tongue, liver, and brains sat on paddleboards, on newspaper. Much louder now, as people spoke over the sound of moving, hacking knives on animal bone. Cleavers came down on blocks made of cut tree trunks, dividing meat, mincing it. Human power. Strong, violent arms of butchers in ritual combat. The hits came at different times, staggered, but loud and menacing, booming, as the sound echoed through the high space. He pinched his nose and hid behind a group of shoppers. Kept out of Dad's sight as best he could.

Dad approached the meat stall of a Muslim butcher; he waited his turn behind three other customers. The man nodded without smiling as he served the first one. Dad paused for a minute or so, studied the slabs of meat, the butcher's space, his young male assistant, who nodded. Flies everywhere. The heavy butcher wore a traditional prayer cap, and a T-shirt over a plaid *lungi* waist cloth.

Fishhead moved in closer but stood well behind his father about two stalls away; he stayed within earshot but did not face Dad's meat stall. A good spot for him, as long as Dad did not turn.

At last the other customers departed. Dad studied the meat, then raised a finger. He meant a kilo. The butcher drew a long knife down on both sides of a sharpening steel rod. Piercing, these cries of metal, and so much of it in here. The man raised his chin, unsmiling. Dad pointed to a hunk of beef, one of five that hung from double hooks. The one closest to him displayed a heap of yellow cow fat, but Dad eyed another hunk, a good choice with no cartilage and few untidy sinews. A generous flank. Red, even.

"My family will eat meat today," Dad said. "One kilo, please."

"Not from me, sahib," the butcher said. "Unless you're paying cash."

Dad flinched and thrust his hands in his pockets. Other customers turned and looked at him. He paused then stroked his goatee and rocked back and forth on his heels, thinking about his next move. The butcher turned to another customer.

Fishhead leaned forward, curious to know what his father planned to do next. The smell, again, something odorous and distinctly predatory, as if the wind moved inside the building to make it alive. The stench. Fishhead came to a fundamental realization that his father loved meat and that his being aligned with the essence of a meat stall, this place. Meat. Meat. Meat. What Dad wanted more than anything, more than the love of his family, more than Fishhead.

"You wouldn't deprive my family of its nutrition, would you?" Dad asked.

"I wouldn't deprive anyone who clears his tab with me, sahib," the butcher said. Most respectful but honest. He took a paring knife and reached for a side of meat. The flies dispersed and settled back on the flesh as soon as he got done. The man measured the meat, moving iron weights back and forth on one side of the large scale. He wrapped the cuts in a newspaper and gave the package to another customer, who paid and left the scene, squeezing past Dad with a sneer. Fishhead wanted to trip the customer, stick his foot out or tap the back of the man's heel as he passed by. Pretend and apologize, a good trick Fishhead learned in school.

"I've been a good customer," Dad said.

"You were a good customer, sahib," the butcher answered. "My meat is good, and I am glad you appreciate it. But you haven't paid me in two months, going on three. If I extended my tab indefinitely with you, I must do it with all my customers. Then how can I make a living and pay my employees? How can I feed my own family? I will be out of business in no time."

"I wouldn't want that to happen," Dad conceded. "I will definitely pay you next week, and that's a promise. Please cut me some meat today."

"Why don't you come back next week when you have the money."

Fishhead moved in closer. A butcher behind him called his attention, but Fishhead shook his head. He stood about six feet away behind his father but slightly off to the side. Then Dad glanced to his right, and Fishhead turned his back to his father. He turned around again when Dad started to speak.

"I have walked far to reach your stall. Will you ask me to turn around empty-handed?"

"Customers clear their tabs monthly, sahib. *That* is the shop's policy, you know that. Must I make an exception for you?"

"I've been coming here for two years."

"I realize that. I have customers who go back five years and more," the butcher replied. He resumed his work.

Dad stroked his goatee and folded his arms. He weighed his options. "I wish to go nowhere else, to no other stall but yours," he said, his voice more pleasant and serious, but lower so other butchers did not hear him. "I prefer to come here," he added, "just as I have been coming here for two years. Two years!" He waved two fingers in the air.

Fishhead could not believe his father's behavior. Dad said more in a few minutes here than he did in a year at home. He became a different man with a different character: charming, without any hint of authority or anger. No drunken slip-ups. A most patient and thoughtful Dad.

"Now you are trying to get on my good side," the butcher said.

"I am your best promotion, don't you see?" Dad replied. "How about that? Go on, do give me that order. One kilo, please."

The butcher eyed Dad warily then gave in. "Okay, but only this time. You pay me next week. I must have your word."

"You have my word."

Fishhead wiped his forehead in disbelief at Dad's victory. He moved away, again, hiding behind customers.

"Let me finish up with this customer, then I will get your order," the butcher said.

"Thank you," Dad replied, pleased. He turned around to face the butcher and observe his method; the power of the man's cleaver cut right through bone and meat, and it wedged into the block of wood each time. Dad raised his chin and folded his long sleeves while clearing his throat a few times to assert his place there. Fishhead watched Dad, cautioned by his reinstated pride and curiosity.

But a few minutes later, and just as the butcher began to cube Dad's order of meat, a man Fishhead had never met called out to Dad as he came up from behind him. Dad turned.

"Balan, sahib!" The man said, his voice raised high in the commotion of the meat market. "It's my good luck to find you here!" He placed a hand on Dad's shoulder. "You have stopped coming to my liquor store. I have been wondering about you. It has been several months. Too long, sahib."

Caught off guard, Dad smiled and began to lead the man away from the stall by his elbow. Fishhead moved in closer, hastened his footsteps to hear their conversation. Too close? This moment of embarrassment. Shame. What, Fishhead wondered, must he do with his embarrassment?

"I have also come to buy meat, chicken actually," the merchant said loudly. "My butcher's stall is there, you see." He turned and pointed to the next aisle.

Dad glanced at the busy stall. "Listen, Ahmadbhai," he mumbled, "I will stop by the liquor store this afternoon. This afternoon, I assure you."

"Yes, yes, I am certain that you will," the merchant said, loud and clear. "Whether you intend to pay me is another question, no, Balan sahib? Must I wait another half year to have your debt cleared with me? You see, I had taken you for a more reliable man. But I am still trusting in human nature."

Dad put his arms out and lifted his shoulders as if to convey his regret in the merchant's lack of discretion. "I promise, I'll stop by your store today," he muttered. "And we can discuss my balance further. But, please, not here, Ahmadbhai. I'm just trying to feed my family."

Fishhead retreated into the next stall. He'd heard a lot, but he wanted to know how Dad intended to get out of this mess. The liquor merchant turned his hands out repeatedly, as if he'd just washed them and tried to rid his hands of the last drops of water; the gesture meant that he'd given up, frustrated, and had no hope for any resolution. He departed with a swift goodbye, leaving Dad alone in front of the butcher.

"Too good to be true!" the butcher exclaimed.

"I honestly plan to settle with him," Dad said, his face an impassive and handsome stone.

"Too good, sir, but nothing doing." The butcher lifted Dad's cubed beef from the wooden block with the edge of his cleaver, lumped the meat together in his hands, and cast it off on the tiled floor. Flies found the meat right away.

"I'm sorry, I cannot help you any longer," the butcher continued. "You may try another stall." He lifted his cleaver high over his head and brought it down swiftly, plunging its tip on the block of the tree trunk with a crack, and the broad blade closed the subject. The man wiped his hands on an old towel, and then got to his feet, as if to leave.

"You mustn't react so strongly to—" Dad began.

The butcher held up a hand. "I cannot extend credit to you anymore. Try another butcher. There are many around you."

"I promised my children they would have some meat today," Dad said. Fishhead could remember no such promise.

The butcher shrugged.

"I promised it to them! What will I tell them now?"

But the butcher had no more to say. He moved his feet around the wooden block and stepped into the tiny back room while his assistant took care of the next two customers. Dad stepped off to one side, and then surveyed the open meat market, as if trying to make up his mind about something. Hands deep in his pockets.

Fishhead crept away to a slightly farther stall but kept his eyes on his father. Three crows fluttered around at his feet, edging close. The stench of meat and blood struck Fishhead again; he looked down at his slippers and noticed that he'd been standing on a piece of soft suet and red cartilage, dropped in a hurry by a fleeing crow. The three birds objected to his presence; he spat on the ground as the smell of the stalls reminded him of the impurity of his days.

Tabernacle for Drinkers

You might insist that only humans control fate and direct it. I will allow you this because it strengthens you and makes you confident, but I know the truth. I know the source of human outcomes. The pursuit of a material dream, a windfall cash benefit, your victory in sport, a promotion, the timely completion of a project, a marriage, the award gleaming in your hands, a published book, that new house—these are purely human outcomes, you say, the result of your vision and hard work, nothing else. You deserve this illusion.

And yet there are those, like Balan, who do not achieve their goals no matter how hard they try, and no matter how long they endure. And Fishhead looks on, a confused, angry son wishing to reject his parent. Is this bad luck? What is luck if not the avatar you assign to me. As with winning, so also with failure. You are quick to blame me for this; you say it's fate that kept you from succeeding. Perhaps you should acknowledge my hand in your successes, but you take full credit. I do know the source of outcomes; I am at the heart of them. Not everyone can take the winner's podium at the same time. Tension is the fate of all energies, good and bad. One thing becomes right, another wrong. One thing becomes visible, another does not. The tension of success requires prospect of failure. Fishhead's story requires his father.

He followed Dad out of the fish and meat stalls. Dad made his way back to the center of the market, a hundred feet or so away, an open square with its peepul tree in the center. A low rectangular cement wall contained the base of the tree. And plastered on the outside of the wall: movie posters, signs, and other hand-painted words in earthen red honoring Hindu gods and the country itself. Paper, plastic containers, and junk food packaging littered the square, a gathering place for the community and wandering animals. A white cow with a distended stomach rested on its side along one wall; the animal chewed on a discarded plastic bag. But Dad ignored the cow, the people, the tree: all of it. A boy on an old bicycle almost ran into him, but even this couldn't deflect Dad's aim: a building on the opposite side of the square.

Open for Business. The Deccan Lunch House. Not the first customer there, not Dad. He approached the narrow cafe and climbed the few stone steps to talk with the owner, who sat behind a small glass-walled counter to the right. Fishhead understood his father's desire to sit down and have a chai and water, because he too needed a drink. But why did Dad stop to talk with the owner? Fishhead crossed the square and approached the lunch house, unsure of himself. Some tinge of regret for following his father like this. Was curiosity a good enough reason? No work, no money, just secrecy. Why all this pretense? Mom had a job that took more out of her than she had to give. Dad had...this.

A male server led Dad in, and he took a seat toward the rear with his back to the front door. Didn't want to be seen or identified. He sat at a white granite table. Seconds later, a young busboy came to wipe it down. Fishhead got up to the steps of the lunch house and hesitated. One foot on the first step. Should he join his father? A cup of hot chai might do him good. No sooner had he started contemplating his next move when the owner called out to him. "You, boy!" Fishhead lifted his head and jumped to his feet right away. The man shooed him off the premises.

Fed up, Fishhead crossed the square and sat at the wall around the peepul tree with his back to the lunch house. He kept turning his head time and again to catch his father's exit.

A boy his age had better things to do with his time, he thought. This life, this curse and suffering, occupied his mind. No space for freedom, no chance to spend time with his schoolmates or with girls. Would this life turn him into an outcast? Why follow Dad like this? Such a waste of time. Let the man do as he pleased.

The longer he sat there waiting for Dad, the more his mind wandered. He imagined the boys and girls social club. Did Anupa go there? Surely she did. Did she play table tennis and badminton? Carrom? He ought to go there sometime.

A series of harsh thunderclaps echoed through the dark clouds, which were rolling in, low and fluffy. Bursts of white light, the occasional bolt of power. Then from the cafe, the crash of dishes. Fluorescent lights came on inside. Fishhead watched Dad nod to the owner and walk out. Dad made a left and crossed the square about a hundred feet away. He retraced his steps through the dirty alleyway and shanties. Too dark for the afternoon. He cut across the marketplace by the train station and went further north and east until he arrived at a small village twenty minutes away. This new direction, this new village, intrigued Fishhead. Unbelievable! Dad managed to uncoil the snakiest destinations in the most unclean places. Fishhead kept his father in sight as the man made his way through a few tight, bending passages with thin, dirty drainage gutters passing through the middle. Standing water and debris. Unpaved passages, alleys. Cemented gutters. More chickens and a pair of mangy dogs. Barefoot children screaming, uncaring about the murky skies.

Soon Dad stepped over the high threshold of a shed with a metal corrugated roof. Fishhead waited a few houses back, feigning a crisis with his footwear, bending to attend to it but fixing his sight on the doorway. And then he walked straight there, a bold and brazen youth. He stuck his head through the door. Adjusted his sight to the dimly-lit interior and looked around in a hurry. The odor of the still, of hooch, choked him, its intensity rising to his head, a stinging whip. The smoke from lit candles. About ten men sat cross-legged in a stupor, facing each other along the rectangular perimeter of the shed's dark walls. Dad took his place among them, just as a server brought him a glass of drink and exited through another door on the other side. Fishhead stepped back, not wanting anyone to question him. Neither in nor out, and, he, too young for a customer. He looked in again. Dad shifted from one butt cheek to the other and folded his legs again to get comfortable. He looked down and crossed his legs as if in a yoga pose, focused on the glass in front of him. He sat as these men did. And in the center but directly on the mud floor, the owner's daily fare: bowls of peeled boiled eggs, potato chips, chick pea fried snacks, roasted peanuts in shells, and three used lit candles standing in their own wax on bottle tops. A shrine, a tabernacle for drinkers. Bottles of hooch and beer stood among the bowls. A display more luxurious than home; no wonder Dad chose not to eat with the family.

Fishhead had enough, more than enough. He pulled out from inside the doorway, disgusted and upset, but just then Dad lifted his head; their eyes locked, but only for a flashing second, perhaps not enough to permit recognition.

Fishhead pushed away from the doorframe and turned around in the dirt passageway outside the shed. His heart sprinted. Did Dad really see him? And if so, now what? The first thick volley of raindrops fell, pounding the metal roof, like he'd just entered an active warzone. Which way should he run? Duck, take cover!

An unimaginable torrent followed, this rain, hurled down from a slate gray sky. People and animals dashed for shelter amidst the deafening downpour. Chickens ran with fluttered wings, clucking. Fishhead pressed his body against the wall of a different shack and stood there, undecided about his next move and unsure still if his father had seen him. The water slammed against the earth and rebounded, pelting and drenching him. No safe place to hide, no safe place at all. The rain stung. He needed to rush home, but not now. He glanced behind his shoulders to see if Dad had emerged. Not yet. The rainwater beat hard against the dirty alleyway and the roofs of all the shacks. Dad had no reason to leave the shed anytime soon. A rain like this kept you indoors and chilled you.

Fishhead edged his way along the walls of shacks, nodding his head to the residents there, all strangers to him. He stood still under the protruding corrugated roof of another shack, a quiet one, dark inside. He waited, unwilling to run home in the downpour, now ceaseless, a brick wall surrounding him for eternity.

Gutters overflowed. The tight passages become troughs of running, cascading water. Eventually Fishhead gave up his post.

He trudged through the shin-high flood racing along the passageway until he got to the main road. But there, the water nearly touched his knees. A violent water to fight against; he struggled to keep his flip flops on. Careful not to lose his balance, he leaned against a post and took his footwear in his hands, and resumed his trek under the pressing rain, the unpleasant warmth. Around him, the traffic appeared to come at a standstill; horns blaring as always, multiplying like a contagion. People crossed the road under umbrellas, in raincoats. A few others unprotected from the rain, like him. Two motorized rickshaws stalled in front of the cigarette factory, stuttering and fizzling out. A taxi plowed ahead with caution.

Fishhead tilted his face to the sky and opened his mouth to drink as raindrops slapped his tongue and cheeks, his teeth, and shut eyelids. His clothes stuck to his body uncomfortably; his dark hair went limp and splayed against his head. He thought of Mom now. His condition did not matter, she mattered. She'd get home from work eventually, but when? He had no way to reach her, and the city began shutting down. His father, so removed.

Soul in Flight

Fishhead took almost an hour to walk home in the endless rain; the flood reached his thighs at times. He watched his footing, stayed away from those deep and dangerous gutters, and his temper dissipated through the soles of his puckered feet. Near home, he could not tell the marshland from the roads. A flawless sea of brown water swept across all property lines without prejudice. The walls and gates, his only markers. He stayed close to them, mindful of the gutter running parallel to the road. At once he knew the state of his home.

He entered the flooded compound with care, then went around the side of the residence to the back verandah. Water had claimed it.

His brothers were doing their best to hold down floating household items and boxes, and runaway pots and pans; meanwhile, Lily stood nervous and trembling but securely at the top of the steps leading inside. She cried for her hunger and theirs. Fishhead felt like all the energy had drained out of him. His wet body shook under his water-logged clothes. He wanted nothing more than a pillow, and rest; he wanted to throw his body down on the sofa. It alone stayed unmoved, its legs submerged, water lapping at the cushions.

All evening and through the emerging night, Fishhead and his siblings pulled as much as they could out of the back verandah, piling what they saved in the front room, until only the sofa and a few disintegrating boxes remained. The clotheslines crisscrossing under the corrugated roof were crammed with towels and clothes. All food ruined.

Dad came around the back of the apartment after nine, holding his flip-flops in one hand in the dark of night. He hiked his slacks past his calves with the other hand as he entered the flooded back verandah. Fishhead noticed him first. Dad showed no surprise and offered no hint of disappointment at the wreckage that lay before him. His head low, eyes down, red eyes, body drenched from head to toe, and dulled into indifference by drink. Dad. Balan George. How he worked to show everyone he had it together! Still on his feet despite drinking for hours. He never wobbled under the weightlessness of his temptation; he did his best to show his plumb-straight control.

He stood in the open entryway, unable to speak or utter words of comfort to his children. Surely he thought of Mom: Where might she be?

Fishhead struggled for answers. He struggled to catch Dad's eyes, but he didn't need to, because somehow he understood the sight and vision of his father's selfish heart, its brooding dream cloud, and the still-beating tension of his errors.

I would impose love on this family, dear reader. It starves for want of tenderness, not food or money. It starves for want of understanding, for salvation. I would impose love on it but for

Balan's corruptions and Eshma's blind sacrifice: between those things I see no room for mutual gestures of kindness and affection. But I see in Fishhead and his siblings few seeds of it growing without light. The flood is a test; watch how they do what they do.

Fishhead pulled a damp towel from the clothesline nearest him and handed it to his father, who, without a thank you, placed his flip-flops on the ledge of the wall first and made his way through the flood towards the front room. Dad surveyed everything but had nothing to say, no anger, no praise. He wiped his head and face. But when he got up on his toes and reached over the sofa to throw the wet towel on the clothesline, something at his feet bit him hard, and he shrieked. In shock and pain, he jumped back and pinched his face. The towel popped out of his hand and slid down the back of the sofa before drifting away below the surface of the water. Lily let out a cry; she placed her hands on her mouth and sobbed.

Fishhead reacted with surprise and, shamelessly, with some relish. Didn't know what to do for Dad, who stepped back and raised his right foot to examine the cause of his burning pain; his two last toes showed the red spotted marks of a bite. Rat or snake? Hard to tell. The bleeding increased. He dropped his feet back in the water and walked away, reaching for his flip-flops on the ledge by the entryway.

"You boys lift the sofa. Make sure you know what it is," he said. "Be careful. Whatever it is, it's alert. Could be a rat or snake. Just be careful." And he left without another word.

"Dad!" Lily cried. "Where are you going? I'm coming with you!"

"Shut up, Lily!" Prem said.

"Yea, just pipe down, Lily. It's too dark to be going out," Fishhead insisted.

"We don't even know where he's going," Pradeep explained. "So be quiet. We have to find this thing."

"Stay back," Fishhead said. "Kishore, get the hockey stick. Or that pole in the corner. Just hurry!" The boys moved more aggressively now, Kishore too, and they splashed the standing water, but nothing moved out from under the sofa. With great care and haste, Fishhead, Prem, and Pradeep heaved the sofa on one end and lifted it high. A snake, thick as a person's forearm, half-submerged, coiled. A menacing look. Black patterned shapes on its back, and the gleaming whiteness of a ceramic plate for its underbelly. They eased the sofa down, and at the very moment when its feet touched the floor, splashing water again, the creature whipped out from under the sofa and slithered away from them, making for the east wall. It moved fast on the surface of the water, clinging to the edge of the wall and heading for the open entryway.

Pradeep started shouting. He grabbed the pole from Kishore and slammed it down, batted the water, but the pole missed the snake and caused a big swell. Prem stood back, displeased. Fishhead grabbed the field hockey stick and whacked away with the hooked end, splattering, again, again. He grew frenzied now, hammering, hammering, and screaming, hitting the wall a few times in reckless fury. He wanted its head, his prize, like Emperor Jehangir had wanted the heads of his enemies put up on stakes by the roadside. The snake's head on a stick, bloodied and full of gore. They batted, batted, batted, two boys in competition.

And suddenly the water turned red, desperate rings of crimson bursting from the clave, and the creature slowed down although its body kept moving, twitching. Fishhead shouted victory. And like his brother, he drew the fierceness of Cain from within his own being and succumbed to his urge to destroy this grace of god. They hammered the being repeatedly until it finally remained still on the frightening, bobbing water. The shin-high flood, yes, no more a folly in earthen brown, but now a cauldron drenched with the color and odor of death. The snake turned face up, straight and light as a soul in flight.

Mom came home around ten-thirty. She brought her hands to her face in disbelief the moment she encountered the murky scene. That one barbarous and rotten corner of red now spread gradually across the settling floodwater. Shocked and disgusted, she almost fainted. A weak body, overworked and underfed. Fishhead took her arm and led her around the side to the front door.

"Where is your father? What happened?"

"He left."

"He did what?"

"He came home and then he left. A snake bit him, but we killed it." Fishhead refused to step into the front room in his soiled state.

"Wash up!" Mom said to him. And to her sons: "You'll never clean this mess tonight. Look at it, just look at it, can you? Just look at all of you. What is happening to us, Dear God in the Heavens. Lord have Mercy! And did you not have dinner yet?"

Fishhead shook his head no. She made the sign of the cross and dropped down to the floor and began to cry.

Fishhead took Lily's hand at the doorway while she sobbed with Mom. "Can't go out there, Mom. Look at the verandah," he said. "Prem saved the stove and some things, but the food is no good. The kitchen is under water, too."

Pradeep lifted the dead snake by its tail and dropped it in a large bottle, filled it with some standing water, then placed in on the ledge. Some specimen, this ex-snake. Bottled so a doctor can identify and examine it.

Fishhead and his brothers cleaned up and left the verandah, unable to do much more until the flood receded. He couldn't imagine how long a cleanup such as this took, with small containers and Mom's only plastic bucket. Drain out the standing water in the back verandah. How many bottles of Dettol might Mom have to buy to disinfect the space?

No telephone at home. No concept of it. The way things happened, the way life coursed through time.

For three days, Fishhead, Pradeep, and Prem went from hospital to clinic looking for Dad, hoping someone had knowledge of his whereabouts. They walked, took the train, jumped on buses, and walked some more, reaching health centers far from home. One hospital called another, which made Fishhead grateful, although he got no answers. Where had Dad gone? Had he died from snakebite? Who found his body? Did the police know? Who reported him? Who carried him away?

Mom decided to take everyone to church. The cleanup had exhausted her, but she'd taken stock of her losses and decided to look ahead. She believed in prayer and trusted its power to alter the course of her life and Destiny. She asked her children to pray with her because only prayer helped to find Dad, even though Dad laughed about it; he disagreed with Mom and nana. No God. A waste of time, he insisted. There's no God. You're all fooling yourselves, he'd said once.

Fishhead carried Lily, while Kishore and Prem stood behind Mom criticizing each other's clothes and appearances. Pradeep stayed back. They walked to the bus stop and waited too long for the crowded bus to arrive and deliver them in front of the church, the one by school. So far away. Mom grumbled at the distance. "God should not be so far away. We'll move closer, and it'll be good for school, too." She refused to walk the three kilometers to church. Their wait drew patience out of Fishhead. Mom tried to pacify Lily when she made a fuss. She suggested that Fishhead become an altar boy; and somewhere deep inside his being, Fishhead liked the idea; it placed him in service clothes before the well-dressed community on weekends, on Wednesdays, and during Christian holidays. Anupa and her cousin went to church. He knew this, too.

Dad appeared unannounced on the fourth day, back to his usual self, unaware of his family's deep concern. The dark clouds departed and made way for the sun, and the heat resumed its form, lifting dampness out of the air. The back verandah took much longer to dry than Fishhead hoped. He too wanted Dad to explain his situation, but Dad neither asked about the cleanup nor talked about his disappearance, even when Mom asked questions with panic stamped across her face.

He spotted the bottled snake on the ledge and laughed, perhaps at himself, and perhaps at the creature's ill-fortune.

"We killed it, Dad!" Kishore said, as if he'd led the charge. "We took our sticks and smashed its head in." Fishhead snickered at little brother's forwardness, a sure sign of Kishore's enterprising nature. But Dad did not care to learn the details.

PART 2

"Prejudice, a dirty word, and faith, a clean one, have something in common: they both begin where reason ends."
    ~Harper Lee

"'I see this with the Gorgon's eye,' the Sibyl called after me. 'It is the Eye which Medusas passed back and forth, the eye of the fates—you have fallen into—'"
    ~Philip K. Dick

The Social Club

Fishhead started spending a few summer afternoons and evenings in the social club for boys and girls at the side of his school building, behind the church.

The place occupied a large public room in a tiled structure the size of a basketball court. Perhaps in a more glorious time of the Raj, it had acted as a garden house before being used as a sports center for cricket, soccer, and field hockey. A fieldhouse. The church had organized the club as a means to bring the community's youth together and keep them out of trouble. Making friendships, building relationships. The east side of the structure had four windows, which overlooked the grounds with its soccer goal posts and chalk-white track rings that always got washed out in the rain. On the other side, an open, narrow verandah gave access to a small compound, used for fetes, badminton, and cricket. The high space of the interior appeared well maintained, with clean walls, good lighting, and ceiling fans. Three ping pong tables stood side by side in the middle of the airy room, while card tables and carrom boards hugged the edges on four sides.

From a window ledge, a shortwave transistor radio broadcast popular film songs sung by Lata Mangeshkar and Mohammed Rafi and, later, rock and pop songs from overseas: "A Taste of Honey," "I'm A Believer," "The Shadow of Your Smile," "(I Can't Get No)

Satisfaction," "Mr. Tambourine Man," and the like. Occasional news breaks announced the state of the world and current Indian affairs: the hard famine, the Vietnam War, Suharto's accession to the Indonesian presidency, De Gaulle's Russian visit, Billie Jean King's Wimbledon title, and other bits of news that fluttered into Fishhead's brain with no real effect. The world did not know his hardship, and he did not know the world. He had no sense of it. He got no satisfaction. Wanted a taste of honey. Heard no rhythm in the falling rain. Did not know a tambourine from a tambourine man.

The social club kept its doors open in the evenings and during weekends, and Fishhead began to like coming here, even as he struggled to conceal his indigence from the other boys from his classes, most of them from well-to-do families in the neighborhood. Did they notice he wore the same clothes day after day? Did they care to understand that, while he moved among them, hunger carved its empire inside his body, against his ribcage and within his flesh, paralyzing his ability to think rationally? His outward appearance meant everything; it made the difference between acceptance and rejection. A state of perfect discomfort. He moved through its space with hesitation but determined to keep the details of his family to himself; his absolute shame and hesitation made him more aware of his poor image and demeanor, which required some expense and care. He had the time for care, but not the expense.

Well-dressed girls and boys stood around in their own groups, talking, laughing, and playing one game or the other. They wore clean, ironed clothes, and showed their grooming and money. A bouquet of fragrance and powder drifted through the air. There were a few from less fortunate families, and Fishhead wondered if they shared similar stories of survival. He received a cool welcome and simply fused in with the crowd, and no one objected to his presence.

In one corner, Anupa and her nameless cousin, the prettier one. Anupa turned around and smiled at him when he stepped inside the club room. How she grew, with the same straight and shiny black hair that fell down her back, going past her shoulders. Her full lips and clean teeth. He wanted to kiss her, and promptly felt guilt for the thought. Her light brown eyes and skin. A knee-high skirt showing her knock-kneed but shapely legs. Good, slender ankles, unlike his bony ones. Shyness prevailed, a prolonged state of diffidence between strangers who edged towards a friendship. A possible friendship.

Fishhead studied the room, unsure of all the budding relationships. Who went out with whom? Which boy wanted which girl? What girl presumed to have the boy she set her eyes on? Anupa's smile calmed Fishhead, although he didn't know what to do with her friendly expression. How must he react? What did she mean?

While Fishhead assisted during Sunday service one morning, the parish priest made an announcement inviting the youth to take part in the choir as it prepared for the Christmas caroling season. Fishhead joined the choir with Pradeep. (Prem's shyness kept him away from youth his age. Fishhead pressed his older brother to join, too, but Prem didn't budge.) Mrs. Sequeira the choir master seemed friendly enough.

And now he stood shoulder to shoulder with these sixteen youth, many of them from the social club. Boy and girl mingled, grouped by voice and height, not gender. He stood near Anupa and caught a whiff of her perfume and scent, the light coconut oil brushed through her silky hair. Her body's warmth, so different than his. She smiled and introduced herself; he did too, awkwardly. Their shoulders and arms touched once during the pre-rehearsal chatter among the group, and he apologized and took a half step to the side. She apologized, too, smiled again, but did not move away from him. Her good, clean teeth, white teeth. Nice breath. How did he smell to her? He shuddered, disbelieving his good fortune. Touched a girl. Touched a girl. Touched a girl in her short gathered gray skirt and white short-sleeved blouse with its round split neckline. Glanced at her moonlight thighs all too quickly. And flames of desire shot up through his body, teased him. He misunderstood his own needs and limits. What next? What should he do? Keep singing. Focus on Mrs. Sequeira, the choir master. What should he do, really? The warmth of this girl. His mind in obvious confusion.

The line between the haves and have-nots made itself visible to him, and he knew where he stood. His camp of misfortune claimed him. He should not belong in this choir group, and yet he did, although he knew the truth: Even acceptance had its circles and doors, circles growing from a most privileged center. He remained in the outer circle. Might Anupa let him in? Bring him closer? Fishhead imagined this closeness and he became uncomfortable with it. He did not know what to do.

All through choir practice, his mind wandered as he pictured her, naked as a Sheesham leaf waiting for his touch, his caresses, fingertips moving quietly along the edges of its trembling arcs, his palms receiving her breasts, his tongue against the heat of them. Wet. The heart-shaped back of her hips. Her neck. Lips like a carnival. Lights going on and off in his head, music ringing in his ears and within the pit of his stomach. But nakedness and private time held hands together, and Fishhead couldn't imagine either one in his life. *Forget it. Just forget it, yaar.* These harsh thoughts scolded the earlier ones. Good thing Anupa could not read his mind. But if she did, what then? Had Destiny marked his fate? Was Destiny setting him along this path? Did Destiny know all that went through his mind? *Surrender. Go with this. The choir. The blessed choir. Sing, and don't be flat. Don't make a fool of yourself. Don't be an idiot, a* 420. *Chaar so beez, yaar. Stay away from that.*

Fishhead walked home in a dreamy state, somewhat disbelieving of his good luck. He'd said little during practice. How did Anupa perceive him? What went through her head precisely now...now, when he thought of her? Did his voice annoy her? No, she gave him no hint of that. Made him happy. She showed no preference for anybody else in the choir group, as if she came alone and went home alone. Alone? A growing girl without sisters or brothers? Where did she live? Surely, some good home near the church. A good church and school: Our Lady of Perpetual Succour. Her cousin sang, too, although Fishhead did not ask her name yet. The prettier one. A couple of rich boys in the group eyed this cousin. She had the same long and silky hair as Anupa, but with a touch of brown in it. The cousin's manner confused Fishhead. She carried herself in a more thoughtful way, a quiet way, saying nothing at all to anyone, shy and withheld, but glowing with some inner light he thought she probably didn't know she had. In contrast, Anupa smiled more and seemed more outgoing and friendlier, and Fishhead liked that in her, admired this quality in her. Did she know pain? Did she know the meaning of hardship? How might he explain his hardship to her? Perhaps she had no interest in knowing it.

No, he'd say nothing to her about it. No one in the group must know the depth of his family's struggles. Although he did not have to beg yet. How his father begged at the butcher's stall! *That* shamed him. But Dad kept a prideful manner about him even then, turning his words and speech and voice into some kind of Bollywood actor's script. Dad had talent and learned how to use it to his advantage. A public figure, better behaved among strangers. He never begged like the beggars. Men, women, boys and girls on every corner it seemed, holding up empty bowls and with such sorrowful faces, the saddest and desperate eyes bathed in dirt and needfulness. Shattering nakedness. Women with infants in their arms. Young girls with infants in their arms and on their hips. Innocence, be gone! Fishhead understood desperation, he did. And if he had to beg, what then? Did he have what it took to hold a bowl in his hands, to have lice in his hair, and dirt in his fingernails? Approach a car with tinted windows? Point at his own mouth. Tell people about his condition. Touch people he did not know at bus stops and train stations, and ask for a few *paise* or food. He did not think he had his father's gift to act like everything was fine. And yet, this social life forced him to keep up a certain appearance of good health. So perhaps he enjoyed the act a little bit, too.

Pradeep walked with him on the golf course road. Neither brother said anything about their real experiences in the choir, about the difficulties of their adjustment to this new social climate. The temptation of new possibilities. Uncertain feelings. Pradeep seemed at ease, as if he'd always known such a life before. Fishhead admired this. He talked about the others: how the others looked, dressed, acted. A running retrospective critique, something they could laugh about. Such talk took their minds off the long walk home along the golf course road.

Hot Type

Dad got a job managing a small printing press with two hot type machines near Dadar, a busy residential and industrial area. The job excited him and he talked about it at home, but not too much. Made Mom happy, although she held her breath and went to work as if nothing had changed.

Fishhead took an interest in his father's new job and wished to see the shop if Dad agreed to take him. Someday, perhaps. He kept asking Dad, kept asking. Weeks and a few months went by. Dad became more confident and moved more surely, but the smell of alcohol on his breath revealed his behavior. His reddened eyes. Quiet moods where he did not want anyone to disturb him in the evenings, while he sat alone in a chair with the smell of printer's ink brushed through his body and hair.

None of these interrupted his taste and wish for good meals. Dad brought home a bucket of live crab, caught fresh for dinner from Mahim Bay, he said. Fresh crab sold at the market along the edges of the train station. However, Mom refused to dunk these palm-sized creatures into boiling water. These insignificant animals with their orange and blue tones, their barnacles, the odor of sea moss and salt. Those roving pill-shaped eyes and snapping claws that tightened around shell as they moved against each other in the bucket, speechless and unaware of their impending demise in this ocean of human need. The home began taking on a different smell, all too familiar to Mom because she grew up on the coast in Cochin, on the coast of southern Kerala. Right on the waterfront with Chinese fishing nets. Sand between her toes, on her lips. Little girl screaming for waves and foam in her hair. Mosquitoes hovering for sweet blood. All past now, her story for naught. And again here, the smell of the sea in every fish she cooked—mackerel, sardines, king fish, shark, pomfret, and too few prawns.

Dad had also purchased a large aluminum pot and new wick stove to boil the crab in one lot. His purchases surprised Mom. What did he mean to celebrate?

She stepped back and let him do the work, stealing a break from the kitchen. Moments like these did not happen often, so why not now? Dad took a bathing towel from the clothesline to grab the large pot, full and hot with boiling water. Mom sighed but said nothing. Fishhead waited for that moment when a good event took a bad turn. It might happen again. Had happened before. He smiled all the same, hunger pinching his stomach. Impatient hunger. Dad took a handful of salt and dropped it into the pot, and watched the water come to a roaring boil. Billows of steam. With iron blacksmith tongs, he transferred each crab from the bucket to the pot and threw the aluminum lid on. He smacked his palms together, pleased with himself, a timer on in his head. A family without a watch, clock, or radio. Nothing but daylight and stars to gauge the late hour. But something different at dinner, at least tonight: an extreme feast.

Fishhead did not believe his good luck when Dad agreed to take him to the printing press for the first time. Now he stood in awe before the two hot metal Linotype machines placed side by side in the narrow shop, each one as tall as a small goods truck, but dark and complicated with so many parts all tangled up together. Pieces of smooth black steel paused and moved into one another, shunting back and forth from side to side and from top to bottom with a single unified purpose; meanwhile, chunky lines of metal letters dropped into a tray to the left of each machine, as its wheels and belts spun. Loud, the clicking and turning of parts. Fishhead inched forward and took his place between the two men who sat in front of typewriters with big round keys. Their keyboards pushed these hot type machines into action. Behind each typewriter, a metal ledge met a square metal wall the size of a chair's backrest, which hid the guts of each machine; the ledge held sheets of printed and hand-marked papers, red pens, pencils, erasers, pushpins, and rulers. Joined to the top edge of the metal wall, another wall leaned back at a sharp tilt and widened at the far end like a flat canopy over the entire machine, and looking very much like a blacksmith's flattened bellows. That blacksmith in nana's hometown. Sweat-soaked ironworker, hammering tools out of shapes reddened under intense heat such as this.

A printed sign hung across the canopy at the top of the machine. *HOT! Do not touch,* it said. Fishhead kept a safe distance. He took a step behind the two men, stood between them, and let his body absorb some of the heat from the machines while he studied these workers. He admired their skill and the objects of their craft. He leaned in and focused on the handwritten sheet of text standing at an angle on an adjustable rack near the operator's hands. The man worked in silence; he did not look up, and kept his sight fixed on the paper while his fingers tapped the typewriter's keys at a steady pace. His left foot pressed down on the pedal, a flat pad the size of a notebook, and the machine kicked into a set of actions.

Fishhead straightened up again, his mind dancing with questions: How did a small printing shop afford these expensive Western machines? Who trained these men? How much did they earn? How many years had they worked here? The same shop, same depressed chairs, same work patterns day after day, the constant clatter. Fishhead liked the smell of printing ink, machine oil, and hot metal. He remembered the materials Dad and Sachdev had used when they'd attempted their screen printing partnership.

At the back of the room, two printing presses clanged away noisily. Dad called them platen presses. Louder than anything Fishhead had heard, especially in such a small place. He did not care to wander around too long and distract the workers. Few seemed unfriendly; they slaved away from wordless hour to hour in the heat of the Indian day, with the shuttered front door of the shop kept open to welcome the outside air. A windblown and dusty courtyard in the center of this industrial complex, set off from the busy street traffic. Structures in need of exterior paint. A cow rested near a custard apple tree and another building at the far end of the courtyard, and two wandering goats edged along there, one straddling the top of the wall. Sunlight pressed down on the courtyard, hard and matchless, softening the fluorescent lights to something more like candlelight.

Inside the shop, Fishhead moved between the different pre-press workstations. Off near the two platen presses, a man used a rag to clean wood blocks with flat copper shapes hammered into them. These copper shapes looked like drawings and images made with small dots, the unwanted parts of the art shaved away like batik blocks. When Fishhead stepped closer to this table, he noticed real handmade drawings on white boards piled up in one corner. The drawings and images had been transferred to these metal shapes, their negative areas dug out with a tool he did not know about. The strong smell of something like kerosene from the wet rags. Cans of turpentine on the table and on a shelf below. So much to see and discover. Then a female servant in a sari began sweeping the floor with a thick jute broom. She covered her head with the end of the sari and did not raise her eyes.

Fishhead took the greatest interest in the two hand-composing stations directly facing the entrance. He got up on his toes and ran a hand across the wooden tray of small compartments. A pair of these trays sat side by side on large wooden tables containing rows of flat drawers, and raised up at an angle like the Bible at church. Two employees worked at these stations. One man peered over his reading glasses and narrowed his eyes but said nothing. Fishhead hesitated then continued. He liked being the manager's son.

Each box in the wooden grid contained piles of metal letters made by the Linotype machines, all letters sorted into individual groups and occupying their own compartments. Vowels took up more space in the grid. As he ran the palm side of his hand down lightly across the wooden grid, the metal letters pushed up against his flesh, tickling him: a feeling not so different from days when he played barefoot on the gravel road in the rented house near the pond. He took care not to get in the way of the two men working here, who were busy fixing the mistakes marked in red on sheets of printed text. The men spoke with their silence, focused on their work.

Dad sat at his manager's desk by the door and read through printed galleys of text, leaving from time to time to offer assistance where needed. On one such absence, Fishhead dropped into his chair. He reached for the small magnifying glass near the edge of the desk, took up a printed invitation, and bent over it to study the printed type; the text appeared sharp and dark without the glass, but through the magnifier the edges of the printed text looked torn and jagged, fibers pulled apart from each other, like passengers hanging from the open doors of packed commuter trains.

Fishhead moved the magnifier over a printer's proof of a black and white advertisement with an image. A young, well-dressed couple made up of many, many black and white dots. The man wore an Indian kurta and white pants, while the woman dressed up in a nice sari. Fishhead envied the woman and her smile. He imagined her life as a model.

Then he took up the metal ruler. He sat back in Dad's chair, slapping his open left palm with the flat end of the ruler; he increased the intensity of his slaps until the workers could hear. He thought of the principal's cane and the pain it gave him each time he went to school late. The older he got, the harder he tried to be on time, but school principals didn't care one way or the other about the age of a late schoolboy. Finally a worker eyed him, unsmiling, from his composing station; Fishhead averted his gaze and scanned the back of the deep and narrow room, looking for his father. Perhaps Dad had slipped out the back door.

Again Fishhead surveyed the desk. Dad had asked him not to interfere with anything. How much did Dad know about this work? Did it challenge him? If he struggled, Fishhead couldn't tell. Dad hid his emotions well.

This new world of printing and commercial art, with so many tasks to know and learn. Such a realization as never before. His father wanted him to be here, to know about all of this. Perhaps he should be more tolerant of Dad from now on. See him in a kinder light. While he sat there in Dad's chair, five schoolgirls went by, dressed in their brown uniform dresses, red ties, and white blouses with collars, and he immediately thought of Anupa. He wanted to see her again at choir practice.

Dad returned about forty minutes later. Fishhead jumped up to surrender the chair. As he slipped past his father in the narrow space between the desk and wall, he smelled alcohol on Dad's hot breath. Saw red in the whites of Dad's eyes. Fishhead said nothing. And he promised himself he'd say nothing to Mom. It might upset her.

He went back to the print shop a week later, closer to lunchtime. He took the train to Dadar station on his own and walked east in the immense heat of the day, the same route as before. Thirsty, but without any money in his pockets, he kept walking along crowded sidewalks. Stores spilled over with their goods. Tea stalls and cafes. The sound of loud film songs drifted through the dry air. Cars, scooters, and taxis pushing up against each other to get somewhere, horns blaring. Cyclists clinging to the edges of the road to avoid the traffic.

After a quarter kilometer of this, he arrived at the shop. Made his presence known to the men working at the compositors' stations. Dad's desk sat empty.

"My father here?" he asked.

"Look in the back."

Fishhead went looking for his father but did not find him. He asked no further questions but came back and stood before the two working Linotype machines. The operators said nothing, but the man to the right turned and nodded. Fishhead stayed there in awe. He took in the patterned sounds of clicks, drones, and hammers flowing out from the hot type machines. The heat and smell of melting lead. Such a distinct atmosphere. Lines of freshly molded metal type dropped into an angled tray near him. He wished to know more, but the workers did not speak to him, and shared nothing with him, no matter how much he believed that he deserved to know. He asked questions; the manager's son with questions. And yet no answers.

Perhaps they did not care to have Dad as their boss. And where had Dad gone, anyway?

At last Dad came up the front steps, carrying a tabbed folder containing sheets of paper. Fishhead said hello, then dragged a stool from the back for himself. Dad opened his folder and read from the sheets of paper in there. A new job. Sketches and notes from some client he had gone to meet in the area. A simple advertisement or announcement. Text without pictures. Another job for the Linotype machines and compositors.

A tea boy came up the front steps with small shot glasses of water and steaming hot chai tucked inside a partitioned, woven metal basket with a wooden handle. The young boy, about eight, also carried a pair of egg sandwiches wrapped in newspaper and tied with thin thread. Simple knots. Fishhead whistled. The aroma of milk, sugar, and fragrant spices tickled his senses. The scrambled eggs smelled so good with diced green chilies and *kothmil.* Cilantro's distinct fragrance. Dad told the boy to put the lunch on his tab, and the boy nodded, then left, singing a Hindi film song Fishhead recognized. The music of Naushad Ali.

After they ate, Dad left his desk to examine a fresh print run at the platen press. Fishhead sat alone now on the stool. The two compositors had left for lunch some time ago, and he eyed their vacant stations. He finished his tea, got off the stool, and walked over there. Scores of metal type bunched up without order in their tiny wooden compartments. He eyed the composing stick, a metal device used to arrange the lead type in reverse, line after line. Pieces of lead spacers. And lead rules between lines. (He put a pair in his pant pocket.) Experts, these men; they had years of experience and could work without lifting their eyes from the proofed sheets of marked-up galleys, grabbing letter after letter from the wooden compartments with some kind of automatic efficiency.

Fishhead had a mischievous idea. He wanted to trick them.

He pushed his body against the workstation's flat files and got up on his toes to reach the angled wooden metal type cases. Near his nose, the smell of printer's ink and lead fused into a strange mixture like camphor balls, but less pungent, and mingled with the scent of the once-polished wood. Something attractive about this place; yes, he liked it very much. The sounds, too. A world apart.

But now, his mischief: he stuck his fingers in random compartments, grabbing pieces of metal type. He raised his eyes, scanned the inside of the shop, looked behind him then checked the entrance. No one around, good. He picked up two or three letters at a time and dropped them into other compartments. The old ink from the heavy metal type stained his fingers, but he kept on, studying the letters before he moved them. Seven lower case pieces of the letter j. Three of the capitalized R. Five belonging to

b. Oh, and the numbers, too. He reached for the 4, then the 9 and took up a pair of # signs and then the & signs. He separated the pieces as he stuffed them all into random compartments, making sure to mix them up afterwards. Such devilishness, and he had no good reason for it.

His father turned around and started making his way to the front of the shop. Fishhead darted back to the stool and hid his stained fingers under the edge of the seat. A few minutes later, one of the composing station employees returned from lunch and put on his messy apron. Fishhead glanced at the man and received a smile in return. He got off the stool and went to the bathroom, where he scrubbed his hands with an old bar of soap. Then he joined the man at the composing station.

For a few minutes he just watched. Then he pointed to an empty composing stick. "Can I use this?" he asked. "Will you show me how to use it?" Fishhead couldn't resist a glance at his own fingers; the soap had cleaned the stain, but it left a lingering shadow of discoloration.

The man did not speak, and wouldn't even nod his head, but he moved his eyes over the top of his glasses like a chameleon. Then he gestured for Fishhead to step back a few inches to keep his clothes from touching the workstation. The man reached for the composing stick and held it up, as if to offer it. Fishhead took the metal gadget from the man, but held it incorrectly. The man showed him how to keep it upright and at an angle so the type would not fall off. Like holding the handle of a cricket bat: fingers wrapped under the base, thumb over the top and pressed against the line of inverted metal type. Fishhead did as instructed; and while he continued to hold the stick, the bespectacled man reached for a lead rule to hold the line of type in place. The man tightened the rule against an adjustable latch on the open end of the stick. Then he reached for a capital letter while Fishhead observed. Working fast, the man tucked the T on the corner of the stick and over the flat rule, pointing the letter's rounded nick up. He repeated his actions with another letter, the h, followed by the next, an e, all upside down and mirrored.

The man finished his line: The Quick Brown Fox. Then, speaking to Fishhead, he completed the sentence: "jumped over the lazy dog." He waited while Fishhead started assembling the rest of the letters.

A new door opening, a strange excitement, a rush of enterprise and discovery. Grateful, Fishhead wanted to kiss the man on his cheek, but thought better of it. Instead, he kept on. The man watched briefly, then left for the bathroom.

Meanwhile, Fishhead disassembled the line of type, put all the letters back into their proper compartments, or into others. Soon, he began to compose his own line: A new door. The reader is watching me.

Fishhead turned and looked up, looking for you, the reader, with a smile. He blew a kiss, tasted the lead and drying ink on his lips; he wiped his mouth with the back of his working hand. "You are watching me, aren't you?"

Fishhead resumed his composing, so proud of himself, although on further inspection, the line actually said: A hew soor ofehed. Sbe miadir es watghing me. He laughed and shrugged his shoulders. Dad paid him no attention.

The process took longer than he'd anticipated, and he continued to make errors; he put the type down wrong, or pressed too hard with his thumb so that the letters tumbled and fell flat against each other. And all the while, the dark stain of lead type and uncleaned ink began to settle on his fingers, but he didn't care. He soon learned how to control the composing stick and hold it in his left hand the correct way. The compositor returned from the bathroom and resumed his work. Fishhead acknowledged him then started another new line, working slowly and deliberately:

Anupa and Fishhead at lover's lane in Bandra. Two of us in—

The words moved up to a third line, so he had to put down a new lead rule for spacing. The other employee came back from lunch, but Fishhead wanted to stay there and finish the rest of his thought, so the man took his place at the other adjacent hand composing workstation. Now the space got too crowded with the three of them. Fishhead stepped to the side while the bespectacled man explained the situation to his co-worker, while the co-worker chewed *paan* and hummed and spat the red juices in the dusty courtyard in front of the shop. (Fishhead liked sweet dessert paan instead, because it did not change the color of his mouth, but he knew the popularity of stimulating red paan. Red stains all over the city in a profusion of waste. Stains on the sidewalks, streets, walls, in alleys, bathroom stalls, and at train stations and bus stops.) Both men talked in Marathi, and Fishhead understood them, although he struggled with the dialect in school. His weakest subject. Poor marks. The other man said something about not refusing the manager's son even when work kept them busy. He clearly did not appreciate the playful interruption.

All the while Fishhead stood there, feigning ignorance, casting a glance now and then at the trays of mixed up type: his mischievous secret.

Fishhead made half a dozen more visits. With each visit he learned how to improve his skill on the composing stick, but he couldn't resist his mischief with the metal typefaces at the hand composing workstations. The proofs started showing up with increased errors, and the workers began to complain.

Fishhead hoped these men liked his father, but it had become clearer to him with each visit that Dad struggled to gain their confidence. Dad never shared a joke with them and did not smile at them, nor did he have lunch or tea with them, often keeping to himself when his managerial advice wasn't needed. Every time Fishhead visited, Dad had left the print shop, and returned with the smell of alcohol on his breath.

At home, Dad kept silent about the trials of work or his relations with the employees. Did they refuse to accept him fully? Did he think himself superior to them? After all, he had worked at the classical music library once and experienced a brief life among people—Indians and Westerners—with status and privilege. The workers at the print shop came from poor, simple homes, and Fishhead saw no difference between his existence and theirs. They too wore simple clothes and footwear, and they all rode the same crowded commuter trains and buses. No matter, Fishhead noticed the distance these workers kept from Dad. He wished his father talked more, but Dad kept a tight-lipped professional manner and seemed comfortable staying aloof. It was just like at home when he drank.

Dad often came home later in the evenings, but just in time to greet Mom after her long day shift at the telephone exchange. The print shop closed its doors at six, and Dad stayed behind until closing time so he could meet with the proprietor and go over the day's workload. And he continued to order food (like the chai and egg sandwiches) from the café near the print shop. He kept a tab for his tea, food, and drink.

Once while Fishhead was visiting, the café owner dropped in on Dad at the shop; the conversation forced Dad to leave his desk and step into the open courtyard. A private chat. What had he promised the owner? How much did he owe, and how had he put off making payments? Fishhead sat on the stool by the front entrance and tried to ignore the clatter and hum of the presses and Linotype machines so he could focus his attention on the courtyard. The employees paid attention, too; the two hand compositors started working slower and slower, and craned their necks to catch the action.

Fishhead did not like the unease that crept through his body. He put his head down and played with his fingers, still straining to hear his father's conversation. Dad's printing press had started to bore him anyway, but at least he still had the few artifacts he'd lifted from the shop; the metal type in his possession had no monetary value on the street, but it made for a nice souvenir. He turned his thoughts to the social club at school; he had a feeling he'd be spending more time there soon, if they'd have him.

Anupa

The first week of December. Still warm in Bombay for the time of year. "You can stand next to me," Anupa said with a smile during a choir group practice session one weekday evening.

"If you don't mind," Fishhead said and stepped next to her, working through the crowd, and his awkwardness and surprise. The middle row of three. He set his eyes to the grassy earth in front of his used canvas shoes and the fraying hem of his jeans. Then with a quick glance, he studied her light brown feet in gray flat-heeled slippers. Those high arches and tapered toes. He took in the fragrance of coconut oil in her long black hair and the slight kiss of cologne on her skin. Anupa took care of herself, he thought; she understood herself and never wore shabby clothes. Today she wore khaki shorts and a light, patterned shirt over them, with sleeves rolled up to her elbows. Her well-shaped smooth legs like milk chocolate, not bony at all, but her knees closer together than normal. How unusual! This feature didn't make her less attractive to him. Why, Fishhead wondered, had he not realized his own nature or cared for himself as these boys and girls did, as Anupa did? They had money and knew the value of their comfort; he did not. Drifting, desperate, he moved without purpose, and always seemed to play catch up with the world, remaining a few steps behind; small distractions held his attention, always those small distractions, aimless trips to Dad's printing shop and what-not. Fishhead wished he had a purpose, as the other schoolboys did— they were big on math, or science, sports, religion, reading even, or they thrived as gang members, or social butterflies. Music and art floated in and out of Fishhead's dreams, page after page of fate and desire and naiveté, rituals molded by survival forever shunting his breath; he felt like a train desperate to leave the depot for newer destinations. Want, his imminent longing: it needed clarity, his voice. And Anupa waited for it. Fishhead sensed this.

As he stood near her, he became aware again of his grungy nature; he wondered about her life at home, its casualness and routine; he wondered if she had moments of despair or fight as he did, a case of obedience perhaps. An obedient child then? She seemed at ease with the world, as if she had no suffering at all; if she did know pain, she hid it well. What were her parents like? He imagined meeting them, and for a moment wanted to shake their hands and impress them so he could whisk her away. He promptly pushed the image out of his mind. Not shy, this Anupa, not shy at all, unlike her good-looking cousin in the front row.

"Do you live around here?" Anupa asked, her face turned to the right toward him and her voice just above a whisper.

He shook his head, unwilling to say too much. Went quiet again.

"Well then?"

"No, not here," he replied, and their eyes met. Her positive but curious eyes. "I walk from the colony on the other side of the golf course. Three kilometers each way." She pouted her full lips as if to whistle, and raised her eyebrows in surprise. Fishhead looked away. What had his confession revealed? That he had no money for a bus ride, no private driver to drop him off and pick him up like the rich ones? No taxis going to the colony where he lived? Yes, he'd said too much. Enough, no more. Surely, others there heard him, too.

The choir master Mrs. Sequeira called the group to attention and passed around the music sheets for caroling. Sixteen boys and girls huddled together on the front lawn of the church, all in their best casual clothes. Colorful skirts, shorts, and blouses aimed at modesty in the traditional Indian way, but clearly threatening to show more skin; meanwhile, the boys wore clean short-sleeved cotton shirts and slacks or shorts, their well-combed, black hair slicked with oil or Brylcreem. They smelled of talcum powder and after shave. Hard-to-find Old Spice, prized Old Spice with its blue logo, the sailing vessel, tapered-neck bottle, and tiny twist off cap. Long-lasting cologne. Nothing like this at home. He recalled the label from bottles displayed in high-prized stores downtown like Akbarallys; his uncle used Old Spice.

Fishhead wore the same pair of torn faded jeans; he'd rolled up his long sleeves and let his white shirt hang loosely over his skinny frame. He glanced at Pradeep standing in the middle row but far to the left; big brother had told him not to make a habit of borrowing his belt.

This choral group challenged Fishhead. He'd learned a few holiday songs during church services, but the caroling list contained compositions he'd never heard before. He paid attention, tried to learn the songs by ear, because he could not read music or play an instrument, unlike the other carolers. He pushed down his embarrassment; he stayed in the last row and made every effort to remain in step and in key. His voice, unsteady at first, surprised him and pleased him, although the better singers and skilled musicians stood in the front rows before him, boys and girls eager to show off their voices above the others.

The choral group took a short break then reassembled again in the evening's fading light; and Anupa moved to the last row, where she stood at the very end to the right, beside Fishhead. Then she changed her mind and switched places with him, so that he now stood at the end. The singing resumed, but all Fishhead's consciousness focused now on Anupa at his left. She held her music up with her left hand and glanced at him often, smiling; several minutes later, in the middle of a holiday carol, she let her arm brush against his and stay there. Soon her right hand found his fingers, peaceful earthworms moving through blades of grass, unseen and curious. She didn't look down, and neither did Fishhead. He felt a delicious cramp around his throat and a tightening of flesh in his groin, but he did not pull his hand away and indulged in this play. His excitement grew; he did not know how to control it. Surely, no one suspected anything; the girl standing on the other side of Anupa said nothing even if she knew. The church compound stood empty in the moonlight, except for the group. The curving high stone wall around the compound hid the neighboring homes and prevented any view from the dimly-lit streets.

The group broke up for the night just over an hour later. Fishhead did not want the moment to end; he waited in anticipation of something, a new beginning, an opportunity to spend just a little more time with her. In the general commotion caused by the group's slow departure and goodbyes, he and Anupa faced each other. Something else desired to be said. A silent parting seemed wrong. Fishhead searched for common sense and the gift to say the right things, his tongue in knotted spate. She spoke first, to him, her voice near a whisper as she leaned in with lips close to his left ear. "Walk me home?"

And his carnival began as he smelled her again, but with clarity now. An aura of jasmine and coconut oil, something he could not put his finger on before. Her long silky black hair fell down over her eyes on one side as she spoke, and her hair caressed his cheek. A waterfall. Blinded him now till the end of the world, and he shut his eyelids but did not flinch or move to evade the silky sweep. Say goodbye to a sad world he once knew.

She straightened up and nodded, smiling. "You won't have to come in," she added, pushing her hair back over her shoulders. "To the gate will be fine. Walk me home then?" She smiled again, more certain of herself than he could ever imagine being.

"Sure," he said, "I'd like that."

She'd cut her fingernails close to the tender flesh. Or did she bite them? Those slender and slightly bony digits. Silver rings. He let his eyes follow her hand in a flash when she dropped it to her side, and he met her gaze. A nervous girl who bit her fingernails? He never did understand why people chewed like that; he'd seen commuters doing it on busy, packed trains and buses. Did Anupa do that privately? He'd never caught her in the act. Nervous girl. Must be a private nervous girl. He wanted to know her story.

She did not live as far as he did, but where exactly? He dared not ask, wondering again about her mother and father and their concern for her safety past sunset. They trusted her to do the right thing. A girl alone, but secure in this group where everyone appeared to know everyone else. Clearly, Fishhead remained the outsider, an outsider lost to privilege and opportunity. He might never see wealth, not the way they did.

While the others departed, Fishhead stayed behind with Anupa as she lingered. He sensed gossip among the departing group. Pradeep took off with two buddies; he wouldn't be going home for a little while longer. Then Anupa's cousin turned to her and asked for company on her walk home. Did they live close to each other? Anupa introduced her cousin to Fishhead. Manju, the more-attractive but silent one. Now he knew her name. Manju failed to hold her smile, and her light brown eyes did not seem welcoming to him. In them he read her need for seclusion, as if the silence of her walls controlled her. She stood as tall as Anupa, and seemed to have the same build; she wore her hair straight but shorter, although it revealed an auburn tinge that he liked. Manju seemed to understand Anupa's gestures and plan, and she turned away to walk home on her own. Fishhead wondered if he should call out to Manju to join them, but thought better of it; if Anupa wanted her cousin's company, she said nothing to that effect.

They closed the main gate and went west along the short stretch of the church road, which fed into the busy two-lane thoroughfare with its high incandescent lights. Anupa made a right and Fishhead stayed by her side as they walked north on the shoulder, safe from vehicular traffic.

"I walk everywhere," she said. "I'll ride the train or the bus only if I have to."

"I hate having to walk," he insisted. "I do it because I must."

She laughed then said, "Hate, that's a strong word, na?"

"Maybe, but it's how I feel."

"Can't you take transit?"

He paused, unsure about stating the truth: his parents could not afford daily bus fare for everyone. "The trains are out of the way," Fishhead said. "I can take the bus, and I have, but the wait is too long, and buses don't stop for me because they arrive full. So I walk. It keeps me fit."

"Yes, and better to see your surroundings."

"This is true," he said, "but we do have to take the trains to go into the city. Mom does. No getting around that." Traffic continued unabated, horns blaring with no good reason even at nightfall. Anupa moved to the inside.

"You don't mind?" she asked, and he shook his head. "My mother says I'm absent-minded on the roads," Anupa added. "She wants me to be more careful of traffic."

"Why, did something happen to you?" he said. "She is right."

"That I'm absent-minded, you mean?" Anupa looked up, an eyebrow raised.

"No, that traffic's very unpredictable. People drive like maniacs."

Fishhead did not know the distance to Anupa's home, but he took delight in this northbound walk with her and counted the numbered side roads, block by block. He checked now and then to make sure they stayed clear of oncoming traffic behind him. Anupa pointed across the road.

"Manju's place, the corner house," she said. "I go there sometimes. We used to spend hours doing homework, but not so much now." From across the road, the wall and flowering bushes hid most of the single-storied house with its brown, white, and gray paint.

"Because you're grown up and doing different things?"

"Yes, you can say that," she answered. "We're in the same standard at school."

"Does she have a boyfriend?"

"Two going after her."

Someone from the choral group? Fishhead wondered. Then: "Where do *you* live?"

"You'll see. We're almost there." Anupa would not touch him now as they walked side by side.

When they arrived at 12th Road, she made a right. Her dimly lit side street, a truly private street that inclined at the far end; it led to the interior and a colony of several three-storied apartment buildings. Fishhead stayed in step with her. Almost every house had gated, walled compounds with outrageous cactus, ferns, and flowering bushes like bougainvillea, rose, kadamba, and jasmine that hung over the walls and filled the compound spaces. Bamboo, lime, and bananas, too. The occasional towering mango, custard apple, guava, or jackfruit tree. A well-paved road with narrow dirt shoulders on either side for pedestrians. Even in this lightless evening, the color and fragrance left Fishhead in awe; he imagined the money and care these homeowners put into their houses. He never came as close to such cultivation as he did now. Anupa led him through this wonder without batting an eyelid or expressing any fascination for the natural beauty he observed, or any interest in the money here behind these walls.

Finally, she stepped up to her own painted wrought iron gate and reached for the latch at the top. Fishhead stayed on the dirt shoulder. The gate mostly blocked his view of the property; he could only see a sliver of a dimly lit brick and stone home, raised about two feet from the ground with a front porch and steps: tiled, he presumed. Smooth concrete everywhere. A light gray exterior with white painted trims, windows, a screen door, and gray front door. Not a big house, not a fancy house, but it impressed Fishhead all the same. A house she called her own. Place, her carnation of pride. He raised his chin to study the terraced roof, the tops of plants above the wall. Three grown banana trees dwarfed the roses, cactus, and bougainvillea plants; their banana flower pods hung low and filled with promise. A high guava tree near the back reached above the roof and hung over the terrace like a well-planned, natural canopy.

Anupa pushed the gate open just enough to let them through, and then she turned, smiling, her head tilted. The streetlamp there lit her face on one side, highlighting her hair, lips, cheekbones, and nose, her medium button nose. Fishhead shuddered to think that she'd ask him in or allow him to kiss her goodnight. Romantic notions in his head. Did he get those from the comics he read, from Archie, Jughead, Betty, and Veronica?

But she did not say goodnight, nor did she ask him to step inside; she just thanked him and waved and smiled gently, and then she shut the gate, showing no hurry.

Fishhead turned and made his way back to the main road, his head in a swirl. He had no idea where Pradeep had gone with his buddies, so he retraced his steps and went south past the church; he cut through the circular median—Diamond Gardens—and stayed on the three-kilometer route for home. He felt no threat on the long walk in the dark, but needed to take a desperate piss, and when he found himself on the long stretch along the desolate golf course road, he unbuttoned his jeans and relieved himself at the edge of the loose wooden fence line. He'd gone past the only house on the golf course property, but a dog on the front porch there barked, setting off two others. "Stupid dogs," he swore. They looked overweight; he imagined their diet: meat, bones, better than his. "Shut up!" He buttoned up, and the dogs barked some more.

He looked forward to seeing Anupa again through the holidays, but he seemed unsure that he could do much more than caroling, because his family's struggles shamed him; and unlike the others, he'd have to wear the same old clothes for Christmas.

In mid-December, Dad stopped going to the printing press. Did the proprietors let him go? Did Dad leave on his own? Had the employees started complaining about his red eyes and the smell of alcohol on his breath? Or did he simply know less about the job than he'd let on when he'd been hired? Fishhead wondered. Dad said nothing. He had his pride, and silence fed this pride; he lived as if he had no obligation to the household he headed. Keep moving, keep moving. What's around the next corner? Go find that.

Fishhead caught the disappointment in Mom's eyes. He shook his head in confusion and frustration. The family's loss seemed normal and reliable; success seemed an unreachable place, too distant most of the time, and too brief when it arrived. Failure, Fishhead reasoned, was dependable; he could perform the actions it demanded of him. Success meant obtaining something, or winning against losers. His skill with marbles. Couldn't use that skill in adulthood, could he? Success: Just another word without meaning or value. In its tiniest shapes, it came as a tease and curse more than anything, as it had in the brief moments of happiness back when Dad had found employment. What had happened at the print shop? Fishhead hoped Mom could get the truth out of Dad, but if she did, she kept quiet, and swallowed this bitter pill. She kept going to work as if nothing had happened.

In Fishhead's growing anger—a more realized anger of a thirteen-year-old—he held on to silence just like the desperate beggars clutched at half-open car windows in the city's chaotic streets. He imagined his life turning out like them, coarse and brutal in their dirt and wretchedness, their near nakedness; he wondered whether his family would share that fate. No savings and no more money to depend on. He flexed his fist to punch the living room wall, but paused: What would that get? A broken hand, with no money to fix it. Instead, he stood at the edge of the marsh and picked up stones from the street, flung them one by one with all his strength; he aimed at anything that moved—dragonflies, birds, frogs, or fish. If he hurt, so should others.

Mrs. Sequeira the choir master increased practice hours and days in preparation for the holiday season. Fishhead stopped going. He missed Anupa, but did she miss him?

Across the Tracks

Fishhead and his family moved again three months later at the end of March, leaving Collectors Colony behind and relocating north of the church to occupy a tiny, beat-up apartment in a filthy tenement block overlooking Chembur Railway Station. A dim space, half the size of the previous apartment, which now lay far south on the other side of the suburb. This move north, however, put Fishhead and his siblings much closer to school—a half kilometer away. Mom had gotten her wish, in that, at least.

Fishhead understood immediately that things didn't look so good. The day his family moved in, he found two rupees (a pauper's sum) folded under an old newspaper that lined a built-in bookshelf on one wall of the front room, and his discovery gave cause for some excitement, and hope for good luck. He claimed the money for himself, but Mom insisted on using it for their next meal.

Fishhead knew that life would never be as good as before. From their front door on the ground floor of this new tenement space, he could see a part of the high roof and steel girders of Chembur station at his left, and the electric power lines running east and west over the two commuter train tracks, which remained hidden from view behind the high municipal wall about thirty feet in front of his building.

Six tenement buildings: cramped, blackening, exteriors decaying from moisture. They stood high behind the municipal wall. These stained cream buildings looked ominous, Old World ships spaced apart from each other; the three buildings in the back made a T shape with the three that stood side by side facing the tracks, but they all seemed poised for some endless voyage, as if hope meant something to the residents here. The wash hung out to dry like aging colored sails from balconies now molding after years of monsoon rain and negligence.

To get to school, Fishhead walked east past four other residents' doors along the common balcony corridor; at the halfway point, he turned right, went down four steps, and crossed the gravel yard to a break in the municipal wall near the other end of the building. He pulled his body through the narrow space and across the filthy gutter, and then stepped over the tracks past the end of the platform to the more desirable side of the community. The main road there opened up to a market. This distant northeastern suburb of Bombay had been expanding, just as the city itself began bursting at the seams. However, its growth felt congested and impulsive. Grocery stalls, hardware and general stores, and vendors selling vegetables, fish, and meat spilled out into the narrow passageways. Traffic, blaring horns, and smog were as eternal as the rubbish.

The main road led straight down to school and church, past Anupa's street on the left and her cousin's house on the opposite side of the road further south. Fishhead hoped he wouldn't run into them. Too much shame. The move here began to depress him. He wanted to leave the city, move to another state. Stop attending school. Did his parents not understand the humiliation of this family's worsening condition? Most people moved forward,

Fishhead thought, into comfort, leisure, and access to good things. His family went the other way. He imagined a future among the shit and stench of the tenement. He noticed his growing indifference as he held on to his silence and anger, which appeared more reliable than his parents, except for one dependable thing: Mom's insistence that her children finish school, no matter the outcome to the family. Finish school, finish school, finish school.

Fishhead turned away from the window. The smell of this stricken and unfamiliar neighborhood cuffed his senses. Debris flung out like confetti everywhere. Blaring film music and stray dogs. The patter of restless, barefoot children. The screech of a commuter train jammed with riders. Soon another would follow. So much chaos. An endless caterwaul, always present.

The heat, filth, and rain of Bombay appeared to wear people down; by evening one could see fatigue and overwork carved on their faces, all deeply lined with despair. How many, like Mom, returned home at sunset then cooked for their families, their hungry children?

She stopped at the market on the other side of the train station and bought a pair of fresh mackerel wrapped in newspaper. Fishhead helped in the kitchen. He pulled the gills open to look for the correct redness and rinsed the mackerel on both sides under tap water; he ran the wet palm of his hand down the length of each side to rid the skin of excess water. The fish glistened in his hands with bright, not chalky, eyes. Flashes of iridescence in the blackish-blue lines marked the silver skin on each side, and the flesh stayed firm to his touch. He trimmed and cleaned the fish on a plastic cutting board, relying on an old kitchen knife that he'd sharpened against a flat spice-grinding quarry stone, which sat in a corner on the floor. Mom had taught him well. The sac of pink eggs from one fish, thousands of them all glued together, made him smile. A treasure. Fishhead ran the mackerel under the sink one final time; he placed each cleaned fish on the cutting board then sliced off the head and put it on a plate, and, using the score lines, he divided the fish into three pieces. He measured and cut the other fish in the same manner.

He stepped aside and watched as Mom prepared the fish with chilies, mango, tomatoes, and spices, while she brought the rice to a slow boil in a covered pot with a lid. He helped prepare the bitter gourd, not a family favorite but affordable and easy to make.

Minutes later, everyone sat down to dinner on the concrete floor. Fishhead crossed his legs in the too-small room. A humid apartment with a musty smell. All units must be the same, he thought, all units in this building. How could he survive here? How could his family endure such a fate? The slowest death. A punishment wrapped in shame and oppression. He'd rather take the pain from one of the principal's cane-whippings. Better swelling palms than this misery.

On the bamboo mat in the center of the room, Mom had spread the pages of a used newspaper as protection from the heat of the dishes. The paper, a week-old copy of *The Times of India*. He knew only his hunger and desperation, which seemed far less important to the world. He could see headlines of stories peeking out from underneath the edges of the kitchenware, stories like cricketer Sunil Gavaskar's century-scoring streak against the West Indies, or the arrival of U.S. troops in Cambodia, or even the deadly earthquake in Peru. It had taken fifty-thousand lives! So much happening everywhere, and he had no connection to it at all, besides this old newsprint.

One tidbit near his plate caught his attention: something about Indian oil and natural gas exploration by Urja Oil and Gas Well Production, the government's young private sector energy corporation. Urja-OGP had been looking for oil and gas in Assam and Gujarat states, and the company turned to Bombay's shoreline as the next attractive prospect. Pradeep had mentioned it in passing not too long before. He'd wanted to become an Indian Air Force pilot, but his poor eyesight ended that dream; now seventeen, he showed an interest in energy and technology.

Fishhead, however, liked art and music; drawing interested him more and more. His brief sessions with the Linotype machines at Dad's print shop had turned on a creative switch in his heart. Usually he sketched and doodled on old paper, on his jeans and shirt sleeves, along the seams, in his schoolbooks. Looking at the old newspaper under the pots and pans, he found himself wishing he could flip past the headlines and study the ads. Some ad designs suggested bad taste and poor skill. The printed photographs in newspapers showed coarse black dots, not fine enough to reveal good details; the dots reminded him of those copper plates of photos mounted on wood blocks back at Dad's print shop. Fishhead had developed a distaste for the crude black and white cartoons in these ads; he knew he could do better.

Dad had pawned off or sold so much. Few things remained in this room: Mom's sewing machine, a folding metal chair, and this cheap bamboo mat, a central piece, valuable now as it brought the family together like this.

Fishhead waited patiently while Mom began serving. The aroma of spices and simple ingredients pinched his stomach. But would it be enough? Fishhead stood at 5-foot-8—too thin in his arms and wrists, with uncut black hair falling across his forehead and spilling over the tops of his ears, and high cheekbones and deep-set, brown eyes that showed his desire to live a better life than the one fate presented him. He wore shorts and an old, oversized T-shirt: almost fourteen, a middle child who adored the sun, who loved being outside past sundown. A growing boy, but ashamed.

Dad had started a new business in this dump, making handpainted holiday cards. He'd purchased paint, brushes, pencils, erasers, glue, and blank cards, and he lined them up against the blank wall. Fishhead did his best to ignore the abundant array of brand new art supplies; he turned his attention instead to this meager feast. Never enough food for this family of seven. He knew he would go to sleep hungry.

I must pause here and point to this intrigue in Fishhead's paradoxical nature, a youth caught at the crossroads of survival, feet planted in the median and unwilling to move as if I, life's cobbler, had nailed inertia to the soles of his feet. Let me repeat, dear reader, that his eyes burned with desire for a better life than the one he faced. These patterns of inaction and vitality are complex, and transferable from parent to child, I confess. Well, is that the case here? Rebellion might suggest an opposite suit of actions, but, in fact, it resembles its origins. Fishhead must be careful. What patterns of behavior is he taking from his parents as he approaches adulthood? Since I am the mastermind of time and a purveyor of the instant in which all feeling and production transpires, I am most interested in how Fishhead lives in the present. I am interested in how he filters this moment, rather than how he keeps tasting the past, the salt of the family's failure on his tongue. He might never understand his family's reason for existence, and yet he has come from it and is a part of it, destined for new motivations: his own Republic of Want. Rice and Sugar. *Chawal aur Chini.* We shall see. The boy is ashamed and desires a better life than this one, which, he insists, I have presented him. But it's this moment that parenthesizes the hour of divinity, the dream of love and fate in the instant, which moves in one direction: forward, never back. Perhaps he will see love elsewhere and know Destiny with the kind of intimacy unavailable here. What you hold in your hands and in your vision is—just as Fishhead holds in his hands and in his vision—a breath of anticipation and expectation. Let us proceed.

A train approached the station on the other side of the wall, as if just outside the front door. A demon at the door. Lily, now six, covered her ears and whined. She, the last child and only girl. Skin like smooth dark chocolate, a beauty in the dumps who resembled her attractive father more than any other sibling. Mom hadn't wanted Lily, but she'd carried and delivered her, choiceless by tradition, by culture; choiceless in a country steeped in convention, ritual, and customs as ancient as seawater. Now Mom and daughter sat apart from each other, saying little to each other, as usual. Lily had become father's pet (Dad had wanted a girl, wanted a girl badly), and now she took her place beside him.

Balan George, father, a dark and handsome man, luckless, guileful. The slight glint of silver in his hair showed his advancing age, but his handsomeness had long ago ceased being an asset to the family. Cursed! His goatee, like a garden shoot. Cursed! He wore black slacks at dinner and a long-sleeved white shirt left unbuttoned to show his hairless chest. That drinking paunch. All cursed to fail. Five children, and more if Mom kept doing his bidding, closing her eyes to resist fatigue in her body.

Fishhead sat next to Prem, who found a spot beside Mom. Pradeep settled between Fishhead and Lily on the other side. Kishore took the floor between his parents. Fishhead glanced at Lily and sneered when she covered her ears. She cried a lot, too much in fact.

"You better get used to these trains, Lily," he said, but she did not answer him.

An unsettling calm held the family together, a life on the edge of a tremor. A tight room, walls caving in, dark. Fishhead glanced at his father, then turned his eyes to the front door. Dad kept it ajar to let the breeze and light in; the still and humid air did not cooperate. Fishhead wanted it closed to keep strangers from showing up unannounced while they ate. Dad's debtors, old and new, always found him somehow.

The heat in the room made Fishhead uncomfortable; he hoped for some movement in the air. Pradeep perspired the most, unable to hide his wet forehead, collar, and armpits. The unit did not come with a ceiling fan.

Mom spooned the curried mackerel pieces and soup over cooked rice on seven tin plates, most of them dented from use. Fishhead kept his eyes on her as she served the best pieces of fish to his father and older brothers, while Lily and Kishore each got half the cooked fish eggs. Lily also got a tail section, the part with the least bones. Mom gave Fishhead the other tail. He nodded when she picked up a head and offered him one.

"You like the heads," Mom said.

Fishhead lifted his plate to receive the mackerel head from her, and he took the extra tail she'd served him and put it on her plate before she could protest. "You know I do," he answered.

"I know. No one else will eat the heads."

"Nasty," Prem said.

"That's for the crows," Pradeep added. "Caw, caw."

Lily giggled. Fishhead smirked. He looked up to this oldest brother most of the time, but not now.

"Then Mom and I are crows," Fishhead answered. "I'll eat the eyes, too. Like this…look," Fishhead put the head in his mouth, crunching slowly and slurping the juices, sucking it all up with tight cheeks and lips pushed out like a fish. He chewed the eyes, gills, cheeks, and bones.

"Tell him to stop that, Papa," Lily cried.

"Your mother named you Fishhead when you were young," Balan said, looking at Eshma. "But you don't have to show off." He cleared his throat, unwilling to discuss the matter further.

Fishhead thought Dad might strike him in front of everyone; slowly he swallowed the juices and spat out the pressed bones in his hand, easing them out gently. He placed them at the edge of his plate. Then he slurped quietly again.

"Does he have to do that?" Balan said to his wife. His eyes narrowed, and his eating hand turned into a fist.

Fishhead stopped chewing.

Mom reached for his arm. "Don't upset your father," she said.

Fishhead studied his plate and said nothing. Head down. He'd earned his nickname, more than enough. But to eat the fish heads without slurping? Hard to do.

Only sleep promised relief from the uncertainties of the day, and he longed to find his place on the hard floor once everything had been put away and the room cleaned, transformed into the family's bedroom. Close his eyes, close them, and drift away. All seven slept in rows on sheets, pushed up against each other in the heat with the front door latched tight. The curtain on the window overlooking the front balcony hung there, unmoving; it failed to keep the mosquitoes away.

Greeting Cards

Just after sunrise, Fishhead woke up to the sound of Mom's voice as she prepared to leave for work. He lay still on the floor, under his sheet, as she stepped over the others towards him. He thought about Dad's single rule: Never step over Dad to cross the living room. Dad meant it. He often got up at sunrise, as he did now with Mom, and took his place in the chair with its back against the wall, a cup of hot chicory and coffee in his hands, his feet tucked under him. A deep-thinking man.

Fishhead stirred when Mom leaned in, her face about two feet from his. "Help your father," she said, pressing down on his right shoulder. "I promise I'll make us cakes."

He did not have to rise as early in the summer; school break had given him free time, but he did not enjoy giving it back to Dad's new venture. He preferred playing marbles with the rough neighborhood kids, a rougher bunch; or hanging out on the school grounds behind the church. Clearly, life put him in an awkward place between the haves and have-nots.

He rubbed his eyes, nodded, and watched his mother make her way to the front door. The rings around her eyes. Those sinking cheeks. He knew her good work habits: be on time, never miss your train, work hard. Work, as long as someone tells you what you should do.–He got to his feet, drowsy but encouraged by his mother's words. *That* could get him through any day.

It didn't please him to work for his father without pay. He sensed that his siblings felt the same. Games of marbles called him, the school playground called him. Soccer. He would stay all day on the field at school if he could, but he resigned himself to playing marbles with the neighborhood boys, later. But first, so much work to do. His father sat ready for him, for the others.

Fishhead put his bedsheet away while his brothers and sister stirred. Dad rested a pad and pencil on his lap, ready to start sketching ideas for his holiday greeting cards. Why not begin early? At last, something he fancied, a path, a vision, an enterprise powered by one mind (his), and many hands. Mom did not put too much faith in Dad's ventures, although she never challenged them openly. Fishhead understood her displeasure.

Hard, dried bread, and coffee with chicory for breakfast. And then the single room became an office and art studio after Lily swept the floor with an old jute broom, half-bent, as if she had a deformed spine. She moved in haste and brushed too hard, but she didn't disturb Dad's materials.

He sketched roughly, with stacks of holiday cards next to his feet. He let Prem and Fishhead complete his sketches and make them tighter on the cards. Fishhead liked this part, at least. He was starting to enjoy figurative drawing. Dad sketched the nativity scene with the holy family, animals, a shed with a roof, candles aflame, glowing in a lightless night. He arranged the cards in order, some finished with holiday images, others near completion. He had cards with white envelopes, ready for sale; blank cards, too, stacked in boxes against a wall behind the chair. But where did Dad get the money for all these? The investment stretched the family's limits thin.

And yet Fishhead appreciated his father's creations. These handcrafted illustrations made with poster paint, glue, broom hair from jute, cotton, glitter, powder, and sand. Dad's clever ideas, good ideas. A few hundred cards now ready to sell, and many more waiting for completion. The dried glue, however, had a mind of its own, because it warped the finished cards; and Dad used rationed rice when he ran out of glue, but this warped the cards, too. He'd put several of the finished greeting cards down overnight, pressed under a kitchen pot filled with baking sand. Best he could do to resolve the matter. In the meantime, keep moving forward.

Pradeep had walked out the door after breakfast, uninterested in Dad's enterprises. Soon Lily and Kishore rested on their elbows, watching. But Fishhead and Prem kept helping, dirty now, hands smeared with paint and glue. Fishhead wanted to understand his father. Dad showed ambition and drive with every little enterprise he touched, but he struggled to kick open his door to success, as if his stars were still ever so slightly out of alignment.

Fate's work then? Balan never acknowledged his Destiny; he did not talk of fate; he rarely talked at all. Just this silent desperation to do something and save his family. He found a goal he liked, and chased it. Pressing, rubbing coins together, *paises*.

What did Balan have in his heart then? Passion—a fruit or shard—but passion all the same, hidden in a drawer in the deep recesses of his flesh. Fishhead had seen this passion in his father, this rebellious emotion, back when Dad had been listening to the classical records from the British Council. A restless man listening to Elgar concertos, compositions by the Schumanns, by Beethoven, Brahms, Chopin, Bach, Dvořák, others. The New World Symphony. Scheherazade. Bolero. Dad had absorbed these, a man in his chair, composed and withdrawn, his body and soul in cursed euphoria, solace, stepping through corridors stricken by mystery and flame, whiffs of alcohol. His unattainable desires and ego.

Why did Dad have such bad luck? Fishhead wondered. His knew that his father wished for something big and unique, something impressive. He saw Dad's passion. But then he remembered Dad's other ventures, which did not last long.

And now this business of cards and commercial art. The apartment smelled like a cottage industry, saturated with the odor of paint and animal glue. It felt unhealthy, lethal perhaps, but Dad opened the windows and door, and they kept working. A minor setback. Better to live with such odors than with the stink of stagnant gutter water or shit wafting through from the outside, he said. The wind shifted from time to time anyway.

Glue, paper, and paint: Fishhead compared these odors to the distinct smell of ink and cleaning liquids at the print shop. If only Dad hadn't left. Why couldn't he hold down a job? A man unwilling to serve. Service pleased others and satisfied a mutually beneficial goal, and Dad would not have that. He could not have that.

By lunchtime, the apartment became unlivable, with scraps of art materials and cut paper scattered everywhere. Slivers of wasted broom pieces dropped and ignored like confetti. Splotches of paint and glue smeared on the hard floor. Dad didn't seem to care if the floor became a canvas, so long as the finished cards piled up, ready for sale.

But Dad's project needed salespeople, too, and Fishhead hated this part of the perfect plan most of all. On Dad's command, he and Kishore cleaned up but did not take their baths. Meanwhile, Prem and Lily continued to watch, learn, and be of assistance as Dad put the finishing touches to his cards. Fishhead waited patiently. Then, long past lunchtime, Dad filled up an old cotton sling bag with the finished cards.

"Sell everything and come straight home," Dad said. "And be careful. Don't lose the money. That will be our lunch money. And if you do well, dinner, too."

Fishhead left with sixty handmade cards and envelopes in the cloth bag slung across his shoulders; he took Kishore with him, and they had just enough cash for their commute, nothing more. Hot off the press! A bag that reeked of glue, paper, and poster paint. The price of each card: five rupees. No one had ever taught the boys how to sell anything door-to-door. Fishhead, embarrassed and awkward about his family's condition, knew it would not be an easy job. Not an easy job at all.

They boarded the commuter train from Chembur, and within forty-five minutes had reached Bandra, a posh suburb on the western coastline of the city. Fishhead knew little of the area, except for its famous week-long festivities and crowded procession with the statue of Mother Mary, which he'd attended with Mom and his siblings. People talked of Bandra's popularity and stylishness, its wealth, and colleges and schools he knew he'd never get into; coffee shops, clubs, *gymkhanas* for the rich, tennis courts, shopping districts, and hotels and mansions by the waterfront. The bandstand area where lovers came to be alone with each other, far from the watchful eyes of censors and traditionalists; nothing but the sea before them and busy Bandra at their backs.

Fishhead told his brother they should split off and double the effort. Kishore seemed eager to do so, eager to grow up fast. A rebellious spirit. A hothead, that boy.

They left Bandra station then tramped on for a quarter mile or so west in the high afternoon heat until they reached a bend in the main road. To their left, the walls of the Jesuit church and school. The road forked; they took the street that veered off to the right and followed that to the rich homes and apartments, a quieter tree-lined section of the suburb.

"Hurry up," Fishhead said, "or we'll lose time." Big brother kept having to wait for Kishore to catch up with him, walk faster. Wet armpits, backs. The day's heat. Beads of sweat piling up on their foreheads, raining down their cheeks. They knocked on every door, entered every apartment building, climbed up to every floor. They tried it again and again and again, going from building to building and home to home. Gates with latches and bells, houses with dogs and without. They went knocking on doors to sell their cards—sell, sell, sell. And all the while, hunger gnawed and twisted

Fishhead remembered to drink water wherever they could find it, in corner cafes and from street vendors. No roadside well or pump in sight here. One resident offered them water but did not need the cards.

By five o'clock in the evening, they had sold forty-three cards, but the trek weakened their knees and legs, leaving them dizzy, parched. Life like a desert.

"Please, can we eat something?" Kishore asked.

"We'll eat later," Fishhead answered. "Let's keep going. Dad will count the money."

He led Kishore home on the train. They reached the tenement building before sunset, glad to be back but desperately hungry.

Inside, they emptied their bags before Dad. Lily and Prem came closer to take a look. Dad kept busy, paintbrush in hand, a glass near him. Not water.

"How did you do?" he asked at last, tugging at his singlet.

"I'm hungry," Kishore said.

"We sold a lot," Fishhead said, his mouth dry.

"How many is a lot?"

"Forty-three."

"You didn't sell everything."

"That's a lot," Fishhead reasoned.

Dad paused. "Go help your brother in the kitchen," he said at last.

Fishhead handed over the cash but stood looking on. Dad counted every rupee and *paise*, two-hundred and fifteen in all; he placed the coins on the floor and arranged the notes near them in proper value, all straightened out and turned face up. So much money did not go far in this family.

Fishhead just stood there before his father and stared at the man's hands, while Kishore went to the kitchen and came back with bread that had been sitting on the dark cement counter for three days. Little brother pinched the few ants scattering on the bread and tossed them away, and he put small morsels in his mouth.

Dad dropped the coins in a shoebox and stood up; he folded the notes and put them in his pocket. Fishhead stepped aside, confused. The work stopped, just stopped without rhyme or reason. Had Dad been waiting for the money all day? All week?

Lily began to gather up the unfinished cards, and Prem swept his cupped hands across the floor to clean it, picking at the edges of paint and glue splotches.

"Get a wet cloth from the bathroom," Dad said. Then he raised his glass to his lips and emptied it—his moonshine, *avaida sharaab*. Slipped on a shirt, buttoned it. He made his way to the front door. "I'll return shortly," he added. "Don't mess up the new cards."

Fishhead nodded. Held back his surprise and disappointment; he wished he'd spent a few rupees in Bandra, for samosas or chai or sugarcane juice. Had Prem or Lily even eaten? Where did Dad plan to go? The market, Fishhead hoped, to the market, please! He'd follow his father again sometime but didn't have the energy now.

But he knew Dad wouldn't go looking for work, not with a handmade greeting card project in full swing. This would all end after the New Year. And then what?

He knew, too, that Dad hated working for anyone. Dad enjoyed being the bossman. Bossman could not stand others bossing him around. Ex-bossman of a printing press. New bossman of a greeting card project.

Fishhead expected the worst: Dad would spend the money, would drink it and gamble it away. He'd pay off a recent debt. He'd leave the apartment and disappear, and return home at night to get his sleep, and do it again the next day. A bossman in charge of his fate.

Something stirred inside Fishhead, begging mutiny. As he watched Dad leave, he knew in his heart that life would get worse before it improved. He knew Dad would send him out with Kishore again the next day, and the day after that, and the day after that. Sell, sell, sell. Get your experience on the job, on your feet, in your empty stomach.

And he knew, too, that he'd do it.

Girls Make Good Ping Pong Players

Fishhead helped tidy up the front room of the tenement, and scrubbed the floor clean with the wet rag, which Prem pulled from the nylon clothesline Pradeep had rigged up in the bathroom. Then he washed himself clean, combed his hair back, pinched out the ants from a piece of dried bread, put it between his teeth, and left the apartment.

He stepped through the gap in the wall overlooking the tracks and crossed the stinky gutter, but he held himself back on the quarry stones there, because a train approached from the east, its roar pulsing through the rails a few feet in front of him. Passengers leaned out dangerously from the doors of every moving car, their bodies pressed tight against each other. Beyond capacity, like all of them, day and night.

Fishhead hesitated. Stay or go? He did not want to wait. So he sprinted across the tracks. The wrong decision, you say? He had a few seconds, this reckless boy. He did, but the tip of his right foot caught the rail running adjacent to the platform, just as the metal horror rolled into the station on his left, its face of two-tone golden yellow and earthen red paint growing closer, getting bigger, much too fast.

His body crumpled; his heart leaped inside his chest. Such fear! His palms burned as he fell partially on the paved ramp. He pulled his legs in with haste, scrambling to get them off the tracks. Would the train stop? Its screech thundered through his being.

But death stalled now, not in his cards.

The train braked to a halt a few feet from him, triggering a free-for-all among commuters to exit and enter. Ram, elbow, hustle! Ants disturbed on the heap. Leaning out from his window, the driver spewed out a long reprimand; and three commuters on the platform, a woman and two men, screamed at him too.

Fishhead heard them all but said nothing. His mind spewed back a response: *No, I'm not mad, and I do look first. I don't have a deathwish.* He got to his feet and examined his scuffed hands while he panted a bit. He'd clean them later.

Other commuters gathered on the ramp around Fishhead, curious about the incident, but he wanted to get away from their questions; he turned south and stepped across the tracks on the other side. There, he went through the space between the wrought iron fence and entered the marketplace. Behind him, the train pulled away from the station, just as another came around the bend from the west.

Central Avenue, the busy paved main road, led south to the school and church. The fifteen-minute walk seemed like no trouble. His palms bled a bit, burned more. He dabbed them with leaves he found under a large mango tree between buildings. He continued on and soon left the shops and apartment buildings behind as he reached a roundabout: Ambedkar Garden Circle. He went around it.

A sea of private homes flanked him on both sides. A classmate's home, Lennie Santos's two-unit brick building, stood to his left, followed by Chembur Gymkhana with its tennis courts on Road No. 16, and then came Anupa's street, also on his left. He saw no one he recognized there. Just as well. No one must know his indignation and shame, not even Lennie. He closed his hands into fists and hid his scuffed palms.

Fishhead walked past well-maintained homes with their gates and walls and flowering bushes, their pet dogs and controlled peace and quiet. The sound of piano keys: who played so well? Classically trained, of course; he knew the sound but did not recognize the piece. Rachmaninoff, or maybe Debussey; Dad would know it for certain.

He smelled home cooking and strong Indian curries—*sambar,* fried fish, pot roasts, and pork vindaloo. Dinnertime, or perhaps the end of it. People were stepping out for their leisure walks, all around him and in every direction. In an hour, the street lights would come on. He went past Manju's very-quiet house and did not see Anupa's cousin there. And then, a tap on his shoulder. Anupa! So unexpected!

She smiled from ear to ear; she'd hastened to catch up with him. He slowed down and let her come at his side; she stayed on the inside, away from traffic. The smell of her perfume and coconut oil touched him. Her sweet skin and long hair. A clean, clean girl.

"I knew it was you," she said, out of breath.

"You surprised me."

"That was my plan."

"Where are you going?" he asked.

"To the clubhouse, where else? And you?"

"I'll join you, if you don't mind."

"I don't mind, but where were you going?"

"Not sure, just walking," he said, and looked at his hands. "Maybe to the school. See if anyone's playing football or cricket." His stomach growled and he almost pressed it down with the palm of his left hand, but stopped. The bruise, and his hunger.

They went down church road on the left and faced its big gates in the near distance. "I haven't seen you in a long time. What happened?" she asked. He turned away for a moment, and she hooked his forearm with two fingers to get his attention when he did not answer. "Is everything all right?"

"My family moved again," he said, but did not offer details. Not worth talking about the dirty and scummy tenement area on the other side of the tracks. His father's joblessness, the family's struggle. Dad's new get-rich-quick handmade card venture. Stupid animal glue.

"I wondered why you were walking down Central," she said. "You took the train, na?"

"No, we moved near Chembur station. It's a really nice apartment." He looked at her, to see if she believed it. "My mom wanted us near school."

"That's good! Glad to have you closer."

"It took too long to walk from the other place. I was always late for class," he said.

"Well, it's good that you moved, then."

"Yes," he said. Then, after a pause, "You look nice! You always smell so good."

She smiled and stroked her hair. "Would you like to walk me back home later? But only if you want to."

He caught her eyes. An invitation! No girl had ever said that to him twice. Could he call her a girlfriend? No. They knew each other as acquaintances, that's all; and across a social divide. Fate appeared to draw him out, he felt, and make time slow down in his blood, make him hum in step with the universe, sing its song of patience. Fate had something in store for him, although he didn't know the details yet. Did he imagine this social divide and make it up in his head? So much second-guessing. He nodded to accept her invitation.

"I'd like to hear you say it," Anupa insisted.

He paused, thinking of nothing in particular, his contemplation, her forwardness and insistence to hear his response. "Yes, I want to. That would be nice," he said.

"That's good. I'm glad," she returned.

And yet Fishhead hesitated. Resistance mixed with desire. Could he give himself permission to take this friendship further? Anupa did not know how he felt. He did not know how to react. So unprepared and embarrassed. Sucked in by his tenement life. And now she reached out to him as they walked. How could he step on her front porch without feeling guilty? He hoped to try. He would train his heart to want it, want Anupa. She treated him like no other person had done, like no one at home ever did or would. She didn't seem to care what others might think or say. She pursued him and no one else, not the rich boys in her neighborhood. Or had he read her wrong? Did she actually have trouble finding and keeping a boyfriend? Must be something wrong with her.

"What kind of neighborhood is this?" he asked. "There's money here."

"Old money," Anupa said. "Portuguese families settled here generations ago. Mine, too. But this is a mixed community, like all of Bombay. We live in harmony. We must."

Her answer did not reassure him; all this wealth and beauty, plus his gnawing hunger, gave him an added sense of worthlessness. Should he bother walking her back home later and risk being seen?

They approached the clubhouse and he raised his hand to lift the latch on the iron gate.

"What happened?" Anupa asked.

His panic. "What?" he said.

"Your hand." She looked down and saw a similar bruise on his other hand.

"It's nothing."

"Not nothing!" she insisted. "You're hurt. How?"

He did not respond.

She lifted a hand to stop him, but he stepped around her. "How? Please tell me."

"I tripped and fell at the train station," he explained.

"Oh no! I'm sorry! See, there's a tap at the side of the clubhouse," she said and pointed. "You can rinse off there. You poor thing!"

She closed the gate behind them while he went off to clean his hands. On the school's sports field to the left, boys played a rough game of cricket with a tennis ball. From across the field, Fishhead became distracted by their shouts and foul language.

"Play ping pong with me, if you want," Anupa suggested. She lead him towards the entrance of the clubhouse. "Why waste your time on the stands watching boys play cricket? You should be playing too, na?"

"I know cricket," he said, "but I can't play ping pong."

"I'll show you. If you can hold a paddle with your bruised hands."

"I'd like to try. Are you any good?"

"I know how to play it!" Anupa said, laughing. "What, you're asking me that because I'm a girl?"

"Oh, I don't know. I suppose."

"Don't be like that, talking nonsense like the other boys. Girls make good ping pong players."

"I wouldn't know," he admitted, flushed with embarrassment. "I'm not sure why I even said that."

"I'll show you then. We'll see who's any good."

He followed Anupa around the side of the large hall and onto the long open verandah. The large room looked empty from the outside, but the sound of ping pong balls clicking against paddles and tables caught Fishhead's attention as they walked in. Beneath that noise, a Hindi film song played through a portable transistor radio. Always the radio. The building stood empty and silent during daytimes when school stayed in session; but the social club came alive after school hours, so that by four-thirty in the afternoon, boys and girls began showing up to chat and play games. Advance their romance and friendships. Be seen and heard.

A group of girls and boys hung out in one corner near two carrom boards, while others played ping pong, leaving the third table empty. Anupa and Fishhead picked up paddles and a ping pong ball off the table top. Anupa spun her paddle around a couple of times in her hand. Then she smacked the ball over the net in his direction. The ball bounced on his side of the table and stayed low; he tried to return it, but it hit the net and dropped back.

He knew he needed more practice and found the game easy to pick up, like marbles, but Anupa had an ease and grace about ping pong which he lacked. His head spun from hunger and his stomach talked back, and his hand still hurt from the bruise. She started a point game soon enough, and, in a few minutes, had beaten him with a score of eleven points; three more games later and Fishhead still hadn't scored ten points in total. He seemed to take his awful losses well, smiling all the while, even while cursing inwardly at his own awkwardness. His bruise stung more now, but he did not complain. His stomach growled again; he hoped she couldn't hear it. No matter, she beat him fair and square. He laughed with her as they put their paddles down. His head spun again, and, uncontrollably dizzy, he turned around and closed his eyes to hold his balance, to stay on his feet. *Anupa must not know.* A shower of stars danced before him; he shut his eyes, blackness closing in through the hunger void.

The others in the room clapped for her. Fishhead felt like he stood no chance. A poor boy from a tenement, stalked by the tigers of privilege.

Anupa waved at him then joined the other girls at the end of the clubhouse. Fishhead looked around to see if anybody else wanted to play: no takers. He stood next to another ping pong table while two boys began a new game with skill and confidence. They played effortlessly.

Minutes later, Fishhead stepped out and headed for the sports field where the cricket game continued. With the clubhouse at his back, he paused on the edge of the grounds and studied himself, his bruised hands, his sunburned feet and flip-flops, torn jeans, and old shirt. Overgrown hair that needed a cut. Everyone else looked so neat, with their laundered and ironed clothes, their colorful outfits, their healthy, perfumed bodies and hair. He would wait and walk her home, if she let him; he would expect no other plans with her, and admit to her that he needed to wash more frequently. His tenement apartment had slow, running water; all the same, he vowed to cut his nails, and bathe every day with help from a plastic water bucket and a green plastic mug.

For now, better to spend time alone on the school's grounds, at the wall by the tamarind tree, or on the spectator stands beside the social club; better to be alone and watch the dusty schoolboys playing cricket or soccer after class. He walked along the edge of the field and sat under the branches of the tamarind tree. He sat on the very spot from where he'd first noticed Anupa. He ate tamarind pulp then; perhaps he needed some now. He reached for the pods and, before he shelled one, dropped a few in a pocket of his jeans for his mother. He peeled away the dark brown shell and veins of the pod in his hand and sucked on the pulp, and he ate its tender green leaves, but the more he ate, the more his stomach snarled.

This seat on the wall gave him a view of the clubhouse and its gate across the field. The cricket game continued, full of energy. Fishhead wished he had a book in his hands. This sudden appetite to read more than ever. Even comics would do; but neither the school nor the neighborhood had a library. The school's bookstore sold textbooks, which bored him. And he missed Jailal Ram Book Stall—the only bookstore selling stories and comics—now so far away on his daily route to and from those previous apartments in Collectors Colony. Could he borrow from his classmates? From Anupa maybe? Did she read much? He ought to ask her. Bite your tongue, hold back shame and do it.

An hour or so later, Anupa stepped out of the clubhouse; she paused between the main door and the gate and looked around. The evening light had changed, and the cricket game had wound down to the last two batsmen, but the boys wouldn't abandon the sports field until it got dark. Fishhead threw his right arm up and waved until Anupa caught sight of him and waved back. He jumped off the wall, feeling light as a feather, weak, and he ran along the edge of the field, going behind the football goalposts and the cricket fielder. He knew Devkumar from class, the boy in the long-on position who winked and whistled. "Lucky bastard," the boy said, but Fishhead ignored him.

A Storybook Home

As he caught up with Anupa, his heart beat faster. Blood rushed through his body and head, freeing him of his burdens, the moral and psychological, the material. Nothing else mattered now.

He accompanied her along Central Avenue and they went north in the direction of her house and train station. He showed her the tamarind pods and talked about food, about ping pong, but when they reached her house, and she unlatched the gate and invited him in, Fishhead became alert and pensive, more aware than ever. Again, he visualized his hardship and his place in the world, but he resolved to make an effort and appreciate the niceness of her home. All the things he didn't have and might never have, right here.

The house looked alive with its windows open and doors ajar, as though it grew out of the greenery that surrounded it. High in the trees, birds chirped their final calls for the evening. Sparrows and a bulbul; the songbird perched on the highest branch.

"Who's home?" he asked.

"Come in and find out!" Anupa said, smiling. She brought the two halves of the gate together behind them and dropped the latch back into place.

"I'm not decent," he said and leaned awkwardly against the railing of the tiled front porch.

She frowned. "Come on."

He let her take his elbow, and she ushered him up to the front door. Two halves and a peephole, a vacant little square cut through the left door with an ornamental bronze grid fastened over it. From the other side came faint evidence of music.

"Do you know that song?" Anupa asked. She reached for the screen door then pushed open the two halves of the unlocked front door. A string of small bells chimed, announcing their presence. *Ghungrus.* She walked in first; no one greeted her. Fishhead followed. The scent of food overwhelmed his senses: fragrant boiled rice, and meat cooked in vinegar, spices, and chilies. Vindaloo! Its red heat hung in the air, even with the windows open. Someone home, but who?

And the music, louder now: a Western pop song, sad and sweet. Fishhead shook his head. "No, I don't know it," he said. The song touched him and made him curious, and it got louder when he entered the living room—a large square area with white walls, neatly arranged with a patterned sofa set, three upholstered chairs, a coffee table in wood, sculptured figurines, doilies everywhere, lamps with soft shades, and framed posters showing a watercolor of a Japanese wave, illustrations of birds, and the port town of "Nazaré-Portugal," with "Fly TWA" printed at the bottom. He held his breath. The sheer window curtains, tied back, brought light into the room. To the left, a tall China cabinet stood between both windows facing the street, with family photographs in their neat frames arranged on top of it; a smaller cabinet, two chairs, and a small table took up space on the adjoining wall. A dark upright piano stood further back against the same wall with its lid up, and a long white cut of linen laid across the black and white keys; this dust cover showed lace-like thread work at the edges. Behind the opened half-door to his right, he noticed a collection of records and a Philips record player, which sat on a polished table against the wall. Two high bookshelves flanked the polished table.

Fishhead scanned the books: Hermann Hesse, Mary Shelley, Agatha Christie, Maxim Gorky, Tolstoy, Solzhenitsyn, R.K. Narayan, Tagore, Jane Austen, Emily Bronte, Lorca, Lope de Vega, Calderon, Byron, Borges, and Shakespeare; also *The Count of Monte Cristo, Jane Eyre, The Scarlet Pimpernel, Frankenstein, Don Quixote*. Three books by Enid Blyton and two by Mark Twain. A dictionary and a pair of volumes about the world at large. And other books and magazines like *Femina* and *The Illustrated Weekly of India.* Three copies of the *Reader's Digest.* Plus records from Hindi film soundtracks by Asha Bhosle, Mohammed Rafi, and M.S. Subbulakshmi.

Anupa's eyes followed him. "My mom has taken a liking to this song," she said. "It's called 'Rhythm of the Rain.' Have you heard of the Cascades? They're an American pop group. She plays this one a lot."

He shook his head again and felt a pang of guilt for his ignorance. No radio at home, not even a little shortwave transistor radio. And, of course, they'd lost Dad's record player.

The song played on, captivating him. Fishhead thought he might remember it for the rest of his life. He moved closer to the record player and turned to face the door. Anupa came and stood near him; she lifted the arm of the player and started the song again.

"I like this," he said, and picked up the record's paper sleeve, listening. A soft hammered instrument played a melody while the lead vocalist sang. Percussive metal, like bells, took him back to the gramophone in Collectors Colony, when he stood silently behind Dad and listened to Tchaikovsky's *Nutcracker*. Songs by George and Ira Gershwin, the emotion in Maria Callas' voice, and the deep tone in Paul Robeson's. He saw Dad in his metal chair, arms folded and focused, not wanting to be disturbed; the man's annoyance.

Fishhead heard Anupa say something, but he failed to respond.

She tapped him on his shoulder. "Meet my mother," she repeated, amused by his attention and contemplation.

He whipped around and almost struck her petite mother with his elbow. She'd come in from the kitchen. An inch shorter than Anupa, she wore a striped blue house dress with short sleeves and front pockets. Her flowery yellow apron at her side. A narrow waist. Glasses, and straight, dark brown hair cut at the nape of her neck and turned outward.

Fishhead apologized and put the record sleeve down then reached out to shake her hand. "Hello!" he said. "Nice to meet you." He had not heard her name and thought it best not to ask for it now. Anupa's mother welcomed him. She looked him up and down, and then offered a smile and returned to the kitchen.

"She liked me, I hope?" Fishhead asked.

"Why wouldn't she?" Anupa said. "Don't be silly." She reached for *The Scarlet Pimpernel* and pulled it off the shelf, and followed that with Twain's *Adventures of Tom Sawyer* and Shelley's *Frankenstein*.

Fishhead shrugged, unwilling to offer any one of the myriad reasons. He studied her intently when she opened a fourth book: *The Swiss Family Robinson*. Anupa's hair fell straight down the side of her cheeks, covering her ears. She pulled it back. So much of her mother in her: the same eyes and smile, the square-ish shape of her forehead, full lips, high cheekbones, the medium button nose, narrow waist, dark hair, and strong legs, but her mother's knees did not behave as Anupa's did; they did not come towards each other when she walked. He observed her back as it curved down nicely, and her short gray skirt fell away with elegance at her buttocks like a bell lamp shade. A subtle, intelligent beauty, rooted in this place of privilege; he thought again of his father and the British Council. This place showed the other side of it.

"Do you play the piano?" he asked.

"No, nah-uh, I'm not good at it." She shook her head. "My mother does, although she hasn't played it in a while. She reads music. I watched her play but it wasn't at Christmas." Anupa fell silent; she lifted the arm of the turntable to play a different song. Fishhead glanced at the record: "Baby Love." The Supremes.

"Where's your Dad? Is he due home from work soon?" Fishhead inquired.

She shook her head but offered no explanation.

"Sorry I asked," he said. Then, moments later: "I didn't mean to pry. I have no right. I'm sorry, I should go now."

She took his hand to stop him. Wordless, pleading, but not desperate. She dropped the books on a chair near the bookshelves. "He left us early," she said, without looking up. Then she reached for Cervantes' *Don Quixote* and paused. At last she looked into Fishhead's eyes. "I lost my father when I turned eight," she began. "But not in that way. No, not that way at all. Worse, I want to say."

"I don't understand," he said.

She glanced anxiously in the direction of the kitchen. "Dad had a good job with TWA," she explained. "He liked to travel a lot, going all over the world, especially to Spain, and to Portugal where both my parents still have family ties." She nodded towards the posters and other tourist items in the living room. "Then I arrived. By the time I turned eight, Dad started imagining things that weren't true. He heard voices that kept him awake at night and that asked him to do odd things, my Mom said. It only got worse. Doctors called them command hallucinations, something to do with…have you heard of it…it's called schizophrenia? By the time I turned eleven, he had to be hospitalized. All the way over in Pune."

"My God!" Fishhead said. "Anupa, that is so sad. I'm very sorry."

"Thank you." *Don Quixote* sat open on her lap, and her hands held down the pages; her gaze stayed down there as well. "I was quite young to know what was really happening," she continued, "but I always felt this…growing sadness. As if things weren't right. Dad began engaging with me less and less. I started asking questions, as any child would, na? He is still there, you know, in Pune. Mom and I go see him whenever we can, but it's always hard for us. We don't have a car, so it's a long trip inland on the Central Railway."

"I'm really sorry. I should not have asked," Fishhead said, his head down.

"No, that's okay. I don't mind," Anupa replied. "But I don't talk about it at school. There are too many gossip-mongers. That's what I don't like, the mindless gossiping."

"Will your mom get mad that you told me?"

"I'm sure she's fine. We only talk about it when we go visit him. She gives me my freedom, which is nice. We have learned to give each other space."

Fishhead thought of his own family in their cramped room, everyone on top of each other. Space, never an option. He understood why Pradeep did not spend much time at home.

"School keeps me so busy," Anupa added. "I don't think of my father as I should. There is less and less room in my head for those memories. My Mom struggles in the same way."

Fishhead remembered that day on the wall under the tamarind tree when Anupa's teacher scolded her, how he'd heard her name for the first time as he sat unaccompanied, eating tamarind pulp to push back his hunger. So young back then, both of them. "Anupa, pay attention!" her teacher had said. Fishhead had carried the teacher's words with him for a long time, although he never understood why. Now he did. Anupa had grown up smart; she depended on her mother's care, but she also supported her mother. How did Anupa bear her pain so well? Fishhead understood, too, the sadness around her smile.

"Do you have brothers and sisters?" he asked.

"No, I have none."

"Do you want some of mine? You can take a pair. Too many in my house."

She laughed. "Are they as nice as you?"

"Not a chance."

"I'll take you then," she said with a smile.

Did Anupa mean this as a joke? He wondered. Perhaps she made conversation for the sake of conversation. Her nature, this directness. He thought too much about it. No one deserved him, he felt, least of all Anupa. He needed to keep her at a safe distance: conceal his shame and pretend he lived a normal life.

And yet he wanted more.

This felt like crossing the deep sea without even a safety float. Courage, he needed courage, and trust. He'd failed to maintain any long-lasting friendships; he knew nothing of romance. What could he offer her, or anyone? And yet he sensed her want in the air. Say yes, say no, or even maybe. Go along with her, give her some kind of assurance. Or deny all of it—No, he could not do that! But what should he do, how should he act? What would any other boy do in his place? *Be calm, be calm. Her mother is here.*

Anupa took the cloth-bound *Don Quixote* and settled down on the sofa; she asked him to sit next to her. She flipped through a few pages and chapters at random, laughing while Quixote dashed across the landscape on his horse, lance pointed at the giant windmills, while Sancho Panza watched in disbelief from his mule. Fishhead leaned in and studied the illustration, and they laughed together.

"Such a fool!" he said.

"You read it?"

"Our English teacher read it in class. Such clever meanings."

"Very true," she replied. "Cervantes even used the words of the medieval knights."

"I had trouble understanding that," he confessed.

"The old English?"

He nodded. "And the part with Cid...Cide Hamid Benen...what's the last name?"

"Cide Hamete Benengeli, Anupa finished. "Yes, it can be confusing to follow all of that. Don Quixote is his story."

"I forgot it so fast," Fishhead said. "Life got in the way." He wanted a glass of water but resisted the urge to ask. So hungry, too.

"Then let's read it together, na?"

"Why not?"

"You can't keep a great book away from me," Anupa said and flipped the pages back to the beginning. "Chapter one." She shifted on the sofa and pulled his shirt sleeve towards her. He moved closer, and she looked at him and smiled then began: "'In a village of La Mancha, the name of which I have no desire to call to mind, there lived not long since one of those gentlemen that kept a lance in the lance rack…'"

Fishhead listened attentively as she read to him for the next twenty minutes or so, her voice never faltering in the quietness of her home. Then she paused and offered the book to him, and he moved it to his lap but let one half of it remain on hers; and he read, slowly at first, getting acquainted with the long Spanish names and descriptions that somehow seemed so natural to Anupa. Moments later, he heard footsteps coming from the back of the house; a flash of yellow moved at the corner of his eye. Her mother checking in. Fishhead kept reading, rigidly focused; he did not dare look up. Anupa glanced up, then back at the book once more, and her mother returned to the kitchen in silence.

"My dad used to read to me when I was little," Anupa said later. "This is his collection. He was the big reader. Mom played piano and sang."

Fishhead paused and took this in. "I'm jealous," he replied. "So many books." Then he closed the novel, bookmarking it with his thumb. "You know, I dropped mine in a flood one morning on my way to school," he added.

"How sad!" Anupa said.

"I'd used my raincoat to wrap the books up. The wet pages dried afterwards, but they got wrinkled. Some stuck together and I couldn't pry them apart."

"That is sad, na? But you saved *Don Quixote*, and the story lives on," she said. "Such a comical character, that Quixote."

"Yes, he's a real madman," Fishhead said and opened the book. "Crazy."

Anupa turned quiet and contemplative.

"Is something wrong?" Fishhead asked.

She shook her head and turned to a chapter where Sancho Panza got tossed up and down on a blanket by lodgers, because his master the knight-errant Quixote refused to make payment to the innkeeper before departing on his horse. "Dad too crossed the line. But in real life," Anupa said. Then she put the book down. She jumped to her feet and let out a big sigh, as if to shake these feelings off her. Fishhead remained seated but followed her with his eyes, anxious.

He got up when her mother came in again. She offered him a glass of water and he took a long gulp. He put it down on the coffee table. Anupa declined. What had her mother heard? Fishhead wondered.

Mother put her fingers together and brought them up to her mouth, signing as if to eat, but Anupa shook her head. Not now.

But how Fishhead wanted food! The aroma of rice and spiced meat teased him, tortured him. Did Anupa not see it? She smiled at her mother then picked up the book again. "Thanks, Ma," she mumbled. Fishhead kept his composure and offered a cheerful expression; Anupa led the way past her mother and through the hallway, past the other rooms and kitchen, past the pantry to the back door.

He followed Anupa outside. Twilight made haste toward an intimate darkness. She shut the door behind them, and they settled on a capped wall on one side of the tiled steps leading down the two feet or so to the backyard. Fishhead glanced at the flowerbeds, the brown clay pots of fragrant roses and marigolds, and flowers he had no names for: carnations, poppies, and zinnias. He and Anupa sat close to each other on the ledge, touching thighs and shoulders; he tried to move an inch or so away to give her room, but she put her hand on his knee and stopped him, said nothing else. He liked it when she kept her hand there. The heat their bodies made; he liked that too Then she opened the book and continued reading until the poor light ended.

"I enjoyed that," he said. "Thank you."

Anupa closed her eyes and settled back as darkness came; the backyard transformed into a shade of the underground, brittle with the signs of nightfall. A few mosquitoes.

"The garden takes a lot of work," Anupa said. "Mom and I both work on it. We get all hot and sticky and dirty. But it looks nice."

"It does," he replied.

"We do need to water the flowers," she added.

"Shall I do it?" he asked, pointing to a black hose lying on the flagstones and on little tufts of grass, snaking between the pots.

"We don't need to do it now," she said.

"I've never done it before."

"We don't need to do it now," Anupa repeated. She moved her hand to the inside of his knee, the inside of his thigh, and rubbed gently.

A rip-tide in his stomach. His heart trembled, failed, and came back again; he wished she'd let him water *that* down with the black hose.

She took his right hand and placed it on her thigh but did not bother to adjust her short pleated skirt as it hiked up a little.

Fishhead stirred, his emotions in crisis. The heat of her soft flesh against his hand. What should he do? *Do something.* The neighbors couldn't see them. High stone walls all around.

She reached up and kissed him, and guided his hand over her. They had all the time in the world.

Make it last, the thought raced through his mind. Make it last. Make it last. Make it last. Dear fate, what should I do? Do more? What if she...? This is a miracle. A real miracle. Please make it last. May it never go away. What should I do? Is her mother watching us? Is she? What if she opens the door? No, I'm being foolish. Let me stay. Let it go on. I must move my hands. Let me stay. Let me stay. Let me stay on longer. A new galaxy is being born this very minute. Isn't this how the universe was made, with kisses? This is what you wanted for me. You brought me here, yes, you did. At first I did not understand any of this, and I can't say I understand it now. Her kiss, this kiss of stars that fill her hair and fall at your feet. Stars make your pillow at night. Will they fill my stomach? I'm hungry but I am here, being kissed. I'll forget my hunger. I'll forget it. Please make this last. Let me stay. Am I doing the right thing? What if I upset her? I have upset her.

"Is it me?" Her voice betrayed frustration. "Do you not want this?"

"I don't know what to do," he admitted.

She smiled, satisfied. "*This* is what you do," she said, kissing him again.

He left in the darkness and made his way towards the train station and the tenement on the other side, frustrated beyond measure and upset at himself. Mad at himself, his ignorance of the world, of her, of love, of desire and want. This Republic, its hostility. *Fate, where are you? Everything is so difficult.* Hunger pains pinching his stomach. Stars dancing before his eyes, pulsing against a bleak curtain. After all that. After an entire evening with her. So much to take in: a storybook home, Western pop songs, literature and foolishness, vindaloo and rice that he couldn't eat, her heated flesh, and sweet kisses pulling stars into his tempest-being.

He walked north on Central Avenue and looked up at the skies; in his dreamy state, he folded his right index finger and placed it between his lips, imagining her mouth against his. Practice, practice, practice. He would do better next time, because he wanted her. So patient, so sweet, the way she led him towards it. He wanted her.

Fishhead kept walking until the main road ended at the south end of the tracks. He stood next to a female pedestrian under the faint glow of the yellow street lights while a commuter train approached from the west, arcing towards Chembur station from the interior of the city. In his dreaminess, it took a few moments to notice his father standing on the other side of the woman

"Oh shit!" Fishhead mumbled, and looked down. Dad stood a few inches ahead of her. Fishhead could reach over and touch Dad if he wanted to, which of course he didn't.

And then Dad turned.

"Why are you out late?" Balan said, glancing at him without surprise, an eyebrow raised.

"It's not late. I was just hanging out with—"

"Don't you have homework?"

"Yes. I was with my friends, outside the church. Our usual thing." The train moved closer, full of passengers, and its wheels screeched along the rails.

"I walked past the church." Balan raised his voice. "I didn't see you there."

"You walked—? I was there, I swear it. You can ask Devkumar or Lennie."

"Are they friends of yours?"

The train roared now, its sound carrying through the rails in front of Fishhead; he said nothing to his father but jumped forward and dashed across the tracks, just as the first car came at him with an ungracious horn blast. Fishhead cleared the metal beast with seconds to spare and found his footing on the slope of the platform, just barely, while the train boomed past inches behind him, and a passenger in the first car leaned out and yelled, "I-d-i-o-t! You got a death wish?" But words disappeared as fast as they came, drowned out by the clatter of rails and brakes. The train screeched to a halt while Fishhead stood there. Heart beating fast, too fast. Another near miss. Good thing he didn't trip.

And yet, who would have cared? Life in this dense metropolis pedaled forward without missing a beat. Would anyone truly miss him? His father, possibly not. Prem or Lily or mother or the others, maybe. Anupa? Perhaps.

He didn't wait for Dad but slipped through the municipal wall; he rushed home and shut himself in the bathroom, with his ear cocked towards the front door.

By the time he emerged, Dad had already returned and settled down with a glass of moonshine in his hand, his shirt off, feet crossed under his metal chair. From the corner of the room, Dad looked at him, ignoring the others. Then he turned away, bringing the glass to his lips.

Fishhead stared at Dad from the doorway. Did his father not even care enough to scold him?

Lily pulled herself off the floor and stepped past him, heading towards the bare kitchen. "Did something happen, yaar?" she asked in passing.

"No, nothing."

"Why ask?" Prem cut in, from up near the front door. "It's got nothing to do with you."

"So. Something did happen!"

"Go mind your own business!" Kishore insisted from his spot on the floor near Dad.

"Your brother's trying to be a dead hero before he finishes school," Balan said at last, taking another sip and looking at Fishhead. "Ask him why. And ask him where he's been all evening." He sipped again.

Lily turned around. "What happened, yaar? Where did you go?"

Fishhead hesitated. "We should have dinner now," he said at last. "I'm starving. Why do we always have to wait for Mom to make it?"

Lily joined Fishhead in the kitchen. He kept his voice low and pointed his chin at Dad, "*He* was standing right there. I crossed in front of the oncoming train. He saw me do it." Lily sighed. Fishhead took a yellow onion and peeled it. Sliced the onion and took a bite, and then another one. He diced some ginger and garlic, and he put the knife down. Rinsed his mouth. He emptied the lentil jar and washed the lentils, and then he lit the stove and began cooking the lentils in water.

Dad did not care to stand in the kitchen and cook for the family. He'd rather be served. Still, having him home this early, before Mom, surprised Fishhead. Often Dad got home long after ten when the shopkeepers pulled their shutters down and when the hooch shack he visited did the same—the owner having coaxed his most intoxicated customers out, before putting away the alcohol and snacks then blowing out the oil lamps. How many times had Dad also been coaxed out of that shack? He kept himself from staggering somehow when he walked through the front door in the tenement. A man and his image, his self-deceptions.

Fishhead thought of these things often.

An apartment without relief. He felt no reassurance at being with his family or seeing Dad's greeting cards and supplies stacked up against the walls closing in on him. This hole for seven people, a vacuum filled by need. Hunger ravaged his insides and claimed his confidence, like black mold did to this place, its streaks and patches visible in the corners by the ceiling. Nothing else mattered, he thought, nothing, except Dad's greeting card enterprise, and the energy it demanded from everyone.

Fishhead tasted the lentils, glad he'd made the dish, at least. He tasted some more, unable to suppress his hunger any longer. Mom usually came home too tired to do much more than serve a simple meal: *dhal,* rice, and lime pickle. Tonight maybe she'd cook a vegetable dish for a change, but chances were that even the *bhaji* would fail to satisfy her family. Mom did her best to improve the dishes on weekends, despite the extra chores she faced. Lily helped. Fishhead did, too. He washed his own clothes on the bathroom floor, hoping he'd save Mom some energy and time.

Anupa stayed in his head and on his skin. Her touch, a torch and spur. His cloud in flames. When she'd kissed him, he'd drifted into a cloud full of heated, eager hands that reached for him and pressed against him from all sides, as time moved like molasses. And now she stayed in his head. He took pleasure in that and allowed this sense to remain with him. Never wash it away; no shower, no bath for a little while. Any other girl would have moved on for some other boy. But not Anupa. Perhaps he understood her reasons for pursuing him and inviting him home. Her kindness and respect, he liked that; she hadn't been upset at him, even when he'd confessed his inexperience.

Anupa hurt, too: Fishhead believed this. She concealed her pain because she chose life; she wanted more and made every effort to move on, but never strayed too far from the memory of her sick father.

Fishhead thought of his own father. His bitterness towards him. Still he felt a bit of gratitude for having a functioning father in his life. He should be glad for that, shouldn't he? Still he resented Dad's behavior, the way it wrapped its coils around everything the family did, subduing it. If given a choice between his father and Anupa's, what would he choose? A hard question to answer.

Perhaps Dad's behavior wasn't all that abnormal; perhaps every family out there had someone in control who acted the same way, and concealed it so that no one suspected the worst. And yet, it brought such immense hardship. The lack of food from day to day, the uncertainty. No chance of a home like Anupa's, which her father had left for them.

Fishhead questioned everything these days. This maturing awareness distracted him from his schoolwork. He'd been enjoying play and time away from home, just as Pradeep also stayed out during the day. But night always forced him to face his family's condition. Candles for reading better at night, candles at dinner, candles to brighten the kitchen, candles in the bathroom. Mom brought them home from church services. Stolen, it occurred to Fishhead. How long had she been doing this? Naughty woman in a veil.

So everyone in the family had a flaw, and everyone dealt with want differently. He'd use his nimble hands, those winning-at-marbles hands; they always brought him good luck.

One Small Victory

He stared at the empty pantry and the open shelves lined with aging newspapers. Pushed up against the corner, five stained spice jars and tins made pockets of cobwebs and dust. Three onions, a small container of sugar, a small plastic packet of tea leaves held together with a clothespin, but no rice or wheat flour. A cup or so of red lentils, if that. No potatoes, curry leaves, garlic or fresh ginger either. No vegetables. And under the sink, a small bottle of Dettol antiseptic, the mosquito sprayer, a mosquito coil, a folded and unused mosquito net with holes in it, some cockroach powder, rat poison, and a pint of kerosene in a clear whiskey bottle with a tightly rolled up paper plug in its mouth. Kerosene rations ended in the second week of the month, and this last cup of cooking fuel remained in the bottle, awaiting its use.

The future held no promises for Fishhead, but life's fantasies came in large quantities, page after page; the newspapers showed a different existence out there, with ads in black and white for fridges, pressure cookers, fans, scooters, cars, gas cooking ranges, blenders (mixies), textiles, modern apartments, gold jewelry, life insurance, new packaged foods, Amul butter, Bata shoes, new film releases, and so much more. Possibilities churned and spun around his mind like an overhead fan, but he knew that, in the end, he'd be better off discarding these images of success and wealth.

His desperation made him want to forget about Anupa. He couldn't overcome his hunger; he'd been eating raw onions, and his breath smelled funny. Surely she'd push him away for that reason alone. And yet he could not let go of the good times he'd spent with her. But what did any of that mean to him after all? The more he imagined a better life like hers, the more upset he became. Desire made him thirsty. The heat made him thirsty. Poverty made him thirsty. Hunger made him push his need down with the easiest thing he could reach for: water. He drank tap water, put it in his stomach, and settled in for sleep night after night, without enough food and without saying much to his siblings, all enduring in some kind of pierced and silent way.

Mom had promised cakes, if they helped Dad with the greeting card project. But the promise had never materialized. And how could it, with everything else she'd been doing? Fishhead had helped Dad, he had, but he also began to realize there'd be no reward.

He'd just turned fifteen when Pradeep finished school in the middle of the year and found a job at Santacruz airport, where he trained as a mechanic with Manitowoc Helicopters, a Canadian offshore company with Asian offices in Bombay, Singapore, and Bangkok. India had begun looking for oil offshore, Pradeep explained, and Manitowoc Helicopters provided a small fleet of Sikorsky and Bell helicopters to support these ventures.

Fishhead still couldn't quite grasp these other possibilities. It seemed impossible to imagine such distant horizons from within the walls of the wretched tenement apartment. Still, Pradeep had somehow managed to break out of this confining shell. He'd somehow made contact with the outside world, a different world of advanced mechanics and aircraft, a world of foreigners with whom he worked side by side, because they accepted him and saw his potential.

Fishhead sensed his older brother's pride, especially on those evenings when Pradeep came home in his orange, greased overalls, sporting the company's embroidered logo on his sleeve, back, and chest. He'd put good meat on his bones, and carried a pack of Dunhill or Rothmans cigarettes and flint lighter in one hand. Girl-impresser walking up and down Central Avenue. Pradeep wanted success and status more than anything else, and this pursuit pulled him further from his family's troubles. Fishhead noticed, too, the glow in Mom's sunken eyes; she believed she'd found a new ally in her first born. Did Pradeep see himself that way? Did she matter enough to him? Pradeep stayed out more and more; he couldn't see how his parents talked less nowadays, how they appeared to drift apart. Mom and Dad lived in different worlds, with different purposes and consequences.

And yet in a troubling way, Mom still colluded with Dad, still made excuses for his habits, his gambles and inaction. Perhaps she had no power to change things. Fishhead noticed something else about Mom that he'd failed to see before: now and then she mumbled ill things to him about his siblings. She did this whenever he helped her in the kitchen while she cooked, and he thought of this when he walked alone on the road to school, troubled somewhat by it. If she did that to him, he wondered, then did she also speak ill of him with the others, with Pradeep or Prem? He did not know; he had no proof. And yet he trusted her more than he trusted Dad; he believed she wanted him in the kitchen with her when she returned home from work in the dark, carrying her meager selection of ingredients from the marketplace for dinner. It pleased Fishhead to oblige her, so long as the food he helped prepare materialized before him, allowing him to feel and touch it in all its reality: the rice, flour, fish, suet, or vegetables. He saw so little in the pantry.

And so little made it to his plate.

This hellish life. His sunburned face and keen eyes didn't give him away, but the pinch of hunger in his stomach took control of his head. He wanted to steal food; it felt like the most natural thing in the world. If he did it, he told himself, he wouldn't do it for long: just until he started to feel full again. He hated the dried, hardened bread on the kitchen counter, bread swarmed by ants. Dhal and rice did the needful but lacked excitement. And to drink: stale coffee made with chicory, warmed on the stove again and again, its bitterness increasing each time. He shared the coffee with everyone until the pot stood empty. He hated chicory and its nasty, dry flavor, but it could be bought in small packets for a few *paise* at the corner shop, and he could always wash away the bitter taste with water. He tore up the old bread and gave pieces to Lily and little brother, pieces he would have rather eaten himself.

But for now: marbles. He leaned against the rear corner of the five-story tenement building, and he put a hand in the left pocket of his old shorts and there they were: three glass marbles, his cat's eye striker being one of them. He loved the game, and he'd become very good at it, some kind of street champion. No other boy or girl in the labor camp could match his aim. Mid-morning, a casual time; Dad had stepped out, still looking for a job, or not; Mom of course was at the telephone exchange. Kishore played outside, and Fishhead had grown bored in the apartment with Prem and Lily. He'd left Prem in charge, even though lately Prem had taken to roaming aimlessly through the neighborhood, deep in thought, accident prone, talking to himself. Fishhead hoped Lily would behave today.

Barefoot, he hung out at the back of his tenement building. He brought his right foot up along the corner of the building and let it rest behind the other knee. He spat in the dirt and pushed back his straight, uncut black hair when it fell across his forehead and high cheekbones.

He spat again when the wind shifted and the smell of garbage struck his nostrils. About twenty feet or so to the left of him at the back of the building lay piles of trash and debris spread over an area the size of a small compound. He spotted two girls he did not know, and Kishore, all sorting through the trash and looking for things to eat in the heat. A pair of mangy dogs pushed their muzzles deep into the heaps.

"Hey, Kishore, go inside," he said. But little brother pretended not to hear him. Fishhead raised his voice. "Go inside. If I find something, I'll bring it."

"No, I can't wait. I'm staying here," Kishore said. "If you can be here, why shouldn't I?"

"Suit yourself," Fishhead replied.

Soon a cow wandered over the garbage piles; it closed its jaws on waste and a plastic bag. Fishhead spat again. Beads of sweat trickled down his forehead, armpits soaking through his blue striped tee in a matter of minutes; and his uncut hair felt like a bag of wet cement on his head and ears. Hunger rattled his mind and distressed him; it made him too conscious of his surroundings. He could hear boys and girls playing in the dusty courtyard up front. Sounds of an argument between two boys: someone had cheated. Fishhead tapped the three marbles in his left pocket. *Such bad players, but they know how to argue. I could show them a thing or two about marbles.* His need to be somebody. Always that need to be somebody. Anupa would like that about him. He spat in his palms and rubbed them together. Then he wiped his hair down, taking turns with each palm. Should he go play? Not yet. He liked to win. He had other marbles at home, marbles he'd won, but each one seemed as precious to him as an egg. He put a few in his mouth whenever he played, but mostly he liked to feel his cat's eye striker on his tongue and under it.

The wind shifted and the stench of the garbage piles irritated him. He snorted and brought his right foot down, studied his feet, and then he headed for the garbage. He bent down without folding his knees as he began to sort through the rubbish. Fishhead had to be careful of used tins, glass, or rusted materials and nails sticking out from pieces of wood. He could usually find something here among the plastic and paper and kitchen waste, but today he and Kishore had company: the cow and the dogs and the two other children.

Near the bottom of a pile, he found an old ear of dry corn eaten away in the center; it had been roasted on a coal flame, probably by a street vendor. A few rows of kernels remained on the ear at both ends. He brushed away the dirt from it and stepped toward his brother to give him the corn, but Kishore had found some old bread; he was eating it, gnawing around the green spots. So Fishhead turned the ear of corn between his hands in a hurry and ate as if the corn would disappear. Then he heard the startled cry of a girl. He stopped and faced her. She had cut two fingers on the lid of a buried can. The girl panicked. Fishhead flung the eaten ear of corn at the cow's back and approached the young girl; she held the cut fingers in the hem of her dirty skirt but didn't know how to stop the bleeding. A golden yellow skirt patterned with green paisley shapes and black lines.

"Hold her hand up, Kishore," he called out to his brother. "Here, like this." And he reached for the girl's hand, remembering an actress in an older Bollywood movie who played doctor with an actor's cut; he remembered the way the fake blood ran down the man's arm. The blood looked real on the silver screen. Fishhead studied the cut, the girl's hand—fingernails lined with a thick film of dirt that contrasted with her soft and brown skin, and she had a burn mark near the index finger and one on the back of her hand, past the wrist. He wouldn't ask her about it. Did she have others?

"Wait here, don't move," he said, and he ran home. He took the jar of turmeric from the bare kitchen counter and dashed outside to rejoin the girl; she stood still near Kishore, frozen. Fishhead opened the jar and lifted a spoon of the yellow powder from the bottom of the jar.

"What is that?" The girl asked. "*What is that?*"

"*Haldi.* Turmeric, don't you know? Open your hand and keep your fingers straight. Don't bend them." He brought the spoon over the tips of the fingers. "What's your name?"

"Nalini."

"This will sting but it will help your wounds to heal," he said.

"Our mother uses haldi for such things," Kishore added.

Nalini shrieked before Fishhead even moved. "What's that for?" Fishhead asked. "I haven't done anything yet." He sprinkled powder on the two cuts and pressed a finger down on each little turmeric heap. The blood soaked through but the bleeding stopped, and the girl shrieked again and cried some more. Fishhead dusted off the excess turmeric, dropped the spoon back in the jar, and closed it. "Keep it on for a little while," he said to the girl, and then he stepped away.

"Where are you going?" Kishore asked.

"Putting this back," Fishhead said, as he raised the jar of turmeric. "I can't stay here. Make sure to check in on Lily later. She's all alone with Prem."

He returned the turmeric to the kitchen and rinsed his hands at the sink. He wiped his hands on the back of his T-shirt as he stepped out. He reached for the front door to pull it shut, but Prem stopped him.

"Where are you going now? I'd like to go, too."

Fishhead hadn't stopped to think about Prem or Lily's hunger; surely they endured the same misery. He had to go find something to put in his mouth, and maybe he might bring them some leftovers. The garbage piles had been picked over too well. "I really need to go out," he replied. "Can I, please? Stay here with Lily and I'll be back soon, I promise."

"You better," Prem said.

"I will," Fishhead replied. He winked at his brother and shut the door behind him but didn't lock it, and he left the front of the building then approached the group of boys, who had settled into a new game.

"I'll be back later for your marbles," he said to them, and he caught a sign of dismay on their faces. He didn't mean to tease them, but it made him feel better to be good at something. He'd played for real money on occasion, when he had a few coins to pass around; it had occurred to Fishhead that he lived as a gambler like his father, but with a difference, he told himself: he wagered on his own skill. And who in the tenement could challenge him?

He followed the unpaved access road leading out between the municipal wall and the front of his building; he walked past the first two tenement buildings and soon arrived at the busy main thoroughfare. Here the marketplace grew as a series of shacks on both sides of the road, with vendors who sold vegetables, dry and packaged items, and lentils, rice, and beans in tall burlap sacks. Other shops sold fried snacks and potato chips, sweetmeats, oil, fresh yogurt and whey in large shallow vats, and eggs, kites, and bangles. A barbershop stayed busy between a bakery and tea stall. Further down the road to his left, the meat and fish market hummed. The marketplace thrived in all directions, extending south of the train tracks, past the gates, then spreading east to good residential homes and apartments around the station and Central Avenue.

Fishhead wondered what Anupa's mother had planned for lunch. How did they eat at the table? Was Anupa proper or messy? Maybe she liked to use her fingers, Indian style. Or did she use a fork and knife? He did not think she'd invite him to eat, and he knew he would not invite her to the tenement. Out of the question. But he ached for her company.

The abundance of the marketplace tempted Fishhead; his stomach pinched him even more. Crows circled above and descended in small groups to the ground. He wanted that life: to fly around, swoop down, and take whatever suited him. To be as clever as the crow. The marketplace had its fair share of wild chickens and flies, too. A cow or goat here and there. The open area smelled of dry earth, waste, and fresh vegetables, and the odor of burning gasoline rose and fell with the flow of motorized traffic. A few people were milling about, but the marketplace appeared far less busy than in the evenings, when the real crowds came; the pedestrian congestion would make it more difficult to move through the area or flee if he lifted something.

Two trucks pushed their way between cars, taxis, and rickshaws coming from both sides, all honking, honking without pause and for no reason at all. Cyclists moved in groups on both sides of the road. He'd become used to the street noise and chaos, which sounded like a rumble, as if storm clouds had fallen from the sky and settled around him wherever he went.

He approached a female vendor who fried fresh mackerel marinated in a paste made from red chili powder, turmeric, vinegar, and salt. She sat on a mat at the side of the road with an old Primus stove and oil dish in front of her, and a wide metal bowl with the spiced fish next to her spice jars. Fishhead could not resist the smell of frying fish, so he walked up to her and stood there; bubbles of oil rose to the top in a frenzy when she dropped the fish in. The sizzle enticed him too much. Crisp, fried mackerel!

"Want one?" She asked him, chasing away the flies and two stray cats. "This is fresh. Two rupees each."

He smiled but offered no answer as he stood there, pushing down the saliva that surged in his mouth. A moment of torture, although he did not ask for a taste.

"Don't just stand there staring like a beggar," she said. "You'll curse my business."

"I don't have any money," he said.

"Then I don't have any fish. Now go."

"I'll give you marbles for some fish."

She laughed. "And what will your marbles do for me? Shall I hatch them? Go!"

Embarrassed, he crossed the road and made his way towards a vegetable vendor a hundred feet south on the other side. Lost in thought, he caught the odor of hot dung, and he saw a barefoot young boy and girl near him with beaten shallow vessels—down on their knees, they used their bare hands to scoop up the steaming green dung into their vessels. "Get that shit out of here," he said to them. The little girl in her tattered clothes and knotted black hair stood up and gave him a shy smile; she put her hand out in his direction, and Fishhead jumped back in horror. He stood there, elbows near his chest, hands in the air, palms out. The boy and girl moved on behind the white cow, its ribs like clean and straight tire marks. Fishhead spat when the girl lifted the cow's tail and thrust her soiled hand against the rear of the animal to swipe away more dung. He understood this enterprise: her family made dried pancakes from it, which they used or sold as fuel. The fresh dung also made walls for straw huts in villages. He remembered visiting a grade school friend whose mother had plastered the waste across the inside walls of her rustic kitchen. She'd smoothed the dung with flat palms that she moved from side to side and up and down. The odor choked Fishhead, and he struggled with his breathing whenever he'd visited this friend's house; the smell irritated his asthma.

He pushed the image out of his mind and closed his eyes for a moment. Then he approached the vegetable shack, staying close to the low table out front with cucumbers, tomatoes, eggplant, and cauliflower all arranged in small heaps in wide, shallow wicker baskets. Three customers waited to be served. Fishhead moved behind them, reaching for a big tomato that sat in the basket, out of the vendor's sight. He leaned in close and pulled the tomato off the basket and let it drop to the ground; he interrupted the fall with the top of his foot so the tomato wouldn't break. When it came to rest, he kicked it gently out from under the table so that it rolled away, out of the vendor's view.

Then he leaned in and bumped into a female customer to create a distraction. "Sorry, sorry," he said, nodding; the customer looked at him with contempt, then turned back towards the shopkeeper. Fishhead raised a hand. "Do you sell tamarind?" he asked the vendor. "Mother needs tamarind." Meanwhile, he dropped another tomato to the ground the same way as before, tapping it away from under the table with a foot.

"No, I don't. Not this week," the vendor said as he weighed a handheld scale with string beans for a customer. The metal scale rang when the iron measuring weights touched it.

"Okay then, thanks," Fishhead said and walked to the neighboring shop about twelve feet to his right, facing north, then he turned around and made his way to the back of the vegetable shack until he reached the spot where the two tomatoes had come to rest. A rooster, hen, and four chicks came up along the wall just as he approached his catch. "Those are mine. Get lost!" he said and reached down to pick up the tomatoes. He stuck his foot out, and the birds retreated with open wings, clucking in a frenzy. He picked up the tomatoes and headed for the snack shop further north. On the way there, he dropped a tomato into the pocket of his shorts and wiped the other one clean on the sleeve of his tee. He took a generous bite; the tomato burst in his mouth, firm and sweet. Juice ran down the side of his arm as he ate, and he lifted his arm to slurp the wet lines, just as a pair of flies landed to take their share.

The snack shop he liked stood near the end of the line of shops on that side of the road, but first Fishhead had to pass the eunuch-transvestite shack. Early in his life, he'd learned the truth about these *hijras*, who'd had their testicles removed at an early age. They walked through neighborhoods in groups to shower their blessings and request money during auspicious occasions like childbirth, weddings, and formal ceremonies. They showed up uninvited if need be to perform chants and dances, or to bless or beg, and beg they did, but with style. Fishhead had learned something else about these members of the third sex: they also behaved like prostitutes and serviced men to earn a living, sometimes marrying men in secret. They lived as outsiders, and he'd felt like an outsider, too. And yet Fishhead became uneasy around the hijras. He avoided them.

The history of the eunuchs stretched beyond his time. He had studied the epic narrative of the Ramayana, had learned to read and write with this written history of his people. In the epic, Lord Rama had bestowed on the eunuchs a special gift—blessing others—because these outcast males stayed with him when he fled the kingdom of Ayodhya in exile. Mughal kings too once employed them in courts and trusted them to keep secrets, often with severe consequences, sometimes a beheading, if the eunuchs betrayed their kings. The eunuchs fascinated and scared Fishhead, and he stayed out of their way even as he admired their bold ways and attitudes, which reminded him of his own solitary behavior.

He approached their shack which flashed with color: cobalt, green, deep orange, and yellow painted on the outside, like the bright female clothes the males wore—flared skirts, saris, and blouses with tight sleeves down to their elbows—and heavy costume jewelry, their long dark hair, the strong makeup, and their bold, provocative conversations and song. Skirts hiked up, hands on their crotches. Three adult eunuchs sat on the steps of the shack with a child among them. An adult braided the child's long black hair. Fishhead looked down as he passed; he did not want to catch their attention. *Chakka, chakka, chakka!* They clapped in an open-handed way that suggested their non-gendered status. Fishhead's heart raced and he began to hurry past the shack, but it seemed as if they followed him with their stares. He became unsteady now, weaker.

"Hey kid, come here," an adult eunuch said. "Come get my blessings, kid."

"Let me sing and dance for you," the child, about ten years old, began. Then it rose from the adult's lap like a dream and moved toward Fishhead, singing. "Let me stroke your cheek and take your hand. Won't you dance with me? Sing and dance with me. Give me one small victory." They clapped together with flattened palms, getting louder, adults engaging now in song. *Chakka, chakka, chakka!*

"No, no thank you," Fishhead said, embarrassed, his voice faltering.

"Come get our blessings, kid. No harm done. We won't curse you either."

"Please, no. Don't curse me, "he replied. And suddenly, the image of the colorful group flooded his vision. Bangles began chinking, bangles chinking, glinting, and voices purring. Skirts went up and down before him, up and down, seducing him. He imagined a thousand arms like the bodies of hairline-thin dark snakes twisting and luring him toward the shack. His knees went limp and he stumbled on a small quarry stone, which shot out from under him like a ricocheting marble during a neighborhood game. He caught himself and quickened his pace; he wished he had wings so he could disappear into the trees like crows.

Past the shack he became bolder, apprehension thrusting recklessness into his heart like a dagger. He soon came to the egg store, three shops down from the snack shop, but the owner had stepped away, perhaps to take a piss nearby. A rusting bicycle stood straight back on its hind stand, too near the doorway and in front of egg cages that almost reached Fishhead's shoulders. He whistled. Eggs in wire and wood cartons stacked high on the bicycle's luggage carrier, two feet tall. A tight mesh of rope held the cartons together. Fishhead thrust his right hand between the rope mesh, showing great care. He freed two eggs and went for a third when he felt a hand grip his shoulder. Fishhead froze and broke into a cold sweat.

"What do you think you're doing?" A thin bearded man asked. The owner. He had a slight limp on his right leg and wore a cream shirt over a plaid loincloth.

Fishhead didn't stop to reason. "I'm dying of hunger," he said. The grip relaxed, ever so slightly, and Fishhead broke away.

He made a dash behind the shacks, where he'd be out of sight; his feet kicked up a cloud of dust, and the marbles knocked against each other in his pocket. "Stop, stop! You shameless rascal...thief, stop him!" the man shouted. "*Budmaash! Beysharam!*"

The foot traffic in the marketplace came to a standstill, as customers looked for the cause of the warning. But the street traffic had picked up, and rickshaws, cars, and trucks moved with horns blaring and motors surging, sputtering. The man's cries fell away. Fishhead ran as fast as his legs carried him, careful that he didn't press the eggs too tightly in his hands. He wound between shops to distract and confuse any voluntary allies of the shouting egg-man. The bearded bastard! The shouting egg-man man did not know what hunger meant. No matter, Fishhead would not get caught.

He'd seen a young thief last year, a boy who'd plucked a customer's package of raw shrimp right out of the woman's hand and bolted from the fish house right into the dazzling sunlight of the open market. Vendors had shouted after the boy, alerting everyone in the crowded marketplace, but he didn't get far before a shopper tripped him. When the female customer caught up with the subdued boy, she swore and snatched her shrimp package from his hand, and she kicked his leg while he lay on the dusty ground, which prompted a girl and two adults in the encircling crowd to do the same. The girl stepped on the thief's right hand, making the boy scream. Fishhead stood in that circle, watching in amazement at justice play itself out. Such a commotion. The young thief begged for forgiveness and got to his feet then hobbled away in shame; someone shoved him from the back and threatened to fetch the police, and they came minutes later then took the boy away, prodding him on and smacking him with their wooden *lathis*.

The very thought of the incident made Fishhead lift his own feet high in the air now, as if he were a thoroughbred at Mahalaxmi.

He ran fast, disbelieving his own speed. Don't get caught, he thought. If Mom and Dad find out... He'd have none of that. No more. As if the shrimp thief boy wasn't enough, how could he forget Mrs. D'Cruz, his math teacher in seventh grade? Fishhead had snatched a boy's hot fried snack and eaten it near the cafeteria, and she'd received word of the incident; during her class, she'd called him to the front and raised her voice up high and said, "Robbing another child's food, eh?" She'd pinched his right ear lobe before the whole class, so hard he'd cried out: "No teacher! No teacher! I'm sorry, teacher!" She'd squeezed both his earlobes like ant-bites as she stood behind him, until he got up up on his toes in extreme pain. "No shame! No shame at all!" A few of the other boys giggled. "What, you don't have enough to eat at home then? I'll speak to your father immediately!" Fishhead had almost pissed in his pants. "No teacher, please don't!" She hit him behind his thighs repeatedly with her wooden architectural ruler, making sure he came to tears; and Dad pulled his belt on him the next day at home. And yet Fishhead hadn't stopped; and so it continued. Sometimes dad used his fist or the back of his hand, but Fishhead liked the stick better; it felt like the principal's oiled cane. But if he got caught now...if the police were involved...

Fishhead's legs grew tired and the air went out of his lungs. At last, he stopped. Panting, he felt an urgent need for air, as an explosion went off inside him. He'd reached an unused metal and stone junkyard with a broken gate a quarter mile north of the marketplace. Somewhere near the quarry.

He felt a wetness at the side of his thigh. The tomato had split open in his pant pocket, and when he reached down to get it, his nervous tense fingers pierced the flesh of the fruit and caused the juices to spurt out. With his right hand he took the messy ball out of his wet pocket and tore the flesh with his teeth, somewhat frustrated by his situation and a bit mad at himself, too. He ate, his breath in gasps, now subsiding. Finally he looked at the two eggs in the other hand. Still intact, good. What a mess that might have been...

In the quiet junkyard he approached a heap of used steel pieces and two painted doors that belonged to different cars. Too hot to touch. So he sat down there under the noon sun with the eggs in his hand. He took the end of his tee and wiped down a flat and smooth area of one car door, all black in color, which belonged to a Premier Padmini taxi once. The door burned. He spat on the painted metal and the saliva dried up seconds later. He spat a few times again and wiped the area clean with another part of his tee, and he pulled his head back to hide from the emerging sounds and squeaks, because his hands rubbed and banged on the door. Now he started to cry and couldn't stop the tears. He didn't know when his next meal would be, but for now, this is all he had. He cracked one egg and dropped its contents on top of the clean area and heard it sizzle and cook; he threw away the wet shell, and watched flies settle on it. He punched the yolk with an index finger and guided the yellow liquid so it wouldn't run on the surface. His finger burned but he paid it no attention. The smell of the frying egg pinched his hunger more, and he couldn't wait. He found a small stone with a flat edge, and he wiped the stone clean with his tee. He scraped off the edges of the egg with the stone and turned the center over to sear it on the door, and then he dropped the sharp stone near him and rolled up the fried egg in haste and brought it up to his mouth. First Fishhead blew on the egg to cool it, but then he ate in a hurry, pushing it with both hands into his mouth and giving himself no pause to breathe in air. He reached for the stone again and scraped off parts of the egg still stuck to the door, and he ate the little pieces.

Then he broke the second egg on the hot door but jumped when a developing embryo fell out of the shell and landed on the dark painted surface. The embryo resembled the yellow cat's eye in his favorite marble, his striker. "Damn you!" he said. "Damn you for being born!" He stared at the embryo, unable to move and unwilling to eat now. "You deserve better," he added.

He scraped the edges of the egg whites that had begun to cook and he nudged the embryo with the flat edge of his stone until it dropped to the dirt. Then he stepped away to a pair of chest-high, fiery paper flower bushes at the edge of the fenced yard, and he pressed down on the ground with his feet. The ground felt dry and hot. He found a short piece of rebar and another sharp rock with a point. He began to dig a hole and remove the dirt, but it took him longer than he hoped. When he reached a gap about as deep as his open hand, he made his way back to the dirt-covered embryo and gently scooped it onto the flat side of the rock. Fishhead returned to the bushes, got down on his haunches, and let the embryo drop into the hole. He buried the egg with the dirt and filled the hole. The glaring sun: its white hot light dug through the sockets of his eyes and pressed against his spine. Turning away as if in darkness, he got up from his haunches and tried to regain his balance, but two marbles fell out of his pocket. Fishhead rubbed his open hands on the dirt to remove any hint of the egg and he patted them against each other to get rid of the dirt. He wiped his hands on his shorts then checked the marbles. They hadn't chipped, good. He put the marbles back in his left pocket, and he picked up the sharp rock he'd used to make the hole. He threw the rock high into the air; it made a wide arc and sank into the shallow valley in front of him. He saw the far edge of the large pond in the valley but did not hear the rock drop into the pond. He turned away.

I can tell you this, dear reader: the perils of hunger strike all corners of the world, pressing deep into your inner cities, and reaching far into the darkest woods, across those stretches of lands, borderless and painted by heat, by snow, mountains, and rainwater. I see how your cities breathe and shriek with new webs of enterprise, awakened to the ageless wisdom of the skies, but designed to ignore those of the *lesserworld* and keep them out of view, keep them wanting. If hunger drums desperation, then desperation often spins wicked rhythms of thievery. Fishhead does not pause to consider his immorality or the imposition on the vendor, because he spars with his want in this Republic. No one is far from reaching such states of urgency. What would you do in his situation? I ask you. Are *you* hungry? Fishhead has nothing. Are his actions right or wrong? Where does one draw the line? Is his drive to steal food more criminal than the thievery perpetrated at the highest levels of business and government? I am aware, I am very aware. The compendium holding this story of Fishhead contains much information from research and field studies of hunger's children and rapacity, and I urge you to read it and find ways to improve your response to need and your empathy in the world.

Fishhead would do again what he did in the market, I assure you; only this time he'd choose a different place, naturally.

And now Fishhead noticed some activity at the other end of the junkyard; he left it and made his way home by taking an unfamiliar path far from the egg shop, where no one would recognize him. He thought of the boys and their game of marbles. He would join them, but the image of the child eunuch dancing and singing and clapping before him flashed in his mind again. Her words, the child's words as she sang to him. He couldn't stop them from forming on his lips while he walked on. He too wished for one small victory.

Back at home, he spotted three different boys playing a game of marbles at the back of the sixth tenement building. He didn't know two of them, but had played with the third one, Pankaj, before—a small, chubby fellow with short hair and bad skin. Pankaj came from the building which overlooked the garbage piles. He'd lost the color of his skin in areas around his face, and on his fingers, arms, and the back of his knees. He had large eyes and an eager smile that made him seem willing to play with anyone.

"Are these your friends?" Fishhead asked.

"No," Pankaj said, "but they've been here before."

"Shall I join you?" Fishhead said to the group. Between them, a dozen or more marbles sat inside a roughly marked triangle in the dirt.

Pankaj looked at the two boys as if to ask them. He did not open his mouth.

"We're in a game. Are you any good?" the older boy asked Fishhead, and he pushed some dirt with his right heel. This boy had an edge to him; he seemed rougher and taller.

Fishhead shrugged and looked away. Then he spat on the ground twice, taking his time.

"Do you have any marbles?" the boy asked.

"I have marbles," Fishhead said.

"I don't see you with them."

"Here they are." Fishhead fetched them from his pocket. "This one, this one's my striker. It goes with me everywhere." He showed his yellow cat's eye striker.

"What are you going to do with two marbles then? Get lost, punk."

"I can play. I'm good," Fishhead said.

"Oh yeah? We'll see about that," the other boy said.

"He's good," Pankaj replied, fidgeting.

"Oh, I'm scared," the taller boy answered with a smirk. "Show us how good you are then. We'll each put two marbles into the triangle and start a new game. What's there to lose, ha-ha-ha?"

Fishhead never thought much about losing his marbles, only his name. He became light on his toes, eager to begin. The tomato and egg helped his focus and gave him back some strength. He didn't respond but kept a straight face, visualizing the triangle area and marbles, and the approach of his strike.

"I'll set it up," Pankaj said, as the three of them removed their extra marbles to start the new game. He let Fishhead add his share, then he arranged the eight marbles inside a new triangle he'd drawn on the dirt after wiping out the old one.

"Okay, you strike first, bigshot," the taller boy said, raising his chin at Fishhead and putting his hands on his hips like a film star. He wore a torn red bandana.

Fishhead nodded but held back a smile. He wouldn't allow himself to lose a single round. A champion on his poor street, at least. He liked the sweet taste of success like the sweet smell of dirt, the dry dirt his feet kicked up in the air as he positioned himself low to the ground to take his shot. He went down on his haunches, with the tenement building behind him, its damp and molding exterior showing the effect of the monsoons. He tossed the cat's eye marble into his mouth to clean it, to make it easier to grip between his fingers. He did this whenever he played with the other boys; marbles in his mouth calmed his nerves; also he did not care to speak unnecessarily, as other boys often did. The sun pressed down like a spectator and Fishhead paid it no attention. He moved the marble in his mouth with his tongue and tasted it like candy. The marble knocked against his teeth and the sound echoed in the cave of his mouth, sending a sensation of wild anticipation through his body. And spit came up in his mouth as he focused on the hand-marked triangle on the ground.

"What's the delay, bigshot?" the taller boy asked, getting closer to Fishhead. "Got cold feet then, or are you just acting?"

The eight marbles stood like wordless soldiers gathered near each other, shiny and colorful, and one beaten and cracked. But Fishhead wouldn't want the beaten ones. Losers kept broken marbles. He didn't know who put that one in, but he knew it did not belong to him. He set his eyes on the triangle, the size of a small ruled notebook, and he leaned forward between his knees, arms in front, hands in formation to strike but not quite yet. He pushed the cat's-eye marble out of his mouth, and he turned the marble against his sleeve to dry it. Just the right size and weight: like a gumball. A too-big striker kept him from slinging it far enough through the triangle; a too-small striker did not have the weight to knock the others out of the space there. The marble striker might even break apart on contact. Fishhead placed his left thumb on the ground and held the marble against the tip of his outstretched middle finger with the other hand. He didn't look up at the boys who watched him closely.

"Hope he misses," one of the others said as he took aim. Fishhead paused. The boy mumbled, "It'll give us a chance, then we can show him a thing or two." Fishhead paused again; he gave the fellow a stare but said nothing. The taller boy scraped the dirt with his heel and Pankaj swung his hand in the air behind him. Fishhead ignored the distractions and lined up his shot, and then he pulled his right middle finger back as far as it would go with the yellow cat's eye striker at the end of it.

He released the striker, his finger pushing forward with a tight springing action. The marble cut a straight line through the air like a bullet then arced, and Fishhead smiled. Just like a MiG jet fighter, that sound. Those curfews during the Indo-Pakistan war he couldn't forget. Just like that.

The cat's-eye marble struck the first ball of glass near him in the triangle, and the force hit the other marbles, splitting the group and spreading the marbles beyond the triangle in a wide circle. His eyes lit up. Holy Mother of God! Fucking crystals! The marble near the far edge of the triangle flew to a distance of five feet and stopped in the dirt. Only one marble stayed inside the triangle, and it had chipped. The three boys sighed and swore and jumped back in astonishment, unable to touch the marbles. Rules of the game, you know. Rules.

"The bastard did it!" The taller boy snarled.

"Yea, sister-fucker, you talked too soon. You talk big," Fishhead said then spat, and he got up to collect his loot.

"What did you call me?" The tall one asked. "Hey, what did you say?"

"You heard what I said. *But I won*," Fishhead said. "I won fair and square. I don't think you want to play with me." He cleaned his cat's eye striker and put it in his mouth. *That should teach them a lesson*. His body went hot inside, light like air filling emptiness in his stomach. He pushed aside the chipped marble in the triangle that he didn't want, and Pankaj scooped it up, smiling as he picked up the chipped marble and closed his fingers around it.

"Want to play another game?" Fishhead asked, tossing Pankaj a good marble; it fell to the ground, and Pankaj scooped that up, too. Pleased, that boy with bad skin. It made Fishhead feel good. He didn't worry about the other boys. Nothing but strangers to him. They did not belong here.

"I told you he was good," Pankaj said, stepping back like a weakling while the others shuffled off.

Fishhead wiped the good marbles clean and stuffed them in his pocket while he stood over the empty triangle. "So you want to play another game?" He asked. He felt the weight of the marbles in his pocket; they'd tear through if he moved too quickly.

Then a sudden movement behind him: a heavy foot landed on his back, just above his right buttock.

"Ughh!" The sound in his throat broke like a brick underfoot, broke like a tricked brick. Fishhead fell forward and choked on his cat's eye striker. He swallowed the marble hard as his body plummeted. He turned his face to the right so he wouldn't break his nose when he fell, and he met the earth with a thud and drone that smothered his heart and stifled him. He moaned, and blood rushed to his eyes, made them scream for hell. Waves of fury pulling him towards a barbaric sun. His attackers came for him, kicking wildly, kicking...

"Stop, please stop!" Pankaj cried. "What are you doing? What—?" They pushed him out of the way.

Fishhead tried to turn on the ground, but the boy kicked him on the back of his folded knee, and then Fishhead felt the kick of the other boy connect with his right shoulder. They kicked him hard in the back over and over and over while he lay there on his side shielding his face and head with his right arm. His left arm locked under his weight, turned away like when he fell running with little brother Kishore. The last kick landed in his gut now, and Fishhead cried out. His left ear and cheek pressed to the ground. His frame ripped with pain—pain, as if he'd eaten shards of glass— and his mouth went dry and coarse with dirt that coated his lips and entered his gums. The dirt smelled sweet.

The boys sprinted off. Pankaj stood there, his feet stuck to the ground, and then he came around and stood before Fishhead. He smacked his left heel on the ground again and again, unable to accept what had just happened and overwhelmed by it. Several more minutes passed, then silence. In the quiet, flies buzzed around Fishhead, around his bruises and cardinal milk. A cow mooed, the bell of a cycle went off, a woman called her child, leaves rustled in a nearby bush under the weight of a lizard. The sound of his own desperate breathing, and Pankaj's footsteps.

"Who are they?" Fishhead said, hurting, his voice just above a whisper. He opened his burning eyes. "Who are those bastards, you know them?" He tried to move but his body resisted.

"I don't know them, I swear!" Pankaj stepped back. "They're not my friends. They just came here once before and we played, I swear." Then he turned and walked away, hands on his head. He hit his head repeatedly to show his regret.

"Ma…Ma," Fishhead moaned as he lay there. "They really got me, Ma."

The smell of frying *pakoras* wafting through the air caught his attention, and he shut his eyes. His stomach ached from that final kick, and from the new indigestible snack: the cat's eye striker. He couldn't eat, not now, but he could smell, and although he often craved mackerel, their crisp fish heads, he loved the taste and texture of fried chickpea batter and onions. The smell pinched his stomach and made him ache deeply. A pariah dog glanced over at him, started to trot over.

Fishhead struggled for a second to get up, but then just lay back down, his breath held inside an acre of time. He closed his eyes, his mind drifted: *Is this my fate? The tenement's a shoemaker's hammer. It beats me down, hammers me like a tack. I will never leave it. Fate, you don't want me to leave this place, you don't. This is how you reply when I call your name. You send a pariah dog to sniff me while I lay here in pain.* He blinked. He looked straight into the dog's monstrous snout, so close that its hairs touched his face. He felt heat: Destiny's curiosity checking his condition. The creature blew out its nostrils near his chin, smelled the rest of him, and then scampered away. Fishhead let out a sigh. He could see what the chickens saw, what the rooster and hen saw, and the fallen tomatoes, too. This world, always bigger and amazing from a new angle. He could go somewhere else, he could. But for now, he knew only *here*.

Fantasies

The ground remains pure, I insist, a respectable place, and there is nothing wrong with it at all, because it feels and moves as you do.

Fishhead has touched it with his skin, his lips, his blood. Is he no different from the countless other hungry children across the globe? How does he pray for his want? How does he pray, if he prays at all? The god his mother entreats is in my benign nature. Fishhead calls on Destiny, and I answer him by means indistinct to his comprehension; these are my ways, which the human mind cannot fathom or predict. He has faith in something. Faith is good. I hope to show him the depths of humility, which is my benign nature. I am amorphous, the impulse of a train, the sea, your country's leaders, an equation, or a mangy dog, but always the spirit of your waking world, always near you and into you, wishing for your contract with me. I have no constraints with the *instant* and keep no hard schedules. When you call on fate, you believe I am reachable, just as Fishhead also believes I am reachable, so know that I reside in the vibrations of time and in the movement of souls. There are galaxies, and there is this, your earth. Both are fated to remain hinged on each other.

What is Destiny to you? What does fate mean to you, and do you pause to consider it? Do you think of me often, and under what circumstances exactly? Am I a probe in your conscience, a driver of your actions, a surrogate of your temptations and ambitions? Do you consider me your ally or antagonist? You would like to speak to me directly, I know, just as Fishhead does, because you believe I am the answer to life's outcomes. You believe I have the answers, just as Fishhead speaks to me through the doorway of his dreams and thoughts, hoping for answers, expecting engagement with me, and with the girl he visits in his need.

He went to her, seeking comfort and tenderness. Where else might he find consolation? He grimaced when she reached up to touch the side of his face near his bruised left cheekbone, the area that met the dirt hard while the boys attacked him. The skin had scraped off there and on his forehead, above the eye. Fishhead turned his face away, but Anupa's gentleness calmed him, fingers urging him to face her. Why, he wondered, had he been so arrogant with those boys? It meant something, although he couldn't say what. He did not want them in his tenement, and perhaps thought that he could stop them with his power.

"Hey," she whispered, while they stood on her open verandah in front. "What are you thinking? I am here."

"Just...going over it, again and again. I can't help it," he said.

"It's over. And you are bruised," Anupa replied. She pulled him close and kissed his cheek. "I'm glad you came."

He put his head on her shoulder, his mind turning still. Why didn't he just walk away from the game? The eruption of words, a hot angry molten torrent that sprung forth from nowhere and scorched all in its path. Clearly, those boys had caused it somehow. And he'd *had* to respond that way. Life on the street. He had to preserve his self-respect, even—especially—in that lowliest of places. He hated the tenement, hated his life. If he saw them again…(Again, the fiery rage. He imagined: pulling back the slingshot, seeing the marble smack into flesh. Or: smashing a bottle, slashing at faces with the broken neck. Cutting and cutting and cutting.)

"I won't ask you how it happened," Anupa said.

He smiled, nodded, grateful he didn't have to explain. "My mother used a clear ointment," he replied, after a pause. "She refused turmeric."

"For obvious reasons, no doubt. You have a nice Mom." She ran a hand along his back. "I would offer a Belladonna plaster, but it looks like you have one on already."

"Yes."

"Oh, you poor fellow." Anupa held his chin, then pushed the hair away from his face. She pulled him closer until their hips touched.

Fishhead did not resist. His body felt numbed by his bruises. She leaned against the gray stone balustrade, pulling her torso back slightly, hips pushed out and mouth open, smiling, aware of his pain. The day's heat pressed down from all sides, and although he enjoyed standing there, he wished she didn't try so hard. And yet he could not resist her arms around his waist. Pain spiked through him. She, soft as a cloud. The fragrant scent on her skin and coconut oil in her hair lulled him into a state of acceptance and cooperation. He knew why he came here, his reasons stacked up in his head like a street vendor's overflowing cart stacked on its four bicycle wheels. Her acts of affection came without conditions, like waves, and he merely had to ride them, unquestioning but conscious of every decision and action. He reached up and caressed her neck, shoulder, and arms. They kissed, embraced. She returned to his bruises.

"So sad, na? Did you get into a fight?"

He nodded.

"You don't have to give me the details."

"It hurts. They kicked me hard."

She moved her fingers across the plaster on his back. "You poor thing. I'm so sorry."

"I am Don Quixote," he said. "I deserve what I got."

She pressed her lips to his and expanded her stance as she pulled him in tighter. "Then I am your Dulcinea. Realizing your fantasies."

"Your hair is golden—" he began, and she chuckled. "Your rainbow eyebrows and rosy cheeks, your alabaster neck."

She smacked him on his left arm. "All untrue! But thanks, really."

He reached down and put his mouth at the base of her neck, and touched his cheek against the side of her face. Received her warmth. Anupa, so soft and smooth. He let her magic work on him. He wanted to undress her there, on the verandah, but knew that she would never allow it, bold as she'd become under the cover of trees in the evening's emerging darkness. The faint street lamp just beyond the front gate and its six-foot-high walls. Her mother, watchful and within earshot! Anupa tightened her arms around him and held him in a precious lock, and his back ached. He squirmed from his bruises.

She made no demands and spoke little of love, but the closeness declared this love. It appeared impossible, unreal. The labor camp, with all its filth and poverty, a life Fishhead knew he would never paint for her. She never asked about it either, as if she knew. As if she actually knew.

He told himself to stop worrying about the impossibility of things, stop worrying about this impractical intimacy. He'd give it a try, give it all he had, even if it did not work out in the end. Anupa grabbed his attention, like soccer grabbed his interest over cricket. Intimacy cost him little to nothing; it required little in the way of gear or special equipment. And what he needed, he could scrounge.

(The school had meager supplies; the soccer shoes in the bin always seemed to be a half size too big, or too small. But Fishhead did not complain, even when his feet hurt. He liked being goalkeeper; he remembered Dad's inspiring stories of his own high school soccer days in that position. Dad sported a scar on his right chest that had healed years ago; he'd said his jersey button had cut him after he'd dived for the ball during a save. Dodging three defenders, the opposing center forward kicked the ball hard from within the penalty area, and Dad had caught the ball against his chest. Fishhead liked imagining his father as a hero.)

Fishhead never talked about the shame. In these moments of closeness and intimacy with Anupa, he anticipated questions about his family, as if she had a right to know now. Did she think she could claim him? He wondered.

Fishhead followed her with his eyes as she retrieved The Man of La Mancha from the living room, then turned on the overhead light on the verandah. She led him outside, left the door ajar, shut the screen door, and eased herself down against the balustrade with the book open in her hands. Fishhead sat beside her, touching, their legs stretched out in front of them.

Anupa's mother came to the door a little while later and asked if she could use the record player. Fishhead said he didn't mind, and Anupa agreed, but she asked her mother to leave the door ajar. Soon Patsy Cline began serenading them with "Sweet Dreams of You." They fell out of reality and into the world of knight-errant fantasies.

Spared You Another Day

He couldn't grasp his place or purpose in the world yet. Getting there seemed possible in due time, but time did not move fast enough. What could he do to please his mother? Pradeep had his mechanic's job at the airport; Fishhead needed something like that. His wish for adulthood screamed with the silent heat of baking sand, and he ached for an honest enterprise to burn his fuel better. Earn a decent living. For as much as he enjoyed tenement marble matches and soccer games at school, neither promised a profitable future. Ambition grew inside him cautiously, tendrils of energy circling around stones and debris, wild tendrils moving between monsters and stolen food. What should he be doing?

His father had felt the same things at the same age, in those tenuous months and days of Indian independence. (Balan George had also shared in India's post-Colonial resentments; he'd shared the citizens' common cause and acted his rebel self, while secretly wishing for a touch of all things English within his reach. Meanwhile the country broke apart, casting Hindu against Muslim in bloody feud after feud. Rage, hate, massacre, death.) Fishhead knew he was asking the same questions. And yet he desperately feared making the same mistakes.

Pradeep seemed content. How had he managed that? What fire burned within him? That determination had paid off, Fishhead admitted; he wanted to believe a similar fire lived inside him; he searched his heart for it, but found nothing. Such emptiness. He had Anupa, but she had no knowledge of his situation. Fishhead would not ask for her help. No, he could not. His fight, his worry. So what if he'd never had formal training? Neither had Pradeep.

Fishhead longed for answers about his future. An average student, he showed no outstanding skill; he kept getting better at soccer, and had a fair competence in literature and art. The Western pop and rock songs Anupa and her mother played—they moved him. They were so different from Dad's old classical records; Fishhead felt drawn to these songs. Could he sing and write that way? Possibly—but he lacked the means to pursue a musical career. He had no direction or guidance. How could he know for sure where his strengths and skills lay? Plus, he'd have to support his mother.

He longed for a sense that fate meant to take him somewhere out of the tenement. His range on fire, a heart in embers, and lives suffocating under duress; it seemed apparent that his family's condition would get worse before it improved. He hoped to change this course—but how?

(If you say fate has a plan for him, you are right; my vision marks Fishhead. His blood carries every facet of his blighted lineage, the good and bad, the cursed, his father's talents and weaknesses, and his mother's diligence and gullibility, the same impressionable characteristics that keep him from shoveling his way clear of the dense terrain of this exploding city.)

What was stopping him? Fishhead asked, wondered. He did not know everything. What was stopping him? He asked himself again and again. This slow, cutting movement through life,

Fishhead swore, and Destiny not answering, keeping prosperity and love down; Destiny dragging prosperity's cross through the dust and rubbish of the tenement block. The sun, he insisted, shined here for heat alone, never for flight and freedom from this darkest of places. It shined on Anupa's home too, but not the same way, not the same.

Destiny, Fishhead said with increasing frustration. Destiny kept him down.

(And I agree, this is my wish for him. I hold him back. I make sure his life moves in a direction unimaginable to him and despite his intentions. His life's path *is* in my hands, as is yours, dear reader. I need Fishhead elsewhere, far away from all that he desires and knows; I need him for interactions with other cultures, with experiences occurring at a different time and juncture which I cannot reveal now. But how will he grow and understand? I send him reminders, as now, but he fails to notice them. A mind like yours and Fishhead's can demand the world, because the mind travels as far as it wants to go, and the more it learns, the more it makes the body follow. But Fishhead's trust in his mind and its fascinations isn't sufficient, and will never be sufficient without the gifts of his pleading soul, which draws him into the subterranean depths of my galactic empathy, its caresses cocooning him away from gravity's forces. Sight unseen. I prevail there in the cellularity knitted by time and matter, and by the beguiling séance domiciled in my agelessness. I assure you, something good comes out of all that he forgoes. Fishhead keeps his mother's welfare in mind at all times. I am pleased.)

Mom didn't have much confidence in Dad's art, or in the little income from the handmade cards he'd created, or in his newest interest: commercial art for the black and white newspaper advertising market. These ventures drained the family's resources, she insisted, and they didn't justify the time and energy Fishhead and his siblings spent to support the work. Mom wanted her children to enjoy their summers.

So Fishhead found himself spending less time outside playing marbles, and more playing soccer. He felt good when he put on his borrowed jersey, gloves, shorts, high socks, cleats, and gloves. And he thought he should earn this feeling. So he practiced hard to be a reliable goalkeeper. He hoped Anupa might notice him in a match or two, but he did not tell her about his games; he knew he'd be ashamed if they lost.

But his team did well. Even Dad suddenly seemed interested in his performance. Fishhead let Dad come to the grounds to watch him train; he choked down his dislike and took tips and guidance from the man. And Dad made good suggestions; Fishhead learned how to anticipate the ball's movement by the position and angle of the striker's foot. "Keep your eyes on the ball always!" Dad said. "Attack the ball; don't let it attack you! Stay on your toes and keep moving!"

The team's successes helped sprout a renewed interest in the sport by younger schoolboys, and Fishhead trained two upcoming goalkeepers. But he still wore the school's over-used gear. And when he visited the social club, in jeans that were torn and patched up from repeated use, he still felt the same. Some evenings, he walked home alone; others, he saw Anupa. She came to the social club often, but not every evening, and he wondered what she did on the other nights. He never dropped in on her mother unannounced, although he had a sense she would never turn him away. She never pressed him for a chance to see his home or meet his family; and he remained surprised and grateful for her reluctance.

One evening in midsummer, Dad unexpectedly brought Lily to the soccer field just as practice got underway. Dad did things as and when he pleased, without informing anyone beforehand. Fishhead thought he'd get used to it. But why come with Lily unless he did not wish to leave her alone at home? Fishhead didn't entirely mind; after a while, he felt pleased by his new audience. He stayed focused on his training, and received Dad's occasional tips from a distance: "Stay on your toes! Don't be lazy!" "Keep your eyes on the ball!" "Anticipate its arc in the air!"

Then an hour into the training, Dad came around to the goalposts with Lily. "Watch your sister. I'll be home later," he said, and left. Yet another awkward surprise, but Fishhead did not protest; he urged Lily to sit on the grass behind the net for the final hour of practice. Every few minutes he turned and checked to make sure she hadn't wandered off from boredom or curiosity.

Afterwards, Fishhead made Lily wait near the social club gate while he shed his practice gear and washed up at the faucet outside the building. Then he changed into his torn jeans and shirt, a process which took several minutes. He tried to ignore the sounds of chatter and table tennis coming from inside.

They began walking to the front when a familiar "Hey!" made him turn. Anupa had come outside, all smiles. She looked at Lily then asked Fishhead, "So aren't you going to introduce us then?"

"Of course! Anupa, this is my sister, Lily." He'd hoped to avoid such an encounter, but fate thrives despite his control. Dad's selfishness weighed on his mind suddenly; he'd brought Lily along, then abandoned her like yesterday's newspaper. What comes next? Fishhead wondered. Lily inviting Anupa over for tea and biscuits? Small talk in their ugly home? Never! Fishhead preferred death.

"You are a beautiful girl!" Anupa offered. "Your brother never said anything about you." She smacked Fishhead on the arm, and he took her correction without protest.

"Thank you," Lily giggled, tongue-tied, inexperienced at receiving compliments. "You know my brother?" She wore a light mid-calf skirt and a yellow short-sleeved blouse with a pattern of soft lines. She walked in flip-flops.

"You could say so. We—" Anupa began.

"We meet at church activities occasionally," Fishhead said.

Anupa got the hint. "Yes, we do." She looked at Fishhead and winked.

"I didn't know he had such good taste in picking friends," Lily said. She studied Anupa then touched her long black and shiny hair, and Anupa did not pull back.

"That's nice of you, na?" Anupa's voice rose at the end. She smiled.

"I owe you ice cream for that," Fishhead said to his sister.

"None for me then?" Anupa asked.

"Sure! We should do that," Fishhead said, quite unsure.

He changed the subject to soccer practice and homework as they continued towards the train station, and soon Anupa split off with a pleasant goodbye. Lily did not invite her home. Good girl.

Fishhead would buy little sister ice cream, he would. Just as soon as he had a job.

At dinner, Lily blurted out: "Fishhead has a girlfriend. I met her, too. She's beautiful! Her name is Anupa."

"She's just a friend," he retorted, with a glare.

The family sat crosslegged on the floor facing each other, the jute mat and newspapers holding few stark dishes before them— rice, dhal, a capsicum and tomato dish, lime pickle. In the stale and dimly lit apartment, Lily's announcement stung; he did not know what to say. He'd never been happier than with Anupa; and yet he felt betrayed by Lily. He glanced at his parents but avoided eye contact; he sensed his father stir. Disapproval? Fishhead could not be sure. Best to sit and wait.

They finished their dinner in silence.

Fishhead started making posters for club events, using poster paint provided by the school. He urged Prem to join him; together they made eye-catching Pop-Art posters for upcoming summer events: dance nights, fetes, ping pong matches, and fundraisers. Art and music posters from the West inspired Fishhead, and he imitated them and learned from them. He enjoyed the work, and made a few extra friends too.

"You'll never earn a living as an artist," Mom said. "Why can't you become a doctor or engineer? Wasting your time chasing after a girlfriend when you don't know your hand from your mouth yet. See how well Pradeep is doing? Follow his footsteps, but don't be selfish like him. And don't be like your father; *that* will take you nowhere."

"Pradeep gets to work with foreigners," Fishhead said. "He's going to be a big-shot man. He can afford a girlfriend. Isn't that what you're saying?"

"It's what I'm saying," Eshma replied. "Finish school and do something with your life. You're failing in Marathi and math." She resumed her kitchen chores.

Fishhead earned his place as lead goalkeeper on the soccer team not long after he turned sixteen. Ambition brought him acceptance with his teammates, just as it did for Pradeep with his co-workers at Manitowoc Helicopters. Now came his chance to prove his worth on the soccer field. His team practiced a lot and played several matches against area schools throughout the monsoons, come rain or shine. The team moved quickly past the knock-out rounds and soon advanced into the semifinals, eventually winning a city-wide victory over favorite Don Bosco High School in the finals.

"You are a star," Anupa said when he stopped by to see her at home a few days after the win. She offered him a Fanta and a slice of yellow cake. "You've made the school proud. You should be proud of yourself."

"Thank you! But I'm still no good at ping pong," he said, laughing.

"Well, I'm no good at soccer," she replied.

The team earned its place on the map, a recognized name in the city. They'd come home with a large shield which the principal kept with great pride in his office, after first showing it off to the teachers and the entire student body during the morning general assembly in the quadrangle. In appreciation, the high school funded a two-week vacation, and Fishhead joined his teammates and coach on a chartered bus.

The private bus took the boys and coach north to the undeveloped area of Virar Lake, more than two hours north of Bombay; they spent a week in the rented cabins by the lake, taking a trip to a rock music festival nearby, and a tour of the commercial chicken farm overlooking the lake. Fishhead unwound in disbelief, a hero among his teammates but still unclear how he'd made it this far with the team. He'd even seen a glint of pride in Dad's eyes, too, after his stellar performance. And yet Fishhead kept his personal life secret; somewhere beneath the spirit of sportsmanship lay an invisible barrier between him and the "haves," Anupa excluded. Others from well-off families were free to cross it, to reach him and accept him, but he seemed unable to recognize such gestures; his condition still tormented him.

At the lake's edge, he stripped down to his *chuddie*, his underwear, and stood beside Coach Agnello, looking at the white cotton against his own dark brown skin, facing a body of lake water the size of three football fields, which spread out from the grassy shoreline at his bare feet. His teammates, impatient for fun, had already thrown themselves in the warm water while he hesitated, silenced by the lake's size and mysterious depth. Too ashamed to open up to anyone. A hero did not show weakness, never.

He had never taken swimming lessons, even though life at home in Bombay meant he could always escape to Juhu Beach on the western side of the city. He didn't visit Juhu at all except once or twice to walk ankle-deep in the surf with his torn-tattered-and-patched jeans, his four-year-old faded blue jeans, rolled up; he never had bus or train fare, and a walk to the beach from Chembur took too long. Too far. Out of the question!

Alone now with his soccer coach standing beside him on a hot April afternoon, Fishhead considered the unavoidable decision: join his teammates in the water or stand alone, safe on land, a lonely chicken, like the clucking hens and chicks housed in the chicken farm up on the high bank, about three hundred feet or so to his left. The other boys paddled their naked bodies out to the deepest center with the screeching energy of children on a playground. Meanwhile, Fishhead stood with confusion amidst their scattered clothes. The lake impressed him, a giant that dared him with its glassy, eyeless coat and swelling shape, a beast unwilling to reveal its secrets and true depth to him. Back in Bombay, the Arabian Sea remained similarly inscrutable, although it dug deeper, much deeper and with more mysteriousness, life, and threat than he could imagine. But what should he do here? The thought oppressed him.

"Go on then," Coach Agnello said, his arms folded. "You're here to enjoy yourself." A young and handsome Catholic priest with wide shoulders and a straight back, the coach wore his white priest's collar, a black short-sleeve shirt, and dark gray, belted slacks. A chrome-plated Seiko wristwatch.

"I'm enjoying myself just watching them, coach," Fishhead said. He pushed the toes of his right foot in the water, wiggling them to make little splashes. A touch of asthma made its presence felt.

"You should join them," Coach Agnello insisted. "They're having a good time, and so should you." He'd coached the team to its championship win and earned the team's trust. In charge of everyone now.

"I'm going, coach," Fishhead said. "Going…soon."

"Don't be afraid. You can swim, can't you?"

"I'm just not ready to go in yet," Fishhead said. A critical measure of reasoning, however untrue. As he spoke, he shielded the nervous tick in his voice by clearing his throat, coming undone slightly with his answer, which came more as an admission of his fear than a denial of the truth: he had never learned to swim, or even float, for that matter. His feet always touched bottom; he made sure of that. He remembered the accidental drowning of a Portuguese couple's only teenage son a year before; they lived on Anupa's street. That would never happen to him, if he could help it. And yet the urge to jump in festered in Fishhead and made him restless.

"You took off your clothes for what, eh? Fashion-modeling your chuddie?" coach said.

Fishhead laughed, but the memory of the boy's drowning silenced him and raised his apprehensions. Still, no point in standing there in his underwear if he had no intention to swim. Perhaps coach didn't mean to put any pressure, but he was doing a good job of it now. Fishhead didn't want to miss the fun.

His coach's words kept pushing him: *Do something.* Fishhead had his pride; he couldn't lose that, not now after the championship. Be one with his teammates. So the next instant, he plunged into the still water without giving any thought of his place or purpose in the world. A sense of light, warm like a slow fire, brushed through his veins with a kind of unnamed urgency. He made a deep splash, and soon his feet found the bottom. He felt reassured. Too easy, this lake; too easy then, just like the sands at Juhu beach that faced the Arabian Sea and great Indian Ocean beyond it. Fishhead pushed up with his toes now. His feet found bottom! He bounced, while his coach observed him from the shore.

Then he kicked his body forward and drove on, paddling as hard as he could, making enormous splashes that ruined the silence of these undeveloped woods around the lake and chicken farm. He imagined the fowl screeching in horror. His coach laughing. Daylight sighed in much the same way as eggs frying on hot car doors. Fishhead did not turn around to look at his coach; he did not know how to, while here in the grip of this watery giant. He released himself from the earth altogether, moving ahead, hard and fast. All that mattered. He did not stop; he could see the heads of his teammates bobbing in the distance. He stayed afloat and kept moving east toward the middle of the lake, far from the shoreline now. He'd join his teammates. But that slight pain emerging in his arms and thighs? He lost sense of time, trusting in the bottom being there if he chose to touch his feet to it.

How long had he been paddling? *This must be the way to swim. Right?* He breathed heavily now as the water pushed against his chest. He kept his head above the surface as much as he could, his face forward, his teammates in view a hundred and fifty feet or so ahead. He spat and pulled in water, and he spat again and again, giving no thought to the machinery in his body—his arms, lungs, and legs—never trained to move this way. Some instinct in his mind had once painted a decent picture of this.

The more he paddled the faster his body glided along the surface, and from the corner of one eye he perceived a great expanse of distance and isolation taking him away from everything which he knew to be true. This is my Destiny, Fishhead thought. I am alone now. Alone! This is better than the tenement, at least. He became sharp, more aware than he had ever been, even in his hours between the goalposts. This newness of silence, water, and color, the sun's hot reflected light—all of it lifted his spirit and closed in on him, and he could not remember a more holy experience, a moment that freed him from the pulls of his world as now. Some kind of grace like he'd never known before, although it seemed to come to him with an increased aching in his arms, thighs, and chest. He worked hard to earn this grace. He breathed hard for it. Getting tired, getting tired.

When he stopped, his feet found no bottom. He had miscalculated. A shock of fear pierced him. He paddled. And he had miscalculated the distance, or perhaps the boys had drifted further away. Still, he kept paddling, but much slower now. And when he reached what he thought to be the center of the lake, he had to stop to let his body rest.

He could hear the splashing and loud voices of the other boys, and he yelled to catch their attention but couldn't be sure if anyone heard him. He turned his body with underwater kicks and pushed with his hands until he faced the shoreline. Then he turned again to face his teammates. Someone called out to him, waved to him. He hoped they cared enough to join him so he didn't have to paddle anymore. Tired now, and all the while he moved his legs underwater every which way and smacked the water to keep his body up, his head up. He smacked, smacked. The surface of the lake reached tight across his neck like arms reaching for a meal, and then it came up to his chin, and started touching his nose now and then.

Fishhead ran out of air. His chest burned. No more strength left in his arms. In a final gesture, he spread both hands out, locked his elbows, and pushed down into the water with flattened palms to lift his body up, which hurt his shoulders too much; when he couldn't do that anymore, he let his arms go limp and turned backwards to face the high sun. He tried to bring his legs up; he kicked to stay afloat, but his body kept dropping.

He closed his mouth and went down, trying to hold his breath, and just before he lost it, he thrashed about and made a push to rise to the surface again with his eyes open wide. Poles of sunlight danced around him, teased him. They'd pull him out of the water, wouldn't they? No splashes underwater, no splashes at all when he pushed, just swirls and bubbles until his head cut through the surface and he gasped hard, letting out a razor-sharp cry as he sucked in precious, precious air. A sudden memory: the sight of those fish in the marketplace, the mackerel and pomfret and snapper with big eyes like distant planets, and mouths receiving the stars rushing through the sky.

He closed his mouth fast as he went down again, but not as straight as before; his limbs would not support him. The water sat on his chest now, forcing him to keep his mouth open like the fish, and he took in water, a long and massive gulp of it. Such a different world down here, more hostile, thick with Destiny's sweat. Destiny! The words never escaped his lips. The more he choked, the more water he inhaled. He pushed hard, thrashed again, but the lake absorbed him. He fought to get to the surface; an explosion tore through his head and torched his nostrils. Dead weight in his arms and legs. He managed to bring his hands and then his head to the surface, but just barely. With eyes burning, with lungs burning and bursting, he lifted his chin high and gurgled and coughed as he pushed out what he had swallowed, but it stole the second or two he needed to take in new air. He had nothing left in him to stay there, nothing more, just inertia, and light surrounding him like columns in God's great hallway.

Far ahead on the shoreline, Coach Agnello began throwing off his clothes. Fishhead closed his eyes as more water entered his mouth. His head dipped below the surface. He could not stay up there. Reaching, kicking in pain as the lake pressed against him, he raised a hand high one final time as if to grab the air above the short, lapping waves, but then drifted down gently into the cavern of the lake's undisturbed depths. Water cooled his flesh, and the doors in his mind clicked shut one after another, leaving him with a few last memories. Bubbles and hisses surrounded him, bubbles...flying about him, rising in shock like chicken feathers, like cotton ripped out from pillows he didn't have at home, from...from......his team's dragged-out pillow fight the night before at the lodge, like the smoke...smoke from pot he inhaled............for the first time there. They'd passed the joint around and he accepted it, wanting to be part of the team............its enduring soccer hero.

It didn't matter why...why Destiny placed the image of this final memory before him, that moment in the lodge when he'd paused............to realize...realize...realize his wrongdoing, but continued on with the pillow fight anyway, all boys jumping.................jumping on their..............their metal cots and thin cotton mattresses in that large screened room in the woods, howling with pleasure, tossing pillows at each other and grabbing them, ripping them more when the.................the thin cotton......................................thin cotton gave way, flinging pillows into ceiling fans running on high speed, and then and then and then...and

then................jumping
into...leaping shoulder-first into
cotton   clouds   billowing   above   their
heads...wit
h   overstarched   sheets   balled   or   knotted   and   tied
around........................around
their...near-
naked...............................
naked..naked
bod.............   bodies............................
bodies......................................or tied to window bars and
metal   headbo
.................................metal................................metal
headbo ....headboards,   and   owls
screeching.........owls that night............owls......owls...

    owls,   so
dark............that..............................night........................
....   that
one...............night...
....
....
...

How much time had passed? It didn't matter, but he opened
his bloodshot eyes; something had wound tightly across his chest
from the side, lifting him up. In the turning, swirling thickness of
lake water, Coach Agnello's shape emerged; he worked with an
urgent power and moved quickly toward the light. Coach used only
one arm and his hard-kicking legs. Fishhead remained passive and

pliant while his body moved up and the water turned warm again. His body shivered, thrashing slightly from the cold still gripping his flesh. Then sunlight struck his face when his head erupted through the surface. Water poured down from his hair, coursing across his ears and eyes, his face. He coughed and coughed, gurgling and throwing up some of what he'd swallowed, and Coach Agnello turned him around while he breathed hard from the effort.

"Take my shoulders. Can you do that?" coach asked. Then he added firmly, without shouting, "Ride on my back and hold on. But be careful, don't choke me. Can you do that?"

Fishhead let his coach take his arms to show him how. He let Coach Agnello come under his chin and nudge him up onto his back, and Fishhead wrapped his arms around the coach's neck but did not wrench it or pull the man backward. Strangely enough, he'd gone past panic, and his still-limp body floated forward as Coach Agnello thrust both hands in front and swept them back to the side in repeated circular movements. He swam back to shore without hurry.

Fishhead didn't let go of his savior until his feet found the bottom. He rolled off the coach's back and stepped ashore and collapsed on his back on the grass, spitting and coughing. His body, heavy as the earth itself, like those fish on white boards in the marketplace. He lay still when Coach Agnello put both palms down on his chest and pumped, meaning to take the water out of his body. Then he turned to his side and vomited on the grass.

"Why didn't you say you couldn't swim?" coach said. He sprawled on the grass next to Fishhead, exhausted, relieved, showing no anger or impatience. "Destiny has spared you another day." He went silent.

Fishhead remained speechless but cognizant. His body pained him and his eyes burned, and while he lay on his side facing the lake, facing his coach, he became aware of his teammates as they all came ashore one by one and dried off, then got dressed in silence, some of them with expressions of shock scarring their faces. They talked in soft and surprising voices:

"We thought he was joking."

"I swear I thought he was pulling our legs."

"Why did he go so far?"

"He should have said something before."

"Coach saved his ass."

"Yea, he was a goner otherwise."

"Okay, boys!" Coach Agnello said, getting to his feet. "Pack your bags. We're going home. It's the right thing to do."

The mood changed, naturally. Fishhead shut his eyes and cried without uttering a sound when his teammates groaned. Ashamed. He'd ended the celebration, their celebration. He couldn't face them. They'd had four full days left on their vacation, and so much more to explore—undiscovered villages with stone and wood carvers, ancient caves, gypsy singers and dancers, and batik makers. If only he could plead with Coach Agnello to let the team stay while he returned home! The lake drained his strength and weakened his confidence. It stole his voice. He had nothing to say, and could say no more in his defense, except to admit to his error. Besides, how would he return home alone? Not on the team bus, the only way home.

He'd tried to be like the others. But *they* knew how to swim. All bodies did not float naturally, no. Dead cows and dogs did. The lake proved his undoing, his Waterloo. He would not go in deep water again; he feared it like an epidemic. Time to return to the tenement, his reality, his Republic of Want.

Back at school, he faced his shame. The principal brought up the incident during the morning assembly, so now everyone—the teachers and students in every row—knew what had happened. Fishhead felt their eyes on him, their pity, and he heard their mumbling. He cared less for what the students thought of him, and more for what the teachers might think. And Anupa, she would find out somehow. She would!

Fishhead kept the news from her, fearing she'd never want to see him again. Sooner or later, she'd get wind of it, from all the talk around the school, the neighborhood, the social club. More reason not to go there. He might not see Anupa again for a little while. So be it.

Foolish Hero-Giri

Life and death, the threat of his extinction at Virar Lake. Fishhead had a momentary realization that he gave up control of everything then. Life imposed new rules on him, he believed, and he continued on as if suspended between loss and desire—strung by need, ambition, and hope, although hope remained as a fragile eggshell around his world.

All around him humanity moved with purpose, drawn into commerce and enterprise by experience, by aims of profitability, and advancing at a pace which *time* and *endurance* dictated. Fishhead ached for belonging but felt deeply that the incident at Virar Lake had severed his attachment to familiar things and people, and that it hurt his spirit and dampened his glory. So sudden, this change. Why wouldn't fate let him have his uninterrupted success? He made a good fit here in this sport. Why did Destiny steal this moment from him? He reminded himself of a crucial fact: facing death reset him; he now had to prove that special sense of daring which the experience underwater had sown in his being. He felt a new sense of recklessness. What should he do with that? He wondered. Go after other interests which might help put money in his pockets.

The absence of money in his pockets didn't keep Fishhead from snatching a ticketless train ride to downtown Bombay, to a music store called Rhythm House, twenty kilometers south into the heart of the city. The ride took more than an hour on the commuter train, always jammed with riders pressing uncomfortably against him. He knew he'd find creative inspiration there, in its imported records and posters, American and European artists and bands playing through the sound system.

He would have liked to go with Anupa, but not this way in rough-style. Riding with no ticket: What would she think? Conditions in the tenement carried enough judgment. Yes, not this way. He'd go with her as soon as he had money in his pocket. Fishhead hoped the owners would not kick him out when they saw him again; he told himself he did not care one way or the other. If they did, he'd have plenty to see downtown. Street vendors sold goods and food everywhere along the sidewalks. No solution for his hunger, however; he could get drinking water, that's all. If he had money, he would see an American movie at Eros Theater or Metro Cinema, or even at Roxy Cinema near Chowpatty Beach, a good distance by foot. Cool off in those air conditioned interiors.

At Chembur station, he waited by the municipal wall for an eastbound commuter train, and stayed away from the platform; he didn't want a ticket collector questioning him. From where Fishhead stood on the graveled space between the ties, his tenement building (just a stone's throw away behind him), towered on the other side of the wall. He couldn't look at it, and strategized the method of the ride in his head instead, ready to jump on board in the clamor before the train came to a halt.

It soon came, barreling into the station full of passengers. The distinct two-tone paint of faded marigold yellow on top and deep brownish red on the bottom. Dad once said that the English had introduced these commuter trains and built the complex railway lines running through the city, and Fishhead had no cause to disbelieve him; he also thought that the English had done so much in India to make their own lives easier. The train screeched and hissed. Cars now jammed with riders—women and children in women's compartments, and men in theirs—people pressed against each other, hanging outside the open doors of every car as they struggled to keep their feet on the footboards while the train ran at high-speed to the next station. They held on tight to the welded door handles and the vertical support steel bars on each side of the wide doorframe. And if required, they grabbed the bars on the windows nearest to the doors, wrapping hands tightly around the narrow edges of the door frames to assure their place on the ride. Always the danger of slipping and getting thrown off the moving train, or smacking one's head against the evenly spaced U-shaped iron beams that ran too close alongside the rails as they held up the electric lines overhead.

Fishhead didn't stand a chance of getting on, but he meant to try.

While he waited between the iron railroad ties, the train loomed past him and over him like a monster in his dreams; and just before it screeched to a halt, some passengers on his side jumped off, landing on the coarse gravel beside him. With two minutes to spare before the train moved again, Fishhead stepped up to the end of the stationary car in front of him and reached for the narrow steel rungs at the back, in the space linking the cars, and he pulled himself up, squeezing between two men who had already taken their positions on the narrow metal ladder. He grabbed a different pair of steel rungs, and the three of them looked like branches of a coconut palm tree.

Fishhead didn't plan on being a railway-rowdy, but this illegal ride had no other definition. The two men adjusted their positions and gave him some space. He clung on while the train let off its high-pitched whistle then jerked to a start. It picked up speed. Fishhead pulled his head and body in to avoid being hit by the steel beams that whipped by, missing him by mere inches. The warm wind smacked him. His arms began to ache from his effort, so he shifted his position on the ladder, careful not to lose his grip or footing. The wind whistled between the cars and blew hard against his clothes and hair; he turned his face away. The two men talked loudly over the clatter of the tracks and the sound the wind made.

The train moved west on the fifteen-minute ride to the interior and then stopped two stations away at Kurla, a vital overcrowded junction on the Central Railway line. Fishhead hopped off and walked along the rail ties with other passengers until he got to the end of the crowded platform, and he went down and crossed the tracks to reach a southbound platform, where commuters stood pressed against each other, more than a dozen rows deep.

He waited for the next southbound train for downtown Bombay. Minutes later, one rolled into the station, already filled to capacity with riders clinging to windows and leaning out of open doors in the heat, and many preparing to jump off even before the train stopped. But the alighting passengers didn't stand a chance, because the waiting crowds on the platform—men before men's cars, and women in front of theirs—started pushing their way into the open doors of the train with a force that lifted alighting passengers off their feet and even carried some back inside like luggage.

Urged on by the excitement, Fishhead ran ahead on the platform, cutting through the chaos until he got to the space between two cars, and just like before, he hoisted himself up on the metal rungs. Four men on both sides of the vacant space hung on the narrow metal ladders, and now two of them climbed up to the open roof and crawled to a seated position near the edge. With a blast of the horn, the train started moving. Fishhead knew the risk, but he followed the men, unwilling to risk an encounter with the ticket collectors inside. He held on to a vent cover as the train gathered speed and the warm wind and dust came at him like an enemy, pressing against his cheeks, hair, and shirt, and threatening to rip his shirt buttons off.

He ducked when the train rushed under bridges, and he kept a constant watch of the high-powered electric lines that fed the train through the flexing pantograph behind him. The power lines hung too low, he thought, too close to his head, and the sound of mechanical parts and motion up there appeared different, raw and unforgiving. What would Anupa say about his reckless lawlessness? He could never tell her. She might never speak to him again.

About twenty minutes into his ride, the diamond-shaped pantograph sparked and sizzled when the train made a sharp bend, and the rooftop lit up as if lightning had struck. Fishhead jumped and reseated himself; he tightened his fingers around the vent.

"Sit straight and don't do any foolish hero-giri!" a man near him called out. "You'll get us all killed with your monkey business."

"I'm not trying to be a hero," Fishhead said. "This isn't my first time up here. I'm just jumpy, that's all."

The ride into downtown took about forty minutes; the train cut through the city and pockets of slums growing along the tracks with a kind of senseless desperation. Might his family go that low? Yes, he thought, not too far from that, not too far at all. The smells changed, suggesting industrial zones, waste dumps, the famous *dhobighat* (open air laundry place), an open-air leather factory, mold-ridden apartment buildings, hospitals, and prepared restaurant food. The pelting wind made his face feel like leather. His blown-back hair. His shirt, now unbuttoned above his navel, flapped like a flag, and ballooned with the onrushing air. His jeans hiked at his crotch and pinched him, but he didn't want to risk relaxing his grip and adjusting himself until he came down from the roof.

Soon the train slowed as it pulled into VT station. The massive Gothic Revival terminal echoed and cranked under slanting roofs of steel beams and sheeting, rising high into the light, where doves, sparrows, and crows settled; the terminus spanned the length of the trains, with platforms—insufficient for the thronging Bombay crowds—lining both sides of each track.

Fishhead eased himself down from the back of the car; his ride-stiffened knees creaked as he leaped onto the platform. Now, a final hurdle: slip through the exiting crowds at the main gates. A pair of ticket collectors stopped passengers at random to examine tickets. Fishhead put his head down and slipped through in the middle of the crowd as it surged forward, and soon he emerged in broad daylight again, relieved. He faced the heavy, reckless traffic on

Dadabhai Naoroji Road; across the street stood the gray stone Times of India building, a relic from the Victorian era.

He hung a left and walked south on the crowded sidewalks while double-decker buses, cars, and other vehicles moved inches from each other with their haste and horns; stone buildings reached over the sidewalks, their columns rising from the edge of the curb. Vendors hawked bootlegged goods, cheap products, and personal items—almost anything one could think of, including "Rolexx" watches, "Chanelle" perfume, and "Ferragama" footwear. Fishhead stopped at a cart to examine hand paintings on dried neem leaves, detailed portraits of lovers and rajahs and half-clad Indian beauties with curved spines and full breasts. He paused at a snack cart to feast his eyes on popular snacks: *bhel puri, chaat, pani puri,* all whipped together with a variety of fried foods and boiled potatoes, chickpeas, condiments, sauces, and spices. He ached for this, for something to fill his pinching stomach, but he refused to beg and face rejection.

He moved on for a kilometer or so. The high-energy of downtown and its tight, loud traffic in the daytime never ceased to amaze him, although the area also seemed unbearably hot compared to home. He wiped the sweat from his brow, thirsty now. To the left: an old banyan tree, and a water tap beside it; a quiet shaded area and a roadside Hindu shrine. A few burlap sheets up on bamboo poles. Orange and white paint. A quiet *sadhu* praying. He went to the tap and drank.

Another half kilometer until the art gallery came in view in an open area called *Kalaghoda* (black horse). He took a left on the side street there and entered Rhythm House, the music store in a heritage building with a round façade. All he wanted.

Fishhead entered tentatively and walked the aisles in awe—a scene so uncommon in Bombay. He began flipping through vinyl records in the waist-high bins, and brushed shoulders with other customers, including a few who looked like college students; he imitated their reactions and movements without making it obvious to them. An unfamiliar song through the overhead speakers: he wished he knew the artist. This kind, he liked the edge of heavy guitars a lot. He wanted more, and wished Anupa or her mother had a taste for it too; the songs they played sounded catchier, more tuneful and less guitar-driven.

"Who is this? Who is this?" he asked.

A student in the next aisle turned and gestured toward the record sleeve standing open on the counter near the register. "Mothers of Invention, yaar. You don't know? It's right there."

Fishhead didn't have a good response, so he stayed silent in his ignorance and kept his ears open as the student turned back towards his girlfriend. They discussed homework and art, their easy-going college teachers and their tough ones. Fishhead gleaned that the girl studied illustration at Sir J. J. Institute of Applied Art. He himself felt his great distance from the city's reputable colleges: a world out of reach, unaffordable even if he should somehow gain acceptance.

These students looked and dressed like Anupa, Fishhead thought. Old money families with history and property in Bombay, or new money coming in from overseas jobs: the Middle East, Europe, or America. If Dad's handmade greeting card business had done well, he and Kishore might have ended up knocking on their doors, in Bandra, Malabar Hill, Marine Drive, Nariman Point, or Hanging Gardens; they had money enough for records and department stores and movie houses and carnivals, and money to eat at fancy restaurants.

Fishhead browsed the bins until he found The Mothers of Invention. His eyes lit up, and he knew he had to come back when he could afford it.

The music changed, and so did the album sleeve on the counter. Fishhead did not know this one either: Black Sabbath. *Masters of Reality.* Not possible, not possible at all. This band did not know his reality and could never master it.

In the back of the store, he studied Pop-Art posters, then grabbed two art books and listened to the next album—B.B. King's *Live in Cook County Jail*—while he read on the floor with his knees folded close to his chest. The two owners kept an eye on him but did not kick him out. Fishhead soaked up as much as he could. A different world altogether, removed from chaos, a sharing of song and culture without hate or prejudice. Images and ideas: the music saturated and inspired him in ways he couldn't fully explain. He could do more. If he attended an art college like J. J., he could outdo Dad.

First, he had to get through high school. Almost there, almost there, and he couldn't wait another day.

He left Rhythm House empty-handed but pleased beyond words; he walked about aimlessly but found himself moving in the direction of the telephone exchange where Mom worked. He studied signs and billboards, and observed foreign tourists and their manners and clothing. Beads, kurtas, bell-bottoms, headbands, tight and loose batik shirts, shirts with wide collars, un-hemmed jeans shorts, Ray Ban sunglasses, showy belt buckles, scarves, backpacks, Adidas shoes and Converse hi-tops—a feast to his eyes. More stores and distractions. A Carnival, a cricket match. Then Anupa entered his mind, and he pretended they walked together. He imagined holding her hand, kissing her.

Later, he aimed further south and went toward the tip of Bombay until he reached Apollo Bunder, where the Gateway of India monument overlooked the Arabian Sea at the water's edge. In school, he'd learned about this stone archway and how the British built it in 1924 to welcome the queen and also Bombay's new governors and viceroys. Bombay, his city, their prize once. Fishhead leaned against the low wall by the monument, pressing his thighs against it, and he imagined the great expanse and depth of this sea, its cerulean beauty and salty odor, its moss, the fishy sting in the air; this great sea ebbed and flowed, more alive than memory. The sea hummed its ageless tunes, if one only listened; a hungry sea, like him. He did not wish to come near the water. He would not let his body touch it.

Why do writers place their protagonists at the water's edge? I believe they should do no such thing; it betrays a lack of originality in the author, and should be frowned upon by all supporters of the arts and by intelligent readers like you, dear reader. But you say you don't mind? It works here? Well, maybe you are right.

Perhaps you'd rather have your protagonist look down a great cliff, or scanning the horizon from some incredible high-rise in Chicago? The open page is yours to sculpt. As for Fishhead, he occupies this page. Once again he came before this great sea which knows my fervor and intrinsic nature. The writer understands this human connection to water as an aspect necessary to Fishhead's character, a feature more important for the boy's survival than the upper middle class life that he pursues. So why not include the scene? Since his incident at Virar Lake, he is less enthusiastic about deep water. I don't blame him. I know water's playfulness and concealed talent for surprise; it wants to remind you of your full dependence on it, or rather its control over you. We are kin, water and I, kin but not the same; although we hum the same universal tune and discreetly talk between us, we speak from different holes in the sky. Water will claim Fishhead at every opportunity it gets, but I cannot release him yet; I depend on him to present my innate personality, my understanding and empathy, my direction of souls as they progress towards the future. Bad or good, all must advance through time, which I hold in my hands.

Fishhead's pathways to Anupa have one obstacle: his struggle to show conditions of hunger among children of global populations. The very encyclopedia containing this title and story sits on shelves in libraries around the world, and at The Cliff Dweller's club. Fishhead's hunger is everything, the same one causing discomfort and desire in the belly of the child and in the flesh of the artist, the writer, the dancer, and musician. An entrepreneur, a laborer, even a pack of lions shows this hunger, as does the thief and *rescinder*. All Fishhead wants is to conquer it.

Never Be Like You

They read *Don Quixote*, and Anupa wanted to take up *The Scarlet Pimpernel*, intrigued by the secrecy of the English nobleman during France's Reign of Terror. Fishhead welcomed it, and he didn't mind that she also read from her father's book of Persian poets, offering—in a slow rhythmic cadence that became Anupa's manner of reading—words by Rumi, Mahsati, Hafiz, Omar Khayyam, Parvin E'tesami, and others. How Fishhead wished he had such books at home, just as he also regretted the loss of Dad's record player from the British Council. He missed those records. Did they mean to chain him to their beauty and hunger forever?

When he spent time with Anupa, he felt special. Her presence put him in a place outside the external world and its stimulations. Life just went by; time rowed on, brushing against him as a whisper or a thump, and he remained mindless of his surroundings, as if in a welcome trance. Anupa's voice, warmth, and breath spilled into his pores, in spite of the dislodged agony of mountains tumbling in his head; he desired burial under all of it, because of her. Everything, all the need and chaos of the tenement, dissolved into meaningless shapes at the periphery of his awareness. Inside her home, a particular quietness and light prevailed, a pleasant sense of withdrawal from the world. She became his mesmeric gaze during their readings and conversations, and when they walked side by side. The sound of her front gates, the warble high in the trees, their footsteps along her street did nothing to take Fishhead back into reality, so that Anupa had to make all the right practical decisions moment by moment (shut the gate, don't step into the gutter, avoid a bicyclist or vehicle and so on), as if she understood his delicateness and vulnerability. Even the unexpected sight of his father approaching in the distance on Central Avenue did not matter to him; it seemed a mirage, until Anupa called his attention to it.

"Why is that man staring at me?" she said. "He's staring at us!"

"What?"

"Do you know him?"

"Know whom?"

"That man who's coming towards us."

Fishhead looked ahead and saw his father approaching; they'd encounter Balan within a minute if he did not do something. "No, I don't know him," Fishhead said. "Let's keep walking. No, let's cross the road instead, now!" And with that he took Anupa's elbow and guided her dangerously through traffic. His rejection of the truth made him flush with shame, and he knew she'd ask for an explanation later, after she caught her breath. This disavowal of his father scarred Fishhead's conscience, and yet it felt necessary.

Anupa glanced across the road. "He seemed to recognize us. Are you sure?"

"Yes, I'm sure." Fishhead felt as Judas Iscariot, and only now understood the significance of the disciple's behavior in the large painting of the Last Supper which hung on the church's wall. He became so quiet that Anupa had to nudge him.

"Are you okay?" she asked. "Is something the matter?"

"Yes, I'm fine. No, nothing's wrong," he said, smiling weakly. The leak in his conscience had begun to pester him. He'd tell Anupa the truth someday, and perhaps she could forgive him.

At home, Dad never brought it up, and Fishhead let the matter stand unresolved. Despite his discomfort, he had nothing to say about it, but the more Fishhead kept the issue at bay the more rebellious he became. He avoided Dad; he had more important things to consider. He became less focused on his studies as defiance grew in his heart, and he continued with soccer, spending time in the clubhouse now and then, where he noticed new alliances and intimacies grow. He felt urges rising in his body. How should he further his relationship with Anupa? Would he have to marry her? Come clean about all he'd hidden from her? She still seemed to want to be with him. Pressing pubic bone to pubic bone, mouth to mouth. Learning the value of touch, the way it resided in his heart and echoed within him. And yet he did not know how to unlock the awkwardness still tying him down. How soon would Anupa tire of him?

Once high school ended, he'd need to find a job, or get into college. And yet he realized he might not make it out of school. The starkness at home filled him with regret and anger. Dad began selling vegetables from a push cart with bicycle wheels; he did it in front of the tenement, which only increased the family's embarrassment. Chained to his shame, Fishhead dare not face his father or remain in the man's company; he felt certain he'd done the right thing by avoiding Dad when he'd been with Anupa. The family fell far behind in the rent, in unpaid tabs for groceries, basic rations, kerosene, clothing, school books, mom's chit fund, personal loans: the list went on and on. Pradeep gave Mom some money to meet the family's expenses, but she complained about it; she felt he could do more. Her sinuses bothered her, and she developed a viral infection in her lungs which left her with an incessant wet cough; it forced her to stay away from work for several days. She gave Fishhead money for groceries, and he cooked. Doctor Rajan came to see her; he insisted they buy a cot, and they got one, a narrow jute cot with a cheap wooden frame. Pradeep paid for it. Pradeep helped Mom and no one else, and he told Fishhead nothing more than he needed to know. Fishhead despised it all. Bad luck claimed Dad.

Fishhead did well in his English, history, and geography exams, and fared poorly in math, science, and local languages. Meanwhile he suffered, his mother suffered, and his siblings suffered. Indians knew how to suffer. But why? He had no control of his fate, and how he wanted change! Pradeep had chosen his own Destiny. Pradeep: happy. Now Fishhead wanted his own way out. But even the liberation he experienced at the end of the school year offered no respite: he did not know how to manage his time.

One evening, Pradeep asked him to attend a party at his friends' house in Anupa's neighborhood, near the gymkhana and tennis courts. Fishhead went, anxious and ill at ease. When they arrived, the full house revealed a casual and well-behaved atmosphere. Popular songs played from a home stereo system. People drank alcohol, ate, smoked cigarettes, and passed around cannabis as night fell. Fishhead indulged. Both substances, the alcohol and particularly the pot, induced a happy effect that took his pain away. But the combination did not suit him. Soon he began to lose his sense of place and the people there. Pradeep cautioned him but did not police his behavior. And then Fishhead became sick.

On the way home, past midnight, he threw up on the public bus; he struggled to stay focused, eyes half-closed, drowsiness clamping down on his head. He needed Pradeep's help to stay on his feet.

When they got back to the tenement, Dad let them in. "Why are you late?" Balan asked, stern and agitated. He'd been drinking, too.

Fishhead had no control of his words or actions. "That's my business," he replied, garbled like he'd put a cat's eye marble in his mouth.

"What are you doing?" Pradeep hissed from behind him. "Don't provoke him."

"Why are you home so late in this condition? Answer me!" Dad boomed.

"That's *my* business. Move your arm and let me in. How is Mom?" Fishhead's stomach ached, and hunger lurched inside him, begging for mutiny in this Republic of Want. Dad: a stranger in his way; and the half-open apartment door, a barricade.

"Apologize at once!" Balan shouted, waking up the family and neighbors. "This is no way to speak to your father."

"What father? You're no father! I'm glad to deny you!"

"Kneel down and say you're sorry!" Balan's eyes bulged, enraged. "Kneel down now!"

"I won't do it. You'll have to make me," Fishhead returned. "Let us in."

Dad threw a fist to Fishhead's jaw; Fishhead's head jerked to the side and he fell back, hitting his head and shoulder against the door before Pradeep stopped his fall.

The noise echoed for a moment in the moonlight and then dropped away, filling the hollow tenement with quiet again. Shadows and disgust closed in on them.

"I saw you coming out of 14th road." Dad leaned over Fishhead. "I saw you with that girl. Who is she? You will stop seeing her at once! I will not allow you to destroy her life."

"As you have done ours," Fishhead said, the heat of the moment turning into spears with fire which pierced the ceiling, punching venom against night's clouds and tearing open the starry Indian sky—it sucked up all the words life had meant for sharing between Fishhead and his father.

Fishhead clambered to his feet and moved weakly to strike Dad in retaliation, but Pradeep held his raised arm back.

They'd argued over college tuition, Fishhead remembered, but never like this. Fishhead hadn't expected any of it. His paleness and intoxication left him all too soon in this tense moment, and sense returned again. He held his jaw and stepped in; his father turned and retreated to his chair, as dark and sullen as bats' wings in the lightless night. Behind him, Mom's silhouette stirred in the darkness. She'd watched the ugly scene in silence from her cot; now she drew the sheet over her head and lay down again, whimpering, defeated, and exhausted.

"I'll never be like you!" Fishhead yelled. "I'm ashamed of everything! Of you! Look at what you've done to Mom! To all of us!" The words spilled out of his mouth, like grains of rationed rice from a hole in the bottom of a burlap bag.

How Fishhead lived under the same roof as Dad afterwards, he could not say. He held his tongue, and refused to even look at his father, and it pained him all the more. He saw Dad differently now: a Quixote on his own weak Rocinante, with a spear of dreams and purpose tucked under his arm, useless against reality.

Fishhead's confusion and frustration began to suffocate him. He stole rides on the train downtown as often as possible; he made sketches and drawings of nature and street scenes; he created three posters for the social club. And before long, he went, portfolio in hand, to see the director at Sir J. J.

On that summer morning he knocked on the man's door, and the director waved him in. A large but sparse office facing the courtyard, well lit, with an abstract metal sculpture in a far corner, and framed paintings on the walls, two behind the director's massive wooden desk and cushioned chair. A government of India flag hung from a pole near the back wall. The man looked at ease in his grey hair, glasses, and clean white shirt; a dark jacket hung across the back of his chair. Fishhead sat across from him and said little after presenting his work; he spoke only when asked a question. The director studied each piece and nodded a few times, rubbing his chin once in a while. Then he leaned back and cleared his throat, looking at Fishhead. He got to his feet slowly and put out his hand. "There is much room for improvement," he said. "But please discuss with my secretary on Monday."

"Is this a confirmation, sir?" Fishhead asked.

"Provide your admission details."

"Have you accepted me then?"

"Yes, please discuss with my secretary on Monday and settle tuition particulars."

Fishhead took the director's hand and thanked him. Then he gathered his samples and left, smiling but surprised at his good luck. Tuition particulars? He had no idea how much his school even cost. Still: a miracle! Now he needed to tell Mom. Maybe she could help him pay.

He saw Anupa later that evening at the social club; they played ping pong, and again she beat him fair and square. "I got in at J. J.," he said, and watched her reaction.

She rushed around the table and hugged him. "What good news! I'm so happy to hear of it. Although I thought you would go to Xavier's for liberal arts, you know, literature and poetry."

"We'll be next to each other downtown," he said.

"Yes, we shall, but I'll miss you at Xavier's."

She beat him in two more games. "Literature!" she shouted across the table while smacking a service ball. "Poetry, great stuff!" Anupa smacked the ball again. "Languages!"

"I see color and song," he replied, reaching for the ball, failing. "I am better at drawing, I swear."

The art school campus of Sir J. J. impressed Fishhead: old stone, concrete, and glass structures spread around the original vine-draped English home of Rudyard Kipling, a simple Old World residence painted in green, and now home to the sculpture department. Fishhead's mother had taken out a college loan from her chit fund; it did not include any extra spending money, but it meant something. He realized his discomfort among students who came from privilege, but he felt at ease with his poorer classmates. Art students hung out in small groups, strumming guitars or listening to them, while others played volleyball in the sprawling dusty courtyard out front. Still others sketched and made art, or painted murals and posters—as upper-level student groups—for movie studios in Bombay.

Fishhead's hunger took him to the tea stall, a shack with few tables and metal chairs at the south end of the applied arts building, with its circular drive and flower garden, and the modern female sculpture at its center. Students visited the tea stall during breaks to snack and chat.

He purchased his art materials on credit from the only art supply store on campus, prolonging the family's crisis even further. Mom negotiated a running a tab at the art store; she privately denounced the concept of the credit system, but Fishhead needed poster paint, brushes, B and 2B lead pencils, a basic Rotring pen set, India ink, drawing pads, tracing pads, paper, erasers, triangles, T-Square, and a ruler—a bottomless pit of art supplies promising self-reward but no immediate financial sustenance. He understood Mom's regret that his art education would never relieve her overwhelming burdens, and yet he moved ahead, believing he'd prove her wrong somehow.

College engaged and revitalized him at first, but Fishhead became annoyed by the slow pace of his foundation classes, the boring instruction. He couldn't focus on theory in color, composition principles, and art history—so much that he did not know. He wanted to make art right away, do big things, as he'd done with his posters at the social club and as those third- and fourth-year students did with their work for the movie studios. But the school curriculum forced him to start at the bottom. Five years upward seemed like such a long road: impossible, even, given his family's hardship.

Meanwhile, he hung out with classmates like Nikhil and other boys and girls who smoked cigarettes; they regularly bought chai and snacks at the tea stall, and enjoyed the comfort of their social lives. Fishhead became distracted by the freedom art school gave him. Nikhil sang and played guitar, and he also purchased rum from time to time in half-pint amber bottles which he hid under his shirt; and they drank together. Fishhead sang with him on stage before a small but discerning art crowd. The rum caressed him from the inside, a warm blanket for the soul, but the drink made him forgot the words to his songs. A few clapped for his courage. Others booed, or simply stepped away.

He admired the talent surrounding him on campus, but felt defeated by the financial comfort and easy hipness that so often accompanied it. And always he had to turn his back on freedom, return to his suffocating life at home, and choke down his silent, growing anger. Dad drank more and stayed out longer, avoiding both his family, and the parade of frustrated debtees who steadily appeared in his absence. Meanwhile Mom, still ill and weak, held down her full-time job with its long and odd shifts at the telephone exchange, sleeping overnight in tight closets when necessary. Somehow she found ways to afford the tuition. Whether Dad went looking for work or not remained a mystery; he refused to discuss his activities with anyone. The family occasionally saw him pushing the vendor's cart around the tenement at odd times of the day, hoping to earn a few rupees, if that. Bring food to the people instead of making them walk to the marketplace. Not a novel idea, but Dad believed in it; people had to like it, he said.

Fishhead couldn't contain his shame any longer. He, too, stayed out all day, spending hours on campus or downtown, and accepting invitations from Nikhil or others to attend free cricket or soccer matches at Azad Maidan, watch movies at the theater, visit street carnivals or fetes, and eat out—always trusting that they'd cover his expense, or at least a portion of it. He thought they would tire of his company. He worked tirelessly to cultivate the barest hint of friendship; he obsessed about how he behaved, dressed, and spent; he molded his behavior to fit in, yet ever conscious of his indigence, especially at the tea stall, where he hoped, but never begged, that the charity of a classmate or two might grace him with tea or a snack.

The art school attracted a contemporary lifestyle and a fashion sense that caused him to retreat further into an introspective self. His college mates embraced rock and pop music and played it on imported cassette players and radios; they smoked, drank, wore new clothes, dated, experimented with drugs, and sang (accompanied by their acoustic guitars) songs from Indian films, and others by overseas artists, like Pink Floyd, Elton John, Neil Young, Joni Mitchell, James Taylor, Curtis Mayfield, Neil Diamond, The Hues Corporation, Cream, Carly Simon, Carole King, Stevie Wonder, The Supremes, ABBA, Three Dog Night, America, The Mamas and the Papas, Jimi Hendrix, and Simon and Garfunkel. So many more. All things beyond his reach, but fascinating just the same. A new time, a new world beyond his shores, so very different from the tenement. A larger hurdle than entering Anupa's world, even: this pretense at college, this need to show face among everyone there. Turn it on in the morning, off at night, and all over again, day after day. He couldn't stand it.

He failed to see the simplicity of his situation—just embrace the poverty. That's all he had to do. Simple enough: be like the other talented students from the backward class, who made stunning artwork, ate simple homemade meals, and spent frugally. But he could not do this; he feared social rejection, and didn't want to abandon all things representing the West. He liked Anupa's world and saw it among his college-mates, and he wanted that more than anything; he desired it and tasted it on his tongue and through the touch of his fingertips. And yet his indigence brought him down further. Empty pockets! Fallen Destiny! Muscle and strength draining gradually from his being, pulling away from his brain and bones.

So with his personal rage clamped behind tight lips, he kept hanging out with the wealthy kids, unaware that they read his poverty with ease and tolerated him. He still had Anupa, didn't he? She'd never abandoned him, although he felt bad that he hadn't made an effort to see her at Xavier's. The more Fishhead drifted from Anupa, the more he thought of her; he missed her and hoped she missed him too. They would bump into each other near Xavier's soon, he believed it.

Then one afternoon, he ran into Anupa on a side street behind his campus; he'd skipped a boring color theory class for a cricket match.

"I missed you!" Anupa said, slipping her arm around his and pulling him close. She looked at him with the same radiance and smile, and then she frowned when he did not return her sentiment.

"I'm sorry," he replied. "Life changes going on at J. J."

"Art school, that's so good, na?" They paused on the sidewalk under the shade of a mango tree. "My BA is coming along nicely," Anupa added, "since you asked." She pointed behind her.

They broke out into a brief spell of laughter. "The sharp one. I missed that about you," he said. "I've been thinking about us a lot."

"Is everything okay?" Anupa asked. She wore a short-sleeved pink tee with a V-neck, a silk batik scarf, sandals, and her pleated gray skirt that stopped just short of her knees. Sexy, he recalled, the way she always dressed. Anupa with her shiny, long black hair and high cheekbones. Her medium button nose and full lips.

"Of course, yaar, it goes without saying," he lied. "All okay." He shifted the topic: "You're so good at that—literature, all those great books. I remember our nice times reading together."

"Too good, no? But you're drawing and painting now."

"Yes, I can show you my work sometime."

"That would be nice. Come over, and we'll read some more."

"I'd like that," he said and waited.

"So, how is everything in college?"

"Fine," he replied. The supplies are expensive."

"Yes, my books, too," Anupa said. If she observed the angst in his demeanor, she gave no sign.

"I believe it. So you're enjoying college?"

"Oh yes, and I saw Ronnie Mistry in concert on campus."

"Bombay's Bob Dylan, I've heard. I should go see him sometime."

"Sure, I'll let you know. Now c'mon, I'll treat you to falooda," she said.

"I don't want to put that on you."

"No, come on, na? I'll be glad to do it." She moved her books to the crook of her left arm. "But not here. Let's hang out at Kyani's."

"Kyani's!" Fishhead said in surprise. Another restaurant out of reach. He didn't refuse her, only because he didn't want to deny her company. "And will you read something to me there?" They walked west on the sidewalk to the end of the road. Soon they faced Metro Cinema at the very busy junction. Horrendous traffic. The rain threatened. A sunless sky, and hot. Kyani & Co. sat on the other side; they had to navigate two crosswalks to reach the restaurant and bakery.

"What will you read me?" he asked.

"I have Borges, Mirabai, Joseph Conrad, and Dickinson. Kalidasa, too."

"You decide. It will be fine," he said. "I really liked *Don Quixote.*"

"Very much so, and *Scarlet Pimpernel,* too."

The traffic surged at the crosswalks. Cars, two-wheelers, cyclists and lorries pressing against the pedestrian white line at each corner, pressing against each other to get going with impeccable restlessness, as a crowd in a soccer match waits in anticipation for a goal. Fishhead and Anupa stepped into the first crossing and hurried to the opposite sidewalk, but just then two young men on a Bajaj scooter at the curb took off, their engine sputtering and revving; the scooter's handle missed Anupa's hip by a few inches, and its foot support scuffed the side of her calf. She cried out and lost her balance, but Fishhead took her arm before she fell to the sidewalk and spilled her books.

"Dogs!" He shouted at the two boys, who took off without looking back. Anupa regained her balance and studied the mark on her calf. A scrape. "Will you be okay?" he asked.

"Yes. Thank you!"

They continued on to the bakery, talking about her close call and the city's bad traffic. When they got there, Fishhead held the door open for her, and they settled at a table in the back. He gave her a wet napkin and she dabbed her bruise with it. Then they ordered their shakes and waited. Anupa couldn't see his hunger; the ice-cream shake would be his meal for the day, a blessing. He looked thin to her, he knew it, but she said nothing. He promised himself that he'd see her again, see her more often.

"My Mom asked about you," she said. "Why you stopped coming to see us."

"You know how college can be. So busy. And I need to find a job." Had he said too much? Did she not care to ask? He placed his hands face-down on the table and played with his fingers. He studied his nails: they needed a trim soon. The India ink stains persisted on his hands.

"Okay, but do come visit us, yes? I won't make you promise. It's up to you."

He nodded. "I just don't want to be a pest."

"You won't be. You never were." She smacked his hands in jest then placed hers on top of his for a few seconds. "Let's have lunch sometime, too. Down here. Will you come see me at Xavier's?"

He nodded but said nothing about his feelings of regret, and his inability to focus on his art, his studies. They drank their shakes in silence. She slurped; he found it amusing. "Who was the other one, that author?" he asked. "Will you read his work, please?"

"Borges? Sure." Anupa read a few pages from *Labyrinths*, from his story "The Zahir." As she leafed through the pages, Fishhead studied her clean hands, wondering how they might touch him again and calm his urges and frustrations. This creature of intelligence and charm. His bookworm. His caring *pusthakon ka keeda...*

"Would you prefer another story? Or a poem from Dickinson?"

"Oh. I haven't read them. Although I do know of Mirabai and Kalidasa."

She read some more.

"I've learned so much from you," he said and waited until she looked up, pleased. "I come from the chawl. Did you know that about me?" His voice went quiet, sounded regretful. She said nothing. "I have no books at home," he continued. "We sell everything—books, bottles, and old newspapers for a few rupees to live on. I'll have to find a job to stay on at J. J." He paused, startled by his confession. "I'm sorry, really sorry. I've said too much already." He looked away past the windows.

She smiled and rubbed his hands. "I'm the one who should be sorry. I was being selfish. I shouldn't have asked you such questions."

"You are my bookworm," he said. "My library." She giggled. "Please," he added. "Continue."

"Okay," she said. "Cervantes inspired Borges, who wrote some things in response to *Don Quixote*, because it's a great piece of literature."

"I like when you read to me," Fishhead said, his voice softer now.

She began reading from the essay "*Partial Magic in the Quixote.*" Fishhead soon understood the difference between reality and imagination in the essay; he understood why Joseph Conrad did not wish to write about unreal things, because life itself contained so much richness and reality that one did not need to depend on an escape into fictional worlds; but Fishhead disagreed on one issue: Why ever write about it, this worthless life? His Republic of Want meant something more.

They sat at Kyani's for just over an hour, and then she stood up. Her afternoon classes would begin soon. He thanked her for the shake and, in his silent heart, for not asking about life in the tenement. He would see her again and wanted her body in his embrace. This, too, of course, remained unsaid.

He forgot the cricket match and went back to class. He endured the daytime hours without food; Mom paid his daily train fare somehow, but the extra twenty-five *paise* she'd started slipping into his hand didn't buy him a cup of tea, let alone a fried snack. He left campus in search of a more affordable roadside snack vendor and imagined his father operating his cart downtown—Dad dishing out snacks in rolled up newspaper cones for his customers, for him, and taking their change, taking his coin, in festering silence. It hurt Fishhead too, everyday; his pain grew like brush strokes in red, like art brushes wasting his blood against the canvas of his decreasing flesh. Every enterprise, he believed, called up a sense of pride; even the shoeshine boy and cowdung girl showed pride in their functions and fates. Did his family suffer because of Dad's pride, or his laziness? Perhaps both. Life as a street vendor presented quite a fall for a man who once ran a classical music library, but perhaps

Dad had come to terms with that. The work supported his drink—moonshine didn't need much money, although Mahalaxmi Racecourse did.

On the way home, Fishhead fainted. This happened often: standing in hot, crammed trains, with commuters squeezed so tight against each other, against him, that he lost consciousness, only to wake up with a jolt as the crowds shifted in and out of the car at each station. He started drifting further away from the circle of classmates he thought might be his friends; meanwhile they sailed through their art classes without any apparent financial trouble. His tab at the art supply store remained unpaid, and it increased when Prem also started at J. J., having made a delayed choice to follow the same creative path. How could Dad and Mom rely so mindlessly in the impossible and unattainable? Fishhead wondered. They already couldn't afford one tuition.

Fishhead lost his focus altogether; he put his own future at J. J. in crisis. He became disruptive in class, failed to turn in his homework, and leaned over his classmates' shoulders to imitate their art during exams. By the middle of the third year, the school found no value in his enrollment as a student and dismissed him.

Mom came and took Fishhead away one weekday morning.

He left without saying any goodbyes, even though a few of his former college mates were playing volleyball out front. He went past them, leaving footprints in the hot dirt; he went out the front gates for the last time with his back turned to the applied arts building, the tea stall, and female sculpture in the roundabout garden.

Tarak Greeting Card Co.

With more time on his hands, and with his body and head burning with indignation, Fishhead took random ticketless rides downtown. He also walked aimlessly on Central, the main road which led south to his old school. He passed Anupa's street but resisted dropping in on her. What might she say about his dismissal from college?

He went past the church and school at times, following the three-kilometer route that cut through the golf course until he arrived at his former home in Collector's Colony. He turned back when his feet started to hurt. This heat, this ridiculous heat. He prayed for rain, glad he didn't have to kneel down in a pew at church. This way offered more freedom in conversation with God, and he felt the brush of nature's wisdom as fresh air passed around him and through him. He believed in fate, however. Or did he?

On a whim, he pored over the "Wanted" classifieds, which ran several columns in the local papers, and soon he took a job as a commercial artist on a meagre salary—a gold mine! he thought—just to stay out of the apartment. He spent late hours at work and didn't take long to impress his young boss, who, Fishhead soon learned, lived with his new bride in his parents' high-rise apartment in expensive Malabar Hill. Fishhead enjoyed his creative responsibilities for this startup greeting card company called *Tarak*

(Star), now entering its third year in business. Greeting cards were not part of the public's consciousness in Bombay yet, but his boss meant to change that. A visionary with bold and urgent ideas, the owner kept imported greeting card samples from Hallmark, Recycled Paper Products, and American Greetings in a folder for inspiration. Fishhead studied them occasionally; he created illustrations and wrote copy, sometimes working in black and white, or with one or two added colors. He soon learned how to make film separations for the halftone colors in his ideas, and he supervised their production in the small printing press at the back of the enclosed office; the shop ran a used Heidelberg Windmill Press and also a Chandler & Price letterpress and die-cutting machine, with a treadle and a big wheel at the side. As well, the company maintained a large format electric paper cutter, saddle-stitching binder, and new embossing and thermography machines—all new revelations and technologies which Fishhead absorbed with zeal. How long would it have taken him at J.J to get so far? Tarak offered a remarkable operation on this little scale, although it still did not compare to the hot Linotype machines, compositing workstations, and other printers' machines at Dad's old job.

Dad—clearly an unrealistic dreamer! And yet Fishhead imitated him, for better or worse: another hungry artist trying to earn a living with some dignity. It had been two years since they'd talked.

Fishhead disliked Tarak's location: a square area tucked away on the second floor of an unsanitary and massive industrial complex in central Bombay, an area called Lower Parel. A primitive fireworks factory ran day and night across the hall, employing men, women, and children whose arms and feet were always covered in black powder. Above and below Tarak, garment factories made shirts and other clothes for foreign buyers. Meanwhile, Fishhead spent his days under fluorescent lights, bending over his artist's desk stacked high with tracing and drawing paper, pencils, Rotring pens, and markers. On one prototype greeting card, he drew a figure underwater, with captions: "Most days I feel like I'm drowning" (on the cover) and "But your birthday is like a breath of fresh air!"; on another, "Help! I'm drowning!" and "Have a bubbly birthday!" His boss rejected those with a frown, and encouraged Fishhead to try something more positive. Sketches and tracing paper littered Fishhead's desk as he explored new ideas; he soon came up with a greeting card character resembling Anupa, but he liked her and respected her too much to turn her into a cartoon; with his Rotring pen, he drew her beautifully on tracing paper and on sheets of acetate, working over various full sketches and parts of sketches arranged one on top of the other, taped down as he saw fit. He put books in a crook of one arm, a Quixote lance in the other. Again his boss rejected it, saying "No customer will go for that." So Fishhead drew another: long dark hair, that pleated short skirt, and knees too close to each other. But the knees did not look so good in the drawings, so he straightened them for the cards. He named his new character Shobha and ended her speech with the expression, "na?", just like Anupa did. Another prototype: Her, on the cover, in reading glasses: "When it comes to happy birthdays…" and (on the inside): "…you've written the book!" His boss enjoyed this one. Fishhead's pride soared. They went to print with a set of six greeting card ideas using Shobha as a market test. Confident again!

Fishhead gave Mom a good portion of his income and saw her tears of joy. He'd worked hard for it, he said to her, just as she also worked hard at her job.

He spent more hours at work than his monthly income justified, because he enjoyed his creative freedom. Sure, there were restrictions: rejections of ideas, plus his employer's practical and economical limitations. Fishhead got used to this soon enough. All ideas encountered some form of negotiation, they had to; he began to see this at his work, and learned how to improve his creative and negotiation skills. His ambition grew with each new idea that he produced on his drawing board. Still, Fishhead wished his paychecks came bi-monthly. A month took too long, he felt, and the money spent too quickly.

When he turned nineteen, he bought new footwear and a pair of light canvas jeans. Mom made cake, and Lily and Kishore helped, while Prem challenged the plan, as usual. Pradeep surrendered a pack of Dunhill's as a gift. Dad presented Fishhead with an office shirt as a peace offering, although he did not say so exactly; he did not say anything. Fishhead thought Mom may have been briefing Dad about the job at Tarak's; had she passed some of his income along to Dad as well? He might never know the truth. He studied his father's expressions. Some hope there. But no smile; no glee for the birthday boy.

He had not expected this gesture by Dad; he felt suspicious. Where had Dad found the money for it? Had he borrowed it? Or gambled at Mahalaxmi? Fishhead took the shirt from Dad, but he looked it up and down as if trying to find a flaw.

"Put it on," Dad said.

"I will," Fishhead answered, and walked away. He wouldn't give his father the pleasure. Maybe later when his mood suited him. Perhaps not.

In truth, it still seemed impossible to Fishhead that they would ever reconcile. So, no use in even making the attempt. He felt it in the blood-red tunnels of his bones. This torn relationship like Palestine and Israel. Or Anwar Sadat and Menachem Begin, without Jimmy Carter to invite them to Camp David. Eternal caution, no trust. What could Fishhead do to get it back? Did he want it back?

What his father did with the shirt, Fishhead believed, was a gambit, nothing more. A means to get them talking again. He also believed that Dad felt no guilt, and perhaps had even abandoned his conscience some time ago. Jealous, he wanted the money Fishhead gave Mom. Yes, perhaps he just wanted his cut.

The more Fishhead thought about it, the more he wanted to burn the shirt. Or maybe give it away to a homeless boy. But then again: Mom might find out. So he kept it but did not pull it out from its plastic sleeve packaging. Let Dad notice.

Fishhead ignored his father for two more months. Finally, he broke his silence again, but only to respond to essential conversations around the apartment. A "yes" or "no," nothing more. Did this hurt Dad? He wanted to hurt Dad, wanted to show him that it took more than a mere man to make a family and lead it—it took hard work and resolve, like Mom had; it took care, and love, and touch, all the things Fishhead missed and wanted.

Anupa had given him those things. He wanted them again. She, attractive and smart, his *pusthakon ka keeda.* His bookworm.

He missed her now, this college girl who had welcomed him, unquestioning and eager. Must go to her, he must go see her.

PART 3

"If you want to use the third eye you must close the other two. Then breathe evenly; then wait."
   ~Margaret Atwood

"Intuition is soul guidance, appearing naturally in man during those instants when his mind is calm."
   ~Paramahansa Yogananda

Destiny, Show Me An Angel

Perhaps you have been wondering about my brief silence, dear reader, occupied as you are in Fishhead's fate, and even as you realize that everything you do and that Fishhead does leads to me. I have resolved to stay present and attentive to his existence, stepping in when necessary, although I must speak now in the sunset of my correspondence—for the jurisdiction of survival in this world is without social, cultural, political, or religious boundaries, and I must leave you soon on other matters taking place elsewhere. You see, I am much sought after for all sorts of requests, good, sad, and evil. I know the voices in Fishhead's conscience, the things he says in moments of anguish, and also the words he spews in regret, or his actions of arrogance when he has won or lifted something without paying for it, always looking for that one small victory. Doesn't someone lose then because of it? Such actions—all actions and intentions like these—are vicious and violent threads that course through life in the tenement. In Fishhead's heart live the words:

Destiny, show me an angel
Let me breathe; let mother live.
I curse the shadows, and people who thrive in them.
Kill patriarchy at once!

I have succumbed to it, and yet I know that I carry it in me.

He had found comfort in Anupa's affections, but he'd been too afraid to ask her to visit his tenement. Little does he know that she does not care to see where he lives, but she thinks of him often, and something in her wants desperately to meet his entire family, his parents most of all.

Unbeknownst to Fishhead, she had observed his brothers and little sister at school and during after-school settings at church and around the neighborhood. She'd seen Fishhead with them, and she'd met Lily that one time. On occasion, she'd seen Pradeep with his friends, too, after he'd returned from work at the airport hangar to spend time with them under the lamplights on Central Avenue. And that man who'd stared at her and Fishhead as they walked together on Central? Was that Fishhead's Dad after all?

Anupa's fate is tied to Fishhead's story in ways even she cannot imagine. I have willed it. Like goodness will do to human beings in sorrow, her goodness has become the enigma of his wishes and all that he wants. The Mecca of his prayers. But goodness behaves like the flame of any candle put in devotion before a cause; the candle, too, loses its glow after some time. However, its duty is recorded in history (I can say this with certainty), and woven through every framework of your world and the universe beyond you—an amalgam of unbelievable and intensely magnified proportions of signs and intentions too incredible for minds to comprehend. But I know of such things, and my name is Destiny, Aka, Brahma, the Moirai, Takdir, Qadar, and Norns—a few names among so many. I know the culmination of every process, thought, and association. Look inside a lotus flower then close your eyes and inhale life, slowly and without haste, consciously. Make yourself aware of the gift you breathe in. This is fate, the fine vibrations pulsing under your skin and through your soul's actions. Every culture has a name for me, for the unknown. What is yours? How will you speak with me once more? I know when you seek me out. You have already said many things in your night's journeys. But the space between? How will you speak with me in the daylight? Make your daylight sing without sorrow or hatred. Tear yourself away from the neurosis, whatever that may be. I am here for you. I have arrived in permanence. Trust me.

Fishhead has kept to his course because he sees a firelight glowing somewhere ahead of him; he must trust something, or he will perish like so many other children around the world. I see such outcomes with sadness. His story belongs rightfully in the hardbound work, *Notes on Conditions of Hunger Among Children of Global Populations*, which Iva (Do you remember this Chicago native?) reads at The Cliff Dwellers Club. As mentioned before, this work contains a remarkable collection of over 600,000 entries on hunger and its consequences everywhere, including insightful information and details, predictive analyses, and statistics from research; more than this are the soulful narratives cradled in a companion collection, evident in the essays, fictions, poetry, drawings, and photographs. But it's Fishhead's story that grips Iva, our citizen of Chicago; the Midwesterner cannot put down the book or insert his bookmark to return to it another time. The story must end so that he can proceed with his own life in the great Windy City.

Confucius, Mencius, thinkers—you called on Heaven's will to mark the movement and decency of humans, whose actions define the progress of time and the realization of those pre-destined steps in their lives.

You too will speak to me again, I know it. You are too busy, but I am here in your awareness. And you will inquire about me as Fishhead does. Why me? Where is Destiny now? You'll pause to ask such questions in that split second of curiosity and need, dear reader. What does fate actually mean to you? Mere names accorded by history and literature have always been insufficient and inadequate to describe me. I am your conscience which communicates during visibility and sleep, and isn't that enough? That same power, that burst of light and heat in your pineal eye, the same face, unseen but leading all beings to their futures and conclusions, their repetitions; I am the space between seconds, the *instant*, living in the unseen folds of cloth, in the air struck inside the palette of a mouth before the utterance of speech, in the fragrance of mint or the aroma of curry leaves that escapes from hands brushing against their leaves; I am the umbilical thread rising, turning from the heart of the lotus towards God's navel; the murmur in the earth before a raging flood that only animals hear; the truculence of blood flowing through ventricles of a hesitant heart; the roar of a deadly king cobra tasting the heat of a human (that unfortunate child) on its forked tongue; a quick moment of awareness when you leave behind your attachment to things and catch the breath of kindness that belongs to God. I could go on, and in all of those things not yet mentioned, I am there, too, marking their conditions and limits, defining their paths before they even know it.

So let me now lead Fishhead and Anupa down theirs—

In Sheets of Gray

Dark clouds one morning in late July, 1976. Surreal light, primordial. The 31st of the seventh month. A day that shouldn't have happened. How might Peter Max paint those thunderous clouds in his pop art posters for rock bands singing songs of lost love, ecstasy, rebellion, or anxiety?

Fishhead left for work early, with confidence in his pockets, under the threat of a severe downpour and darkened skies. Then the rain came, a twisting rain that bit down like a rabid dog, tearing umbrellas and turning them inside out. Commuters ran for cover. Bolts of electricity lit up the blackness, thundering their woeful calamity across the city's hot and sticky landscape, now swarming with office-goers and artisans. His Chembur buzzed with activity. Even animals ran for cover, the wandering cows and pariah dogs, snakes. Couldn't tell night from day. Why shouldn't his greeting card company shut its doors at times like these? Because jobs awaited completion, profits made, and money earned. And if they were closed, no way to find out anyway. Most residents owned no phones, no landlines; a privilege of the upper middle class and wealthy, a rare and true luxury, which the government approved and furnished following hefty paperwork, costs, and legal formalities that often took months, years to pass. Even Anupa had no telephone at home. And certainly his family couldn't afford one.

Mom worked for the telephone exchange, an international operator no less, and still—no phone! Out of the question. If Fishhead wanted to check in at work, he'd have had to walk to the market on the other side of the tracks first, and use the "subscriber trunk dialing" booth, provided it had opened. Too much effort.

He jumped on the packed westbound train at Chembur station, but couldn't squeeze his way away from the open door, the rain; soon the train arrived at Kurla junction in the center of the city, about fifteen minutes away from his tenement, but still far north from his workplace. Now drenched, he pushed his way to the interior. The heavy rain continued. Screeches of water. A train hammered from all sides by a torrential shower. Sheets of gray obscuring vision, dulling all sense of hearing and direction. So loud, better not to speak at all. Let nature do the talking. Nothing stayed dry, nothing at all. Rainwater gathered everywhere, already ankle-deep on the ground and rising, moving and churning dirt, debris, twigs, blue tarps of the slum-pawns. Water, moving like a brown restless serpent in search of lower ground.

When he reached midtown just over half an hour later, Fishhead pushed his way through the packed car and almost lost his right slipper when his foot got entangled with someone as he alighted at Lower Parel station. He couldn't keep his balance and went face forward on the cemented platform, his unopened umbrella still in his grip. He smacked his torso on the drenched, dirty surface; bruised but not hurt. "Bastards!" he said aloud. "Shit!" He got up without help from the impatient passengers on the platform; they stepped around him, as if he did not matter at all. Kickable, this boy.

He tidied himself and stood there as the train departed, and then he made his way up the stairs of the overhead pedway, which spanned the width of four tracks and opened up to the busy elevated main road on the other side. Vehicles moved in a thick stack at his left, so Fishhead went down the sidewalk of the paved bridge and walked south for a little while. He raised his eyes to the clouds above him; in the distance, the sky lightened and gave him hope. He cut through a few cross-streets and passed row upon row of shops and tea stalls; he did not stop until he arrived at work.

He took the stairs to the second floor and caught the stray glow of fluorescent office lights leaking out from under the shop door. He didn't keep a key, but the shop workers always began early. He entered the glassed-in front office, ready to get to work; he could hear a couple of pressmen moving about in the back. (A client's brand identity order, for delivery in the afternoon. Fishhead had designed it a few days before.)

The shop door opened. "Go home," his coworker said. "The boss left a message that we should all take the day off. Because of the Hindu festival."

"I don't mind putting in a few hours," Fishhead said. "I'm already down here."

"We're going to leave soon," the coworker said. "The brand identity project is done."

"Well, let me take a look, at least."

The coworker shrugged; Fishhead followed him into the back and looked everything over. He didn't entirely mind taking a day off, come to think of it; after nodding his approval, he turned and left the premises with his desk untouched, eager to spend his time in other ways.

Outside the building, an idea: take little sister and Mom out to the carnival; the rain would stop soon enough. Then again, Mom wouldn't be home until after sunset, tired and hungry, weak. Could she take a little break to join them? Her job imposed a schedule she couldn't escape, even after years of government service; promotions arrived as regularly and infrequently as Halley's Comet. All day long she'd remain on a top floor of her building, cut off from the city below; and she took her naps in a closet then went back to her overtime—eager to pay down her loans for the chit fund the art supplies, to pay tuition, buy rations, food, text books, clothes, soap, and transit tickets. An endless list.

On his way back to the station, a second idea: invite Anupa, too. Then again, he didn't know her schedule. She might be in class. But hadn't she been glad when he'd last come to campus? She'd even suggested lunch. And why hadn't he taken her up on the offer yet? Questions unanswered. Should he track her down at college? Would that seem strange? She might be at home. How could he find out? And what about Lily? He'd have to go back to the tenement to get her. Would Dad allow it? Would he even be home?

The rain came again, a sudden spurt; he opened his umbrella and ran towards Lower Parel station. When he reached the top of the paved bridge, he looked down over the four tracks and watched the rain smack the weak roofs and tarps of shanties on the other side. An array of slums. They grow anywhere if given a chance, he thought.

He measured the two distances in his head: his sister remained the closest; the ride south to Anupa's college downtown would take a lot longer. So he jumped on the next homebound train and stood by the door during the ride north; and when he got to Kurla junction, he hurried up the wet steps and took the pedway over the tracks, eager to change trains, careful not to slip.

Fifteen minutes later, he reached Chembur station. The distinct odor of his tenement: shit, filth, and overflowing gutters by the tracks. He hated returning in the heat and trickling rain, in his wet clothes, with jeans sticking to the backs of his thighs and calves, and brown pudding and puddles under his feet. Oppressive indignities. He didn't earn enough to have his own apartment in a decent neighborhood; besides, Indians didn't do that—they stayed with their families through thick and thin, until marriage took them away, or until family conflicts or job reassignments forced a separation. Burdensome obligations. Fishhead questioned all of this; he often considered leaving home. But that, too, would summon unpleasantness: gossip, questions, and frowns.

Late morning now and a drizzle. From the platform he faced the tenement and considered his options. A change of plans: Lily would have to wait. He turned around, opened his umbrella, and went south across the tracks. Central Avenue and the marketplace seemed quiet after the rush hour, not so closed-in and chaotic. He took a deep breath and walked further south towards Anupa's house.

He paused, doubting his intention, when he saw her curtains drawn shut in front. A quiet street, a much quieter place, except for the rain which came down again in a steady downpour. He unlatched her gate and locked it behind him; it squeaked a little. He went ahead, stepped on the verandah then closed his wet umbrella and let it stand in a corner; he watched it puddle as he approached the front door. Raindrops broke through the foliage around the house. The lusty smell of clean, wet earth, almost choking. He knocked, thinking Anupa's mother would greet him, but after a pause, Anupa answered. He recognized her eyes as she peeked through the peephole. She let go of the hinged cover on the inside and released the slide bolt latch holding the two halves of the door together.

He caught her surprise. She stood before him in a casual *lehenga choli* outfit with short sleeves, her long hair tied back, and nothing on her feet except for a pair of toe rings. A spray of rain coasted across the verandah, and Anupa closed the door in a hurry to keep the spray out then opened it again; she stuck her head out, glancing to her right and past him with a raised eyebrow.

She leaned back. "Hi!" she said. "This was unexpected."

"Yes," he replied. "I took a chance."

"Look at you. This rain is unbelievable."

Fishhead nodded. Sunless conditions, an awkward hour of the day: he stood prepared to leave if turned away. A drenched pariah dog jogged on the road past the front gate, whimpering, as if mocked by hostile raindrops. Anupa smiled clumsily; Fishhead returned it but did not move from his spot on the verandah. He became uncomfortable. She looked like she was about to motion him in, and he moved at last, but she put a hand out, holding it against his chest to stop him from entering in his wet clothes, and her bangles chinked. He felt strange, a ridiculous suitor tripping over his common sense to get into her dry home.

"Wait here," she said, and left him standing there.

Self-conscious now, he kicked off his slippers and looked in through the open door to her living room, impressed as always by the order and cleanliness. He listened for Anupa's mother, but he heard nothing. Anupa returned a couple of minutes later with towels; she dropped one on the floor by his feet and watched him step on it, and she gave him the other towel then helped him wipe his wet hair and face.

"I'm getting your clothes wet," he said, not thanking her yet.

"Who cares? It doesn't matter," she replied; she ushered him in and shut the door, engaging the slide bolt. "I got dressed for classes but decided not to go. Look at it outside! I have the wrong outfit on. So stupid, na? Should be wearing shorts or a skirt and gumboots in this weather. Not this…like as if I'm going to a party."

"I like it. You look like a film star."

"Thanks!" she said. She made him turn around.

"So are you…were you…going to a party?" He asked, facing the door.

"Silly green bean, no! And I like college, but it's no party, not in the least, let me tell you."

"You don't have to convince me," he said. "I had to quit J. J., so I took a job."

"What? I had no idea!" She reached for his shoulder and turned him towards her.

"I'm so embarrassed about it. It's the tuition…and trouble at home…"

"So sad. That happens sometimes," Anupa replied. "So, tell me, what *are* you doing?"

Was she disappointed? He couldn't tell. "I make greeting cards for a small company in Lower Parel."

"That's nice, yaar!"

"I'm enjoying it a lot, but I'm not doing much reading."

"Then we'll have to do more together."

"Sure…yes, we will. Anything you like. I miss it." His response prompted silence, a pause, while he took the towel from her and continued to dry himself.

Then Anupa quoted:

Be still, sad heart, and cease repining;
Behind the clouds is the sun still shining;
Thy fate is the common fate of all,
Into each life some rain must fall,
Some days must be dark and dreary.

He shrugged, mystified by her memory. The right words at the right time. The shame in him now, for being so inadequate. His greeting cards did not compare; they sounded petty and playful. Perhaps Shoba should speak like a poet, just as Anupa did.

"Longfellow," she revealed. "A perfect poem, 'The Rainy Day.'" She studied him, satisfied by her effort.

"Tell me another one, please."

She looked up at him and then down at the floor, turning away for a few seconds, thinking for a moment; he thought he'd offended her. Fishhead hadn't yet seen this side of her, this dedicated side. Then, another quoted passage:

A sobbing flares up to tremble in my soul
And a savage elation…tempting?
No…embracing the sky,
Frenzy of a child frightened by the moon…
…as if archways of mist drank the clouds
And drop by drop dissolved in the rain…

"Now you've really got me," he said, eyes wide, his arms limp at his side with the wet towel in one hand. "How do you do that? Who is that? Tell me."

"Badr Shakir al-Sayyab," she said. "Do you know about him? Great Arab poet of Iraq. But I think I missed a few words."

"No, I don't know about him. You learned all this at college?"

"Yes, and so much more. But tell me about your work!"

A pause. "Perhaps you've heard of Tarak's? I'm an artist there."

"The greeting card company? They sell cards at Akbarallys. I've seen them."

"And a few other places," he answered. "Definitely a growing business." He did not tell her about Shobha. He felt embarrassed. He'd mention it next time.

"I'm very happy to hear of it. I'm sure you're an A-class artist."

"I'm doing my best."

"Of course you are," Anupa said. "I'm glad you came. Look, I'll make you some tea." She did not wait for his reply but began walking toward the kitchen, with her lehenga skirt in her hands so it didn't catch on her feet.

"I know it's an odd time of day to drop in on you like this," Fishhead confessed, studying her back; it showed through between her short choli top and long skirt, which hung low at her waist. Anupa gave no response, but he knew she'd heard him. He did not move from his place by the door; he wondered why her mother hadn't made an appearance yet. "I thought you would be at Xavier's, and I wanted to go there first when I left work," he added, projecting his voice across the hall. "Boss called in this morning and told everyone to go home, but I only found out after I went in." Still no response from Anupa as she disappeared into the kitchen, so he continued: "I'm glad for the day off! It's nice, but this rain must stop!"

She stuck her head back in the hallway and laughed. "My God, that's so inconsiderate of me to leave you standing there like that! Please, come inside."

Fishhead stepped into the living room; he edged closer to the hallway but did not enter it, worried he'd surprise Anupa's mother. "I thought I'd take Lily to the carnival in the afternoon. Will you join us? I'd really like you to join us."

"But the rain?" Anupa lifted the skirt again as she moved. Her feet slapped the floor, and her bangles rang with a light sound. Her toe rings accented her feet and ankles.

"Maybe it will end by lunchtime," he replied. "So will you come?" He wanted to take her feet in his hands.

"Maybe. Actually, yes, I'd really like that." She gestured for him to leave the towel in a corner of the hallway.

"That's great! Let's hope the sun comes out soon," he said and dropped the towel as instructed. She backed into the kitchen. "Mind if I join you there?" he asked then added, "I'd like to say hi to your mom."

"Sure...but I'm all alone," Anupa confessed. "I thought you knew that by now."

"I'm sorry, I couldn't tell exactly."

"Like most Indians, no amount of rain can stop my mom from going out. But she will come home looking a lot drier than you."

Fishhead chuckled. "I fell at Lower Parel station. And I ran in the rain."

"How sad," Anupa said, reaching for a tin of black tea. "My mom is attending a choral group rehearsal that will go on until lunchtime. They're preparing for First Holy Communion services, and the fathers have asked her to play the piano and organ...the pedal organ." She spooned leaves of tea into a tea ball infuser and set it in his cup, with the chain hanging on the outside. She closed the tin and put it back on the shelf.

"Rehearsal in this weather, oof!" Fishhead replied. The kettle steamed and let out a long hiss. Anupa had placed it on a clean Shakti triple-gas burner; a thick hose connected the burner to a red gas tank below the counter. Two tanks there, one being a spare. He came and stood beside her, but leaned against the counter with the side of his hip, so he faced her when they talked. He studied her kitchen, impressed by how clean and complete it appeared with light, tiled walls, a thick granite counter, a Kelvinator fridge, baking oven, cabinets, Sumeet blender, stainless-steel sink, lights, matching dishes, utensils, knives, and silverware. Dish rags with that new look, as if they'd never been used. Pots and pans, several to choose from. A ceiling fan. Jars of spices and a hanging basket filled with onions, garlic, green chilies, ginger, limes, okra, brinjal, tomatoes, and fresh herbs. Bananas and guavas in a bowl. A cast iron hand-cranked meat mincer clamped to one edge of a counter close to the wall. On the floor below the sink stood the coconut scraper with its wooden footrest. He wanted his own mother to have all these, exactly what a normal kitchen should possess. How did Anupa's family afford all this, with a sick father in a hospital in distant Pune? He wondered. Old money, new money, investments. It had to be so. The kettle whistled.

Fishhead caught himself glancing down at Anupa's navel, and she caught him doing it, but said nothing. She turned off the burner.

"Dancer-like," he added, "the way you're dressed. So *deshi*."

"C'mon, yaar, I like Indian outfits! Not just bellbottoms and western clothes," she said, pouring hot water into his cup. She placed the kettle on a jute trivet that sat on the counter. "Soon the West will be copying all our styles! You'll see."

He placed the back of his hand gently on her stomach, barely touching it, and then he moved his hand over her navel, caressing skin, if only for a few seconds. The navel pointed in. She flinched and held her breath. He retracted his hand, unsure if she'd push him away or, worse yet, ask him to leave. When she flinched, her stomach moved with less grace than a belly dancer's form, but he liked its response to his touch. His cool hands from the rain, his still-wrinkled fingertips.

"I am true," she said. "I am as real as you are, Fishhead." She reached for his cup, but it trembled against the saucer, and she blushed. His tea went black.

"Yes," he agreed, and he turned his hand, going palm-side down against her flesh, her stomach, and then down the side of her hip. He wouldn't look her in the eyes. "You and I are very real," he added, "and everything else fails to exist. This is ours, yes, Destiny?"

Anupa giggled. "Only *we* exist," she repeated. "And nothing is ever what it seems until you and I make it so."

He stepped close and touched her mouth with the same hand. Then he brushed his lips against hers, pausing; he studied her eyes and waited for an adverse reaction. Anupa faced away from the counter and pushed her pelvis out, denying the air between them, and she pressed her mouth on his, lips moving. So tender and warm, their kiss. And more. Lushness, like a silver sleepless moon, melting and foaming into his heart. A wave of desire swept him from within and caught in his throat. Shut off his thought-valve. His chakras turned, a carnival raw with desire. That Republic of Want. From the base of his spine to the top of his head, his chakras went spinning, twisting, as *naga* would do inside him and inside you too, dear reader, spinning through history and back to the blazing divans of Vatsyayana's carnal philosophy.

Fishhead moved his right hand to her side and brought it around the natural curve of her smooth hip and skin, attempting to tuck his fingers under the decorative hem of the lehenga and the hidden drawstring passing through it, not tight, just there, low on her waist. His teasing and curiosity. Unresisting, she let her arms fall to her sides and studied him, the movement of his searching hand.

Would she step away? Say "Please, no!" He thought of her mother, who might suddenly knock on the door; he imagined Anupa putting a stop to it, just because. But she stood still instead, as if, he believed, as if she wanted this, as if she had been expecting it. He eased his fingers down under her hemline, and he brought his hand back gradually around her hip and towards the front, drawing the heat of her lap through his touch. She shuddered, stepped closer, and took his forearms. Then she placed her toe-ringed feet on top of his feet and raised herself up as she wrapped her arms around him. Moments later, Fishhead moved the same hand behind her, still restrained by the hem and drawstring, and he spread his fingers out at the soft base of her spine, reaching, now with both hands. She took his face and turned it to meet hers when he edged the low hem of the lehenga away from her waist and let it slip to the floor.

Mirroring the Abyss

Creation brought them together as sure and steady as the rain over their heads; Fishhead believed it. Where did this benevolent universe materialize from? How did it perceive its own unfolding manifestations? He and Anupa belonged to it; something very special, I will admit. He and Anupa belonged, and they move fundamentally through time and memory because of it. Actual beings, Anupa said so, and Fishhead remained certain of this feeling. Actual beings destined for solidarity.

Something changed in him, in her, as if miraculously they shared an indelible fascination for each other's presence and for living, without judgment, for linking and not wanting to let go of each other; the glow in their bodies, a sparkle like those beams of daylight which appeared suddenly through the parting clouds over the city, as if granting Fishhead's wish for a brighter afternoon and carnival. A day as clear as fate's reflection in every puddle of water left standing near his hasty feet.

An enthused young man. Encouraged by light. He went to fetch his sister from the tenement on the other side of the station wall; they'd meet Anupa on the platform, an arrangement that suited him. Bound for good times, all three of them. Anupa suggested leaving a note for her mother with the neighbors before she left home.

Fishhead could not let little sister ride alone in the women's compartment, and he did not want Anupa and Lily to ride together without him. Crowded commuter trains ran full of desperate adults and crude, ravaging children; clever pickpockets mingled in all sizes, genders, and dispositions. Lily would rather be out on her own, but she displayed no signs of adult behavior, nor did she understand how to confront the bold manner of the world with polite fierceness. She, like adolescent girls her age, would fall prey too easily, Fishhead thought, and break down crying, unable to resist any harassment from strangers. So he purchased three first class tickets, although it made no difference to their comfort while traveling, because he knew they'd find no empty seats among those cushioned green benches with their stamped logo patterns. Bedbugs resided there, too, but not as many as in the other general second- and third-class compartments. In any case, Fishhead didn't care for a seat when he traveled through the city.

Lily beamed when she approached Anupa, studying her with awe and curiosity as before. Pleased but cautious, Fishhead wondered whether little sister might become disagreeable and cranky along the way. Instead, Lily surprised him. She touched Anupa's clothes and hair, and complemented her on everything, especially the jasmine fragrance she wore.

"Can you get me bell bottoms like hers?" Lily asked Fishhead.

"Maybe when you finish high school."

Little sister pouted.

"You're short!" he said. "I'll get you other things."

"Like what?"

"Yes, like what?" Anupa smiled.

"I don't know! What should I get her?" he asked Anupa.

She laughed. "You got yourself into this mess, you get yourself out!" But she chatted happily with Lily for the rest of the train ride.

Sometime later, they reached the end of the southbound run to Churchgate Station. The western side of downtown. They stuck together while exiting the too-crowded terminal, not far from Mom's telephone exchange, and outside they found a restaurant populated by college crowds. Anupa knew this one and waved to a couple of classmates as they entered, but she did not go and talk to them. The restaurant served local and northern *thalis*—stainless steel platters with vegetarian dishes and yogurt, accompanied by rice, roti, sour pickles, *papads* (lentil wafers), and a sweetmeat for dessert. On Lily's insistence, Anupa sat next to her, so Fishhead took a chair across from Anupa and faced the interior. They ordered their meals and received the dishes within a few minutes. Fishhead dived in with his fingers and so, too, did Lily and Anupa. The restaurant buzzed with activity and with the accompaniment of local film songs playing through overhead speakers.

Lily placed her empty bowls on the table, outside her main tray. Fishhead helped himself to her leftover curried coconut and string beans. And he ate Anupa's share of mixed pickles; she did not care for the tartness and spices. For dessert: *srikhand,* a strained, thick yogurt dish sweetened to perfection. Lily finished hers but then reached forward and stuck her spoon in Fishhead's dessert bowl, helping herself to some of it. He frowned, but let her.

"You can have some of mine," Anupa assured him.

He let his ankles find hers under the table. A thank you. If he could have a moment alone with Anupa...then again, seeing her walk arm-in-arm with Lily softened his heart. Lily needed a sister she could look up to. Living with a houseful of boys hadn't toughened Lily; she was less shy and timid than she might have been, but she cried a lot for being teased.

Anupa put the small empty bowls on her plate and took a long sip of iced water. Then she took Lily to wash her hands in the women's sink, a narrow open trough in the back of the restaurant. Fishhead watched them go; they acted like they'd been friends for a long time.

The girls soon took their places at the table, and he departed to wash his hands as well. By the time he came back, Anupa had ordered coffee for everyone, delicious South Indian Mysore coffee. She pulled a book out from her bag and began reading. Fishhead did not interrupt her, but it made him curious. He dipped his head sideways to look at the cover—*Fishhead: Republic of Want.*

"Listen to this," she said, and read; the words resounded, echoing a whisper in Fishhead's consciousness—Yes, dare I say it: Destiny awakening him from his dream. The words of the story sounded like his own life, exactly like his life from moment to moment in the way he'd been living it, only that he did not remember every past detail until he heard it fall from her lips. He listened, his eyes on her lips as they moved line by line:

"Anupa, pay attention!" he heard the teacher say to a girl in straight black hair that fell down past her shoulders. Anupa had faced away from the group and fixed her eyes on him. He didn't know her but he liked her clean uniform, black saddle shoes, and white socks that went up her nice smooth calves. She had dark eyes and pretty legs, a square-ish head with long and straight hair, silky black hair. Some of her classmates started to giggle, and they too looked at him. One girl reached over and pulled Anupa's shoulder back to make her face the teacher.

"Come on, yaar," the girl said to Anupa. "Don't upset the teacher."

Fishhead turned a corner of his mouth up and swung his head back in the direction of his school; he made sure to keep his balance on the wall, as he extended his reach to grab on to a branch. Then he stepped off the wall with the branch in his grip, saying "Anupa, pay attention...Anupa, don't upset the teacher! Anupa, pay attention. Come on, yaar." His weight took the branch down and bent it. He never let go and pulled his body towards the thinner end of the branch, until his feet touched the ground several seconds later and even as the branch began to resist. The branch meant to spring back and slip through his grip. He held on to it as it went away from him gradually, and he pinched off six long tamarind pods in the process, dropping them at his feet. Then he clutched some leaves just as he let the branch whip back to its original place above him with a whoosh. It cut through the air, leaving a bunch of tiny leaves in his fist.

He liked the name Anupa. Didn't forget it. He named the tamarind tree Anupa. Anupa, fresh like the leaves in his hands. A sweet and sour girl? Sweet and sour worked well for tamarind, but he didn't think he'd like that in a girl. Anupa had better not be sour, not to him...

Anupa giggled as she read, and then became more serious as she learned about him and the way he'd lived, paragraphs of hunger, want. A decrepit existence. The tamarind tree. The scolding. They looked at each other, while Lily studied them both oddly, full of questions. Her eyes lit up when she heard her brother's name.

"Am I in there, too?" she asked when Anupa paused.

"It's our story, yes," Anupa said.

"But you weren't born then," Fishhead said to Lily. He sat before them in disbelief. Yes, he'd lived through all that. And there in her hands: his own life in print. How awful! Who else might read it? And then almost immediately he thought of the future; he wanted to get to the end of this novel.

"Shall I read more? This is fascinating," Anupa said. "I found it at the bookstore at the Centaur Hotel. Near the airport."

"How does it end?" he asked, then stopped her. "No, don't read it. I don't want to know."

"Do *you* know the ending, Anupa?" Lily asked.

"No, silly! I just started it yesterday. Shall I look? Although I have to say, I don't like skipping ahead."

"Please don't," he begged. "Not now. Later."

"Okay." She closed the novel and dropped it inside her bag.

"We should go. Free up the table."

"You know I never forgot seeing you up on that school wall," Anupa said as they got up. "When you pulled that branch down and jumped off, my teacher said you were up to no good, just like all the other boys. She said you'd amount to nothing."

"If she only knew how right she was," he laughed.

"Don't say that! It isn't true at all. You *were* hungry, my God! It upset me, what she said. It was mean of her. I never liked her. Nobody liked her. Not worth mentioning her name, na? Some teachers like their power and control. They beat us behind our knees and on our knuckles with bamboo canes and wooden rulers.

But good teaching goes beyond textbooks and homework. God should have told her you were hungry."

"Still, look at me now," Fishhead said. "No better than I was."

The words hung there. At last Anupa spoke: "I wouldn't say that. Anyway, thank you for naming the tamarind tree after me. So nice of you."

"I scratched your name in it somewhere," he said.

"Really? I'll look for it the next time I visit the school. It's been a while."

And with that they made their way out of the crowded restaurant. Not yet three in the afternoon. They went east and walked past the public gardens. Then, at Fishhead's suggestion, they headed north on Mahatma Gandhi Road to do some shopping. At a sari store, Fishhead picked out a simple printed sari for Mom; he bought his sister a blouse and floral skirt. For Anupa, a set of glass bangles. Not much: all he could afford.

Next came a shoe store, where Lily picked out a pair of sandals. But the heat soon tired them, so afterwards they stopped for falooda at Harilal's: cold milk shakes, made with ice cream, rose syrup, vermicelli, tapioca balls, and basil seeds. They took their time drinking them.

"Best in the city," Anupa said. "As good as Kalyani's."

"My classmate Mira's mother makes really good milkshakes, better than the shops," Lily said. "That's what she told me."

"Have you tasted them?" Fishhead asked.

"No, she doesn't invite me to her house."

"Well, that's no friend. Why believe her?" he said. "You're drinking the best in the city. Don't bother with what Mira says."

"She's always showing off," Lily added. "The driver drops her off at school, brings her lunches, and picks her up. Her uncle is an actor."

"Well you're drinking a better milkshake than she is," Fishhead said.

"Hey, doesn't your Mom work nearby?" Anupa asked.

"Yes, she does. Let's go see her," Fishhead replied. "I'd like you to meet her. And we'll get her something to eat." He ordered two vegetable samosas from the snack counter, to go.

"I want to see her office," Lily said.

"Will they let us in the building?" Anupa asked.

"We'll see," Fishhead said.

They walked on sidewalks for several minutes in the heat and stayed off the busy roads until they approached the old stone Standard Chartered bank building, where they had to cross the street to get to the telephone exchange. A daring act, crossing here with the chaotic rush of speeding wheels and blaring horns. One car came rushing towards them from the left, swerving around a scooter and a lorry. Without warning, Lily dashed out into the street in front of it; Fishhead gasped, but somehow she got to the other side. (The driver honked furiously as he passed; Fishhead caught a glimpse of his arm flexing as he banged the horn, muscles tensed under his white shirt, a pack of cigarettes folded inside his rolled-up sleeve.) Fishhead took Anupa's arm, and they rushed forward into the next gap in traffic. The air held the heavy scent of spent gasoline. Once they reached the opposite sidewalk, Anupa had to stop and catch her breath. But they made it.

The twelve-floor glass government building stood out from the surrounding heritage structures. The two policemen at the entrance let them in the lobby after a few questions, and Fishhead led the girls up the elevator to the eleventh floor. The clock on the wall of the main lobby marked the time at almost four.

"Mom works here?" Lily asked.

Fishhead nodded. "I came here twice before on my own," he said, "and she brought me and Prem here one time three years ago. We saw the telephone boards and the operators. Everyone wears headsets and talks at the same time, and they move cables out from one place and plug them in elsewhere on the board. Mom, too. Connecting families, I guess."

"Is your mother expecting you?" Anupa asked.

"No, she isn't." They approached the receptionist, who worked behind a wall with a sliding glass window. He introduced himself; she asked them to be seated and then disappeared inside.

Fifteen minutes later, Eshma emerged from a side door, which promptly closed behind her. Fishhead jumped up and approached Mom, unable to acknowledge her anemic eyes, sunken cheeks, and bony frame. This hardworking woman, drawn to sacrifice. He kissed her on the cheek, and Lily did the same, while Anupa hung back and watched.

"Oh, what's all this? I hardly expected you at all!" Mom coughed. She brushed a lock of hair away from her daughter's face, and then reached for Anupa's hand. "And who is this wonderful human being? Who have you brought to meet me?"

Anupa stepped forward and kissed her on the cheek.

"This is Anupa," Fishhead said. "She's going to Xavier's."

"I finally get to meet you," Anupa said, beaming.

Mom returned her smile. "Why has my son kept your name from me? Why has he waited so long?" She coughed a few times. "A beautiful girl like you?"

"I've met her," Lily added.

Fishhead shrugged. "She spends a lot of time reading. Literature, poetry…" He held back from stating the obvious: he'd been too embarrassed to bring anyone home to the tenement, Anupa most of all. Maybe Mom had resigned herself to it all; maybe she believed her children should accept it without question as she did.

"Anupa's super smart, Ma," Lily jumped in.

"Your son calls me his bookworm," Anupa said.

"That's a nice thing to say." Mom looked at Fishhead and cleared her throat.

"It's true. So how are you, Mom?"

"Good, good. I didn't expect you here!"

"I'm taking Lily and Anupa to the carnival," he explained. "We just ate thalis at Churchgate. Did you eat?"

"You ate thalis? That's excellent," she said and coughed. "Yes, I snacked."

Fishhead knew she probably hadn't eaten at all. Or maybe a banana and a roti. Never enough. Never ever enough. Life ate her strength with its hunger. Doctor Rajan said she lacked sufficient iron in her body, and that she didn't eat enough. Fishhead handed Mom the small brown paper bag with the two fresh samosas.

"For me? Thank you!" she said. "I thought I smelled something good. I'll eat them on a break. This is so nice of you."

"Would you like to join us at the carnival?" Fishhead asked, suddenly feeling guilty; he knew her answer as soon as he posed the question.

"I can't leave yet, son. The boards are lighting up with international calls. I must stay."

He reached out to take her arm when she coughed again. "That's all right, Ma. I…we wanted to see you. I wanted you to meet Anupa. And…" He nodded to Lily, who presented Mom with the sari they'd picked out.

"What's this? Oh…!" Mom smiled and pressed the gift gently. She frowned, unclear if she should unwrap it in front of them. "I better not open it now," she said at last. "But I'll take it with me, okay?" And then she sang the next statement, "I think I know what it is. Thank you…thank you!"

"Shall we come pick you up later?" Fishhead asked.

"No, you better not wait. I'm not sure when I'll be done. My lunch time is over and I have one break left at four-thirty. A long day, like every day." Then she added, "I'll see you at home. Enjoy yourselves, and be careful. So nice to meet you, dear. And don't let him keep you away from me so long next time."

"I promise I won't," Anupa answered, taking Mom's hands in hers.

Fishhead kissed Mom goodbye, then Lily and Anupa did the same. He stood by Anupa's side and waited until Mom disappeared behind the door, still smiling and clutching her gifts in both arms. Then he led them out of the building. The pace of his mother's life weighed on Fishhead. She would keep working until the government forced her to retire, or until some external force compelled her to stop: her health would give out, or Dad's debtees would start tracking her down at the telephone exchange. A sick and simple woman with little joy, confined in her workspaces, unaware of the larger world. Still, Fishhead saw the light in her eyes briefly, in small moments like this. He believed his mother might hold this picture of Anupa in her memory forever, and he liked that very much.

I'll admit, I enjoy such moments the most, these precious seconds of kindness and morality, unburdened by violence or the crises continually upsetting families and societies around the planet. The universe is love and violence, yes, love and also violence—properties inherent in everything that occupy its spaces, the actual and ideal, that's in you and in your world most of all. Like Fishhead, you have your heart and intelligence to help navigate your way across time. Its permanence and irreversibility should make life less complicated, it should—but changing conditions alter his perspectives, and they will affect yours, I know. You have want, as Fishhead wants. Every desire, dear reader, faces its just conclusion. I desire, too, if you must know. I wish for solidarity and union more, because love brings light and life, not malevolence or emptiness; but each click forward in time is a determination of associations past and present, of confronting forces. Coalition or control, such is the nature of matter that exploits time. Selfishness, greed, and manipulation, or the oppression inflicted by one soul against another soul will—like all actions of empathy and understanding—mark the eternal movement of souls through time (yes, I have used this phrase "movement of souls" before); each experience is webbed to so many others, and so on it goes, lives moving through the unknown with separate destinies, but tied to the same outcome. This is true awareness. And do I reside at the periphery of your awareness? I ask you. I must, I know I must, because you have a conscience. What does it ask of you? Does it prompt you for risk, or safe reward? Does it blindside you with the unfamiliar? Perhaps it leads you towards the unexplored. I *am* the unexplored and the unknown, as I have said before. Do you see me on the gilded edge formed by small miracles, or in opportunities awaiting your grasp? The things that happen to all. The things that happen. You might say it is fate's cruelty or kindness; but there, under the next step you are about to take, lies a tapestry woven by the elements which will draw you away from all that you know, and from all that you have known.

How nice when good things happen, wouldn't you agree? How nice for love, Fishhead thought, that his mother had seen the three of them, and said the things she'd said, touching hair and flesh, smiling, and embracing this new memory.

Now Fishhead moved with appreciation, a young man grateful for his wakefulness and speech, his movement, and situation; and he moved with an understanding that he lived in the unknown and could never truly separate himself or his behavior from those instructions of the unknown, because I have invited him there, the three of them in fact. And you, dear reader, what are your instructions from the unknown? What is your hunger?

Carnival

They left the telephone exchange building behind and walked north, charged by the spirit of their happy encounter.

"Do you think Mom will wear the sari to work?" Lily asked.

"Definitely," Fishhead said, "All the ladies come to work in nice saris. The men dress up, too. Clean shirts and slacks, even suit jackets if they are bosses."

"Do you think she liked me?" Anupa asked.

"Yes!" Lily interjected. "I know she—"

"Didn't you see how bright her eyes got?" Fishhead asked. "Of course she liked you."

"She's very sweet," Anupa admitted. "I can still feel her touch. So warm. Those hard-working hands. You're lucky to have a mother like her."

"You've got a great mom, too," Fishhead said. He squeezed Anupa's hand. He needed water, thinking the girls felt the same. The heat zapped their zeal but they stayed on their feet.

Lily locked arms with Anupa and they matched steps on the sidewalk. "I'd like to meet your mother."

"I'm sure you will," Anupa said and smiled.

They arrived at the vast public grounds and cricket park about fifteen minutes later; the park appeared empty now, with several patches of rainwater on the grounds. A carnival had been going on for a week, tucked away on one side of the park by the main road; in the distance Fishhead could see its Ferris wheel reaching high into the sky. Nothing could stop a carnival, not the rain.

As they approached the colorful main gates and the welcoming arch, they could hear music floating out from inside. They went to the ticket booth: ten rupees each. Anupa insisted on paying for hers; Fishhead asked her to buy him a snack instead, and she agreed. He took her hand and pulled her close as they walked inside together, squeezing through families and groups of teenagers. Such excitement! By sunset, it would be as crowded as the rush-hour train stations. Triangular flags and helium-filled balloons in bright colors flew over game stalls and vendors; they sold food, sweetmeats, handicrafts, magic oils, ayurvedic potions, clothing, fabrics, footwear, cosmetic jewelry, bangles, makeup, perfumes, toys, kitchen items, music cassettes, and other goods. A distinct aroma of fresh food and fried snacks filled the air, braided with the scent of oils, potions, and fragrances.

Screams, hoots, and shouts came from the giant wheel ride. Fishhead urged the girls to watch for puddles and wet patches, even though the rainwater began drying up quickly in the heat. Behind the giant wheel stood another tall fabricated structure, round and colorful with cheap artwork, over two stories high and just as wide, with thick wooden poles leaning up against it on all sides for support; it looked like a giant wooden barrel built of tight vertical planks. The Well of Death. Two metal stairways rose on either side of the round structure. In another corner of the carnival grounds stood a stage for storytelling, performance, and puppetry. Film songs blared from cone-shaped loudspeakers hung crudely on wooden posts everywhere, connected to each other by a string of dangling wires; the posts also held clusters of vertical fluorescent lights facing downward. Colorful bulbs hung everywhere, shining dimly in the afternoon sunshine. Lily took Anupa's hand, entranced; she couldn't decide where to begin. They bought cold drinks—Limca and Fanta—and sipped them through straws, and debated what to do first.

Finally, they tried their hand at darts, then proceeded to the ring toss, the duck pond game, and the ball toss. No luck for any of them, but they were having fun; they ambled the stalls and ate cotton candy. Then, a puppet show; they sat for a little while to rest their feet, and afterwards lingered to watch the singers. Nearly an hour went by.

Lily didn't want to go on the Ferris wheel, but Fishhead convinced her to check it out by telling her she could sit in the middle. They all held hands and screamed with excitement, and gripped the edges of their seats; at the very top, they saw the crowded, sprawling city as if for the first time. Lily had to sit down afterwards; Anupa felt lightheaded, but recovered soon enough.

After walking around for a while, they jumped on the carousel with the giant cups and saucers and fell into bouts of laughter and more screaming; as their cup whirled madly, Anupa threw her arms out with no care in the world.

"I'm going to throw up!" Lily cried. She stuck her tongue out, and her loosened hair went up in the air behind her.

"Are you having fun yet?" Fishhead shouted to Anupa over the screams from the other riders. "You're stuck, yaar…you're stuck to the wall of the cup!" He laughed and gripped the handles.

"Get me off, get me off!" Anupa cackled. "No, let me sit here and go to the moon! Take me to the stars, Fishhead. Let's take this cup and fly away!" She let go and reached for his waist.

"Okay!" he shouted, wrapping an arm around her. "Just hang on—"

And they sat locked in this embrace, this centrifuge, unwilling to let go. The ride eventually slowed and stopped, and Fishhead got off with the world spinning around him. Lily grabbed his shirt to keep from falling, and Anupa took their shoulders to remain on her feet. They found a table with four chairs at the edge of a snack stand near the carousel. Fishhead enjoyed seeing Anupa and his sister together, acting as if let loose in a valley of flowers. Full of wonder and innocence, free from worry.

By now the hot sun had begun its descent, and visitors continued to fill up the carnival with its high wooden poles and exterior canvas walls, all painted with festive signs and colors. The lights came on and soon flooded the grounds, and the songs played unabated one after the other from the overhead loudspeakers. The open spaces of Azad Maidan and downtown beyond the canvas walls of the carnival seemed subdued by comparison, as if the well-lit celebration had arrived like a festive ship on an ocean of earthly sorrow; this city might never corrupt the carnival's euphoric mood. Fishhead checked the time: almost seven. He planned to leave when Anupa and his sister reached a point of exhaustion. Although he didn't mind prolonging this experience, he did not think they'd want to stay out until the 10:00 closing time. Besides, he needed the extra hour for their train ride home to Chembur, plus the added time required to walk Anupa home. And Dad would want Lily home early enough. A bit of a quandary, this management of time and travel. For the moment, the carnival begged them to carry on.

"Are you tired?" he asked Lily, and she shook her head, but also rubbed her eyes. "Is it getting late for you?" he asked Anupa.

"Not at all. I'm having fun." She pressed his hand in hers. "And my mother knows where I am."

So he suggested they visit the game stalls again and get some food afterwards. Anupa offered to pay, and he accepted. This time, Lily won a stuffed tiger at the ring toss, a striped tiger the size of a large purse, and she hugged it, hugged it like it held all the pleasures of the world that she did not have. Anupa also won—with steady hands at the buzzing wacky-wire challenge—a stuffed blue unicorn with glitter sewn into it, smaller than Lily's tiger, but flashier. His bookworm, this one who'd led him through a pasture of prose and wonder as he'd never experienced before—and, suddenly, without warning, he had a desire to know the ending of the book in her bag: *Fishhead. Republic of Want.*

"Can I see it?" He held out a hand while they walked to a snack stall.

"See what?"

"That novel in your bag."

"Are you sure you want to know?"

"I want to know," he insisted.

"Please, don't!" she said. "You'll spoil everything."

"Don't, brother!" Lily added.

Fishhead waved his hand to show his insistence, so Anupa took the book out and handed it to him. He began flipping through the novel at random; but when he searched the end of the story for its climax—a young man now lost in his want and curiosity—she loosened a button on her shirt, then snatched the novel from him. Turning away in the dust, Anupa tucked the book inside her shirt, right below her left breast; the book dropped to her waist and settled near her navel. She buttoned her shirt again with the book there like an unusual body part just above her gabardine bell-bottoms. He dared not retrieve it in public.

"Why did you do that?" he asked with widened eyes. "You cheeky thing, you." He moved his right hand forward as if he meant to retrieve the book from her, and she made a half turn away from him then ducked.

"Please don't spoil it! Please."

"Yes, brother," Lily interjected. "Let's just be here." She pressed the side of her face against his shoulder and tugged at him.

He checked himself, not wishing to make a bigger scene. People stopped and stared. Anupa straightened up then slipped an arm inside his, and she planted a kiss on his cheek which drew strange and judging looks from attendees nearby. Sweat appeared in his armpits and on his back, and the constant noise had made him restless, but he hid his unease well. He let the incident go but went silent for a minute. Then he turned to Anupa and said, "You're right."

"I know," she said.

Well of Death

They ate savory snacks at a busy stall, and sipped icy, fizzy lemon-lime soda right out of the bottle. Then Lily said, "Let's go up there," and pointed to the round barrel-like structure in the opposite corner of the carnival grounds.

"*Maut ka Kuaan*?" he asked, studying her weary eyes. "Are you sure?"

"I want to go up there, too," Anupa said. "I've been thinking of it all evening. And now it's calling me."

The massive painted barrel stood with its crude wooden poles pressing against it from all angles, and the two attached wrought-iron staircases wrapped around the curved sides, going all the way to the top, to the spectator rim. High, he thought, but not as high as the cranes on the offshore oil rigs they always showed in the papers. He thought, too, of traditional construction sites in the city with their roped scaffolding of bamboo and wooden poles, and the workers who climbed like iguanas at their own risk, producing floor upon floor of new concrete, stone, and glass. Such human danger to make ends meet.

"Can I buy some bangles first, like Anupa's?" Lily held up her thin wrists. "See, nothing here, no bangles."

"You're too young!"

"C'mon, brother, please?" Lily reasoned. "Girls in my class are already wearing bangles and trying on makeup. Let's ask Anupa."

"Ask what?" Anupa said.

"Did you wear bangles when you were my age?"

Anupa looked at Fishhead and then turned to Lily. "I was a little older. Didn't care so much for jewelry at first. But my Mom allowed me to wear one to school, just a plastic one on each wrist. But never glass bangles like these." Hers chinked when she shook her arm.

"Please, brother?" Lily begged. "Besides, it's bad luck for a girl to buy her own bangles."

"It's bad luck for a young woman to buy her own bangles," he corrected her.

"So I'm growing up, then!"

"Yes, I suppose you are."

"See? And I'm a good student. You'll be proud of me."

"My sister, the brightest! I *am* proud of you," Fishhead said, and tousled her hair. "Let's get you some bangles. Then we can go up there."

They approached a well-lit stall, with four men behind three long tables stacked with a surplus of plastic, glass, and metal bangles, most of them wrapped in light brown paper and newspaper and paired in half or full sets, all packaged in small cardboard cartons with lids. On these stacks sat the open samples for the customers. On the walls hung painted boards with hooks showcasing other, more expensive bangles and designs.

"Bangles, *choodi*, get your bangles here!" a vendor said, when Fishhead and the girls approached. "Best in city!"

Fishhead felt overwhelmed, all that glare and glitter, that shine. In a few minutes, Lily picked half a dozen blue plastic bangles, and she let the vendor slip the plastic ones over her fisted hands, three on each wrist. The man used a lotion when the bangles got stuck over her knuckles. He worked expertly, and she never felt any pain.

"Young girls are wearing bangles these days. It's become fashionable," the man explained.

Anupa nudged Fishhead and winked. He smiled back. Lily said nothing, engrossed in her experience.

"Can I see those glass ones? The textured ones there in green and yellow." She pointed to the samples on top of the box to her right.

"There is no Indian wedding without bangles, no married woman without bangles on her wrists," the vendor explained, now looking at Fishhead.

"Even toddlers at home are adorned with gold and silver bangles," Fishhead said.

"Yes, sir, but glass bangles have special meaning to new bride."

"Can I get these two glass ones?" Lily asked, turning to Fishhead.

"Mom won't approve. But okay."

"End of honeymoon when last glass bangle breaks," the vendor added.

Fishhead smiled and turned to Anupa. "Want to try?"

She shook her head. "I like what you bought me."

He paid for the two bangles. Lily dropped them in her plastic shopping bag from the clothing store and picked up her stuffed tiger, and they left the stall. Done with shopping.

Fishhead bought three tickets for the Well of Death. They waited in the long line at the bottom of one wrought-iron staircase; the one-way climb to the top, with thin handrails on the right and narrow steps wrapping around the barrel. Guides eyed the eager crowd, keeping them in check; they counted how many people could go up the staircase. Fishhead and the girls made it through. He asked them to stay ahead of him.

"Hey, how wide is that?" someone in line asked a guide.

"On the inside, thirty-five feet, more." The guide shuffled a deck of used playing cards, coming up with a joker each time. "And more than fifty feet high, even higher. That's how *we* build it, but it can be less if no cars are used. We drive cars here, you'll see."

"How many cars?" Fishhead jumped in.

"You'll see, sir, and be amazed."

"And this started in India, didn't it? *We* created it?" the man behind Fishhead asked. People in line closed in, tightened the space, eager to listen above the carnival noise, this raucous defiance of the city's indigence.

"No, sir. Wrong, sir," the guide answered. "First started in Am'rika. In New York before World War I. Am'rika is great entertaining country. In Am'rika, is Motordome. In India, is Well of Death." He shuffled and had Lily pick a card; she drew a ten; the man shuffled again and asked a young boy next to her to do the same, and the boy drew an ace of clubs; the man looked at Fishhead next, but then turned to Anupa, and she drew a joker. He promptly dropped it in his pocket when another guide signaled for the line to go up the staircase. The people moved with impatience, sometimes shoving but always pressing forward, and the staircase shook with the weight of the crowd. Fishhead stayed close behind the girls, his hand on Anupa's waist.

Others followed behind him, until the guides cut off the line. People booed and complained; some decided to leave and return; others simply waited their turn, determined to catch the show before the carnival closed. Fishhead took Anupa's hand as they ascended, and Anupa did the same for Lily. The staircase rumbled but held steady. And soon they reached the top and stepped on the spectator rim. A loose cone-shaped canvas roof sloped gently above them from a center pole. Constructed like a boardwalk, the rim of tight wooden planks went in a complete circle around the lip of the well, along with a thigh-high painted railing with thin metal posts aligned flush with the wall of the well. Fishhead felt uneasy. Everything shook under him, mild earthquakes of crowd motion. Three guides gestured for everyone to spread out and distribute the weight evenly. A light net about a foot and a half in depth hugged the inner lip of the rounded well. Fishhead and the girls followed the crowd as it stepped around the rim, and the narrow space filled up quickly. Curious spectators jammed together, leaning over the railing as they looked down the well. Somehow in the shuffle, Anupa ended up on Fishhead's left with Lily to his right. He didn't think too much of the change.

Just hard ground at the bottom. Dirt inside the round well with its center pole. And wide, vertical planks of cheap, dark wood expertly joined together for the wall, which presented a straight drop to the dry earth below. Vertigo for anyone uncomfortable with heights. An angled ledge skirted the base of the well; built also like a circular boardwalk, the ledge acted as continuous ramp wide enough to fit a small car. The ledge included a hinged door—now open—cleverly cut out from the wall. The tall wooden center pole that supported the roof also held a set of bright fluorescent lights, which pointed down, just like the lights on the carnival grounds. Six men entered, four walking their motorcycles through the door. Fishhead recognized two Jawa bikes, a Honda, and a Royal Enfield "Bullet" without its rear separate passenger seat. Then three small cars—two black, one red—drove through the door and waited at the base of the pole, idling close behind each other and facing the direction of the ramp. All in such a tight space. So well-rehearsed. How many times had they run through these motions before? Fishhead wondered. A man closed the ramp-door and made sure it locked tight, and the drivers took their positions. Fishhead struggled to hear their conversation. Moments later, two motorcyclists fired up their engines.

Spectators looked down, excited. Sound and exhaust fumes rose from the base of the well. The roar, the boom. Lily covered her ears. The crowd shifted around Fishhead, and the girls stayed close to him. His anticipation grew. Anupa threw her right arm around his waist and he took her shoulder; on the other side of him, Lily hugged her stuffed tiger. Fishhead moved to the left a bit to give them a few more inches on the rim. Two other motorcyclists fired up their bikes, and the four riders went around the pole and three cars twice, casually, and then edged up the ramp, racing their engines. Within seconds they were roaring round and round and up and down the circular wall, and the force of their turns, their wheels and power, began pushing the whole structure of the well out and then in several inches again and again, and the spectator rim swayed with it, too. Anupa gasped, and Fishhead tightened his grip around her. "It's like a hula hoop!" she shouted. The crowd let out a unified cry, full of delight and shock. Lily screamed with them, and Fishhead looked at her briefly.

The four bikers came together, one below the other in a single row, and then broke away on the inside wall; they joined up in pairs, one right behind the other. Moments later, one rider pulled away from the group and dipped down to the lower part of the well while the three other riders came together again near the lip at a steady pace, close to the red line and net, too close—defying gravity and justice, defying fate; they rode alongside each other while the fourth rider went around near the bottom at a slower pace. The three riders at the red line raised their arms up and touched shoulders and went a few rounds at full speed this way, hands free. People clapped and whistled, shrieking...shrieking with pleasure, and they leaned forward over the wooden waist-high railing and looked down. Fishhead did, too. What daring entertainment, such precision! No room for error. The bikers finally grabbed their handlebars and sped away from each other but continued to go around. They took turns doing seat stands on their hands, and other tricks, but they never fell or faltered.

Fishhead became entranced with the sound and fury, and he blinked, unbelieving, as the remaining two men jumped in the cars while the three drivers started up their vehicles below. Could he ever have the courage and skill to pull off something like this? He couldn't be sure. The wooden well, a vertical cave, echoed its monstrous sounds, filling the area with a light gray smoke that made them choke and cough. Only moderately more chaotic than Bombay's streets.

The car drivers raced their engines and shot up the ramp one after the other; they joined the bikers on the vertical wall, moving at the same high speed, turning the well and its crowd into a tight death trap. Fishhead released his grip from Anupa's shoulder and leaned down with his hands wrapped around the railing.

How much time went by, he couldn't tell; time itself seemed without a beginning or end, and he felt the weightlessness of his thrill pull him into this vortex. His heart and body throbbed with the pulsing and moving well. Vibrations crawled up through him, displacing anxiety and fear. Anupa, too, leaned over the railing and gripped it, but Lily stood up straight and tugged at Fishhead, as if begging him to stand back up. A most dangerous game. Bikers and motorists with lives on the line, brave souls, daring souls. Fishhead's mind wandered. How did they do it? What if an engine failed, or if they made an error in judgment? Catastrophe hung in the air, just fractions of a second away. Destiny watched, waited.

The bikers rode to the lower end of the well and slowed down, and the three cars took over, racing as they came near the lip; they took positions side by side, riding close together while their passengers leaned out the windows and waved. The crowd applauded and hooted. Fishhead looked at Lily; she stood speechless, her eyes wide open with amazement, and he wondered if she had swallowed her stuffed tiger. Anupa stayed leaning over the railing. Fishhead took her shoulder and tried to pull her back, and she stood up; but moments later she leaned over the railing again.

The three cars at the top moved away from each other but kept in sync with the bikers below. All three cars and bikers then staggered their paces and places as they went around the well in confounding, kaleidoscopic whirls. Then a biker on a Jawa raced to the top at high speed and met up with a single car speeding round and round just a foot or so below the lip of the well. The biker aligned his bike with the speeding car and then pulled his front wheel about two to three inches away from the car, and he kept the same speed as the car while he stood up on his seat. He reached for the top of the car with his right hand, put his left hand behind him, and went round and round with the car, hands free of the handlebars. The crowd went wild. Fishhead clapped and whistled, and Anupa pressed down on the railing, transfixed and in awe, while Lily stood still and silent, unable to watch, while two other bikers and cars repeated the trick below.

Then they all broke away from each other, and the last biker, the one who had stayed at the bottom all this time, now pulled his bike behind the left taillight of one of the cars, the red one, as they both cut through the pack and came speeding around to the top of the well, just as the two other cars angled down the ramp and settled on the dirt floor. The three motorcyclists circled below, poised for a final round. So much going on at the same time, and time itself a paradox of experiences, flooding both thought and feeling. Each vehicle and driver fulfilled a purpose in the show. A complex pattern. Fishhead lifted his head to survey the crowd; he felt the same way they did. This Well of Death. *Maut ka Kuaan.*

Now the biker and red car both circled around the inner wall and then came up to the lip in front of him, roaring and sputtering, going counterclockwise turn after turn. Several spectators leaned forward on the railing like Anupa; she seemed locked to it, entranced like them. Fishhead joined her, and Lily took his arm but remained standing. The biker stayed near the left taillight of the red car as they went around fast. Then he touched the fender of his front wheel to the car's taillight and rode two rounds behind the vehicle while doing a handstand on his handlebars.

The crowd applauded, whistled, shouting cheers. Clearly an incredible, impossible feat. Calling death, inviting it. Fishhead whistled, but Lily tugged at his shirt anxiously. He turned for a moment and winked at her, and finally saw her crying. She shivered, and he rubbed her cheek; then he turned around again to face the show.

The biker sat back down, then raced his engine, attempting to cross over and switch places with the car near the red line and lip. They made a quick turn together to initiate the switch, and the biker began pulling his way up from behind the red car, which moved down gradually to make room for him. Both so close to the red line. A pair of charging, roaring bulls moving too, too fast. Fishhead stood and watched; Anupa still leaned on the railing, mesmerized.

Then the unexpected horror...as if time hesitated and shifted to create a rift through which existence plunged. After the quick second turn, the racing car choked and fired, letting off a boom; it sparked and spat oil against the wall from under its chassis, and the driver aimed downward for the ramp in haste. Losing momentum. Ready to drop like a fruit if he didn't hurry. The warm smell of expulsion—

Somewhere an apple falls; a hungry child reaches for it, linked invisibly to the tree.

The crowd gasped and screamed. The biker reacted to the boom but could not see the spill, could not see the car's trail of splattered oil angled against the wall, and his wheels skated over the oil. Anupa moved as if to lift her torso up, as if she knew the outcome, this calling, in that split second. Fishhead jerked back and yelled, but could not complete the cavernous wail emerging from his body. Humans are never fast enough, except in their minds.

In a lightning flash, the biker gripped his handlebars tight as he lost control, an asteroid thrust aimlessly through the all-encompassing air; his motorcycle a projectile shooting through a second's funeral, soiling time with the unthinkable energy of its oncoming destruction. A caterwaul like no other. The wheels danced and shimmied, reaching for free space past the restraining lip of the well. The frame spun out, spun up and flung the biker against the net, tearing it up, while the bike aimed for Anupa and the person at her left with its maximum impact, its tail end reaching into them first. A young man in a kurta turned to his left when the biker, free of his bike, came toward him. Anupa tried to stand, to duck, but she had no time to scream or even take God's name. No time at all in this accelerating bolt of doom. Fishhead gripped Anupa's arm and pulled their bodies back; he pushed into Lily and the crowd behind him. Not fast enough, and no room at all. The rear of the bike caught the side of Anupa's head and smashed her into Fishhead. She went limp, lifeless. The thrust forced her into his embrace as he fell back against the rows of onlookers trapped behind him; he screamed…screamed into the emptiness, and the sound of thunder is all he heard echoing down the halls of the unknown. Lily screamed, reaching for Fishhead through restless bodies. Everyone screamed. The bike, deflected, rose straight up towards the conical canvas roof and then fell free in an arc down the well; the dislodged biker tore through the net; the pole holding the net at the lip snapped in two and tore through the right shoulder of the young man in the kurta, injuring him badly. Crashes and yells ensued below. Pandemonium. With a monstrous crash, the bike dropped like a stone on the roof of a stationary car and bounced off, rattling its twisted frame onto the ground. Onlookers at the top of the well stirred in high-pitched emotion. Surprise and shock, shock and despair. So much damage done, blood everywhere, on Fishhead and in his soul, and Anupa feathered silently in the cradle of his arms, his regret. Chaos reigned in the Well of Death and rippled out quickly through the carnival grounds.

Bookworm

The frenzied crowd made way for emergency medical assistance, and the police arrived several minutes later. Two inspectors from the criminal investigation department began their inquiries, while paramedics helped the wounded and moved the injured to Bombay Hospital nearby. Anupa's covered body made its way in an ambulance to the hospital. Too late. The motorcyclist had suffered serious injuries from his fall, but would live. For now he lay there at the bottom of the well next to his mangled bike and the dented and damaged cars, amidst shattered glass, twisted metal, and the yelling of his frantic coworkers; one of them had the presence of mind to throw open the ramp door, lest a fiery explosion consume that wooden prison.

Fishhead couldn't go far away enough. Her memory slept with him every moment of the day like a silent, dreamy spouse. *Why didn't the universe slow down time in a catastrophe, as it did to create life?* Fishhead became distressed by the thought that he might have been able to pull her away.

Anupa. His bookworm. *Pusthakon ka keeda.*

He felt responsible. He couldn't face it much longer, this gaping hole in his chest. Did the novel in her bag end this way, too? The bookstore at the Centaur Hotel carried few popular vinyl records and the newest bestsellers from publishers around the world, and he thought for a second that he might ask Pradeep to stop and look for the book there. But then again, seeing their tragedy played out for the world to read—that hurt would cut him deep inside. And an alternate ending would taunt him with lost possibilities. Let others have that pleasure, or not. Either way, that book would soon lose its way in the vast ocean of literature, floating aimlessly, forgotten, and useless, a yellowing edition in some suffocating corner of the world. Other books, better books, would take its place everywhere: a cycle of want and despair.

Maybe he should get away, go work on an oil rig. The dangers of life at sea appealed to him more now; he did not care if the water consumed him. Let it. Let it wrap its swarthy arms around him and drag him down. Let it open its gaping mouth and swallow him whole. He figured he deserved a fate worse than Anupa's. What could that be? Make it his.

Every inch toward Anupa's front door disturbed him. He felt cold shivers throughout his body, but he had to go there, stand face to face with her mother and explain every moment.

"Tell me everything!" she wailed. "Everything! I wish to know it all."

Her unkempt hair. She punched her head with fisted hands when he began talking. Even as his words faltered, she reacted as if struck. He could offer no more than his own pain. Memories from school, the tenement: the suffering of Saint Sebastian. Her arms shook: timbers in sorrow, bending fast under death's hurricane. She pressed them again at her sides, slapped them again and again against her sides to restrain herself, and stomped her feet on the floor. This ecstatic motion. What else could Fishhead do? This hole he'd left her, a tangible relic of a once-incomparable motherhood. He suffered, too, but knew he had no right to expect any acknowledgment of that.

"I swear it, I swear I'm telling you the truth!" he cried, tears streaming down his cheeks. "How could we know such a thing would happen? We were just spectators. I loved her, you must believe me. I loved her like the sun!"

She wore black from head-scarf to toe, covered every part of her Christian self with severe modesty to dwell in the darkness of her daughter's passing, while Anupa's body lay sublimely calm with her books, dressed in grieving lace within the dark, decorated casket with its white satin and lace. An open casket raised on a table in the center of the living room, with all the furniture rearranged to permit the stream of neighbors, relatives, classmates, and friends who came to pay their respects, bearing flowers and wreaths. Windows stripped of their curtains and doors left open. Let the light flood this darkest of houses. Members of the church and choir stood in a corner with candles in their hands. Candles lit everywhere; Anupa's mother grieved for three whole days and nights, unmoving from the side of Anupa's casket, refusing even the comfort of the chair provided for her there. She threw her body down repeatedly across the casket and pressed the side of her chest and face against Anupa's silent frame with her arms out, black rosary in hand, a dark veil across her eyes, crying, reaching for her only child, the child she'd created and nurtured, clutching and pleading with her god to resist this cold passage through time.

"Return my child to me, return her, please!" she cried. "My Anupa! My baby! Return her to me, I beg you!"

She did not eat or drink, even as guests attempted to feed her and calm her. The parish priest came and blessed the home, blessed the body with prayers and sprinkled holy water. Roses everywhere, raising the fragrance of reverence and condolences to an unreachable ceiling, scents of affection trailing past the walls, the open windows and doors. For three days, Fishhead stepped into her home like a stranger, and each day he set his eyes on a tall and somber man standing in his dark blue suit beside Anupa's mother and the casket, a man Fishhead had never met but seemed to recognize. Anupa's sick father from Pune—her features resembled his as equally as mother's. The man remained silent and erect; he wore a TWA pin on a lapel of his suit, with matching gold cufflinks.

Fishhead felt reassured with each visit to the house, glad that Anupa's mother never chased him away. She did not even notice him among her guests, it seemed. The police blamed the carnival, filed a report to state that fact. Would she want to sue anyone? A suggestion not on anyone's mind.

Fishhead's thoughts cycled through the events of the incident over and over like the needle on a long-playing record. He remembered their final embrace. The disorder of spectators pushing and rushing to exit the Well of Death. Falling from the winding wrought-iron steps. The stampede. These images of madness might never escape him. He hadn't wanted to leave her alone on the narrow deck; he and Lily had been forced to cower from the panicked crowd that trampled around and over them, over Anupa's bludgeoned body in that confining space—her belongings strewn about, stepped on, crushed in the red. Fishhead had clenched his fist around her long hair, but in the madness of the surging crowd he'd been forced to let go. Let go! He refused to leave. Others had been hurt, trampled on, pounded by the heat of anxiety and hysteria, but no one else had passed away, just Anupa. His bookworm. He wondered if her brief periods of silence and distance on the carnival grounds had indicated something: that she'd somehow received her instructions to witness the unknown. Had she not been thinking of the Well of Death since they entered the carnival? "Now it's calling me," she'd said. It had called her, and she'd answered. Had she actually read something in the joker she'd drawn from the deck of cards? Or in the ending of the novel in her bag? Had she known about it all this time?

She'd offered herself to him completely, welcomed him without guise or guilt, without expectation or judgment. No one would replace her, no one; he believed it. And this realization devastated him more than hunger or tenement life ever had. Fate had snatched her away, and he failed to see any purpose in it. Useless! Fate had made a mistake. Did Destiny have no feelings, no regret, no conscience? He himself no longer felt alive. "Do you not see this?" he asked aloud, his eyes to the heavens. Fate had spared him, but why, and to what end? More suffering in the filthy tenement? More purposeless labor?

Lily cried and cried. She woke up with nightmares, mystifying Mom, who'd met Anupa, and Dad, who had not. They did not speak to Fishhead about it; he suffered their stony stares and wondered how they felt. And then he found the letter, and he knew.

The onionskin parchment had been folded in an envelope, and sealed and placed under his jute mat at night, so that when Fishhead woke up, folded his bedsheet, and rolled up the mat, he would see it. He got dressed and left the apartment with the letter; he left his siblings behind, and he let his feet take him to a tea stall in the open market south of the tracks. There he ordered a chai and read it:

Oh! My DEAR Boy, (what a hypocrite word this "DEAR" is!)

When your mother and I reflect back to your nineteen years, our present tattered, sad memories recall the time when we so lovingly picked-up Fishhead as the 'apple' of his parents' eyes and a bastion of the family (Pradeep notwithstanding) on whom everyone in the family placed trust and hopes of rewarding anticipation. The words you said echo through our ear-drums – BUT TIME has now taken its toll and we hear a new phrase of discontent through the present circumstance of this young woman's death, which you have caused by your recklessness and disparity of self. OH TIME, is your name frailty or do you only act in extremes? You, TIME, have altered all our aspirations into mere illusions, even though you are the best healer of all wounds. Couldn't you, TIME, have been more sympathetic and considerate with us and shortened our agonizing anticipations? Or is this the penalty TIME has imposed on us for our indulgences?

Both your mother and I have seen in our life-span
Pleasure and pain,
Security and fear,
Solace and Anguish,
Happiness and Sorrow,
Good and Bad,
Plenty and want,

Riches and poverty,
Achievements and Disappointments,
Prosperity and misery,
Evitable and the Inevitable,
Miracles and Despair…

This long list, we thought and hoped, would have ended with the trust we place(d) in our 'growing' children. Nay, TIME has now added strange correlations:

Extreme Hope into extreme Despair
Extreme Love into extreme Hatred and Denial.

Somehow, our laments don't seem to end here because our wounds are ongoing and fresh, and into these fresh wounds you have rubbed more salt. Despite your acute criticisms of me, your father (yes, I was that!), and my misfortunes, I had asked you to stop seeing her, this girl now dead because of you, whom I had never met. You did not wish me to meet her, I know this to be true in my heart. Perhaps you knew I would never have approved of your mismatched (social and economic) situations.

Still you carried on—behind my back! You were willing to put your own family's welfare second to your own needs, just when your mother and I believed, and hoped, that you (and Pradeep) would assist us and help bring the family out of its hardship. Now this DEATH! This price on our heads. And the loss to all. May it reside in your conscience until you see the truth of your error-full ways.

May be the 'adult-child' still lacks the manly composure of maturity – or may be, because the 'tongue' being in a wet place, the 'adult-child' doesn't want it to dry and keeps it in constant ambience. (isn't there One word for this as

'CALLOUS'?) May be the 'adult-child' is yet to realise that discretion is the better part of valour – or it may be that the 'adult-child' has yet to realise that love is not platonic or Utopian and must be expressed naturally and materially – or perhaps there exists in the innate self a psychosic urge for an indulgent emphasis and expressions –

I close my eyes in self-sacrifice and retreat with a heave of sigh and with the parental charity, 'cause TIME is running out on us. Lo, whatever it may be, your mother and I have witnessed this PLAY for too long a time without reprieve from your disobedience and disrespect. It is with a heavy heart that I must bid you ADIEU and say I no longer consider you my son. You may see your mother as you wish, if she will receive you.

AND SO BE IT.

–Balan George

Fishhead put the letter down and rubbed his eyes. He ordered another tea. How could he go back to work? How could he return to the tenement? Had he been wrong for wanting more? Such dramatic words from his father; he read them again, absorbed them, lay awash in them. The insanity and intensity of the man; the oppression of the machine. Fishhead felt as a victim, but also as someone who had measured his own role in this very machine. How much farther would it carry him into the future? He did not want it, wishing right then and there for a newer society with a different name and means, anything but the oppression which patriarchy imposed on him now. This prolonged illness. And what about his own sense of loss? Why did his parents not feel for him? Where did their sympathies disappear to? He felt pain in his chest and in his limbs, as if drowning again. The tea did little to help. He needed a stiff drink to calm his nerves.

He called the office and took time off from work, and he stayed out all day, with his father's letter in his back pocket. He checked into a hostel for young men, in an area just north of Sir J. J. that placed him deeper within the bustling city but far from the tenement in Chembur; as he rested briefly in bed, he read the letter twice again. Then he got up, stuffed the folded letter in his back pocket once more, and went to the water's edge at Apollo Bunder. He stood near the Gateway of India monument in the day's heat, mind focused not on his family, or the city careening around him with purpose and determination, but on the emptiness before him.

Thoughts pulled him back to the chaotic vibrant country. A swelling of prosperity and discovery (on land, in the air, at sea), a hungered culture motivated by some oncoming global enterprise— what role could he play now? Without Anupa. With an interrupted college education on his resume? He thought of his greeting cards, and Shobha, the character he created based on Anupa; he could never face this character again. So: time to move on from Tarak's.

He looked down at his hands, his empty hands and heart. He'd need to learn something new. No more life in the tenement. Was this what he'd always wanted? He remembered swallowing the cat's eye striker. The fights. His wins. His family going nowhere but down, down, sunk by father's pride; his sick mother struggling as if trapped—with her gills and fins and overcast eyes—in a fishing net. A father drenched in his dreamlike stupor and suffocating in it. And siblings, some escaping, some floundering. Now, one lost to sight and touch. Just a memory.

He turned his head when he heard a motorcycle engine racing away behind him, his heart pounding now. So much for daring, he thought, so much for daring.

Think, now, dear reader, of those would-be heroes on the threshold of the unexplored, the novel, inviting danger and urging *me*, Destiny, to open doors for them, demanding access to the unknowable. Souls straddling boundaries between the physical and intangible. Fishhead has suffered, but suffering is the soul's burnishing. He will realize this hard truth: A door closed pushes open another. You already know this, dear reader; you have heard it before. And the door that opens could be the one facing those vast unreachable spaces spreading out on all sides within the great universe, where time and light acknowledge me. And how do *you* float these days? Head first or feet first, tethered or untethered? Do you soar? Fishhead remains an infant still in the motherhood glow of the cosmic tree, and she will cut the cord sometime, she will, I know. It has begun now.

His tired, sleepless body capable for now of nothing else but a review of events running through his mind, haunting him. A receptacle for rebuke and guilt, but soon he will empty it out. The horizon far ahead of him tugs; places and experiences beyond might perhaps be his too, he wanted to believe it. Life offshore, on an oil rig. He steps away from the monument and its basalt Victorian arch, and he leans over a stone ledge there to face the mossy waves. Then he takes the letter from his back pocket and rips it into pieces, releasing them all to the benevolent air and warm, murky saltwater. He sees Anupa before him. Waves of foam and rapture. Those keen eyes, full lips, dark silky hair, her small breasts, flat stomach, and lush thighs. All of her. What else? Her pining mother. He looks up at the sky, as if making a silent promise. And what else? Yes, the books, Anupa's countless books, that vitality; shared music and stories from around the world thriving beyond his reach and filling his heart. A well-deserved education: this knowledge at last that life thrived because of pain and loss, like familiar layers of death and decay on the blackened forest floor nurturing fresh green shoots until they burst forth under an umbrella of rain and sunlight. Those patterns lived in him, too, lived everywhere. Yes, Destiny.

∞ ∞ ∞

ACKNOWLEDGEMENTS

This full-length novel first began as short stories during my MFA program at Northwestern University (NU-SPS). *Fishhead. Republic of Want.* is a daring experiment in my effort to reach a place in life with finished manuscript in hand. I received sound advice, got awarded, was rejected, and also stumbled along the way on particular inspirations that appeared as crucial opportunities rather than roadblocks. I followed those internal prompts, unsure of the outcome but always trusting with my heart, patience, and with a sensible knowledge of craft most of all, which, I believe, seems insufficient to the writer's compassionate and critical eye.

Writing is a process condoned by allies and critics alike. This process could not have been realized without the support and guidance of many, to whom I remain eternally grateful. In particular, I give thanks to Bernice Mennis in the Adirondacks for your early mentorship as I began my writing career with so much uncertainty; to all my well-wishers and friends at Vermont College (now Union Institute & University); my excellent graduate teachers, workshop classmates, and university associates and friends at Northwestern, especially Amy Danzer for your tireless support of the literary arts; my thesis advisors Laurie Lawlor and Christine Sneed; Reginald Gibbons, for your guidance and valuable insights, and for sharing your love of Indian food; Ragdale in Lake Forest, IL, for affording me the time and space to create; La Casita residency at el Ranchito Cielito con Nopales in La Union, NM; and Sunday Salon Chicago and writers' conferences for welcoming my literary citizenship.

I would like to thank the editors of the following journals in which excerpts from from the novel first made their appearance in a different form: *The Sunday Rumpus*, *Third Coast Review*, and *La Tolteca Zine*.

I know I am forgetting others. If I have failed to mention you here, know that I am always thankful for your help and friendship.

Blurbists, you're the best! Indie bookstores, you rock!

Thank you to my editor and publisher Jerry Brennan at Tortoise Books for your guidance and vision. Vindaloo *is* awesome!

Finally, thank you Cynthia Kerby for your support, love, and partnership.

<Write-or-perish!>

ABOUT THE BOOK

Amidst the teeming tenements of 1970s Bombay (Mumbai), a hungry teenage boy struggles through life in a poverty-stricken family ruled by a domineering alcoholic father, when suddenly he faces another challenge: the affections of an upper-middle-class girl. In this exploration of poverty and pleasure, patriarchy and tragedy, Fishhead's titular narrator must search for ways to bridge the gap between two seemingly irreconcilable worlds: the life he longs to live, and the one chosen for him by Destiny.

ABOUT THE AUTHOR

Ignatius Valentine Aloysius earned his MFA in Creative Writing from Northwestern University's School of Professional Studies. Born and raised in India, he is a naturalized U.S. citizen and lives in Evanston with his wife. Ignatius is a lecturer, designer, and musician. His writing has appeared in *Triquarterly*, *Third Coast Review*, *Newcity*, *The Sunday Rumpus* and other venues. He is a co-curator of Sunday Salon Chicago, a bi-monthly reading series in Chicago, and serves on the curatorial board at Ragdale.

ABOUT TORTOISE BOOKS

Slow and steady wins in the end, even in publishing. Tortoise Books is dedicated to finding and promoting quality authors who haven't yet found a niche in the marketplace—writers producing memorable and engaging works that will stand the test of time. Learn more at www.tortoisebooks.com, find us on Facebook, or follow us on Twitter @TortoiseBooks

Printed in the USA
CPSIA information can be obtained
at www.ICGtesting.com
JSHW022204140824
68134JS00018B/848